THE WAGES OF SIN

Kate A. Knight

First Published by Khaton Enterprises LLC, United States of America,

January 2015

ISBN: 978-0-9896468-7-1

Library of Congress Control: 2015935781

For Christian

PROLOGUE

Richard was waiting, dressed in slacks and a button-down shirt just inside the front door. His casual dress shined a mocking spotlight on the formality between them. It had been a month since he had last laid eyes on the woman he claimed was like a daughter to him.

"Amy, how good it is to see you," he said slowly and without warmth. "It's been a long time." His slur was almost gone... making progress everyday.

"I'm not on the list," Anne replied, but smiled to take the sting away. She moved easily into his arms and pressed a kiss to his cheek – proof that the years under his tutelage had not been a total waste.

"Todd is not here. You've made a long trip for nothing." But what he meant was *why have you uselessly made a long trip?*

"So I've been told," she replied, casting an eye around the entry hall, a pointed admonishment of his cold reception. "It's not entirely pointless however."

"How so?" His direct stare would have been unnerving to those unaccustomed to Richard's manner of stripping away pretense.

"I wanted to see you, of course. It's been too long."

There was a lingering air of expectation, as Richard waited for the prodigal to reach across the breach. It never came. After a long time, he gestured to the entry hall's half bathroom. "Come up to my study when you're done. We'll catch up."

Anne took advantage of the small space to give Richard the time he needed to make the journey up the stairs. It suited her purposes for him to collect and arm himself. Let him think he held the control. Allow Todd the opportunity for discovery.

Anne splashed water on her face and carefully dabbed her skin dry. Her eyes were bright despite the shadows etched deeply by days of lack of rest.

"Not a day more," she said to the woman in the mirror, and watched pleased, as the fire burned brighter.

Richard was predictably seated behind his desk, his contingencies firmly in place. The indifference he exhibited was feigned. He was never nonchalant when in his place of power, cushioned leather at his back, a sea of mahogany between him and his subject, firearm within easy reach.

Anne pulled a pen and an envelope from her purse. The pen was heavier than most, endowed with recording capabilities only people like them would anticipate. The envelope was larger, meant to draw the eye away from the camera.

"What is this?" Richard asked with barely more than mild curiosity.

"My answer to a question not yet posed," Anne said, easing her considerable bulk into the hard seat facing him and drawing closer, so her props were easily within reach.

Richard laughed. "It's not like you to be so cryptic, Amy." Anne waited in silence until his false humor melted away. "Why don't you tell me why you've come? How is that for a question?"

"I want you to tell me who killed my father," Anne said.

Having held Richard's gaze without pause, the shift in him was plain to see. He grew harder, colder, and far more attentive to the woman before him. His gaze narrowed, the lift of the corners of his mouth arctic, making even the brown eye appear blue.

"Are you sure that's where you wish to begin?" he asked, tilting his head to the side. He had discerned a change – the subtle difference between the woman before him and the one he had raised. He could not tell precisely what it was, but he was intrigued.

"It's seems as good a place as any to start. After all, you did promise."

"Of course you would think so. You never developed an appreciation for nuances. It is always black or white with you."

Anne shifted into the hard-backed chair, as if it were made of the deepest plush. "Why don't you teach me, Richard? Then I'll show you what I've learned at your knee."

ONE

"Richard called."

I was practicing not being so practiced with Todd, and so released the sigh I would have otherwise bottled up. Todd wasn't boasting. His carefully chosen words, although delivered with an abruptness that might have indicated a certain amount of don't-give-a-shit, were in fact a deliberate prompt. Todd meant to inspire some emotion in me, whether shame, remorse or jealousy. He wanted to me to pick up the phone and make a call he clearly felt was overdue.

It was a sign he was becoming comfortable with my feelings for him. He forgot my condition did not allow subjugation to those types of weaknesses. Anger I could feel in spades. Jealousy I did not at first recognize, but had taken root like a weed in rainy season. Guilt, remorse... these were hinged on my consideration of another's feelings, and so did not come naturally to me.

Amy Koehler is a sociopath.

That Richard had chosen Todd over me was more a blow to my competitive spirit than a blow to any tender sentiments for the man who had once aspired to replace my father. Uncle Richard had raised me after my parents were murdered over a decade ago. He watched me grow into a woman, blaze my way in a male-dominated career, and make a name for myself. Then he watched me marry the man whom he now chose over me. Another woman would have been resentful, angry, jealous. I had made my peace with the fact that Todd Birch was an asset Richard wished to control, but my position as his wife was also one of power. I could leverage my husband against Richard, just as Richard thought he could control me through Todd.

It would have been so much easier if our relationship were all business. I was as far removed from the handler I could have been, as night was from day. Firstly, I was in love with him, which compromised my objectivity. The only mitigation against that vulnerability was my awareness of it. Secondly, I did not know what moved him... why he claimed to love me.

"Amy," his voice came again, "I said Richard called."

"I was waiting for you to get to the point," I said, hoping the quiet timbre of my voice took the bite out of the words. I sighed again and sank deeper into my pillows, tucking one edge of the down comforter under my body. I switched the phone to my right ear in a renewed hunt for comfort. There was none.

It had been many years since I had slept in this bed. It was the one my father had awakened me from the last time I saw him alive. The memories made me cold. In contrast, the site of the injection I gave myself half an hour before flared on my hip. I could feel the solution that was designed to force my body into ovulation at work. Coming only weeks after my first attempt at clomiphene, and against my doctor's counsel at that, I was prepared for the worst. Debilitating nausea and blurred vision were nothing I could not push through to bind Todd to me in a way Richard could never manage.

"He's disappointed, Amy. You've been there five days and you haven't called." And beneath the deep resonance of his voice was the weight of Richard's expectations. Regardless of the message I loved Todd's voice. It never failed to awaken something warm and liquid in the pit of my belly. It made me *want* to please him.

"I've been busy moving back into my parents house and preparing for this interview."

Todd was quiet for a while, giving me hope he would drop the topic of Richard. There were better things to talk about. I had not seen my husband in nearly a week, which meant we hadn't touched in as much time. The caress of his gaze across my skin wasn't nearly as potent from behind the screen of a video call.

"They've been gone for a long time now, Amy. It's your house."

Anything but that would have kept the flame in my core alive. But those words had not only awakened darker memories, they breathed new life into the bitter emotions that were never too far from the surface.

"Tell me again why you love me," I said, the combative edge not hard to discern.

Todd groaned. It was a familiar sound that was usually accompanied by his thumbs being pressed painfully into his eyes. "Not this again."

"Make me understand."

"What's not to understand, Amy?" His hackles were up now. Good. We matched.

"Why –"

"No," he interrupted. "Not why. How. You don't understand how I could love you, because you don't think anyone should."

It wasn't true. I had only never *cared* that anyone might have loved me before. There were reasons why they would. My training and conditioning made me very good at my job. My family left me well connected in the intelligence community. Richard, as the Director of National Intelligence, was everyone's boss. And my father had a star on the CIAs Memorial Wall. But Todd claimed his declaration was entirely personal, which was beyond suspect.

"Just admit it," I breathed into the line. "I wouldn't blame you."

"What do you want me to say, Amy?" There was more defiance and frustration than resignation. Definitely not the victory I was looking for.

"Tell me the truth."

Jesus, I was cold. It was twenty-one degrees outside, and the only thing preventing snow was the lack of precipitation. Winter was here and it had been years since I had lived through one. However, as much as I wanted to adjust the thermostat, my hip burned too much for me to move just then.

"What were you doing in Jamaica?" "

"Amy, we've been through this before."

Todd had told me one thing; the embassy cables said another. One version claimed he was meeting a Cuban contact with ties to the Defense Ministry, so we could get the jump on Cuban sales of Cold War military hardware to North Korea. The other version proposed Todd as a peace broker between Santo Domingo and Kingston missions, as the State Department centralized some of its Caribbean functions. Apparently, the smooth operator had special skills required to keep the ambitious Ambassador Woodbridge from creating waves.

If I pushed him now, I knew what answer I would get. This was an unsecured line, and married or not some of our secrets were not ours to share. The Cuban case was still active, and there was no reasonable justification for him sharing those details with me. No one would care that, in order to preserve our marriage, he was forced to confess his sexual history with his source's sister.

"Did Richard send you?" I finally asked, then rushed to quiet whatever vulnerability peeked through. "I would understand if he had. I know he wants us together, because he encouraged my decision to be with you."

I did not need to put into words Richard's reaction to my other lovers. As the only man I had brought home, Todd knew he was unique. Plus he was extremely uncomfortable with my sexual history, despite his understanding that some of my proclivities were the result of my ... condition.

The sharp inhale and slow exhale sounded harsh across the line. Todd was coming to the end of his patience.

"Nothing short of a direct order would have made you pursue me with such dogged determination, Amy." His words were a hiss in my ear, the words melting together as if swept in on a single wind. "Did you think I didn't know?" Todd asked without anger. He had swatted away my confession with the confidence of a lion dismissing a gnat.

There was once a time in our relationship when I thought I had the upper hand. Todd had been the one who pushed for more and I had reluctantly yielded. Of course Richard's endorsement of him as a partner had smoothed his way, but that fact I had closely guarded. Then I found myself foolishly in love with the man, of which he became aware. Faced with my decision to cut out the cancer before it completely incapacitated me – I had left him – Todd finally lowered himself to match me.

He loved me, he said, but his love and mine were too different to ever be equal. Our chemistry was undeniable, but Todd had never been stripped bare from a need that surpassed the physical.

"Did Richard tell you?" I forced through cold, hard lips. I shivered once and it felt as though it started on the inside of me. Everything but my right side burned as if touched with hot coals.

"Richard didn't have to tell me anything," he said, which didn't mean that Richard hadn't. "I know you, Amy. And I could never forget how determined you were to forget me before you suddenly couldn't be without me."

From his tone it seemed we had both hurt each other. A weekend alone with him, days and nights of unrivaled sexual bliss, culminated in a catastrophic foray into the open. I was entirely unprepared for the spotlight he had cast on me, as well as the threat he and my reaction to him posed to life in the shadows. The uncertainty of wanting him and knowing he was bad news for someone with my social anxieties and in my field compromised my judgment in the eyes of others. So I lashed out at him. I cut him off like a gangrened limb until Richard opened my eyes to the merits of the man.

It should have occurred to me then that Richard's turn at Cupid would not have been a one-sided affair.

"It is all up to you," he had responded to my objection that Todd Birch had a lot going for him and that a potential relationship was beyond my sole discretion. Had he known that because he had already secured Todd's agreement? Was I the real reason for Todd's visit to Jamaica?

"Richard didn't tell you to fall in love with me. You did that on your own, Amy. So why can't you understand that I fell in love with you for you?"

Because you are you, a part of me whispered so low I almost missed it. Todd Birch was by far the deadliest man I had ever met. He was beautiful by any objective account and wore his appeal comfortably like a favorite t-shirt. The piercing nature of his dark blue eyes had a way of stripping me bare, then caressing me from the inside out. After the initial shock of his physical appearance, his eyes lulled his captive audience into a languorously sensual daze. I had seen him do it to complete strangers with just a glance. His gaze was both invasive and entirely too intimate.

During the days, pitch black hair was slicked back into a smooth shell. Behind the gel-tamed furrows was incredible depth. Once tucked away from the public he shed the gloss and allowed his thick curls to blow free. Either way, Todd's hair had a way of twisting itself around my fingers, luring me deeper into the mystery of the man.

He was hard, lean and sinewy. It was a physique that was required for his career with the Marines. He now employed it with devastating effect for his cover as a senior US diplomat. Although there was no ban on sex appeal, officially, it was forbidden to use sex to get our jobs done. But the man I had married was renowned for his sexual appetite, and there was no rule against consenting adults fulfilling their needs without compromising their positions. Todd had fucked his way through his postings, a fact I was unprepared to handle when I was sent to join him while on probation for killing a host country police officer in Jamaica.

"There was something between us from the first time we met. You cannot deny that, Amy. And you can't manufacture it either."

God, he was right. Our chemistry ran deep, but it went deeper than just a physical reaction. Case in point: Colonel Robert Townsend. I was also attracted to Todd's nemesis, and as sexually compatible as we were, I had yet to act on that attraction. And it wasn't for a lack of opportunity or reciprocal feelings either.

Before I had met Todd, Colonel Townsend and I had made plans to meet and relieve some of the sexual tension between us. It was ironic that the man who had stood me up – in my opinion to protect his marriage, but according to him because the Narcotics Affairs Director had run interference – had spent the next two months in ruthless pursuit of me.

The history between Todd and Colonel Townsend was a rancorous one. Childish competition between grown men had led to bruised egos and one dead fiancée – Todd's Mona. Knowing the man I had married, I wasn't convinced his hands were as clean as he claimed. But I had decided almost from the start that it didn't matter.

Was I afraid of him? Yes, but not for the reasons one would think. It wasn't his temper that kept me away from his rival; it was my weakness for my husband.

So yes, he was right about our start and our feelings for each other. It didn't answer the question however of what Todd was doing in Jamaica, at an event I was almost guaranteed to attend because my ego wouldn't allow me to accept such discourtesy, even from a full bull.

"For God's sake, you're the only woman I can even imagine fucking while we're fighting."

"I'm the only woman who fights with you," I clarified, and some of his tension eased.

"And I'm so fucking hard right now. I wish you were here. I would give my left nut to have my cock in your mouth right now. And as you know, I'm pretty fucking attached to my nuts."

"Todd..."

We had a mountain of issues that could not be leveled over a midnight call while separated by hundreds of miles. But at least we could find a middle ground, a refuge from the secrets and mistrust. Our breaths slowed in tandem, gusting on a slow exhale, whispers of budding desire. His need for me soothed like a warm drink on a frigid night, and the certainty of my response was like a physical caress to his heated flesh.

"The first time I laid eyes on you I thought you were so beautiful."

I had put extra effort into my appearance that night because of my plans with Colonel Townsend. What were the chances Todd would not remember why I'd been there?

"You were angry. It gusted off you in waves, but you were so fucking beautiful. I couldn't stay away. I knew there was something there, something special about you."

"Because I was angry?" I never thought of myself as beautiful. It wasn't what I wanted to be remembered for.

"No, because you were more comfortable with your anger than you were in a yard full of people would have swan-dived into an empty swimming pool just for the opportunity to make you smile. If only you would have given them a chance."

Friendships had never come easily for me. My father had stressed self-reliance. I had never needed anyone for purely personal reasons before... until Todd.

"When he touched you, the way he looked at you, the possession in his eyes nearly broke me."

We both knew who 'he' was. Colonel Townsend had approached, separated me for my company, and apologized in an unapologetic manner for standing me up.

"But you kept dodging him, and I knew he was the one who upset you. The more he pushed, the more you pulled away, and if ever there was a woman in need of rescuing, it was you."

That was new. I had never before felt as helpless as I did with Todd. He had ways of finding all my hidden, tender spots. It had something to do with his eyes, his voice, his very presence, and the intensity with which he used them. As much as I understood the danger of him exploring the parts of me I kept hidden, sometimes I just couldn't help it. Other times I could only deflect.

"I thought you came over to protect his wife."

"I came for you. Tammy made her bed when she married him."

Life was unfair. I had walked right into Colonel Townsend with my eyes wide open. If there ever was a victim – a woman in need of rescue – it was Tamara Townsend. She didn't deserve her husband. In fact she would not have "made her bed" with him if Colonel Townsend had not chased her to punish her sister. The sister was the one who got away, the woman who had broken him by sleeping with Todd.

Todd must have been thinking along similar lines, because his next words were thick and bitter.

"That was a long time ago. I knew what he had become and I didn't want him hurting you. I had to save the beautiful, broken girl."

My breath escaped me in a hollow bark. "Broken? You took one look at me and decided I was broken? Because I wore leather pants for a married man?"

"First of all I love those pants on you. Secondly, I didn't just take one look. I spotted you the moment you walked into that yard and fuck me if I could look away. If the hottest girl walks into a party and not one dick twitches, she's either knife-to-your-balls psychotic or she belongs to someone dangerous."

He barked a single, humorless laugh. There was no one there more dangerous than Todd.

"Townsend couldn't claim you with his wife next to him, but his interest said you were free. The more I watched, the more I could see that you were on the outside, Amy... there, but invisible. You trained them not to see you, because I had to have asked half a dozen men about you, and no one had anything to say. Imagine, no interest from a bunch of healthy, horny Marines, and no reason why."

"The pack doesn't piss on the alpha's spot."

Todd scoffed. "But he hadn't fucked you yet. He wouldn't have put his hands on you for all to see if he had."

"Because of his wife?" It was my turn to jeer. Tammy couldn't have stopped him from getting his dick wet. Knowing their history made his disregard understandable, albeit inexcusable.

I distractedly rubbed at my chest where the burning sensation from my hip had spread. In a blatant disregard of the laws of gravity, the heat ignored my toes. I curled them into my soles and burrowed them deeper into the duvet.

"Because of his command. He could touch you and deny there was anything going on, and that would have been the truth. But the minute he put his dick in you, it would be hands-off in public."

Todd released another drawn-out breath, slowly defusing his frustration. It was a consistent reaction to the mention of anything Townsend related.

"The thought of him owning your body was driving me crazy. I was going to take you away before he could claim you. I never expected it to be that night, but I wanted you invested in me to cut him out of the picture once and for all."

I smiled at the memory, and to the realization of how easily Todd had accomplished what he had set out to do. Less than an hour later he was buried deep inside me, filling a need that had been building for nearly three years. Todd had given me the reins to our relationship... let me think I could control where we went and how I felt, and the whole time he had been chiseling away at my defenses.

"When you first looked up at me, I felt you inside me, Amy," Todd said, so softly that at first I thought I might have imagined it. But then he continued. " You were like a shot of some drug. You fucking rocked me and I couldn't remember a woman moving more than my cock. You were hungry for me and so helpless to hide it, you couldn't keep a straight face. You looked at me, and Townsend could have fallen off the edge of the earth and you wouldn't have noticed. How could I let you go after that?

"When I'm with you I *feel*... feel things I haven't felt before. It's fucking intense. You drive me up the wall; your lack of faith in me is infuriating, because there isn't anything I wouldn't give if I knew it would make you whole. I want to understand you, but the only time I feel you're opening up to me is when I'm fucking you. I wish I could spend every waking moment inside you... I wish life were that easy, because I fucking love you, Amy. But it's never that simple.

"So I take the little you give. I put the pieces together, trying to make sense of the terrible things that happened to you. Your parents were murdered and I know you feel some responsibility because you survived. It's called survivor's guilt, Amy, a symptom of PTSD for which you self-medicate, because you need a clean psych file to work."

I had to break in before he said things that could not to be unsaid. "You don't understand anything. You don't know what you're talking about."

"I do know, Amy. And Richard knows too. You probably learned that shit from his wife," he barked.

Of course Todd saw more than he said. The pull of the void was one lesson I had learned from Aunt Abby. My first Valium was taken from her stash. And what had started as self-destructive behavior became a coping mechanism.

But what pulled me up short was the disapproval of Richard that stuck out of Todd speech. Why would he save nearly all the condemnation for his mentor? Was Todd playing me? Only after the seconds had ticked into a full minute did he exhale a rough breath, and with it, the burst of raw anger.

"I get it, Amy. He let it go because he didn't want to hurt you. I disagree with his methods, but I understand why he chose to do what he did, because I love you too. My point is, you were a child dealing with issues most adults never get over. I don't blame you for learning how to cope. You did what you had to do."

"This is about Adam."

"It's about all of it, Amy."

"Do you think I put myself in the position to be raped because I felt fatalistic after what had happened to my parents?"

"Do you think I would blame you that, Amy?" Todd shot back. "Adam Rutherford was a predator. I blame him for being a rapist. I blame Richard for being satisfied with a cover-up."

Why didn't I just hang up the phone? Why did I allow Todd to resurrect long buried memories? Why did I allow him to wring tears from a deeply buried part of me? I remembered being that broken little thing, crippled by the weight of my father's dying wish, and the realization that I would never see him again. I would never have him to lean on. I had never been in that position before, and I was afraid I would fail. I was lost and alone for a moment, and then Adam happened.

"Adam Rutherford gave me purpose. He made me want to live." Because faced with the prospect of death as his cruel hands squeezed the breath from my body, I knew I couldn't let my father down. I had to live.

"He raped you, and Richard compounded the situation by pretending it never happened. You were a child, God dammit, and he thinks of you as one of his own. But if that had been my child, I would have done everything to protect her, and I would not have put my job above her. He was wrong, Amy, and I wish I could fix it for you. I wish you would let me help you."

In our brief time together I had seen Todd broken twice. The first time, he'd found me half naked and covered in blood in the midst of three corpses. The second time, I had left him and he realized my heart was ready to give up on us. It had always been the fear of losing me that could break him. But tonight behind his sob was a desperate anger. It moved me, because that emotion was entirely my own. He had never felt it for anyone else, not even when he killed for them.

"Okay," I said, and it was almost as quiet as the night.

"Okay what?"

"Okay, I want you to help me. Would you help me fix it?"

Even as I embraced the power to sink him to the depths of desperation, I welcomed too the power to save him.

"Jesus, Amy. I would do anything for you," he said.

That was still questionable, but we were building a future together. I was building a case for Todd to choose me. Today he might have killed me if asked, but tomorrow I wanted him unfailingly on my side. And like he said, Todd would put his child above everything, even his job.

I massaged the burn on my hip with cold fingers. My body would rebel against the fertility drugs I was secretly taking. And this time, the battle would make last month's reaction to the clomiphene pale in comparison. I would give him the one thing Richard could not and use it to keep him by my side.

"And I would do anything for you," I said.

TWO

"Name?"

I looked up at Bert through the miniscule crack of my rental's window and swallowed the bile seeping up from my stomach. He had been part of Richard's security team for about two years now – an uncharacteristically long time to be babysitting. There were only two reasons I could think of that explained his prolonged assignment. Either this was all he was good for – protecting a man who could damn well protect himself – or Bert was just riding out his time, waiting for retirement or a book deal. Neither theory sat well with me, and I didn't try to hide my feelings from the one who inspired them.

"Minnie Fucking Mouse."

He looked up at me from his clipboard – a fucking clipboard at the end of 2011! – when his colleague who was busy checking the undercarriage of my rental chuckled. It was dark, but I hadn't recognized him from the glow of my headlights. Since my last encounter with Richard's team was only a couple weeks before during a quickie Thanksgiving visit with Todd, I figured he was new. Unlike Bert, with his thinning hair and liver spot hands, who had outlasted five team members so far.

"Is there a problem, Mrs. Birch?"

I gritted my teeth against the rise he was aiming for. Married or not I would always be Amy Koehler. "Are you going to let me in or do I have to get Richard out here in the cold?" For effect I thumbed my phone.

Bert flicked the collar of his coat, turning his back to me before getting the all clear from his side-kick and buzzing me through the gates.

The front door was unlocked, so I made my way through the eight thousand square foot house with the ease of long familiarity. This used to be my home. I had spent nearly three hours running here the night I escaped my parents' murderers. I was moved here after that night. I returned here the night Adam gave me purpose, then every holiday and most weekends off from West Point. Then when I turned twenty-one, everything my parents had owned was released from trust to me, and I was able to come and go as I pleased.

I had married Todd Birch outside my father's study window just months ago. And if everything went according to plan I would conceive a child in my father's house at the end of the week. Todd was coming home – to my real home – for a weekend, at which time we would negotiate our long-term plans. Christmas was only a couple of weeks away.

I found Richard on the second floor, adjusting the settings on a treadmill. "Too old for real run?" I asked in greeting.

Richard didn't look at me. He was busy choosing between a California redwood park trail and the Grand Canyon. "It's freezing outside."

"Great. I don't have to listen to you whine about the fucking heat."

He stopped poking at the buttons and threw me a stare over one shoulder. Grown men had pissed their pants under the point of Richard's one blue eye. I pressed the heel of one sneaker into my glutes in a much-needed quad stretch. Our bouts were mostly psychological, but I enjoyed warming up with Richard.

"You're never going to keep a man with a mouth like yours."

I rolled my eyes and made no attempt to hide it. Richard may have been responsible for bringing us together, but Todd and I had put the work in that would keep us that way. Of all my faults, a potty mouth was the least likely to derail that.

"Hurry up, old man. At your pace it will be noon before we're back. I have people to see, places to be, and a ton of shit to do."

Richard turned and hit me with the brown eye too. I switched legs. After a full minute he gave up on trying to eyeball me to death. I braced myself for the next the blow: preying on my self-consciousness. I slung my leg up on an incline bench and pressed hard until my hamstrings squeaked. Richard stomped past me, heading towards his bedroom presumably to change into thermals.

"I'll radio Bert to gear up," I announced to his retreating back, still waiting for a jab below the belt. He might have looked older than at Thanksgiving, but Richard never changed. He was just taking his time, making sure he caught me off-guard.

"Bert stays at the gate. Tell the new guy to grab the quad. I don't want to have to worry about the two of you keeping up."

I was shocked by the tame rejoinder, but hid the surprise as I sank into a straight leg stretch. "You know it's not a punishment if he likes it, right?" I would never understand why Richard put up with Bert. He gave his own kids a hard time for being complacent in their jobs and their lives. Andrew, his second son, had been branded as lazy for hitting thirty as a bachelor.

Richard's head reappeared from behind the half closed bedroom door. "By the way, you look like shit, Amy," came the overdue shot. "Put some lipstick on." Then he was gone, fully expecting compliance at 4 a.m. on my way for a run through the woods.

When Richard joined me on the back porch a few minutes later, I was more limber but still bare-faced. Nick, the new guard, confirmed our itinerary with Richard then set off ahead, shivering in his light coat. It was his first run with me, for which he was grossly unprepared. For three hours he would scope the trail before us, then double back to keep a closer watch on Richard. In about fifteen minutes he would regret the convenience of riding instead of running. Without a hot beverage, the wind chill would have him frozen to the bone in no time. Richard didn't find it necessary to warn him, so neither did I. Whatever he had done to irritate his boss – and by the chill behind the older man's easy smile, I could tell he had an axe to grind – was their business.

We were soon on our way, jogging at an easy pace to get the blood flowing. The first five miles should have been warm-up, but Richard cut it back to three.

"You're definitely going to lose that man of yours if you need half an hour to warm up," Richard offered, rocking me with a near debilitating bout of nausea. So we picked up the pace for the next six miles, partly because I needed to escape the idea that Richard had given any consideration to the mechanics of my sex life.

He matched me well enough as we alternated short sprints with longer recovery paces. I eventually slowed so we could run shoulder to shoulder without giving away the tiny concession to his deteriorated condition. At sixty-five Richard was in excellent shape, but that morning he didn't move as vibrantly as I remembered on our previous runs together. I blamed it on the cold air, which although dry, was harsh on the body. I filed my concern away to be examined another day.

My own nostrils were abraded by each breath, my cheeks singed and my lips cracked. It was a struggle to keep my muscles from clenching taut from the cold. At about the halfway mark, I was forced to break stride and seek the support of a rough barked pine. I rubbed a sprig of pine needles between my hands, inhaling their fragrance. But no matter how hard I tried to tighten my diaphragm or calm the roiling contents of my stomach, the urge to retch grew more powerful.

Bile burned its way up my throat. I held my breath to avoid aspirating the stomach acid, and a wave of lightheadedness almost knocked me over. It seemed to go on forever until finally, starved of oxygen, my leg muscles cramped and I collapsed on all fours, heaving onto the forest floor. The man who had raised me since I was seventeen years old stood several yards away, pacing with his back turned. Nick caught up to us on one of his double-back loops, but Richard waved him away. I could count on Richard to preserve our image.

After a few more minutes of empty retching, the contractions eased and I was able to stand. I brushed the dirt and leaves from my hands and knees, then took to the trail in a slow jog.

"Sorry," I offered Richard between wiping my mouth and catching up to him.

His gloved hand on my arm pulled me up short before I could get my momentum going. He stared at me for a while, blue and brown eyes mapping the sharp edges of my cheekbones and the hollows of my face. In better light he would have checked my pupils, trying to assess whether anything more powerful than endorphins tainted my blood.

"You look terrible."

"I'm fine," I told him, but let him look his fill. The fact that I allowed the probe should have been proof that I was clean. Todd's words from the night before awakened an old realization in me. Richard knew I self-medicated; he had always known. He just didn't want to hurt me, or rather, my career. But now that he had me where he wanted me – married and home – to what lengths would he go to keep me there? How much was he willing to keep on ignoring?

"What did you take?"

"Nothing. It'll pass. My stomach is just a little unsettled," I offered, deliberately misinterpreting him.

"You know what I mean, Amy," he said sharply, his fingers tightening on my arm for a moment before dropping to his side. "You're a married woman now. You should be having children, not polluting your body..." His words gently faded into nothing. The same nothingness he had pretended for all these years.

I turned away and mumbled so he could just make out the words. "What do you think I'm trying to do?"

He caught up to me in two strides, because I wanted to be caught. He spun me around because my reluctance was only an illusion.

"What did you say?"

"Nothing." I clenched my jaw. I met his eyes, which were wide with anxiety, with my own defiant stare.

"Are you pregnant?" His fingers squeezed my forearms on both sides, proof of his desperation when moments ago he had been so careful.

"That's none of your business."

"Amy!" He shook me gently, much gentler than I would have expected before this conversation began.

"No," I answered, and watched with keen interest as the light in his eyes began to fade. "Not yet anyway. But I'm trying."

"You are?" He asked in wonder. And then his eyes clouded over with suspicion. "How do you expect to get anywhere when you're here and your husband is not."

I pulled away from his fingers that were becoming more insistent by the second. "Not that it's any of your business, but I'm taking fertility treatments. It only takes one try, you know, if we time it right."

"What's wrong with you?" Richard asked, his eyes resting almost accusingly on my empty abdomen.

I rolled my eyes. "Nothing's wrong with me. I'm perfectly capable of having children. It's just that I've been on some serious birth control and haven't ovulated in over a decade. It takes time to come back naturally." Here I offered a short, humorless laugh. "The side effects are a pain; the nausea is unbearable, but I don't want to wait."

Richard's understanding caught up to my intent, and his urgency knocked me back a step. His voice was pleading, his gloved fingers caressing like a whisper across my chin and cheeks. "Do you want it, Amy? Really?"

I had never seen him this soft before, except perhaps the night twelve years ago when I had run to him. Even then, he was gentle but firm, taking charge of the situation, promising answers. From his lips justice had sounded like vengeance. I had never heard this pleading quality when he asked me to trust him back then.

"Yes, Richard. I want Todd's baby."

"Why?"

I thought about what would make Richard happy, what would put him in a giving mood. Perhaps my brief pause came across as reluctance, which my would-be father recognized as a precursor of the truth, raw unfiltered and entirely too revealing. His eyes were hopeful.

"Because I love him."

Richard melted like stone, slowly even at extremely high temperatures. But in that brief moment, he looked at me like a loving father, and all the hardness was gone. He was liquid in my hands. As he hugged me, his laugh echoed with genuine joy and relief through the empty forest. For years he had waited, sometimes despairing that I would ever come around to his vision of happiness for me. He had allowed me the freedom to go my own way, and now like a prodigal child I had returned.

I wanted my fatted calf.

"You can't tell Todd that I am on fertility treatments."

"Why not? You can't get pregnant without him, and I can assure you he wants children as much as you and I."

I could feel my lips thinning as Richard all but confirmed that he had no intention of keeping my secret. "I don't want him to think I'm pulling him away from his work in Santo Domingo." Again Richard dismissed my objection with a breezy wave, the same ease with which I blotted the tip of my nose on the sleeve of my thermal.

"But of course he will come home," came his all too easy offer. He also turned us around, wrapping an arm around my shoulder as we walked back to the house. I pulled away to face him, forcing us both to a stop.

"Not on my account, Richard." His delight dipped a notch when confronted so openly with the might of my immovable demand.

"Alright. Then on mine." He made to step around me, but I blocked the path. This was my gift, getting what I wanted without the most astute subject realizing it.

"That's your professional prerogative, but I don't want him to know what I'm doing."

"What difference does it make? Don't you think he'll find out soon enough?"

"February is soon enough. His birthday is the eighth. Hopefully by then I'll have more answers."

Richard looked concerned, his eyes straying to my abdomen again. If this was what being pregnant was like – being stripped of privacy for the sake of other people's curiosity – I would hate every second of it, starting now.

"What other answers? Is there something wrong, Amy?"

I shook my head and crossed my arms over my stomach, ineffective shield that it was. "With the drugs, there is a risk of multiple births." A wide grin cracked his face in two as he shook a thick, gloved finger at me. Richard cupped my face and kissed my cheeks, the momentary warmth replaced by the stinging cold air.

"You beautiful girl. You've never done anything halfway." Richard pulled me into his side with an arm around my shoulder and we resumed our walk towards the house.

"Promise me, Richard. You won't say anything to anyone?"

He nodded, but I could tell from the near empty chuckle that his mind was already weaving a scheme. "I won't say a word, but he must come home. I want you both home for this, Amy."

I allowed myself to be led down the path, kicking absentmindedly at a stray pinecone. "I'm not sure where I'll be, and I wouldn't want you to interfere with Todd's career. If he knew, he might resent it and grow to hate me."

"You have an interview in the next couple of days, don't you?"

I pulled away from his embrace, but kept up the pace. My only response was a noncommittal shrug, consistent with my history of resisting Richard's interventions. He was my boss' boss' boss, but I had gone to great lengths to conceal our personal relationship from casual onlookers. Everything I had accomplished thus far was through my own merit.

"Do you still have your heart set on Paris?" Richard was fishing. Of course he would not give me Paris. He never intended to, so I had tried to win it without him.

I shrugged again. "To visit someday, but I realize now that's not where my strengths are." I wiped my nose again, but this time it was meant to conceal what little Richard could see of my face.

He tossed his head from side to side thoughtfully, but kept staring at me, casting his line then reeling it in to see what was at the end. With only my profile to go off, it was an effort in futility. He never imagined that the pupil would one day outshine her teachers.

"You will like what Don has to offer. The opportunity couldn't be better if it was made for you." And I had no doubt it had been made for me. I held my silence though. Better to have Richard think I had fallen unwittingly in line with his plans for me.

"And he's wanted you for some time now. Don likes your mind."

Don Blitzner liked my mind so much he had set me up. Because of him, a kill-team headed by a corrupt cop had tried to exact payment for a failed drug-and-guns run out of my skin. I was uncomfortable, to say the least, working for a man whose idea of an entrance exam was surviving a death squad while protecting my unsuspecting fiancé. All with no notice.

"I confess," Richard continued his musings, "I like your mind too, Amy."

He fell quiet and I left him to his thoughts. I knew our conversation wasn't yet over. For one, we were only walking, although at this pace there were two full hours ahead of us.

"So how likely is it that there will be multiples?"

Of course he would want to know that. Probability was their domain; it was the lifeblood of the intelligence community, which was why I had the answer readily available.

"Thirty percent." I could tell he liked the odds, even if he didn't smile.

"Never satisfied with half measures," he repeated with what sounded like pride. "Don't you worry about Todd, Amy. You just give me one boy with a head on his shoulders like yours and his daddy's, and everything will be all right."

No pressure.

Richard turned his eyes away from the future and his visions of dynasty to pull me back into an embrace. I felt his breath against my ear and his hands soothing my back. His breathing was deep, but his body stiff, and I knew to prepare. He was only ever like this right before a flaying. Richard couldn't face the rawness he exposed. He hated the reminder in my eyes of his own failure... failure to fulfill the promise he had made to me twelve years ago.

"Your daddy would have been so proud of you. We raised you to be the woman you are now. You took what we taught you, found yourself a worthy man, and you're gonna share that with your boys. Between you, me, and that man of yours, we're going to make them great. One day, their daddy is gonna have my job. I promise you, Amy. You just keep on doing what you're doing."

By the time he pulled away to assess the wreckage that was my composure, the tears had frozen tracks on my cheeks. He rubbed at them with his gloved thumbs and I watched his Adam's apple bob with the struggle to clear away his own.

"Don't cry, Amy."

How could I not?

"He asked me to take care of you, and haven't I done that these ten years?" It was twelve, but I nodded just the same and pulled at my dripping nose. "I feel guilty that you and Todd haven't had a real honeymoon. Let me take care of that for you. It's what your daddy would've done."

I focused on the improbability of Richard ever experiencing guilt, which made me laugh through the tears.

"The first time you brought that man of yours home you told me your daddy would've wanted you to go experience Paris before you started having babies."

I lifted my eyes sharply to his, all thought, all hope frozen in that moment. Of course I planned on going to Europe. I had someone there I had to kill. I had even confided in Todd that there was someone in Europe who might know who ordered the hit on my father. He probably dismissed it as the wishful thinking of a broken-hearted girl, but he had agreed not to mention it to Richard.

It was only the details of Blitzner's offer that kept me from purchasing the ticket weeks ago. A long weekend was more than enough time for me to bring my plans to a close. Sergei Afanasenko was a dead man walking and he didn't even know it.

"I think you're right. So would you let me do the right thing and send you both to Paris for your honeymoon?"

It seemed too good to be true, which meant it was. I knew better than to be tempted right out the gate. "We won't have the time. If I accept Blitzner's offer he may want me to start right away. Plus Todd doesn't know when the new ambassador is taking office. He might still be head of mission this time next year. It's risky enough that he's taking off this weekend to come home…"

My protests were feeble and trailed off as Richard shook his head. "Leave everything to me, Amy. You can even call it a honeymoon Christmas gift. Just say yes."

"Richard…" I sniffled, pressing my sleeve to my nose again.

"Say. Yes."

He was so ardent I knew the offer was spontaneous. I had done that. I had wrung honest emotion from his stone-cold heart. There was a swelling inside my chest that I was afraid I could not contain. I answered quickly before it fed more tears.

"Yes. Thank you."

Richard kissed my cheeks again, then stared into my eyes. "Good girl," he said with the same affectionate smile he gave his prize

Dobermans. It didn't last long though. Such expressions of emotion were a source of embarrassment to both the giver and the recipient. "Come on, we'll run back. It's cold as a nun's tit out here, so try to keep up."

I stared at his back for a short while as he took off along the dirt track, confident that I would follow and Nick would realize we had deviated from the itinerary.

That was always the problem with change. It was insidious, slowly, methodically chipping away at the foundations of the old establishment. As I took off behind him, catching up easily, but deliberately holding back, it was clear to only me that the pupil had surpassed the teacher.

THREE

Donald Blitzner repulsed me, and I couldn't understand why. There was nothing objectionable about his physical appearance. His hair was grayer than I remembered, but his new role as head of the CIA's counterterrorism office may have had something to do with that. His eyes might have once been a crystalline blue. Now they were just glassy with unshed tears for all the people he had fucked over. After all, he had almost gotten me killed.

The longer he talked, pointy chin resting on top of his steepled fingers, the more mobile my skin became, desperate to move out of his line of sight. More than repulsion with his Charles Montgomery Burns brand of sleaze, Don Blitzner terrified me. I was afraid of him because I knew nothing about him, and even after three years of being stationed together in Kingston's small mission, I could no more guess at his motives for wanting me on his team than I could understand why he would set me up.

I was not satisfied with his account that I was being tested. Stress positions and calculated circumstances were one thing. Tipping off a corrupt cop and his drug trafficking enforcement team of my role in the interdiction of their organization was another. There was no way Blitzner could have been certain of the outcome, when in the first instance, they had come for me when least expected. Only the paranoia that went hand-in-hand with my condition had saved me. And in the second instance,

Blitzner had failed to mention to me that I had been marked. Even a casual warning might have changed things.

Maybe I would have handled things differently... been more discreet in eliminating the threat once the element of surprise was placed in my favor. Maybe I would not have been booted out of country and my name and reputation shredded. Maybe I could have been on my way to my Paris posting where I could personally direct the apprehension of Sergei Afanasenko. Instead I was managing the operation through the eyes of an asset who at any moment could turn on me, as well as layers upon layers of mercenaries whose main value to me was their disposability.

And it was all because this man who had nothing to gain, and if what he was saying now was true, risked a considerable loss from my demise, had almost had me killed. Perhaps the reason he terrified me so was the fact that I had to trust him. I could not read him, had failed for years to divine his reasons, motives and next steps. So the only way left to get the answers I deserved was to pose the question to him. I could accept or not his answer, but either way I would have to trust this man.

"Why didn't you tell me I'd been made?"

I didn't care that he had been in the middle of reciting the role and responsibilities of the Center for Terrorism Analysis under the Directorate of Intelligence in the CIA. I needed an answer to my question before we went any further. If he had acted on a whim, or perverse sense of humor, then I was ready to walk away from his job offer.

And maybe one day I would show him how to really kill someone.

Blitzner leaned back in his chair, the leather so fresh it squeaked under his gabardine pants. The sickly sweet smile he always wore never dipped, but his sagging lids did, hiding for a moment the reptilian quality of his eyes. As if I would ever forget...

"Why, Amy," he began, deliberately slow while he brushed off the speech he had rehearsed. Of course he knew this would come up. He had to. "In our line of work, you are not always forewarned of the consequences of your actions."

I could not stand for the deflection now. I cut him off. "You pushed for me to identify Vargas."

"I certainly did not. You volunteered. I simply endorsed your offer."

"Without which Lowe would have refused. But that is beside the point. You leaked my identity to the locals. You knew they would come for me, and you kept that information to yourself. I want to know why."

Blitzner's hands disappeared below the polished surface of his desk. Without those pencil-thin fingers, the surface appeared bare.   It was home to two desk phones, a stack of pencils turned tip-up in a tin container, an empty organizer, and three three-ring folders that had no labels, one of which was my personnel file. It was his way of letting me know I had competition for this job.

Someone – possibly Richard – forgot to inform the bastard that I wasn't really looking for a job. And even if I were as desperate as he imagined, Don Blitzner would have been my last choice. The wide smile he offered, which was in fact a baring of overused, tobacco-stained teeth, displayed his unfamiliarity with genuine emotion. Without practice it was impossible to do justice to pleasure when suffused with its opposite.

"How strange it must be for Captain Amy Koehler to be so wrong," he drawled, either betraying deep Southern roots or affecting them. With Don Blitzner, one could never tell. I remained unmoved by his sarcasm. "Your time on that island was up."

I held my silence, something that was working for me more and more lately. Never mind that his latest assertion was news to me – and hardly anything that happened in our Kinston embassy was news to me. I had been posted there for two and a half years and intelligence was my lifeblood. My term should have ended at the end of the year, not the middle of summer.

"Why, Admiral McDowell was convinced you had outgrown that assignment."

The man's eyes darted from my file to his GSA-approved tiles. Without carpeting there was one less home for covert recording devices, so his shiftiness had to be a sign of prevarication. Or with Blitzner, that too might have been calculated.

"And it appears he was right. There are certainly more worthwhile pursuits for the spouse of Todd Birch than chasing dime-a-dozen traffickers. If you were honest with yourself, you would be the first to admit that your forays into the operational fray were counterproductive to your new position. Yet you would not take Lowe's word for it. You had to experience it for yourself."

The man was a liar. He had to be a very good one to be sitting behind that desk. But the best lies were the ones hinged on truth, and all lies were not made equal. Sometimes the ones left unspoken were the most powerful. The things Blitzner left unsaid were too convincing to be ignored.

"You're a first class analyst, Amy," Lowe had told me on a sunny Sunday afternoon at the Kingston yacht club. *"You have a combination of guts and natural instinct that I haven't seen in someone your age in a long time. You'll go far if you don't get careless, and distractions will do that. I don't think you're the woman to manage Birch, and you've got too much on your plate right now anyway."*

That meeting predated my decision to reach out to Todd, after two weeks of pretending he had been wiped off the face of the earth. It was after that conversation with Lowe that I had appealed to Richard for help on an obstacle to one of my cases. Not only did Richard impress me with his knowledge of my sex life, I was surprised by his assurance of Todd's interest in me.

"Amy, think about it," Richard had said. *"He's a rising star in the State Department, and there's a good chance he'll be a career ambassador one day."* That had been a lie… one I excused because it was a legitimate cover.

I was aware at the time that the Richard and Lowe each had different ideas of where my career should take me. Lowe saw me as an independently superb analyst. Richard's vision was more traditional – a breeding mare for the next generation of people like us. But Richard had sweetened the deal with what Lowe did not know me well enough to offer: free will.

"I'm not going to tell you what to do," Richard had lied, *"but I will say, this could be a boon to both your careers."*

The only way Don Blitzner would have been privy to those plans was if Richard had shared them with him. But there were at least a dozen layers of separation between Richard and Blitzner, and no acceptable reason for direct communication between them.

Additionally, Blitzner's new role as section chief in the Center for Terrorism Analysis was a quantum leap from his last role as chief of the Narcotics Affairs Section in a tiny embassy, buried deep in the Crime and

Narcotics Center. His determination to have me was also troubling. Only Richard's intervention could make perfect sense of such a climb or Blitzner's sudden infatuation with my career.

Strange as it might seem, I believed Blitzner today. He wasn't lying when he informed me I was wrong a few minutes ago. There were so many things I could have been wrong about.

Knowing Blitzner's shiftiness, I also recognized he would only commit to the question I had posed.

"You knew they would come for me, and you kept that information to yourself. I want to know why."

"How strange it must be for Captain Amy Koehler to be so wrong. Your time on that island was up."

He hadn't kept it to himself. The decision to move me had already been made.

He had shared with Richard.

Richard knew I was a target in an attack that resembled the one in which my parents were killed.

Lying in bed next to Todd that night, I recalled listening to the end notes of the rain. It brought back to mind that night twelve years ago when the execution squad came in from the lake, wiping out our guards; when I forever pulled the scent of the damp woods and moist air into my lungs as I ran for three-and-a-half hours; when the cold rain soaked through my pajamas and into my bones and deep in my heart.

They shot my mother in the back as she ran to my father. My father was tortured. Three broken fingers on one hand, one bullet nearly amputated his leg at the knee, then another that ripped off his skull on exit, and my life was irrevocably changed.

Richard knew another team, albeit amateurs in the task of killing, were coming for me and he did not warn me. All to teach me a lesson? To push me into a decision I would never have made on my own. How pleased he must be now to see me falling in line.

The man sitting across from me had traded up on my back.

"You did very well, Amy, better than anyone could have expected in fact," Blitzner had said at the scene of my refusal to lie down and die.

The bodies of the three men who had tried to kill me were still warm and Blitzner already had the next steps in my career mapped out.

"Now you, young lady, should expect a very interesting offer very soon. We need people like you, Amy."

Of course his promotion was paid for, a reward for aligning himself with Richard.

But Blitzner wasn't the only one blossoming under the glow of Richard's favor. *"I came for you,"* Todd had said two nights ago about the first time we met.

Now Blitzner's revelation put that confession in context. It made sense that Richard had been certain of Todd's interest in me. It made sense of Todd's 'love'. He too was part of the conspiracy.

Truly I was not surprised. A man like Todd Birch had no business falling in love with anyone, least of all me. It was not disappointment that twisted my insides into tight knots. The waves of nausea and the surge of bile creeping up my throat were only the result of the things I was doing to my body. It was suffering I would have to endure, because flesh and blood and bones were my battlefield.

And I fully intended to use it to beat Todd at his game.

FOUR

"Why, Amy, I hope I haven't upset you."

I could have laughed at the irony. This man had gone to considerable trouble to court me for an analytical position on his team, but could still treat me with the kid gloves required for handling the hysterical female. I would have been offended if not for my history with Richard.

Men like my father's best friend belonged to a different generation. Women had their uses... their place... and it was a man's responsibility to protect that. My father had blurred the lines with me. I was an only child, but I never felt my sex was a disappointment to him.

My father raised me as his heir, and yet he seemed to preserve the old ways with my mother. So while I was aware of the role of women in the lives of powerful men, I also knew I was an exception.

When Richard took over, it was hard for both of us to adjust. He had never had any daughters – just three sons – and he looked to me to step into that role.

For him, everything my father had taught me was to be used to bring a good man home – and only a man in our small community, adept at deceit and unflinchingly loyal was good enough. In fact, I was little more than a vetting tool for Richard's heirs, and a womb to house his legacy. That was where Richard and Blitzner parted ways. Blitzner wanted me because I was good at my job.

"A combination of guts and natural instinct that I haven't seen in someone your age in a long time."

Not only would it be an injustice to every woman in the intelligence field to allow my prospective boss to see how shaken his revelation had left me, it would have also been a personal embarrassment.

"No, you did not upset me." I swallowed hard to keep the bile down. "Just getting over the flu, that's all."

But like a shark in bloody waters, Blitzner's attention was fully centered on me. The blue eyes beneath the thin gray lines of his brows were distinctly predatory.

"Well, I imagine it must be unnerving to learn the 'love match' between two of our brightest stars wasn't as spontaneous as you had first imagined."

For a moment there was real pleasure behind his smile. And if ever I had had any doubt, it died under this man's gloating.

The government seemed to like sociopaths. It was what made us good at our jobs, even if we were terrible human beings. Blitzner, for example, seemed to genuinely enjoy the hurt he imagined to have inflicted with those words. He had no other motivation – nothing at all to gain – from informing me that my marriage was one of convenience.

Lucky for me, anger was a natural antacid.

"If you are hoping to confess to having orchestrated my meeting with Todd, let me apologize in advance for stealing your thunder."

"Orchestrated?" He made a tut-tut sound with his tongue against his teeth. "I'm afraid I can't take that credit."

Blitzner… afraid? Not yet. But soon.

"You monitored my communications. You knew I was meeting Colonel Townsend that night. You ran interference – came up with a bullshit distraction to keep him away, then put him in my path later that night. You knew I wouldn't let it go, that I would confront him. You also put Todd at that party. And aware of the history between them, you knew Townsend's interest in me was like waving a red flag in front of a bull. That, Mr. Blitzner, is orchestrating."

His shoulders met his ears in an expression of chagrin. He was no way apologetic of his role in the conspiracy. In fact, his Cheshire cat smile oozed pride. "So you know…"

"I have always known, Mr. Blitzner. You've misunderstood me from the start. You see, I know you are someone else's tool, and this –" I tilted my chin towards his bare desk and even barer office on the second of eight floors – "is your reward."

I had the satisfaction of watching the glee melt from his eyes, even if his smile never dipped by a millimeter.

"You surprised me with all the work you put into using me to build your position. You should have simply asked me to join your team. The path of least resistance is only ever the path of the loser in a zero-sum game. But my career, Mr. Blitzner, benefits us all."

I watched him exhale slowly and quietly, struck mute for a while. He had only ever seen me behind my bosses, when my future was on the line and it was better to get along than to make waves. That had gotten me nowhere. The assignment I had worked so hard for would never be mine. And all along, everyone – everyone! – had been using me, manipulating me for their own purposes.

I would make it to Paris without them. I had found my father's last prey through my own devices. I was married to a man who had lied to me from the start, who had spurned my offer of forgiveness and chose to perpetuate the deception. I might as well get some mileage from their scheme.

"I want a thirty percent raise. I work from my home office unless I absolutely need to come in. I want my current expense account doubled." Not that I needed any of it, but power was only an illusion if left unused.

"Why, Amy, you haven't even seen my offer yet." His fingers met in a steeple under his chin again. Blitzner was mostly unreadable, but I recognized his 'game on' move.

"Like I said earlier, you are someone else's tool. He knows what I want and is prepared to give it to me. You have only to ask. The home office is entirely within your purview. Have the offer revised and I'll pass by this afternoon to sign. You can tell me what you want with Detainee 28211 then."

I pulled the strap of my purse over my shoulder and made my way to the door. He needed his privacy to put back the pieces of his pride, and I was more than willing to give it to him. But before I went, there were a few more things we needed to be clear.

"Once I start working for you, Mr. Blitzner, I expect to work for only you... not Admiral McDowell. I would appreciate it if you did not bring your arrangement with him to bear on our working relationship. In return I promise you the same courtesy."

"Of course, Amy. I wouldn't have it any other way."

I mimicked his humorless smile. "The next thing is my husband. He is not your concern and our marriage is off limits. You can tap my phone, tag my car, have me followed, sniff my piss. I don't care. But I want it all off when I'm with my husband. You should also know that I have the Admiral's team sweep my house, and I'm sure Todd will want to bring in his own people too, given the CIA's reputation for overreaching.

"You have my number. Call me once the request is squared away. I'll come in to sign, and discuss Mohammed al-Mohammed."

I walked away with a calm I did not feel. I made it to my rental and drove four blocks to the nearest Starbucks. The closest parking was a disabled spot for which I beat out a septuagenarian. I made it to the toilet, emptied my stomach, and was back in my car before the old man could make a second tour of the parking lot. I was me again.

FIVE

Mohammed al-Mohammed was born Mohamed al-Qasim in Tyre, Lebanon in 1963. He was one of half dozen children born to Hasan al-Qasim, an engineer and renown bomb-maker for Hezbollah during the Lebanese Civil War. As I pored over his nearly two hundred-page file, I tried to calm the ever-deeper pounding in my chest.

Mohammed al-Mohammed represented a life I thought I had given up.

He was raised in terror. Terror was all he knew, and the only cure for someone like him was death.

I used to hunt men like him. I used to gorge myself on any piece of information available, then I would delve inside their minds, looking for that one thing that would break them. The ability to reach into the far recesses of minds and hearts like theirs made me undeniably good at my job. It was why Blitzner was willing to put up with me. The problem with navigating the labyrinth was the price I paid each time I did it. It was the reason I'd wanted to give it up; it was the reason I'd left Military Intelligence.

I knew I was getting lost. I could feel chunks of my humanity slipping away each time. And I didn't exactly have a surfeit of that. The risks I was willing to take, the sacrifices I was okay making, devalued human worth. Like my targets, the mission transcended everything, and the lives I took and the people I destroyed were weightless in my skewed balances.

Traffickers were different. Their devotion was to a physical thing, and their faith was rooted in their five senses. If they could not experience their rewards in the here-and-now, it did not exist. And nearly nothing was worth dying for. Even if the best of them had to be ruthless, the lengths to which they would go were always checked by the risk their actions posed to themselves. The need for caution, to preserve their wealth, power, and lives had become their conscience.

Visions of divine reward had stolen Mohammed al-Mohammed's earthly conscience.

While on the hunt, I was not very different from him. I had nothing to lose and neither did he. Still, he and I were far from invincible. For years, my father had been my weakness, and only recently had there been a rival.

Scouring the tome before me, I was convinced Mohammed al-Mohammed had no weakness. But I was sure Mohammed al-Qasim did.

He was twelve years old when the war in Lebanon began. His family was one of thousands displaced by *Operation Litani* in 1978. Israel had invaded South Lebanon in response to PLO militant attacks. The family found little refuge in West Beirut during a conflict that launched the car bomb as a weapon of war.

Of the more than three thousand six hundred car bombs employed during the conflict, Mohammed's father, Hasan, was reputed to have been involved, in one way or another, in the construction or deployment of over twelve hundred of them. Hasan was implicated in the 1983 bombings of the US Marines barracks and the French Dakkar barracks in Beirut, as well as the US Embassy bombings in April 1983 and September 1984.

For all the anarchy that surrounded them, and despite their father's reign of terror, the al-Qasim children were all well educated. At twenty-six, Mohammed and his older brother, Saad, had both earned PhD's in engineering and chemistry, respectively.

One would think Mohammed al-Qasim would never have had a chance to rise above his circumstances. Being raised by a terrorist in an environment where he witnessed terror and desolation on a daily basis was not conducive to healthy psychological development. However, annexed to his file was his brother's. In Hasan's eyes, Mohammed al-

Mohammed was The Good Son, because at their father's behest, the eldest had been the subject of a *fatwa*.

At thirty-three years old, Saad al-Qasim had married a Maronite woman with whom he had led a secret affair, and to whom he was now married and living in exile in Paris under the name Selim Haddad. In exchange for asylum and the protection of the French government, Saad had become the primary intelligence source on his father's illegal activities. So when in 2003 a US court awarded damages to the families of US personnel killed in the embassy bombings in Lebanon, the decision was based on Selim's testimony to French intelligence agents that his father had acted in concert with Hezbollah and Iranian agents.

When the family disappeared in 1990, it was Selim who pointed the finger at Iran. After two decades of living off the radar close to Tehran, Mohammed al-Mohammed reemerged in Iraq in 2007. He was arrested in Baghdad, and eventually identified through DNA provided by his brother, Saad, and subsequently transferred to Guantánamo.

At the time I was sifting through his file, Mohammed al-Mohammed was one of the one hundred forty-nine remaining detainees, having been classified in the 2010 Task Force final review as one of the forty-eight detainees who were 'too dangerous to transfer but not feasible for prosecution.'

Mohammed al-Mohammed was also the most uncooperative. For a man who claimed to have nothing to hide, he was unusually tightlipped. Four years after his arrest, the man knew no one, lived nowhere, and was resolutely ignorant of his father's whereabouts. It was almost as if he had gone to sleep in November 1990 and awoke seconds before his capture. He was a mystery that endured through two hundred sessions of interrogation, some of which lasted a full week; three sessions of enhanced interrogation; and two overnight visits to Camp No. He was a mystery Blitzner thought I could solve.

It took me three days to work through Mohammed al-Mohammed's file, but only an hour to conclude the pointlessness of my visits to Guantánamo. After eight days of total sensory deprivation, the man had claimed 'light' as his favorite color, and 'silence' as his favorite sound. The next week it was rock and roll and barking dogs. After that the fun and games had truly begun, but to no avail. If he hadn't cracked under pressure in four years, hadn't screamed a name while under severe psychological duress, and had withstood both Dr. Emily Crofter's traditional and experimental treatments, then I was not going to sweet-talk him into telling me where his father was hiding.

I was never in denial of my own failings, and empathy was beyond my emotional grasp. I knew Mohammed al-Mohammed had been abused, caged, demoralized. I even respected his defiance. However, there was no doubt the man had to be broken, and ultimately, I believed he should die. As should his father.

Mohammed al-Mohammed had already lost three fingers, some sensitivity in his right arm, and one-eighth of his face to bomb-making. Nothing short of completely losing his mental faculties would stop him from following in his father's footsteps should the opportunity – even a moment of freedom – arise. There was no safe place for The Good Son but the grave.

The other brother was the only real hope we had of breaking Mohammed al-Mohammed. I did not think Saad in fact knew where his father was, but I doubted the French had tapped him out completely. There had to be a chink in Mohammed al-Mohammed's armor, and if anyone knew what that might be, it would be his older and only remaining brother.

If there was anyone who could get Saad – or Selim Haddad, as he was now known – to talk, it was I. He had a laundry list of vulnerabilities: a wife for whom he had abandoned his family; children he undoubtedly loved; a peaceful existence in a beautiful city; the freedom to quietly practice chemistry; and of course, a bounty on his head. I had no conscience that would stop me from shaking the earth beneath his fragile world. And that was exactly what I began to do.

Adeline Haddad was an interior decorator, and a suspicious woman. The lessons of her past were hard learned ones, so she refrained from visiting the home of first-time clients. Through an asset in Paris – an expatriate, who after nearly a decade living in the city for a multinational was more Gaul than Wisconsin – a pretext was created to draw Adeline to rue de Liège. I was budgeting a couple of weeks to incite confidence, because as wary as Madame Haddad wished to be, wealth was a wonderful leveler of obstacles.

I was pushing the limits of Blitzner's budget, but if the ploy worked, the reward would be worth every centime.

SIX

The last four days had to be the longest of Anne's life. Between short shifts of napping at her father's desk, the hours of poring over target files had blended into seemingly endless cycles of work, eat, hunt.

After months of monitoring, Sergei Afanasenko's schedule was known by rote. There were the odd instances when businesses or family emergencies warranted straying from the routine, so for the last few weeks most of Anne's efforts went into risk management. That was just as well, because keeping a handle on her father's old asset and her current, though reluctant, talent acquisition specialist, Blerim Nesimi, was almost a full-time job. Moving around the watchers to avoid detection, ensuring she had a cleaner on standby, and establishing boots on the ground, namely Angelika Prokop, rounded off Anne's list of top priorities.

Three weeks of 'home study', affording her the opportunity to learn about her presumed adopted homeland had ended with Angelika's relocation to Paris in early December. Her apartment on rue d'Assas in the sixth arrondissement was a few blocks from the Russian tea shop where Sergei Afanasenko and Ivan Baranets met on Fridays. The location was another few blocks from the dance school where she was enrolled for the upcoming calendar year.

As much as the former gymnast-turned-prostitute-turned-student would have liked to believe her purpose in Paris was to fulfill her lifelong dream of becoming a professional dancer, her mission was in fact to secure employment within the Baranets' household. So far she had made her presence known at the tea shop, stopping by every few days for a drink with pointe shoes hanging from her bag by their laces. She had inquired about a job one Friday afternoon while seated two tables from the man who would soon become her employer.

Michel Baranets' birthday party was scheduled for January 7, and the second shift nanny would quite suddenly become unavailable during the Christmas rush. It was Anne's intention that Angelika would fill the role, a task she had been working on assiduously, well into Saturday afternoon to achieve.

While the need to conceive was urgent, ensuring the hunt for Sergei Afanasenko remained secret was paramount. So as much as Amy had been disappointed by Todd's decision to cancel their weekend together – the first they would have in her parents' home – she was also grateful for the time apart. Since the prostitute had been stolen from him in the first place, Todd was well aware of Angelika's move to Europe. However, as far as he knew, all ties with her had been severed, and she would eventually return home to the Ukraine.

Todd's change of plans was especially welcome as Anne caught a glimpse of her reflection on the way to the kitchen. She poured herself a bowl of cereal. The mainstay of her diet over the past week was almost all gone, but instead of a grocery run, Anne's plans for Saturday night were limited to changing out of the sweat bottoms and a sweat stained tank top she had been wearing since her shower on Thursday night. The acne flares from the fertility treatments had turned her cheeks, chin and neck into an angry swath of broken, inflamed skin.

With no plans to see or be seen by anyone in her current condition, and considering her present workload, the insistent peeling of the gate intercom was an unanticipated interruption to her evening. If not for the persistence of the call, she would have been tempted to wait out the intruder. The vehicle displayed on the surveillance screen was unfamiliar, but the thick head of jet hair, chiseled cheekbones and square jaw line had been forever etched into her consciousness.

Todd was home, and Anne found herself in an unfamiliar position: caught completely unaware.

With the security system disarmed, it would take Todd approximately two minutes to make it to the front steps, unload his vehicle, and pass through the front doors with whatever baggage he had in tow. That gave Anne only two minutes to find herself under a steaming shower with a toothbrush clenched between her teeth.

By the time he had peeked into most of the lower floor, journeyed up the stairs, and in and out of a few empty rooms on the second floor, eight full minutes had passed.

Hair wet and freshly shaved, Anne emerged wrapped in a terry robe just as the doorknob turned. The light puff of vapor carried with it the spicy notes of her shampoo, ordered ritually from Neil George. The familiarity of the scent, which he had always known as his wife's, fulfilled its purpose. Without more than a cursory glance, he pulled her into his arms, breathed her in, and began to lose himself in weeks of longing.

"I've missed you," he gasped, firm, smooth hands breaking the seam of the robe, mouth hungry as it devoured hers. His breath was warm, warmer than the moist air that left beads on their skin.

"You said you weren't coming," she breathed into the billowing swirls of steam floating above them. He should have been pleased there was no rancor behind her words, because Amy's default was to eke a betrayal of sorts from this gift.

"I wanted to surprise you."

Amy hated surprises.

The belt of the robe was knotted one second and pooling around her ankles the next. His lips and tongue grazed swiftly yet expertly across her jaw, flicking for a moment along the shell of her ear before moving along the column of exposed flesh that stretched into her clavicle. The subtlety of the moves had her skin alight, igniting wave after wave of thrilling tickles that rested heavily in a pool of moisture between her legs. Anne moaned, head tilted back in a lazy arch to give him all the room he needed. Her hands were frantic in their quest for skin.

"You did," she answered. Then on a sigh, as his deadly hands slid smoothly over her body, "But I can't find it in me to be angry right now." The snap of his jeans, the slide of a zipper, and Anne could fill her hands with the hard globes at the base of his spine. A slight nudge and his pants fell to his thighs.

With a swift two-step, Todd had her backed into the bathroom and shifted positions so her back was pressed firmly against the door. The suddenness of the move made her lose her breath for a moment, then again when his hungry mouth closed around a breast.

Anne's moan crescendoed into a single cry, shocked by the sharp ache of his mouth pulling deeply. It was a pain her body was unprepared for, and Todd too, judging by his reaction to the flinch. His hands stilled, one on her thigh, the other just beneath the wounded breast. His gaze was fixed on the soft peachy tone of her skin and their raspberry tips. Although it felt like a fire was raging inside, Anne knew what he would find. No mark, no bruise to indicate he was harsher than normal. And Todd knew his wife liked the bite, relished rough play.

"They are maybe a little bit fuller," Todd mused, weighing both breasts in his palms.

Anne ducked her head as he raised his. She could not look him in the eye without him knowing the truth. The man could run an interrogation as much with those eyes as his smooth tongue. She sought refuge in the crook of his neck where the scent that was all Todd – tobacco, sea and sun-bathed sex – was strongest. Nimble fingers slipped inside the waistband of his plain white briefs, imitating the stroke and caress of a rhythm Amy knew by heart.

Todd's answering groan rumbled deeply in his chest, echoing with his widening expanse as he fought to maintain control. He only pulled his wife's fragrance deeper into his lungs. The familiarity was intoxicating, blurring the lines between what was and what should have been.

"Wait," he gasped, only to have her efforts redoubled. It was that giving, the unprecedented sacrifice that was foreign to the woman he had married, and which gave him pause. He very much appreciated the change, loved in fact the skillful play of her hands on his engorged flesh, and too, the teasing whisper of her breath against his pounding pulse. But Todd had always been endowed with a will that overshadowed hers.

"I hurt you," he said, as he braced against her shoulders, trying to pull away. "I barely touched you."

Anne slipped from his halfhearted grasp, sinking to her knees before him. Determined fingers tugged on his underwear, which she smoothed down his calves. The tip of his arousal bobbed before her lips, nudging for a second her cheek. Todd could not deny that he wanted her; the string of moisture that joined them was proof.

"It would kill me if you don't let me suck you."

His rock hard thighs quivered as she took him into her mouth, pulling until he hit her uvula then beyond. A slow, slippery release was followed by a feathering lave of the tip before she swallowed him again. The throbbing at the back of her throat intensified as the muscles of his glutes and thighs bunched beneath her fingers. Todd's cry was as blunt as his fist slamming into the bathroom door, making her jump. The fingers of one hand dug into her scalp, pulling tightly as he wrapped her chocolate locks around the fist, torn between pushing her away and thrusting deeper still.

"Fuck!"

Anne could hardly resist the need to witness her effect on him. She tamped down the urge to gag, pushed away the initial panic that accompanies the fear of suffocation, and opened her throat to him. Head tilted back, her chin brushed his bunching sac while she watched him in his primal glory.

Todd was undoubtedly the most beautiful man she had ever met. The pride she felt in stripping away the urbane layers of the diplomat, revealing the brute at his core, was a powerful aphrodisiac. His entire body tensed, Todd rocked gently back and forth. The thrusts of his hips became more pronounced, building faster, deeper each time. His head was thrown back, his breath sawing harshly between clenched teeth and locked jaws. He seemed to grow before her eyes, chest expanding while a deep blush climbed to his neck.

She was on her knees, but there was no doubt as to who was the dominant.

At the earliest opportunity for breath Anne seized it, then lost it again in a moan as Todd tugged harder at the knot of hair wrapped around his hand. The fist clenched against the door moved to cup the underside of her jaw, holding her in place at the perfect angle to meet his thrusts. His hips pistoned in perfect timing with his gravelly groans.

"Fuck, fuck, fuck…"

Anne was enthralled, her body melting in awe. How selfish was Amy to keep this to herself! It was no wonder women fell for him; it was no wonder Amy had fallen for him. Even without true love, even if this was all he had to give, it would do. Anne was in love with him too.

Momentarily distracted by her musings, Anne did not see the curtain of jet lashes lifting. Then it was too late. The piercing blue eyes she had searched in wedding photos stared too deeply into her, and of course, as was always the case with Todd Birch, the man saw too much.

"What the fuck!" He exploded, simultaneously raring back and pushing her away. He stumbled into the shower wall while Anne tumbled backwards into the door, landing on her tailbone, elbow and shoulder.

"What the…who the…"

It had to be the first time he had ever been at a loss for words. His equilibrium shifted along with the boundaries of the possible. Frantic hands struggled with his clothing to cover his waning erection. There was no hiding Anne's shrinking spirit however. It wasn't she he wanted. She gulped down her disappointment, wiped the traces of his desire for another woman from her mouth, and waited. The rejection burned when she should have been terrified of the power she had given him.

"What the fuck is this?" Todd asked quietly, stuck between rage and disbelief. "What is going on?"

"You tell me," she answered through stiff jaws and swollen lips. "You don't want me."

"You are not my wife!" he shouted. He was an astute man, because without being told he seemed aware of the need for secrecy. He lowered his voice in an angry whisper. "You are not my wife."

Todd had had his suspicions. In a moment of anger he had thrown them at Amy. He thought she pretended, had created a world in her head to deal with difficult times and painful memories. Now it seemed he realized how wrong he had been. There was no pretense here between them, and Anne refused to insult the man. Still, the truth was too much for him to accept, especially with his dick wet and the smell of his wife thick in his head.

"Are you?"

His disbelief even in the face of his own certainty was disarming. She loved him, and the man clutching at the edges of their reality as desperately as the towel to his front, had pain etched into the fine lines around his eyes and the grooves of his brow.

"You know I am not."

He breathed deeply for a moment, then peered harder at her, inching closer. He tried to disprove with his eyes what his sense of scent told him was there. The difference he sought would not be in the lines he traced now, even with those all seeing eyes. The damp weft of hair he had tousled in his haste to get away had fallen into her eyes, but she left it there.

To push it away would have been too revealing: Anne was left-handed, Amy used her right; together they were ambidextrous.

"You won't find a difference, so let's just pretend," Anne said, although to say the words created a hollowness in the middle of her chest.

"No."

"There is no reason for you not to want me," she protested, unwilling to try and unable to hide the hurt of his unequivocal rebuff. She was not Amy. Pulling herself up, she brushed her hair aside. "Why don't you want me?"

"You. Are. Not. My. Wife." As if the question angered him... offended him... maligned his character.

Anne scoffed at the irony. The man was a whore. His exploits were legendary. Few people had expected him to marry. Less had expected him to choose someone like Amy. No one expected him to remain faithful. Why else would they buy him a prostitute and deliver her to the home he shared with his wife?

"You are no saint, and in the dark we are the same," Anne offered, one hand waving along her exposed body, displaying the lines he had so recently crossed.

"You are nothing alike. I know my wife, and I would know it even in the dark. You look like her, you smell like her, but underneath..."

"Underneath, I am the woman you deserve. Amy is selfish; all she does is take. She will use you up until there's nothing left to give. She doesn't know any other way."

"You don't know her. You don't know the woman she's become." Todd was either too angry to be repulsed, or his mind had begun to accommodate the truth. He moved closer, so close in fact that he had crossed the space between them without conscious thought to do so. He pulled Anne by her arms, the chest and shoulders she had admired minutes before now boxing her in. She knew not to be afraid; he would never hurt them. Still, his much larger frame crowded her, forcing her to shrink back in caution. It was further proof of the differences underneath the skin.

Todd's wife would have pushed back, combative to the end of her control.

"I want my wife back," he seethed, fueled by the softness before his eyes, so different from his wife. He pressed harder against her body until she was flat against the door, arms trapped between them, legs locked into place by the powerful thighs she had caressed.

"You can't have her."

"You don't get a say. Now give me back my wife."

"You are wrong. She needs me, because I protect her. Just as our father meant it to be. She will always choose me." Her voice shook, belying her defiance. Todd fed off her weakness, his hand closing around her throat. The threat of violence was evident even in the gentle caress of his fingertips.

"Anne," he whispered, in his element with danger, "give me back my wife."

He knew her name. If she had surprised him with a revelation of their father's role in this, Anne could not tell. But Todd shocked her with how much he knew. She was crushed that it made no difference. How could he not want her? His soft shaft was pressed against her belly, and the pressure of his fingers increased. The threat was fast becoming a certainty.

How could he love someone like Amy? She was hard and unyielding, a sociopath. Except with him. Amy might have poisoned him against her, but Todd had found some softness in stone. Somehow, despite her conditioning, Todd could make her yield, exposing tenderness she was never meant to have.

"I'll kill her first," Anne spat, angry enough not to care how she might have hurt him, or how badly she might damage the hope of reconciliation.

Todd squeezed, and Anne fought back. She tried at first to pry his fingers away, then beat at him with ineffective fists. As a last resort she scratched at him with nails she had cut that same day so she wouldn't pick at her face. But Anne was not built for the fight. That was all Amy. Anne was designed to yield and that was what she did, sinking heavily into the darkness.

SEVEN

It felt like daybreak, but the light streaming through my west-facing window announced mid-afternoon. It wasn't much in the way of light; the sun had lost most of its luster fighting through a layer of clouds, thick with the promise of sleet. Yet behind my eyes, the weak light glimmered as if bouncing off a hundred mirrors, hitting me where it hurt most.

My head pounded to a steady beat, so heavy that it almost dulled the ache of my sore body. Everything above my navel was stiff as if I had fallen asleep trapped inside a tiny wooden box. That in itself was strange, because I knew without opening my eyes that I was in my own bed, floating on the latest cloud technology the mattress company had to offer.

The headache echoed through my body, sending spasms to the pit of my stomach. I was hungry too. I could not remember my last meal, and the warmth of the churning acids inside me warned of an ulcer if I didn't get something to calm them soon.

As urgent as it might have been, food would have to wait. The saliva I had pushed down to cool the heat was burning like a river of lava down my throat. I opened my mouth to gasp, but closed it just as quickly. The thought of swallowing air had my stomach gases on the move, smoothing the way for the acid to follow.

'Move, move, move,' I urged my board-stiff limbs, but it was like wading through knee-deep tar. I didn't dare open my eyes, relying instead on memory to find my way to the ensuite bathroom. Besides once stumbling over what felt like my robe, I made it safely and in the nick of time too.

It was painful, so painful in fact I risked opening my eyes to verify I wasn't throwing up stones.

It hurt to move; it hurt to stay still.

It hurt to breathe; it hurt to hold my breath.

I gasped at the sheer helplessness and could have cried at how broken my voice was.

What the hell had happened to me? It felt like I had been repeatedly run over by a slow-moving cement truck, and that I had screamed through the whole ordeal.

There were footsteps. As much as it felt like death, I froze. There was someone in my father's house.

I was in the process of lifting my head when the overhead lights flooded the room. The geeks at NASA claimed light has no sound. So why the fuck was there thunder in my head, so loud it drowned out the voice that followed? Thankfully it didn't last long; the lights went out again. I wished the flashes behind my scrunched up lids were as easily put out.

The good news was the intruder was friendly. That should have been a source of relief, but it didn't explain why I was so beat up.

"Here's some coffee." Definitely friendly.

Gratitude surged through` me like vomit, but I wouldn't have been able to utter a thank you to save my life.

Todd was home. I didn't know how to feel about that. The last time we had spoken was Thursday. He had already told me he wasn't coming home for the weekend. The new ambassador to the Dominican Republic had presented credentials to the president and had taken office weeks sooner than Todd had expected. Although he, I and a select few knew Todd's role as Deputy Head of Mission and Chargé *ad interim* was a crock full of shit, appearances had to be maintained so he would not be revealed as a spy on later missions. Todd had to stay and perform critical hand-over functions.

Now that he was standing less than a foot away from me, I wondered if I had missed something. I had been preoccupied with the Mohammed al-Mohammed case, but I would have taken note of something as important as Todd's return home. Right?

Obviously he was here. Obviously something had happened. Why couldn't I remember? My mouth tasted like nothing – no wine, no food, nothing at all. I was not hung over. Could my present condition have been a side effect of the fertility treatments? What the fuck was going on?

I managed to open one eye without ripping my head off. It was just in time to see the hem of Todd's pants and the light shining off tiny drops of moisture on his boots as he turned and left.

He didn't sound too happy to see me. He had been exploring long and hard enough to make his way outdoors. He had been here long enough for something to happen.

I was as glad for the coffee as the slight reprieve his sudden departure granted. But I knew my husband well enough to understand that his silence was a gift of only a few moments for me to collect myself. It was the least he could do. We were like fighters sent to their corners to strategize. Not knowing what we were fighting for left me at a distinct disadvantage. And Todd wasn't the type to pity an opponent, even his wife.

I dragged myself across the cold tiles to pull my arms through the robe. Getting to the sink was an even more difficult task. I was surprised my shaky knees held me up. Bracing myself, I hit the lights, but it was a long couple of minutes before I finally opened my eyes.

I nearly knocked the coffee over, which wouldn't have been a great loss. I didn't need coffee; I needed a doctor. The person staring back at me had already gone a round, or ten, with Todd. Or maybe it was that cement truck.

My left eye had had a small bloodstain on the cornea since my encounter with a killer cop in Jamaica four months ago. Now both almost matched, with broken capillaries in and around the sunken holes. If there were any doubt I had been air-starved, the fingerprints at my neck obliterated it. It also explained why my throat was a gravelly mess, and why I sounded as if my breathing tube had been ripped out dry. The trail of broken and discolored skin stretched farther south. My shoulder, my arm, and sections of my back were a shocking tableau of reds, blues and black. And although my face had been mostly spared any bruising, my chin, cheeks and neck appeared to have been burned with hot water then painstakingly picked over.

I was dismayed at the prospect of hiding all this. Fortunately, the season would play in my favor. I could hide the worst of the body damage with a long-sleeved turtleneck, and a little conditioner could fix my hair. But my face was another matter. When and how had it gotten this bad? It was pure irony that the fertility treatments had had such a disastrous effect when the point was to get my husband to fuck me.

I rifled through my medicine cabinet with the ridiculous hope that scientists had discovered fresh-skin-in-a-bottle, and by some miracle I had some in stock. Instead I found aspirin. I counted out four and swallowed them with the lukewarm coffee just as light footsteps sounded nearby. My headache intensified as I bent to wash my face, but I really needed the cold water to prepare for round two.

The silence stretched endlessly between us long after I knew he was there. I took my time drying my face, then stalled even more under the pretext of finding and pulling a brush through my hair.

"What did you take?"

For a moment I was afraid of the question, simply because I didn't know what had happened last night. Then Todd shook the bottle of pills.

"It's only aspirin, Todd."

I eventually turned to find him examining some pills he had spilled into his palm. I knew I had earned that distrust, but it touched something painful inside me. I wanted him to know it. My stare was a silent but heavy and intrepid thing.

"You look like a meth-head, Amy, and you have a sharps bin full of needles." He didn't even look at me as he continued sifting through the pills. He managed to level my audacity as casually as he was dressed.

Tan slacks, brown boots, a thick, cream, wool sweater over a blue button-down shirt, and he was as beautiful as dressed in one of his suits. His hair was free of its shell; soft, thick as sin, and black like the doubt that hung between us.

"It is Amy, right?" He asked, his face a blank, uncaring slate.

How could the heart inside me continue to beat when it felt like a block of ice? Anne. Anne had happened.

Todd had the high ground and I was trapped in an indefensible position. I waited for the start of the assault. He slammed the aspirin on the counter next to the coffee that mocked me. The few sips I had had soured in my stomach when Todd finally raised his eyes to mine.

"This is a lot for me, Amy... Much more than I ever imagined." One hand plowed furrows through his hair, an ineffective means of relieving his frustration. His fingers massaged his temples.

It was not the beating I had expected; it was resignation... surrender. I would have preferred the assault. I never wanted Todd to give up on me.

"I don't know what to do," he said. "I don't know how to help you."

"You said you weren't coming." I was surprised the words came out so clearly. My heart was pounding in my chest, making it hard to breathe.

"What does that have to do with anything?" Todd protested, sensing a challenge when the truth was simpler. I was lost without him as my compass and didn't know where to start. "I wanted to surprise you."

"I would have protected you. You would never have..."

"You can't control this. You cannot self medicate a mental illness, Amy."

"I'm not insane. You just don't understand."

"No, I don't!" He shouted, but at least he was still looking at me. At least there was a chance he would see me shaking, willing but afraid to explain. "Help me to understand. Please convince me I didn't marry a lunatic."

What was crazy was the fact that Todd was still standing there, hoping for the best when this beat anyone's definition of the worst. What was even crazier was the fact that I would do it; I would make him understand. If only I could figure out where to start...

"She said your father did this."

I hated that I couldn't remember. Without all the pieces I couldn't risk lying. Todd knew enough to push me... More than enough to hurt me if he wanted to. But he wouldn't stop until he had everything. He was angry and confused, but at least he cared. Otherwise he wouldn't be standing there trying to understand, pleading with me to trust him. It was etched in every line of his body, from the top of his perfect hair to the tips of his fingers gripping the edge of the vanity as if holding onto his sanity.

"I'll show you," I said, quickly before I could change my mind. This was unparalleled for me and Todd seemed to understand the weight of trust I was willing to put in him. His Adam's apple bobbed as he digested my decision. Todd nodded and so did I.

I returned the hairbrush to its place, and as the rest of my body warmed up to our pact, I tightened the robe around my bruised body and led the way. Out of my bedroom, down the hall, past my parents' bedroom and two doors down into my father's study. I could feel Todd's steps falling lightly behind me in the creak and groan of the wood beneath our feet – too lightly for a man his size. His tread could hardly be heard over the drumming of my heart.

It seemed my whole life my father had prepared for his death. When the time had come he chose to go calmly, eschewing the relative safety of the panic room hidden behind the bookcase. He knew the people who wanted him dead were not strangers, and they would not have been deterred by our security system. Betrayal didn't come from strangers; it was always the ones we held close. I never wanted to forget.

I caught Todd staring at my father's restored desk. When they shot him in the head, the bullet had passed right through and lodged in one of the panels. CSI had sawed through the wood to extract the slug, but weeks later I had reclaimed the broken pieces and made them whole again. I might have been able to disguise the work of the killers and investigators, but that had never appealed to me. Someone accustomed to killing without a trace would recognize it. Todd recognized it.

As per my father's instructions I had emptied the contents of the safe as soon as I was allowed inside. Men from his office had come and Richard stood by my side as I handed over my father's work. But there was a second safe no one had known about.

Our panic room was a steel-reinforced box slightly larger than my bedroom. It was bare except for a small, dry pantry; a rack holding four rifles, six handguns and several boxes of ammunition; and a wall of surveillance, ventilation and communications equipment, all powered by two separate auxiliary power sources, each with about three days of juice. The bank of screens that provided visual oversight of every square inch of the estate was dark now. They were automatically powered on when the panic room was sealed from within. A distress signal once went directly to both the local Police Department and my father's office.

There was also the vault – a safe core accessed by biometric scans, which was our final recourse should the main doors be breached. Inside the vault was my father's personal safe, hidden beneath a single screen from which we could monitor activity in the outer room. At the time of his death our security was the best of its kind, but my father knew it would not have kept us safe.

Over the years I had pored over the work my father had left behind. It had failed to shed any light on the reason for his death, but it was full of what Todd needed. I collected the files and left the inner sanctum. Todd had not followed me in. He was enthralled by my father's study... my father's desk.

"Todd," I broke through his thoughts. His brow was twisted into a severe scowl, his eyes dark like the Pacific in the midst of a storm.

"What happened here?"

His unspoken thoughts were heavily tinged by sadness, whether for me or my father was yet to be seen. He was both reverent and terrified, like a visitor inquiring about a house of horrors, uncertain who had suffered more there. Those who had died, or those forced to live with their ghosts?

Todd wouldn't understand that I had been my happiest here. True, this was also the home of my deepest anguish, and for that reason alone it might as well have been haunted. But I loved this place, and now that I was so close to finishing what my father had started, I was no longer afraid of being in his presence. It was infinitely less painful now, knowing I had not failed him.

"This is where I grew up."

"Not the house," he interrupted sharply. "This room... This is where he...?"

He could not say the unimaginable. Imagine how I felt living it for twelve years.

"This is where my father was murdered."

"Why do you keep it like this?"

"Why do we celebrate bat mitzvahs, quinceañera, and sweet sixteen parties? This is a living memory of the night I stopped being a child. This is my coming-of-age, Todd."

"That desk –" he charged, finger pointed at it, as if it were a living, breathing offense.

I sighed. If he couldn't understand this, the rest would be impossible. "This is my father's study," I began to explain. "It was forbidden to me while he was alive, but every now and then I would peek inside and watch him work. He knew I was there, but he let me watch. It makes me feel closer to him to keep it this way. And now when I sit in his place, I can feel him watching me."

A flush of disapproval crossed his face, but he dashed it away before it could grow roots. In its place stood reluctant understanding. "They never found those responsible."

We had been over this before. It was a simple truth with which I had come to terms, as far as Todd knew. It should not have made me uncomfortable. But in a moment of weakness I found myself shifting from one foot to the other... restless.

"No," I answered simply.

"Is that something that would help you get better?"

"Better at what?"

Todd only looked at me... into me. Ah, he was back to the question of my mental health.

I might have winced if in his question I had not surmised his desire to make me whole. If finding the murderers would help, then he would do it for me. Frankly, I didn't see how Todd would ever find answers where Richard had failed. But that was if I took his offer at face value. And if there was anything I had learned about my husband this past week, it was that he did not live his life for me.

So why was I willing to share with him my father's work...one of our deepest secrets?

Because I had no choice. Todd already knew enough to be dangerous. But by staking my career on the trust he wanted me to have in him, perhaps I could keep him bound to me. It was the only way to buy myself some time – at least a few weeks until I could unmask the man who had betrayed my father, the person ultimately responsible for setting him up. I was so close to finding Sergei Afanasenko's American backer.

"I will never feel better about what happened here. This is as good as it gets." I balanced my father's files on my palms and offered them to Todd. "You have to decide if you can live with that."

Todd crossed over to me, but for a long while did not take my offering. As one moment yawned into another, the files seemed to double in weight, pulling down my arms like invisible anchors. Todd stared into my soul, and I allowed it. Finding nothing but openness, he turned to the files.

They were old-fashioned—a throwback to my father's hey-days working at the CIA. There were some typed notes in crisp Courier font; others were handwritten, as if recorded in the field. The sheets were organized in black five-ring binders, labeled according to the date, subject and series, which were in turn tucked inside large leather envelopes. Each was secured by a piece of string wound around a small, raised nub. The envelopes were waterproof and coated in fire retardant, but otherwise it was pretty low-key on security. My father had trusted it, because it was always intended that these files would be tucked away inside his safe, inside the vault, inside our panic room.

And here I was handing them over to a man who was close enough to betray me, but in many respects was still a stranger.

I pressed his answers into his chest, and reflexively Todd held onto them. There was only the briefest touch of our hands during the transfer. It might as well have been a volcanic eruption for how affected we both were. Our eyes met, and everything we wanted to say, but could not, was there, clear as day for the other to see. But somewhere along the way our receptors were broken and the message eluded us. I broke away from the impasse. I collected myself, tightening the robe around my middle, and walked away.

"Where are you going?"

"To my room. You have a lot of reading ahead of you, and I need to take care of myself."

"No more running, Amy," he cautioned, bringing me to a dead halt. I turned to find him still clutching the pile to his chest.

"Where would I go?" I asked. With a wave in his direction, fanning him from head to toe, I said, "You have everything now."

And then I left him to decide whether he still wanted my love.

EIGHT

I took a long shower, but for most of it I simply stood under the steady stream of near scalding water, trying to piece together what had happened the night before. The deeper I dug into the barren well of memories, the more my headache intensified. My mind was a maze of brick walls, which was understandable because frankly the memories I sought were not my own. I gave up just shy of giving myself an aneurysm. At the end of the hour, I was clean, but no wiser than when I had first stepped in.

I was pink all over, except where I was flaming red, and black and blue. The better part of a bottle of moisturizer and a tube of concealer went into covering the damage to my face and neck. The good news was those bruises offered some perspective.

I was well acquainted with Todd's fingerprints around my throat. This time however, I wasn't as sore as if we'd had sex. So it seemed he had been confronted by Anne, who had had the control taken from her.

The mental image was so powerful it sent a shiver coursing through my body. Todd was the physical embodiment of my fantasies. Furious, he both titillated and frightened me. I mourned the loss of not witnessing firsthand that anger. Instead I had been faced with the carefully composed shell, the civilized façade of the leashed animal.

I was left to compose myself... construct the illusion of meeting my husband on an equal footing.

I never considered myself to be beautiful, but I did not want to especially look like shit either while married to a man like him. For his part, Todd had been so cold and unfeeling in his censure that he hadn't yet looked at me as a woman today. I was a puzzle he was determined to solve, and after he read my father's files, I doubted I would ever be anything more to him.

After fourteen days of follicle stimulating hormone injections, I had had my HCG shot late Friday night. Tender breasts, this morning's bout of nausea and a body temperature of 98.6° were pretty good indications that I was ovulating. But it was all in vain. Todd Birch was not going to touch me for love, wealth or power. The remaining twelve-hour window for peak fertility would be wasted, because I had given him all the power he had been searching for over the past six months.

So I was surprised to find him just outside the bathroom door, calmly perched on the edge of my childhood bed. The new mattress was softer than what he liked, but I had bought the adjustable sleeper as a compromise. Based on the fact that he still wore his imperturbable mask, and my father's files were gathered into a neat pile next to him, I doubted very much that we would be exploring his sleep number settings together.

"These don't have your name," he said, one hand coming to rest on the top of the pile while the other remained flat against his thigh. It was an unnatural position, as if he had deliberately decided on the neutral pose. It disturbed me, because I had seen the shell of the man, had experienced the deep chill of the killer, and this was the worst he had ever been with me.

"No," I answered simply, because I could not judge his state of mind. Did he think I was holding back, that I was lying?

"If I read them will I find Anne?"

I held my breath. He had not read them? So, why was he even more distant than an hour ago?

"Yes," I answered his question, again refusing to offer more.

"Make me understand, Amy," he said, and it sounded like a plea.

For a brief moment in time the mask slipped and I saw the cracks beneath. My breath escaped in a rush. It was as if I couldn't get enough air inside me. My heart raced, pounding in my temples again, reigniting the familiar pain.

"Why don't you read them first?"

He did not answer right away. The sound of a wheelbarrow rolling by caught his attention. Besides the initial distraction, Todd did not seem overly surprised at this indication that we were not alone. So he had met Mr. Bankowski, the gardener my father had hired twenty years ago to attend to his roses. He was a one-man landscaping business who had maintained the property as my father had left it with nearly zero direction.

"I can't," Todd finally answered, and this time when his eyes met mine there was no hiding the profound sadness. His fingertips brushed across the smooth surface of the thick leather envelope on top, while he inhaled deeply and slowly. As the air left his lungs, he seemed to deflate too, virtually shrinking as the fight that had held him up dissipated. He looked tired, perhaps resigned, which unglued my feet from the polished wood floor.

We had both worked so hard to hammer the pieces of a life together. For him to give up on everything he had bargained for seemed unfair and a personal blight. How broken was I to break Todd too?

"I've tried, but I cannot." Todd's voice broke and from some deep recess tears pricked at my eyes. I squeezed every muscle in my body taut, all the way down to my toes, trying to keep them in.

"You're in here," Todd said, stabbing a finger at the pile, "but you are 'The Subject'." He bit out the words, his anger and disgust apparent. "You were his only flesh and blood, and he called you 'The Subject'."

I dashed away the tears that had broken free, before they wrecked my cover-up job. I hated that he would judge my father, but I held my silence, because Todd would never understand. And it would only show how hopelessly, irrevocably damaged I was if I defended him.

"You were a walking, talking, breathing experiment for him, Amy. He was your father. He was supposed to love you. He should have protected you."

"He did," I whispered, because it was automatic.

"Don't say that!" Todd shouted, and with an angry swipe of his hand sent the pile of files flying across the floor. It was probably a disappointment that the parcels remained intact, and no sheaves went fluttering everywhere. "He broke you!"

It required visible effort to calm himself, but there were simply too many emotions to check the raging tide.

"How old were you?"

I hesitated, because Todd did not need any more fuel. He raised his eyes to mine.

"How old were you when it began?"

"Eight."

If Todd thought he saw defiance – and yes, pride – in my raised chin and flashing eyes, then he would have been right. He may not *want* to understand, but I *knew* my father loved me.

The balled fist resting on his knee clenched tighter. In contrast, his free hand tried to wipe away his aghast expression. His eyes came to rest on the folders scattered across the floor, then suddenly jerked away as if burnt by the sight. His fingers worked at his jaw, massaging the strained muscles.

"I'm not sure I want to know this, but give me the Cliff's Notes version of why." Todd really did not want to know. The stiffness with which he faced me, arms crossed over his chest was a defiant stance. But here was my chance to make him see from my father's eyes.

"You know what my father did for work?" I began, choosing my words as carefully as picking through a minefield.

Todd nodded briskly and singly, as if to assent might have been misconstrued as approbation for my father. I pushed on.

"He believed there was no better future for me, no nobler cause than to serve my country. For whatever reason my parents had no other children, so I was his heir. My father was determined to groom me to follow him, to make me the best and ensure that I would survive."

"Don't try to convince me that he wanted the best for you, Amy. I won't believe it. Just tell me why he did it. Tell me what he did to you."

"My father understood the vulnerabilities inherent to my sex. He wanted to ensure that if ever I had been caught, that if I were to fall into enemy hands, I would have more recourse than death or dishonor."

I took a deep breath as I watched Todd recoil.

"I know it sounds bad... crazy even... But you have to put it in the context of his career, and the times. He fed on the Cold War, and at the same time Europe was decolonizing and it was as if the world had gone mad. He was revolutionary in his methods, but that was also true of his dreams for me. I was going to be more than a powerful man's wife or a hole to be fucked in a trade for secrets."

I might not have said the forbidden word, but it was a defense of my father nonetheless. One that snapped Todd's patience.

He sprang and I refused to back away. The hand that had worked to soothe his tense jaw muscles minutes ago now seemed intent on quieting me. Todd cupped my chin, fingers feathering across my lips with just enough pressure to stem the flow of words. His touch was gentle even if his presence was meant to intimidate.

It was a trick that might have worked on Anne last night. By the flicker in his eyes, Todd seemed to understand that I was an entirely different animal. Anne would have cowered, but my fists were up, ready, pressed casually for now above his heart and diaphragm.

"He trained me to fight and I'm good at it."

Todd, with a flicker of his gaze at the balled hands between us, understood that I would fight... that it came naturally to me. But, either he was confident in his own skills, or he had no intention of forcing a physical confrontation between us. So gently the move was incongruous with the tension between us, he caressed the sides of my throat where beneath the layers of makeup his fingerprints marked my skin.

"Anne yields."

"You're different, like night and day," he whispered now, because with his lips only inches from mine, I could feel the words on his breath.

"And separate," I added, drawing his eyes from my lips to my eyes. "Separate identities. Thoughts, memories, secrets are linked to a separate consciousness. She cannot tell what she never knew."

"How did he do this to you?"

"Conditioning."

Todd's eyes closed for a moment, shrinking away in the face of his fears. Determinedly his gaze returned to mine, silently urging me to explain.

"Psychotherapy. Hypnotherapy. Memory processing."

"What kind of conditioning?" The pressure of his fingers increased at my hesitation. I swallowed hard and he relented, his eyes following the motion. The last thing he wanted to do was hurt me more than he thought I had already endured. "What kind of conditioning, Amy?"

"Physical... chemical."

"Sexual?"

"Never." He was determined to think the worst, although I had denied a similar allegation months ago.

"Then how..." He started, but had to stop. His eyes appeared glazed and I marveled that this man would cry for me. "Last night, I hurt you." By the caress of his fingers and the journey of his eyes, I knew he was mapping the fingerprints.

"That wasn't me."

He struggled still with the concept. His brow crinkled as his mind refused to bend. He nodded anyway. "I never wanted to do that to you again. Doesn't matter how much you like it, I can't..."

"That's different. When we..." Todd's eyes flashed back to mine, "when we played, I never lost consciousness. It was always me. It's a release for me, that's all."

"A learned release," Todd persisted.

"Yes. I learned it from Adam Rutherford III, my rapist." Todd flinched. He closed his eyes and pressed his forehead to mine. Against my fists, his chest heaved and his breath ghosted against my lips. "I know what rape is, Todd. I know about dubious consent and persuaded consent. My father never did any of that to me."

"I don't understand. I don't understand what happened."

God, I hated feeling his pain. It shook something loose inside me and I did not know how to put it back in its place. Like these silly tears.

"The trigger is control," I whispered, because my voice was thick with an unnamed emotion. "Should I lose control I lose my consciousness... my identity. When we play, it's my trust that I give you, but I always retain control. There's a difference."

"Explain how she knew about me. If you are separate, how does that work?"

"Over the years, we have developed ways to communicate. But where you are concerned, it's been different and I'm not sure I know how to explain it to you."

"Try."

"I've never been in love before. I don't think my father prepared me for these feelings either. Somehow she feels them too, both the emotions and the physical."

Talking about it was like setting fire to gasoline. His touch burned, the sensation sizzling all the way to my core. My breasts grew heavy, the tips tingling with each breath. It was painful and I loved it.

As he stared into my eyes, the heat spread. His throat worked hard at keeping the desire down, but Todd burned too much to hide. His hands moved over my skin like tentative kisses, trailing down my front until they eased the edges of my robe aside.

"Do you know we did this last night?"

I shook my head. It was more than just a denial. I did not *want* to know. It was my body; it was insane to feel proprietary over Todd enjoying it with Anne.

"She wanted me to fuck her."

"I know," I breathed, because I needed him to stop. I did not want to hear this. I reached up on my toes to fuse our mouths together, but Todd pulled away. His hands gripped my hips, holding me steady. All hope was not lost however.

"Doesn't it bother you?" he asked, head tilted back so he could read me.

"It would solve the problem," I forced out.

"Why is she a problem if you can control it, as you claim?"

"Because you drive me crazy, Todd. You make me feel things I had never hoped to feel. Why wouldn't she want you too? We are in love with you, for God's sake!"

"You never answered my question. Does it bother you? Would you mind if I fucked her? I mean, it's your body, technically it would be you."

"Yes, it bothers me," I cried, slapping his hands away. He caught me by my wrists before I could pull away.

"Why?" The strength and abruptness of his anger surprised me. Where was the leash, the mask… his control? My core melted.

"Because you're mine," I panted, desire rendering me breathless. "You are mine and I'm selfish and I never want to share you."

Our eyes and wills clashed for only a moment, because in the next Todd had me pressed deeper into the wall. His mouth crashed onto mine in a frenzy of lips and tongue and teeth. I pushed him away just far enough to get my hands on the buckle of his belt. His hands that had proved to be so gentle before tugged fiercely on my robe.

"Say it again," he breathed.

"You're mine."

"You're fucking crazy," he said as he stripped me. His pants were just about undone, and while I continued to work on the zipper, Todd lifted me by the back of my thighs. "But I love you."

The bed was only six feet away, but he was buried inside me, my legs wrapped around him before we got there. The thick, soft wool of his sweater scratched my overly sensitive breasts as if it were made of steel. It was painfully delicious. I arched into him, relishing the abrasion and the fullness of having him firmly rooted inside me.

There was something inequitable about being completely naked, my legs spread wide apart by his hands at my knees, while he remained almost fully clothed. But the beat of his heart, the way he closed his eyes and gritted his teeth to savor me; the quiver of his belly as he raised his hips to withdraw inch by glorious inch, were proof of his enthrallment.

"Todd," I cried, surprising myself with the need in my voice. He was poised above me with only the tip of his erection joining us. I had never felt a wider Gulf. "I love you so much," I said, my hands framing his face making sure he could see me.

It would have been nice to say he kissed me sweetly as we made love. It would have been perfect if we could have extracted some tenderness from the storm around us. But the reality was even better.

He was not gentle. Rising to his knees then sitting back on his heels, Todd pulled me onto his lap and thrust deeply. The blow echoed through my body, and before I could fully appreciate the aftershock he had pulled away.

The fabric of his clothes abraded my skin as he slammed into me again and again. His fingers dug harshly into the flesh of my hip on one side, and my shoulder on the other. His pulsing length hollowed me out, and I craved him even more. I raised my hips to welcome him.

"Look how wet you are!" Todd moaned, eyes fixed on his glistening flesh pistoning in and out of me. I couldn't see, but God I could feel how slick we were! The sound of our bodies as we came together was a thick slurp that could be heard above our labored breaths and the pounding of our hearts.

"So fucking tight... and hot. God, it's like you're burning up inside."

"I am. I burn for you," I whispered, surprising us both. I enjoyed Todd's commentary of the marvel that was our bodies welcoming each other. But I had always been content to silently savor the sensations.

"Please don't stop," I gasped as Todd, ever appreciative of the tiniest progress I made, moved relentlessly in and out.

"Cum," Todd urged over and over again. His hair was falling into his face, the tips sticking to his skin where beads of sweat had broken out. "Cum, dammit. I'm going to blow."

And yet he redoubled his efforts, drawing me closer, tilting my hips higher so he could sink deeper, tightening his hold so he could pull faster. My fingers were twisted into the sheets as I tried to hold onto something... tried to stop myself from being swept away by the wave of unparalleled ecstasy. My core trembled and wept, my muscles closing involuntarily around him, grasping his throbbing shaft tighter, refusing to let go. The pulse seemed to echo through my spine as I came powerfully, my limbs locked in a painful arch, my muscles vibrating like the wings on a hummingbird.

"Yes, God!" Todd forced through clenched teeth, his own body held taut, veins bulging and head hung low as he too was rocked by our most powerful orgasm yet. I felt him emptying inside me in thick streams that kept coming and coming. Just when I thought it might be over, my core spasmed, only to have Todd jerk and spill even more inside me.

By the time I found my voice and recovered control of my body, perhaps a full ten minutes had passed. Todd had collapsed on top of me. Our breaths kissed as we were both too spent to shift.

"What the fuck was that?" Todd asked, garnering just enough strength to shift to his side. He carried me along with him. I snuggled into the woolly softness of his sweater, filling my senses with the sight, sounds and scents of him. There was a faint strain of tobacco from the cigars he loved, but the rest was spicy ocean blue, sunshine, sex, and me. The buckle of his belt pressed into my belly, but I let it, too afraid to lose the connection to him should I move.

"This is how it should have been," he said between breaths. "Last night, this is how I wanted it to be."

"I'm sorry," I whispered, forced to face him when his fingers tilted my chin.

"You didn't do anything wrong, Amy." Looking into his eyes I could have lost myself in their endless indigo depths. "You couldn't help what was done to you. None of it was your fault... not what your father did, and not what Richard covered up."

I knew better than to try to change his mind. Perhaps if I wasn't so broken I might have understood his perspective. I believed my past had made me stronger, while Todd obviously questioned what I might have become without my father or Richard's influence.

"Obviously this will change some things between us," he said, then rushed to finish while staving off my protest with a finger pressed to my lips. "I don't know what and I won't pretend to know how. I just know things will change and we will have to make adjustments."

I thought of the fact that he had just come inside me. He was still inside me, my leg hooked over his hip. If everything worked out as I had planned, then indeed there would be changes ahead.

"But the bottom line is I love you, and I don't want to live without you. We can make this work, but you have to want it as much as I do."

He didn't need to try so hard to hold me in place. I wanted this. I wanted us. I needed him. As our breathing synced, the calculations behind our union didn't matter as much as the way he filled my heart. Todd could have walked away and I would have understood. He could have used what I had given him to break me, but instead he was using it to keep me.

"I do."

"Swear it."

"I swear it on my life," I promised the one man who could easily exact payment.

Todd shook his head. "Swear it on your father."

There was no payment to be had should I renege on this promise. But he had at least taken away one simple and irrevocable lesson from our confrontation. I loved my father above anything, possibly even my husband, and I would never tarnish that love with a lie. It was the only honor I had.

"I do."

"Mean it, Amy." The words escaped his lips as a plea, but as he lowered his head to mine, closing the gap between our lips, there was no way I could have missed the warning in his eyes.

"I do," I whispered and accepted first his kiss and then this breath, his body and soul into mine.

NINE

"All women are crazy. You just have to find the one whose crazy you can live with," Todd said.

I resisted the urge to take offense. It would have been an instinctive response for most women. But I wasn't like most women, and I knew my own shortcomings. I also knew Todd would not have resurrected a subject we had laid to rest in my bedroom several hours ago in the cereal aisle.

"Or one who is more hot than crazy," I clarified.

He tilted his head from side to side as if weighing my contribution. "It's the same thing. Your way just sounds more shallow."

I rolled my eyes and didn't try to hide it. His political correctness when in public, even during a private conversation, was irritating. He grinned and pulled me close so he could nuzzle my neck.

"As much as I love your tight ass, soft tits, and sweet pussy..." he whispered in my ear. I nodded my approval and we laughed softly. "I don't think I can live with *this* type of crazy."

Todd was referring to my side of the shopping cart. My staples were Cocoa Puffs, coffee, peanut butter, sliced bread, milk and Snickers bars.

Todd's arms snaked around me, settling in the rear pockets of my jeans so he could hoist me up against his front. We had not wasted many of the hours spent in my bedroom on talk, but judging by the pressure resting against the crux of my thighs, Todd was ready for more. As was I. He nestled in the crook of my neck, displacing my turtleneck to nibble at the sensitive underside of my jaw. He scratched my bruised skin with the rough edge of his new stubble.

I visibly struggled with this contrived life. Under the eyes of the public, the genuine became unwieldy in its unfamiliarity, like the picture of domesticity we were portraying. Bundled in thick sweaters, denim and boots, a love-struck couple nuzzled in the snack aisle, their cart left unattended nearby. Last-minute shoppers determined to beat last call maneuvered around us, belying the invisibility they had accorded us on account of our disturbing display of affection. Old people smiled their approval as they clutched tighter to each other, seeing in us younger versions of themselves. They had never been more wrong.

Their normal was alien to me, and Todd with his uncanny astuteness knew I wanted nothing more than to run away. But he wanted this – communal carts, petting in public places, approbation of an audience. And if I were serious about wanting our marriage, then I would have to accept them too.

It wasn't much to ask considering I, with my Mriya cargo hold of baggage, wasn't much of a prize. So I relinquished my hold of the instructional manual on the presentation of a normal couple and simply breathed. At rest, my body's functions – respiration and heart rate, were borderline low, which my father knew could confuse most lie detection mechanisms. My body's reaction to Todd was foolproof anyway. I had only to focus on him.

"God, I want you so much," I murmured into his ear, snaking my arms around his neck. I felt his smile against my throat a moment before he retreated to arm's length. He examined my face and I let him see while my fingers twisted casually in the hair at his nape.

Finally he said, "I like you like this, Amy." I wished he had left it like that, because next he added, "I love you, but you are not an easy person to like."

It wasn't anything I had not heard before, but it was still a swift blow to the gut. Instead of digging through to find the positive in his declaration, I let Todd see me. This was part and parcel of our openness, wasn't it? He couldn't keep kicking me when I was down and expect me to take it.

As if doused by icy water, the heat from moments ago was gone. I released him and stepped away, breaking his hold on me too.

"You know what we need?" He said to my back as I assumed carts duty.

I had a number of suggestions, starting with less compulsion to say whatever came to mind. Instead of reaching for the bait, I focused on hoisting the tub of cat litter someone had left around a blind corner that I had to hoist out of the path of my cart.

"We need a housekeeper," Todd continued, relieving me of the bucket of sand. I disagreed with his observation, just like I didn't feel the need to hold hands and push a cart like conjoined twins. But I wanted us to work and a big part of that was making my home Todd's.

"Yeah?" I asked, waiting as he browsed the frozen vegetables on offer.

Already the cart was overflowing with living and recently alive things... things that hadn't visited my kitchen in years. Fresh fruits, vegetables, potted herbs, fresh meat, fish, eggs, cultured milk products, including "buttermilk for pancakes," he had said with a look that questioned my mental faculties. What was the point? He would be leaving tomorrow or the day after anyway.

"What are you going to do with the housekeeper during the three hundred and fifty days when you're at Mission?"

I agreed it was a big house for just the two of us. When I was growing up, my mother had supervised a housekeeper but had made all our meals with her own hands, because that was her job. My job was to succeed my father. Even so, I thought I did a good job of keeping house for myself with the help of a monthly cleaning service. And regardless of Todd's concerns about my diet, I had survived all these years living alone.

Todd however needed staff like he needed a dry-cleaning account.

"About that..." he said, leaving the air between us pregnant with anticipation while he perused the limited wine display. His casualness pricked at my skin, sending the small hairs standing on end.

"About what?" I asked, holding my breath. Richard immediately came to mind, but I quickly pushed him away. Todd could not know what I had done.

It was probably suspect that I had not asked how he had managed to make it home. With the recent accreditation of Ambassador Castillo-Mendez, Todd should have been in Santo Domingo supervising his briefings. He told me as much on Wednesday when he called to cancel our weekend. But here he was with me, and I hadn't questioned it or his explanation of "I wanted to surprise you".

However, it had not been an uneventful reunion. Between explaining my dissociated identity disorder and sealing our pact with a series of mind-blowing orgasms, I simply had not had the opportunity to raise the question.

"I visited my parents on Friday."

Todd's parents lived in a retirement community in Boca Raton, Florida. I had met them for the first and only time at our wedding. He on the other hand visited them on his way Stateside, time permitting. It was unusual however, for him to spend a full day out of a weekend trip on the detour. So whatever had prompted a visit to his parents also accounted for our overflowing supermarket cart late on a Sunday evening.

A whole, deboned roasting chicken, prime rib and a rosemary bush would have rotted in my refrigerator if left to my own devices.

"And?" I prompted with impatient hands. The man grinned even though he could clearly see my heart was throbbing in the V between my clavicles.

"I'm coming home," he said, unrepentantly toying with me. "I've been offered a home-based position."

"With the State Department?" I asked dubiously.

Todd shook his head. His evasiveness set my heart pumping to the beat of 'home, home, home'.

I grabbed him by the front of his shirt, the hard plains of his stomach grazing my knuckles even under two layers of fabric. "Tell me," I said, stretching on tiptoes to catch the words as they left his lips.

"Deputy Director." He whispered it directly into my ear, tickling me with wisps of my hair. That had to be the reason for the pang in the pit of my stomach. "Intel J2."

Todd was giving up his cover, or more likely, Richard wanted him to live straight. Still, the Directorate for Analysis in the DIA where Todd's potential new position resided was, among other things, adviser to the chairman of the Joint Chiefs of Staff. Either Todd was better and more important than I had imagined, or Richard had taken succession planning on a rocket trip.

It was too much to process in the back of a supermarket where the lights were being dimmed to urge shoppers out. My lips were cold when Todd pressed his to them.

"What's wrong?" he asked, snapping me out of my shock, opening my eyes to the fact I was raining on his parade.

"I can't believe it," I said, which was a terrible recovery that Todd did not miss. I shook my head, trying to dispel the haze... and yes, jealousy. "I mean that's fantastic."

"Tell me what you really think, Amy," he said. The light had dimmed with his smile and it was my fault. But he had dropped a bomb on me against the wine racks in a supermarket for God's sake!

"Tell me you accepted," was all I could manage.

Todd shook his head "I wanted to talk to you about it first."

Here? Really? I rushed into his arms because I was at a loss as to what to do with myself. "It's great. I'm proud of you. Congratulations," I said, wincing at how trite it all sounded.

"This is good for us," he said sedately, pressing his hands against the small of my back. He was too sober, as if he meant to convince me. Didn't I sound convinced?

"Of course it is," I said, then pulled away because it was obvious I wasn't fooling him. "This is new to me," I said, letting go of the urge to conceal the uncertainty. "Were you expecting it?"

I was better at deflection. It gave him something else to think about, and when he looked at me his eyes were infinitely less suspicious.

"No."

"But you've had how long to think about it?"

"The offer was made on Thursday morning."

Richard, I thought. What bargains had he made to achieve this in less than seventy-two hours?

"Give me a minute. I've only had two seconds to get over the shock." He seemed to relax before my eyes, "I am happy for you. I'm glad we'll be home together. I just haven't had the opportunity to think about all the facets."

Todd nodded his understanding, then reached for my hand. "Trust me, Amy."

"I do," I replied, but it stuck out between us like a naked lie. I wasn't sure whether I should have tried to convince him or allow some time for the idea to settle in. To his credit, Todd didn't want to keep ramming my lack of transparency down my throat. There was only so much humble pie anyone could eat before throwing it up over his self-righteous shoes.

"So the cover is done?" I asked, because it seemed like a safe enough topic… as safe as could be in such a public place.

Todd nodded. "I'm dusting off my birds."

There were minefields everywhere. It would have broken the ice to invite him to fuck me while dressed in full Marine Corps regalia, but my attraction… flirtation… connection with another Marine Corps colonel was destined to unsettle the dust that was slowly falling into place between us.

We left the supermarket even more subdued than when we had entered. And as the clerk rang up our stock, each beep an accusation of or disregard for her working hours, I could not help thinking about the other 'facets' of Todd's new role. It occurred to me that perhaps it was his new job that accounted for his willingness to understand my condition.

Todd could never have me committed without hurting himself. He would have to kill me to leave our marriage unscathed.

TEN

I was a prisoner and in the moment, I was okay with that. More than okay, in fact. I might as well have been chained to the bed, as the scene before me unfolded. Todd Birch dressed in a suit was magnificent. Todd Birch in Marine Corps service alphas would have had me creaming my panties, if I'd been wearing any. I wouldn't have given up the view for anything.

"What's going on in that head of yours?" he asked, checking his tie and insignia placement.

"Not much," I answered, then because we were more than just *practicing* being open and honest, I said exactly what was on my mind. "Just wondering what a girl has to do to get fucked by a full bull."

Those Eagles – wings spread like my legs while Todd ate me out, head turned in profile with olive branches and arrows clutched in their talons – had nothing on the man wearing them. They mocked my peace of mind, declared war on my libido.

I was afraid Todd would make the association with Colonel Townsend. He would be mostly wrong. I wasn't attracted to Townsend because of his rank. As a former Army captain, and having been surrounded by military men all my life, I didn't buy into the fantasy of a man in uniform. Perhaps he had derived his confidence from his position, but it was Townsend's raw maleness that drew me – the man beneath the uniform.

Our eyes met in the mirror. I stretched, back arching, toes pointed to make room for the unraveling of the coil of desire in my belly. I should have been sated. I was already sore from his tireless ministrations. And Todd should have been wrung dry. But if the sudden light in his eyes was an indication, he was equally intrigued by the picture I had drawn.

Todd turned to face me, fingers already loosening his khaki belt. By the time his knees hit the edge of the bed, three buttons of his coat were free, his tie loosened and trousers hanging around his knees.

"This has to be quick," he cautioned.

" I don't mind." I scooted down to meet him, legs hanging off the edge of the bed.

Todd shook his head. "Turn over, ass high," he directed and my core trembled with the first string of an orgasm.

Todd's primalness was definitely no by-product of a uniform. The ease with which he commanded me, mastered my mind and body bordered on casualness. He was so composed as he entered me that I would never have imagined that he was already hard and throbbing, a bead of moisture glistening at his tip. But as he pushed inside, palming my ass and spreading the cheeks, he could not hide how badly he wanted me. Again.

"Sweet," he groaned, squeezing a moan out of me too.

I sank into a deep arch, pressing my shoulders into the sheets that reeked of our all-night play, taking him deeper. I twisted to catch the sight that had consumed my imagination as he had pulled on the trappings of command. It was everything I had imagined and more.

His head was thrown back and eyes closed to better savor the moment. But only for a little while, because he also didn't want to miss the view from above with his big hands opening me up to him. Our eyes met as he slowly withdrew, our bodies vibrating as he tried and failed to contain the pleasure. With our visual connection in tact, he sank into me again, and even if I had wanted to, I would not have been able to hold back the cry bubbling up my throat.

Todd growled, and the juxtaposition of such a primitive sound coming from *this* man awakened something light, airy and feminine inside me. I did this to him. I was capable of stripping away the façade he showed to everyone else, even Richard. The power titillated me so much I couldn't help the smile that spread across my face.

From his answering grin, I could tell it pleased him to see me like this, spread out and vulnerable but fine with that. It satisfied the core of his maleness in a way my orgasms had barely touched. That reaction too intrigued me.

"I love you," I said, experimenting with my newfound powers, also clenching my muscles around his erection.

Todd squeezed the cheeks of my ass and pressed deeper into me, rubbing his pubic bone against the smooth skin of my backside. He never answered me with words, but there was no need. I could see. I knew.

The light in his eyes deepened, but the smile on his face melted away. Those eyes that had always regarded me with suspicion – or perhaps that might have been my imagination – were now completely open. They revealed the depths of Todd's desperate need for me. It reminded me of what I felt for him.

"Ass higher," he said, which was scant warning before his open palm cracked against first one cheek then the other. I lifted higher for him, my eyes catching his. "Are you ready for this?" he asked with a grin. "I don't want to be late for work."

"I wouldn't want that either." I finished on a gasp, because Todd hadn't waited for my permission. He found a quick and deep rhythm that echoed throughout my body. He filled the hollowness, hitting a nerve that had my body alternately pulsing like a heavy heartbeat and fluttering like the wings on a hummingbird.

Firm hands gripped my hips, pulling me back to meet each thrust, working in perfect counterpoint to the thrust of his hips that pushed me across the bed. He had me spasming around him in under a minute.

"That's right," Todd cooed without easing the pace. "Milk my cock. I'm going to fill you up. I want you dripping with my junk."

At this rate, I would be feeling him for several days. But the combination of pleasure and pain had me peaking again before I had fully recovered from the first orgasm. And as my walls tightened around him, I felt Todd swell inside me. Beads of sweat dripped from his brow onto my back. Todd rubbed them into my skin, marking me with more than just the semen surging inside me.

Powerful hands pressed me firmly against his body, a willing recipient for everything he had to offer. I took it, then more, stealing a clenched teeth cry from so deep inside him his abdominals contracted tightly to push it free.

I was dizzy with pleasure, my mouth flooding and tongue heavy as my craving for the man soared unchecked. We remained joined for long moments after our release. Todd sagged against me, propped awkwardly against my backside, trembling knees barely holding him upright. Neither of us wanted to break the bond.

He watched the fall of his perspiration onto my back, enthralled by either their pattern or the unrelenting nature of our desire for each other. Despite the issues he had never imagined would plague our union when he had asked to marry me. I swallowed hard then cleared my clogged throat.

Our eyes met and for a moment I was unsure again. He had earned much from our alliance, but I was asking even more from him. I was uncertain whether he was satisfied with the balance, or lack thereof.

"We can't keep doing this," Todd said, but didn't make a move to disentangle from me. His thumbs were busy massaging his scent into my skin.

"Why not?"

"Because for one, we're going to kill each other." He pressed his thumb into one of the dimples at the base of my spine. From the way he caressed me, I could tell he wasn't serious about stopping at all. Even as his erection waned, he pressed deeper into me, desperately trying to maintain our bond. I squeezed my knees together and lifted higher to accommodate him. Like fuel on dying embers, Todd stirred.

He moaned. "And secondly, I don't have enough shirts." The one hanging loosely off his shoulders was soaked around the collar, sticking to his skin in places hidden under his green coat.

I arched and stretched, rising to my elbows in a fluid motion that piqued his interest even more. My flesh tingled and my muscles throbbed from his assault, but I would have taken more of him if he had demanded.

"You have to admit this is worth the dry cleaning bill though."

Todd hummed his assent and I had never heard another sound more rife with regret. He withdrew with infinitely more care than when he had entered, his eyes flickering between my face and my swollen lips. He sighed at the picture. He replaced his erection with his fingers, rubbing his essence around my clitoris. His fingers burned. Slick with both our release, they massaged our juices into my flesh. It was as if he couldn't stop marking me.

From the bedside table my phone buzzed, breaking the spell. The haze of arousal lifted at the sight of Don Blitzner's name. Todd released me, stripping off his coat and unbuttoning his shirt as he went.

"Koehler."

"Amy, good morning," he greeted me, sounding entirely too cheerful at 6a.m. for this to be a call I would enjoy.

"How can I help you?"

"We have a briefing. Meet me at my office in one hour."

I held back on a quiet sigh. "Unless you have a helicopter on the way, that's not going to be possible." I bid a sad farewell to my hopes of getting a short run in before work. It was a solid forty-minute drive to Blitzner's office in the best weather without contending with Monday morning traffic.

I caught Todd's headshake as he pulled a fresh undershirt over his head. He rubbed at his neck again with the old one, catching any sweat he might have missed on the first pass. Jamming the phone in the crook of my neck, I beckoned for him to toss it my way. Catching the shirt one handed, I buried my nose deep into the folds of the moist garment and breathed him in.

"Make it quick," Blitzner urged, not in the least put out by my polite refusal. "We're going for a drive and you don't want to miss this." Then he hung up before I could press him for details. Having effectively piqued my curiosity, he had no need to hang on the line to be peppered with twenty questions.

"Change of plans?" Todd asked. He knew I was mostly working from home now.

I nodded. "Blitzner wants to go for a ride. I don't know why."

Todd nodded without pausing in his redressing, I was content to enjoy the double feature.

"Amy." Our eyes met in the mirror again as he pulled on his coat.

"Hmm?" I was in the middle of a stretch.

"Neither of us has the time. Get up, get dressed and meet me in the kitchen." He finished his belt, made a few final adjustments to the full picture, then reached for his cover.

"We could skip breakfast and make time."

Todd never did answer. He left the bedroom, but it wasn't just my imagination that detected a drag in his step.

"Baby," I crooned, "your love is addictive."

Todd shook his head, but refused to look at me. His only response was a quiet chuckle I had to strain my ears to catch.

Scientists claimed sex was good for the complexion, which led me to believe I hadn't had nearly enough. After a quick shower, I slathered on some over-the-counter acne cream under copious amounts of sunscreen and concealer. It wasn't a perfect camouflage job, but I was just glad I didn't look like a scalded cat anymore.

I pulled on a Monday suit – black pencil skirt, blue shirt, black pumps – and scraped my hair into a ponytail. A quick mirror check revealed the darkening bruises around my neck – a definite no-no for work. I scavenged a thin turtleneck sweater from an overstuffed suitcase of clothes I hadn't worn in three years. Ovulation had done a number on my boobs too, because although I hadn't gained any weight since my last winter residence, the sweater clung indecently to my chest. A long blazer was added to preserve my modesty, but it couldn't cover up the smell of old clothes.

I threw my sweater into the dryer with a dryer sheet, then headed for the kitchen from which wafts of cinnamon and coffee emanated. Todd was hanging an apron over the back of a high chair, having recently transformed bread into French toast. Dressed in only a bra, a skirt, and a smile, I took the seat across from him.

"We really need to get someone in here to help," he said, handing me a fork and doing his best to ignore my dishabille. He pushed a shaker of powdered sugar and a jar of maple syrup towards me, before cutting into his plate of toast. I followed suit but was unprepared for the warm buttery sweetness that brought out the starving urchin in me.

"Why?" I asked around a mouthful of food, while adding a generous dose of both the sugar and syrup. The man was clearly talented. "This is amazing!"

Almost as much as the sex, I missed Todd's cooking. A less selfish woman would have felt some guilt at the imbalance in our relationship. A less understanding man would have lost patience with my selfishness. Todd only laughed.

He took a final sip of coffee then passed the cup to my side. In a flash, he pulled me halfway across the table to chase the cinnamon and maple flavors in my mouth with his tongue.

"You're sweet," he murmured against my mouth. Our eyes met as he licked my lips. The heat was strong enough to singe the hair on the back of my neck where his fingers caressed me. He kissed me again, lips pulling slowly and sweetly, tongue stroking leisurely against mine. My toes curled and back arched as desire awakened in me.

"I have to go." Todd pulled away with a rumble in the back of his throat, totally self-satisfied.

Briefcase in one hand, he turned back to me after a few steps, and I smiled at the realization that he needed the length of the kitchen between us.

"Call Abby on your drive to work this morning and raise the question with her. I'll discuss it with Richard as well later this afternoon."

I tried to keep the smile from melting at the mention of Admiral McDowell. I centered my attention on maneuvering more toast into my mouth. "Why bother with Abby then?" I tried not to sound petulant, but may have missed the mark.

Todd shifted from one foot to the other, impatient to go or fed up with my obsession with his relationship with Richard. I couldn't really tell while focusing so intently on the food, wondering where the sawdust taste was coming from.

"Because you'll catch more flies with honey than vinegar. It doesn't take much to make Abby's day, which you can mine later for a favor. It wouldn't hurt either having Richard think you're playing an active role in managing our household."

As usual, Todd saw too much. He had seen right through Richard... and me too. He crossed the distance between us and turned me to face him. His fingers at my jaw were firm but not in the least painful. Just insistent, like the way he was staring into me.

"He's from a different generation; his expectations are more traditional. For the record, I couldn't care less if you didn't know how to boil water. That's not why I married you."

Of course not. He married me for my connections... for Richard, the Secretary of Defense, and the men like them who remembered my father and had loved me as a child. He married me so he could be exactly where he was now... so the highlight of my day could be discussing staff recommendations.

"That's not why I fell in love with you," he added and this time when he looked into my eyes, he gave more than he took. In one glance, he shared with me the depth of his feelings for me – and whether they were in spite of his better judgment was irrelevant. He opened up for me to see and believe his hope for our future.

"I don't care for anyone else's opinion on our relationship. But sometimes, it doesn't hurt to pretend to value them when there's more to gain. So smile, pretend you're June fucking Cleaver, and behind closed doors, I want you to continue being the woman I adore. OK?"

Well, when he put it like that...

All the anxiety that had been building at the mention of Richard's name was strapped to the back of a sigh that rocketed out of me. "OK."

Todd kissed me again for good measure, whether to seal our deal or prevent me from thinking too deeply, examining all the facets of his strategy.

God knows I would have found something else to distrust. But when his mouth took possession of mine, when his breath gusted against my face and all my senses were flooded with him, all reason chased after that rocket. I wanted nothing more than what we had in that moment.

Yes, Todd's effect on me was not unlike the human brain on meth.

ELEVEN

Don Blitzner was an asshole and I was beginning to think my social anxiety disorder wasn't as rare as originally thought. Based on our early morning conversation, I knew he had a brief planned and that a drive was somehow to be incorporated into the equation. Based on the sensitive nature of our work, it wouldn't have been too far out of left field to conduct our chat session in a moving vehicle to minimize the chances of being overheard.

The reality turned out to be an experience in terror.

Blitzner met me in the parking lot of our building. With the attention of the conspiracy theorists firmly fixed on identifying secret CIA buildings around McLean, our location in Herndon was relatively quiet. It was slightly out of the way, too far west for anyone not heading to Dulles. So I was both intrigued and yet not at all surprised when Blitzner loaded me into his blackout Chevy Tahoe, and headed east on the 267.

The ride was mostly quiet, which was disturbing considering Blitzner hadn't shared our location and had his sickly-sweet smile firmly in place. It was like taking a secret ride with the Joker – the Heath Ledger one – and I had left my Sig in the lockbox in my car. The only part of the forty-five minute drive that was more awkward than the first twenty minutes of silence, was our attempt to break it.

"Have you given any thought to our dilemma?" Blitzner began, tone and comportment in direct conflict. He was dressed like a funeral director in a plain black suit, black tie over stark white shirt, dead eyes staring blankly ahead. But his voice was almost lyrical, it was so upbeat.

"What dilemma would that be?" So far, I had only the Mohammed al-Mohammed case open. But with Blitzner, it was never OK to assume.

"Why, detainee 28211, of course."

Of course, my ass. Mohammed al-Mohammed was many things, but a dilemma was not one of them. He was contained and would always be. There was nothing pressing about his case.

We merged onto I-66, heading east. I began to doubt this was an aimless drive. Nor was he taking the long way around McLean. We soon blew by the Church Falls exit, which left Arlington and everything south and east of that. It was next to impossible to guess our destination. And the closer I peered at Blitzner's purposeful driving style, the more I realized he did indeed have a destination in mind. He couldn't stop watching the clock and double-checking the time on his watch.

"So, have you?" he pressed. "Given any thought to..."

As if I wasn't being paid – and quite generously too – to eat, breathe and sleep detainee 28211. "I have," I answered, then allowed the conversation to lapse again.

It was a full five minutes before anything was said again. "I think you should see him."

"Why?"

His smile stretched wider. "There's nothing like looking into a man's eyes while picking apart his secrets."

And with that, Blitzner managed to conjure the image of his head on a vulture's body as he picked at human flesh. "We've been picking at him for four years now. There's no point in going to see him."

That ended the conversation for the next ten miles. We had nowhere to go but east into D.C or south towards all the military installations. Todd was at one of those military installations, but I hadn't asked where he was working. I knew he would be receiving his new command today, which might have been at the DIA headquarters at the Joint Base Anacostia-Bollings, or the Pentagon. My unease mounted as Blitzner began humming quietly under his breath. I tried and failed to recognize his point of reference for the melody. But the radio was off; the only sounds inside the car were the drone of the tires eating up the asphalt, the wind, and the unknown tune in his head.

"Do you have a better idea?" he asked, and I struggled to recall where we had last left the discussion. It was the most painful ride ever.

"I do," I answered, but didn't volunteer any more than that. Just like he would not volunteer any information on where we were headed. My only consolation was knowing Blitzner would have warned me if he wanted me working with my husband. I had been clear on that score.

In addition, Todd had not yet received his command. He would not be prepared to give a briefing just yet, and most likely he wouldn't actually be the one conducting the exercise in any case.

Besides, Todd would definitely have given me a heads-up if I had suddenly appeared on his calendar. To be sure, I checked my phone for any messages. There were none.

To compound my anxiety, I could not imagine what new intelligence could have surfaced regarding Mohamed al-Mohamed. There hadn't been anything in years, which was why I had been assigned the case. I was tasked with wringing blood from stone.

So why the mystery?

My heart rate kicked up a beat when Blitzner signaled on the approach to Exit 75. In a minute we were heading south on SR110. A few minutes after that, we merged onto the Pentagon Access Road. The chips fell abruptly into place as we bypassed the southeast side, with its concourse, metro station, and the visitors' entrance. We continued north towards the River Terrace entrance to the Reservation.

Blitzner's preoccupation with the time made sense, as did his insistence on taking his car. The Pentagon Force Protection agents checked and double-checked his vehicle information, performed the required undercarriage inspections, then directed us to our assigned north parking spot. Blitzner continued to hold his cards close to his chest however, and I refused to ask. He didn't need to know that my heart had lurched into my throat and almost choked me.

"Ready, Amy?"

I was anything but ready, but I smiled and nodded. Following his cue, I placed my cell phone in the glove compartment and exited the vehicle. I had no clue what I would find inside, but I hoped it wasn't Todd.

I had had the experience of working with him only once before. We had already hammered out an understanding of our personal situation and committed ourselves to each other with a joint kill. The victims were rapist, drug and human traffickers who had tracked down Angelika inside my Santo Domingo apartment. They deserved everything they got. However, there was something to be said about killing people and disposing of the evidence as a husband-wife team. So, yes, our commitment to each other had been sound.

That was a good thing too, because a few days later I had had to face Todd across an embassy conference room with Colonel Townsend at my side. The colonel and I had collaborated and recently concluded a trafficking case involving senior Dominican military personnel, and Todd, as acting head of Mission, had to raise the matter of arrest and prosecution with the country's political leadership. Colonel Townsend had tried to exploit the opportunity, inferring a level of intimacy in our work that we had certainly skirted but never in fact achieved. The relationship between Blitzner and I was different, but I wanted that man as far removed from my marriage as possible.

I wasn't much for hoping. I planned and accounted for every possibility. But in my present situation, I had no recourse but to hope our Pentagon field trip remained Todd-free. And I had good reason to expect that it should be. The building was spread over nearly thirty acres.

What were the odds of my accidentally running into my husband when the floor plan covered seven floors and over six-and-a-half million square feet?

I dutifully trudged behind my boss as we headed from the parking lot to the twenty-foot portico, the lagoon and Bollings Joint Force base behind us to the southeast. If I seemed to be on the lookout for some hidden threat, then that wouldn't have been very far from the truth. What I found from forty feet was in every sense a danger.

Clad in service alphas identical to the ones featured in my fantasy come to life this morning stood Colonel Robert Townsend. It was not just his physical appearance that distinguished the man from my husband. Where Todd was dark with a full head of luxurious hair, Colonel Townsend was golden, blond spikes compacted into a high-and-tight. His eyes were blue too, but a clear crystalline hue that evoked images of the sky on a cloudless day. Todd's reminded me of the deepest part of the ocean.

It was my objective opinion that Colonel Townsend was formidable too. But while my husband had a certain sleekness to him, his predatory quality came more from his aura than the lines of his body that were always carefully cloaked by tailored clothing. Colonel Townsend on the other hand was a brute who wore the trappings of aggression proudly. He was hard and corded everywhere, one hundred percent animal on the prowl, which appealed to me on an evolutionary level.

We were sexually compatible. I enjoyed the play between pleasure and pain, which I knew he could deliver. After all, I had secretly recorded him putting Angelika through her paces. When he had looped his belt around her neck, holding tightly to the reins while riding her hard from behind, I knew the cruel universe had intended for us to be together... or meant for us to lust after each other from a distance.

"Ah, Colonel Townsend," Blitzner greeted the man, managing to sound both surprised and unsurprised at the same time. As if he hadn't planned this well in advance, possibly since last week while I was bulldozing him in his office. They shook hands. "You remember Amy Koehler, don't you?"

We saved ourselves the pretense. Colonel Townsend did not offer, so I kept my hands firmly rooted in my coat pockets. I had to admit though, the soft wool had nothing on the ice blue eyes staring me down. That gaze still had the power to warm me up and turn me on.

Blitzner had saved me once from making a colossal mistake, because I had soon learned that Colonel Townsend was incapable of discretion. He would have broadcasted our physical relationship to anyone with eyes to see, regardless of what that would have done to my career. This time, I wasn't so sure of my boss' intervention however.

"Amy," the colonel said in greeting, one edge of his thin but inviting mouth arching teasingly... sensually. "I thought you would have been a Birch by now."

It was an old dig at my husband for my insistence on keeping my father's name.

"Either will do," I answered with a smile I hoped was more breezy than board stiff.

Blitzner rocked back on his heels with both hands in his pockets. He had baited two dogs – one of them in heat – and was content to observe the scrape that followed.

"I'll remember that," Townsend replied, and just as easily pressed his hand to the base of my spine to escort us inside. Blitzner not only allowed it to happen, he unexpectedly stepped aside, giving the colonel all the space and unspoken permission he cared for. "It's good to see you again, Amy."

He would call me Amy and I would have to call him 'Colonel Townsend' or 'sir'. He would press his arm caressingly along my body, flirting with the upper curve of my ass, painting a picture for the onlookers to interpret as they wished. And I would have to ignore it, pretending it wasn't happening and didn't mean anything. I really hoped Todd was at Bollings and we didn't run into anyone we knew in the labyrinth of corridors.

"Please don't tell me you've missed our Mission days so much you've been keeping tabs on me," I jabbed at him over one shoulder. He was staring at my ass, and if I wasn't mistaken, that was his pinkie I felt through two layers caressing me. "First Santo Domingo and now here."

It wasn't far-fetched. The gleam in his eyes as he returned his attention to my face – my mouth, more precisely – backed up the accusation. Colonel Townsend wasn't above stalking me if it meant he could hurt Todd. And all this was over a woman who had played two friends against each other.

Jesus, they were overgrown children!

"You'll remember Colonel Townsend was Military Liaison Officer," Blitzner interjected, suddenly eager to offer an explanation. "Well, we all worked so well together that when we ran into each other a few months ago, I mentioned I was building a new team. And as it turned out, Colonel Townsend was also looking for a new command. It's our good luck that our plans coincided."

Back in the D.R. Townsend had mentioned spotting Blitzner here a few months ago. Blitzner was throwing a squash match in the Pentagon Athletics Center against Bill Beecher... obviously courting Bill's boss – Uncle Richard. How Townsend had explained it however, implied a distant sighting, not an actual encounter.

"Colonel Townsend is going to be our operational liaison."

At some point Blitzner was going to have to run out of surprises.

How the fuck was I going to explain this to Todd?

The parking situation alone belied it being a spur of the moment field trip. He would never believe I had had no idea we would be working together. He might even suspect I had had contact with his rival in the week prior to his arrival.

The window of opportunity to give Todd a heads-up had closed. I had no cellphone. We cleared a security checkpoint, then boarded an elevator heading for the restricted mezzanine level.

I was so preoccupied with keeping one step ahead and out of reach of Townsend and his roaming fingers, that I completely missed the ambush awaiting me up ahead.

My Monday morning had become a comedy of errors. Except there was nothing amusing about the surprises awaiting me today – all of them in service Alphas. In my line of work, surprises could be deadly, and the one standing outside Room MC4 had already tried to kill me once.

TWELVE

"Do you two know each other?" Colonel Townsend asked.

It was a reasonable question. Major Ed Cummings had absent-mindedly shaken Blitzner's hand upon introduction, but neither he nor I had been inclined to approach the other beyond the briefest chin lift, too wary of each other to force civility.

Did we know each other? Ed was fond of calling me 'cunt', and for good cause.

"Yes," I answered at the exact moment Major Cummings answered, "No, sir."

I left the explaining to him. Colonel Townsend was Marine Corps and Major Cummings was Army, but this was obviously a joint operations team and it was never a good idea for an O-4 to lie to an O-6.

"We've met," Ed said tersely, hazel eyes narrowing, darkening to the pure brown as he stared me down. "But how well do you really know anyone?"

Ironic, considering Ed knew me better than Townsend ever would. The last time we had laid eyes on each other was in Kuwait three years ago. Ed had once claimed to love me, without really knowing me. I believed he was in fact enamored of my connections to Richard. Pity he had never been able to tap our full potential.

I had video evidence of Ed acting out one of his rape fantasies. He'd caught me stealing it from his hard drive. And if there had ever been any doubt of his feelings towards me, Ed had sent someone after me three years ago. I had disposed of his recovery and enforcement personnel. In turn, Ed was responsible for the murder of one of my assets, Matt Boone – alias RageMan 96253 – a former CIA hacker.

I would never forget Ed's last gift to me: Matt Boone's autopsy report and photo. The MD had pinned the death on a motor vehicle accident, but I knew better.

Between Ed and I, there were more secrets and lies, broken hearts (Ed was married with two kids at the time of our liaison), and dead bodies than a Martin Scorsese production.

Now both Townsend and Blitzner were watching us, and Ed lacked a sophisticated bone. He was all brash and bluster, incapable of controlling his reactions to me. He continued to stare daggers at me, jaw ticking, body tense, cheeks flushed. He was either strangling me in his head, or remembering how Anne had pulsed around his cock as he pinned her down – hands bound behind her back, cries muffled by a gag and the flax sack he had pulled over her head.

I entered the briefing room ahead of the men, shrugging out of my coat with casualness I didn't feel. Colonel Townsend followed, his hand never straying more than a heartbeat away – a fact that neither Blitzner nor Ed could have missed. Exactly as Townsend intended.

"I didn't take you for a tag-chaser, Amy," Colonel Townsend murmured as he pulled out a chair for me. And yet the statement implied he had come to exactly that conclusion.

"Don't be mistaken, Colonel Townsend. You've only ever seen the back of me and not the way you've wanted either."

I shrugged from under his touch while pulling my chair closer to the desk. It was useless trying to establish distance between us with a public brush off. Particularly when he did his best to hint at a private, more intimate relationship. He took the seat to my left, scooting close enough that I caught and held his scent, leaning so close at times that the soft down at my nape stood on end.

There was no denying my attraction to him. The way my body reacted to his proximity made what had passed between Anne and Ed seem like a harmless infatuation. And Ed was aware of this. In spite of our tragic history, he seemed upset at the fake intimacy Townsend was advertising.

Ed and I had both worked in Military Intelligence. I had impressed him with my knowledge of Arabic and Farsi, and he and Anne had bonded over sexual bondage and S&M. It was during a phase of my life when I was focused on collecting favors. The video of their encounter had become a bargaining piece in the hunt for my father's killer. In exchange for what he naïvely thought was the only copy, Ed had passed on information regarding the whereabouts of Samantha Windsor – a CIA operative and Matt Boone's wife who had disappeared in Baghdad in 2006. Grateful for the first news of his wife's whereabouts in five years – she was a guest of the Iranian government – Matt Boon had led me to Blerim Nesimi, who in turn led me to Sergei Afanasenko, who would eventually lead me to his American backer – my father's killer.

Too many facets of my life were coalescing in this little room. One slip from Ed would have Townsend and Blitzner salivating over the opportunity to hurt Todd, or curry favor with Richard.

For that reason, I tried to relax, falling back on a tried-and-true strategy to conceal vulnerability – distraction. That Townsend provided in spades. It wasn't as difficult as I would have wanted either. Our connection was like metal to a magnet.

"I don't get it," Townsend whispered too close to my ear. I felt his breath as a tickle on my skin and smelled the coffee on his breath. "What do you see in him?"

"Saw," I whispered back, turning my head slightly to the left. It left only a smidgen of air between our lips. "It was a long time ago. I was young. He was no longer my Commanding Officer. Maybe it was a mistake."

"You do know…" he said, inching his chair even close, adjusting the seat of his trousers around his growing erection and using the movement to conceal the action. I pulled the edges of my blazer around me. The extra layer hid the peaking of my nipples even as it seemed to rub the aching points raw. "You do know it won't be like that between us, don't you? When I bury my cock in you, there will be no mistake. And you're going to beg me to fuck you every way 'til Sunday."

I didn't doubt it... if he could actually get his cock inside me, which was a huge condition considering I couldn't look at him without thinking of my husband. And what falling for Townsend would do to our marriage. Todd couldn't blame me for my body's reaction to the man, but he would hate me for giving in.

I was counting on Todd being as reasonable as I was giving him credit for, because Blitzner was watching Townsend and me like a hawk. He wouldn't interfere, not when he had nothing to gain. But it was information he was filing away. Thankfully, there was no news here. That Townsend wanted to fuck me was no secret. I just had to make sure we weren't ever left alone.

Ed for his part, did his best with the briefing. He laid out the latest intelligence report on Hasan al-Qasim and his sons between watching intensely for every movement Townsend made in my direction. He hated me; he had tried to kill me once, and would attempt it again, if he thought there was a chance of success.

And yet he was not only distracted by Townsend's attention to me, it seemed to infuriate him.

That was a disturbing picture of the type of man who drew me... that even in his hatred, Ed was still possessive of me.

The briefing was all pointless torture for Ed and I. There was no news of Hasan al-Qasim's whereabouts. We suspected he had trained his son in bomb making, then sent him into Iraq to teach the insurgents how to put together a real bomb. Mohamed al-Mohamed was rumored to have been the chief explosives report to Moqtada al-Sadr's Mahdi Army. The brief was more of a tally of American lives taken in bombings that were being laid at Mohamed al-Mohamed's door.

If it were Blitzner's intention to justify holding Mohamed al-Mohamed, it was pointless. I didn't need convincing.

So for nearly two hours we sat, watching slide after slide of the wreckage of the Mahdi Army's attacks on the transport convoys, mosques, markets, and government installations.

Mohamed al-Mohamed's arrest in January 2007 had followed the arrest of a handful of Iranian intelligence officers in December whose communications had given away our detainee's location. He was caught empty-handed, but his old injuries – blown off digits and nerve damage – had identified him by his trade.

Following a month when one hundred and fifty US soldiers had died, most of them in bombings and shootings that had followed bombings, Mohamed al-Mohamed had booked himself a one-way ticket to Gitmo. He had no one to blame for his position but himself... and perhaps his father.

Now it seemed Hasan al-Qasim was at it again, training explosives trainers for deployment to Iraq. His signature had made a reappearance in fourteen bombings since May of this year – eleven in Iraq and three in Afghanistan. Officially, Operation New Dawn had ended yesterday, December 18, with the withdrawal of the last US military convoy into Kuwait. The war in Iraq was officially over, but we expected Iranian sponsored attacks to continue harming US interests in the country.

The point was to shut down the al-Qasim bomb factory, and the only way to do that was to kill Hasan and as many of his pupils as possible. Mohamed al-Mohamed was our GPS to his father, or so Blitzner hoped.

Technically, Ed was on loan to us, and it was Townsend's responsibility to ensure he was returned in the same condition he had been checked out. Once I found a way to crack Mohamed al-Mohamed, the information would be fed to Ed who would filter it to the operational team that would target Hasan in Iran, or somehow lure him away from his refuge.

Townsend was the bridge between Blitzner and the Department of Defense, having proved himself useful in the capacity of Amy-wrangling. He wasn't the sharpest knife in the block, but he had the memory of an elephant and believed in preserving relationships. That made him good at his job as liaison, but also meant he disapproved of my methods.

Someone didn't want me abusing DOD resources.

It wasn't my intention to do any damage, but Ed clearly had other ideas. He seemed intent on cornering me at the end of our session. While Blitzner and Townsend conspired to make my life hell outside the conference room, Ed lingered unnecessarily, inviting me for a tête-à-tête with a raised brow and a tilted head. Because the day couldn't possibly get any worse, and because I knew Ed would have his say one way or another, I opted to reduce the chances of it occurring at a more inconvenient time.

I gave Townsend's pinkie a much-needed leave of absence, abandoning the hand at the base of my spine to hopefully quietly hear

Ed's rant several feet away. He used to be discreet. We were able to carry on a deep flirtation for months without his wife or anyone in our company or HQ suspecting. To say that I was banking on more of that discretion was a gross understatement.

Unfortunately, Ed was worked up by either my blackmail or Townsend's possessiveness. We had minimal shelter in the small alcove of a locked door only paces away from my boss and my would-be lover. A few feet in the opposite direction, another corridor bisected ours. And while our hallway was mostly deserted, traffic crossing the intersection was steady. Every now and then, uniformed military personnel passed by, some moving leisurely and others a bit more briskly on their way to their engagements.

Whether to provide some privacy from the pedestrian traffic or a last ditch attempt at intimidation, Ed had me backed up against the door, crowding me from the front with an inflated chest and the same cologne that had seeped through the flax sack. Even in the dark I could identify Ed by his fragrance and the cinnamon gum he favored. Even hours after he had gotten rid of it, the spicy note still hung around.

"Back for more, are you?"

There were several candidates for what was on Ed's mind. Had I come back to fuck with him? In both the literal and figurative sense, based on his anger and the faint strains of musk wafting off him.

God, how could he be aroused at a time like this?

I didn't want to tangle with him by any means. My life certainly didn't need the complication. Working with Townsend again was more than enough.

Speaking of the colonel, I turned my head to see if his possessiveness extended to bringing a premature end to Ed's ambush.

"Don't look at him. Do you really want to drag him into your drama?"

"My drama, Ed?" I asked. He was the one putting on a show. It was also a challenge though, because if Ed ever opened his mouth about Matt Boone, or what Matt had stolen from him, he would be out of a job, and living on borrowed time.

But so would I.

"Yes, you. Drama cunt." Ed licked his lips, sucking on his full bottom lip while running his eyes over mine. "Maybe I should tell him what he's up against. You were hot for it... your pussy one of the best I ever had, but nothing is worth your degree of fucked up."

And yet Ed seemed to be caught up in the memory of the fun times he had had with Anne. His cinnamon coated tongue peaked out again from between his front teeth.

"Why'd you have to fuck things up, hm?"

"Stop it," I hissed at him, aware of more than one pair of eyes trying to find me from behind Ed.

"Why? Because of him?" He tilted his head in the direction of the conference room door. "I know he hasn't fucked you yet," Ed continued, knuckles cracking where he had them braced on the door on either side of me. I didn't push him away. I didn't want to touch him, didn't want to encourage him in the least. "But he wants to. So what's the hold up? I bet that bird on his collar has got you creaming."

Ed laughed in an angry imitation of humor.

"I think he knows you'll fuck him over once he's stuck it in you. And for no other reason than you being a crazy fucking bitch."

The sad reality of the liaison with Ed became more apparent as he continued, shifting from one foot to the other but always limiting the breathing space he allowed.

Anne didn't fuck him so I could later blackmail him. The deception had only come after.

Ed had gotten his; it was only fair that Anne got hers too. It was this inseparability of anger, desire and dominance that had appealed to Anne's submissiveness, and my craving for purpose. It was no coincidence that the men in her life were all dominants with anger issues and near uncontrollable impulses to bend us to their will. The military was full of them and for years I had used it as a recruitment ground. The ones who had stuck around had wills that were stronger than mine: Todd, Colonel Townsend. Ed, not so much.

"You need to back off," I said slowly and deliberately, willing the caution to clear the fog in his head. "We're even now. So do us both a favor and stay away from me."

Ed laughed. It was quiet, dark and humorless. "I'll stay away alright. After I bleed you, you fucking cunt. You ruined my life. And before this is played out, I'm going to take yours."

"You're welcome to try again, Ed, but don't expect me to take it lying down."

Ed laughed again. His threat assessment had always been piss poor. "You're going to take it when and how I decide to give it to you," he said, which sounded awfully like something he would have told Anne years ago. "And this time there's nothing holding me back."

The danger with Ed's particular proclivities was their evolution. It was naïve to expect his rape fetish wouldn't one day spiral into something deadlier than role-play. It seemed in the intervening years those urges had progressed, and the thing that had always held him back from going too far had slipped away.

Suddenly I wasn't as interested in whether there had been actual victims, because something far more dangerous than Ed would hold him back. In fact, it almost passed us by without first realizing the mistake. But old habits died hard and Todd Birch could not resist an opportunity to face off with his old rival.

"Well, if it isn't my good friend, Bob," he said as he backtracked from the intersection into our quiet hallway.

His target was Colonel Robert Townsend, but it was Major Edward Cummings who jackknifed to attention and saluted, leaving me exposed. Todd probably would not have given Ed more than a passing glance if he hadn't spotted me in such revealing proximity to him. Our eyes met and held even as he addressed Ed.

"Major Cummings, do you know my wife?"

If ever there was a good time for the roof to cave in on me that was it. But I was never so lucky. Never was, never would be.

Fuck!

THIRTEEN

If my heart weren't about to beat out of my chest I would have found Ed's bug eyes comical. A heart attack was a distinct possibility as the four men I never wanted to meet were converged in an ever-tightening circle around me.

It was a classic Mexican standoff. Colonel Townsend was armed with the surety of my attraction to him and the confirmation of my history with Ed. Ed was locked and loaded with my association with the hacker Rageman 96253, that had resulted in one of Ed's Iranian assets being compromised. Todd knew more than any other single person alive – which would destroy my career if disclosed to any of the other three. And Blitzner... he was entirely too close to Richard for comfort.

In the absence of a plan, I had to fall back on that fickle hope again.

I hoped they would stick to old agendas.

Blitzner was a bit of a wild card. I had to minimize his participation to that of a detached observer. Townsend was a one-trick pony, almost guaranteed to try to piss Todd off. Since our history was no secret, it was a certainty he would try to play the Ed card. The fact that Ed was standing at ease at Todd's direction, and that Todd had not yet given Townsend a second glance, meant my husband was determined to get to the bottom of our acquaintance. So Ed it was.... If I couldn't escape without mentioning our informal association, I would play up the fact that it was unfair of Todd to judge me on my history that predated us.

"Major Cummings was my CO years ago," I offered promptly, stepping from under Ed's shadow.

"I didn't ask you," Todd easily deflected without the courtesy of even looking at me. Objectively I couldn't blame him for directing his question to Ed. Ed couldn't lie to him and get off scotch-free; while I had given Todd cause to doubt me time and time again.

"How do you know my wife?"

I swallowed hard and watched my husband transform before my eyes. He became harder, and not just in terms of the tension in his jaw. I had only witnessed this shift in him once before. It was the night we had killed together. This was the man who kept a kill kit in his car, complete with a small arsenal of firearms, suppressors, gloves, duct tape, a hatchet, plastic sheeting, knives and lots of cash.

"I was Captain Koehler's CO at NGIC, sir."

I might have believed him that our only association was through the National Ground Intelligence Center, if he had been firmer in his response. But Todd was already suspicious, and Ed's inability to think on his feet made it clear he had conveniently picked up on my hint.

Todd wasn't about to let Ed off the hook so easily.

I interjected. I could handle Todd's wrath, had courted it before and had dealt well with the consequences.

"Todd," I said softly without compromising firmness. I touched him too. I felt his stomach tense under my fingers. Judging by his expression as he peered down at me though, it was more of a flinch at the unwanted contact than a response to desire. His eyes were nearly black as he stared through me.

"Don't," I said, so softly only he could hear. He stared intently at my mouth, perhaps waiting for more, possibly a denial of his suspicions. I offered none.

With the barest excuses, he pulled me away from our audience. His fingers were hard against my arm. He held me away from himself, as if contact was to be avoided... as if I was soiled. My face flamed beneath the layers of makeup I had applied to conceal the ravages of the weekend. I couldn't bring myself to assess the others' reactions.

We didn't go far ... just around the bend. If Todd wasn't careful, the audience we had just abandoned, or any number of the men who passed in the hallway with brisk salutes, would overhear us.

"It's not what you think," I preempted the second my back hit the wall.

"What do I think, Amy?"

That was a rhetorical question if ever there was one. I could feel the fire in him like a physical blow to my face.

"Tell me you didn't let him put his dick in you."

"Stop it," I hissed at him, pressing my hand into his chest. It was a defiance of his intent to create distance between us. When he tried to step away I followed.

"Do you know what this means?" he spat at me, and all I could see and feel was his anger. But the words implied hurt too.

"It means nothing, because you don't know what happened." I tried buying myself some time with defiance.

"I know you!" he seethed, pressing me back into the corner and slapped my hand away. Not sharp enough to be considered a strike, but forceful enough to get me away from him. "I fucked you within an hour of meeting you."

It was my turn to flinch. I was too surprised to hide it. I had never been ashamed of my sexuality before, not even when confronted by Richard at seventeen. Later I used it to survive… to reset the ticking time bomb inside me. Now here was Todd using my past to define me. Even though he was no saint, I was the dirty one.

The flash of regret across his face was too little too late.

"You're slut shaming me?"

"I didn't mean it like that," he said, which was no apology at all, because he did mean it like that. But it did drop an opportunity for deflection in my lap. Pity it actually stung.

"I don't have time for this. I'm working."

I was successful in pushing away from him, partly because of his insistence on distance a few moments ago, and partly because he was too absorbed by guilt to react in a timely manner.

"Amy," he called after me, which I ignored.

Blitzner and Townsend were still in quiet conversation, a clear pretext for awaiting the outcome of our confrontation. And Ed had retreated to the conference room, hiding. He blocked himself into a corner because Todd followed me back into his corridor and Ed's only escape was through him.

My cheeks still flamed from Todd's verbal slap, even though he belatedly tried to portray a united front to the audience. He shook hands with Blitzner and Townsend, suddenly intent on keeping a possessive hand at the base of my spine. I was going to be bruised there. I maintained eye contact with a point above Blitzner's right shoulder through the tense greetings with his rival and brief introduction to my boss. No one was fooled.

When Blitzner realized there was no gain to be had beyond the mounting awkwardness, he signaled our departure. Townsend, our escort, was forced into abandoning his witness post to the impending confrontation between my past and my future. And there was no doubt there would be a confrontation, as we left Todd standing outside the conference room.

I wasn't one for wishful thinking. I was a planner. Wishing I could have started the day over would have achieved nothing in any case. I could not have refused to accompany Blitzner to the Pentagon. I could not have avoided Colonel Townsend or Major Cummings, and since it was Townsend's presence that had lured Todd to our corner, I could not have avoided our discovery.

Would I have warned Todd about my history with Ed? Between confiding in him about my father, and making up in his service alphas, there had been no opportunity to ease him into the topic of my sexual history. What would I have said anyway?

"I've never had a colonel yet? Made the rounds with a couple of majors one of whom you might run into some day, but mostly stuck with company officers."

"Are you OK, Amy?" Blitzner asked as soon as I settled in next to him in the car.

I had floated through our parting with Colonel Townsend with a numbness that persisted. I could not even blame the cold. We had been spared the frozen rain splashing against the windshield by a few seconds.

"Fine," I answered, sinking deeper into the absence of feeling. I met his dead blue eyes, now alight with ill-concealed interest. As if I would ever confide in this man.

He nodded without answering and started the car. I thought we had dropped the topic, because we drove for twenty minutes, all in silence, before he picked up where we had left off.

"You're very quiet. Is there something on your mind?"

I would have laughed if I'd had the capacity for humor just then. We had made the entire journey to the Pentagon in near silence and my reserve on the return was suddenly a cause for concern?

"Actually, there is," I said, mentally switching gears. "I have to go to Paris, preferably in the next couple of weeks."

I kept my gaze straight ahead, but could feel Blitzner's surprise as he divided his attention between my face and the slippery road ahead. DC metro area had a love-hate relationship with winter. Everyone wanted a white Christmas, and yet they were shamefully ill prepared for it, especially when it came to driving in it.

"What's in Paris?" he asked. At least I was working for someone with an open mind... open but devious. If it were either of my old bosses, Lowe or O'Brien, they wouldn't have been too keen on hiding their skepticism or suspicion.

"Saad al-Qasim. Mohamed al-Mohamed's brother."

I glanced his way to catch the swift rise and fall of his brow. I had managed to surprise him. Blitzner wasn't just a shit-disturber now. He had an office to manage, which included budgetary accountability.

"I don't think he has any idea where his father is, Amy. And finding Hasan al-Qasim is our main priority. You should focus on a way to break Detainee 28211."

I nodded, but kept my eyes fixed on the skating rink that was I-66. "I know what my objective is. And that is why I need to go to Paris."

He reverted to silence after that, but our confinement was thick with expectation. I felt Blitzner pondering my request, attributing the seriousness it deserved. That spoke of his respect for me... professionally at least. His insistence on my joining his team made sense; I represented more than just securing Richard's favor.

"If you think it will make a difference," he conceded after a long time.

"I do. And I'm going to need a car bomb too," I said and braced my arms against the door. As anticipated, the SUV skidded, veering dangerously close to the median wall. To his credit, Blitzner quickly brought the vehicle back under control.

Somehow, I didn't think his muttered "Jesus Christ!" was directed at the blare of horns behind us.

FOURTEEN

It wasn't over between us. It would have been naïve of me to think that a short separation would mean the death of what had begun between us almost six months ago.

As Todd had so hurtfully thrown at me, I had slept with him within an hour of our meeting, and that was indicative of a personal failing that would plague us throughout our time together. He would never forget; and I was unapologetic. But he had married me knowing I was terribly flawed. That his ego had brushed aside all his better judgment was no fault of mine.

He should have had the foresight to weigh the consequences of my lifestyle choices when he'd struck his bargain with Richard.

Of course I hadn't forgotten about that. I conveniently ignored it when it behooved me to do so, but I would always remember that he had used me as much as I had planned on using him too. In truth we should never have lost sight of that which was the foundation of our union.

As I watched from the relative safety of the security monitor, Todd pulled through the gates of our home. It was barely 7p.m. and full dark. I had had hours to prepare. Our confrontation wasn't anywhere near over, and I was ready for the waters between us to become even murkier.

I wasn't sorry for my history with Ed, and not just for what it yielded in terms of solving my father's case. What had happened between us before my marriage was irrelevant. Todd was a whore and shouldn't have been throwing stones.

But the humiliation of being stuck in a Mission that my husband had fucked his way through was still fresh in my mind. It was embarrassing to be confronted daily with proof that your spouse had been around. And that was where Todd incited feelings in me that were foreign.

I understood his dilemma, and even empathized.

The fact was I loved him. I didn't want to lose him.

But I was angry too – and justifiably so, I felt.

Here, in the privacy of our home, I would give him all the answers he could stand. And I wouldn't throw the fact that I had been less than thrilled at the suddenness of his marriage proposal – a mere four weeks after our first meeting – back in his face. If he didn't know nearly enough about me, then I was not the only one to be blamed.

I didn't have long to wait before he found me curled up in my father's old chair. The leather was old and familiar, enveloping me in the warmth of my father's memory. Without Ed, I would not have been able to meet Matt Boone's price, and I wouldn't be weeks away from getting my hands on Sergei Afanasenko.

Despite the trying interruption to our day, Todd looked as fresh and delicious as if he'd just pulled on his uniform. Except for the dark stain of fresh beard that stood out starkly against his perfect features. His skin, bronzed by the Caribbean's perpetual sunshine, shone like a beacon in the frigid Virginia winter. His eyes were bright cobalt. And I knew mine weren't the only appreciative ones that had devoured him all day.

"I'm sorry for the things I said today," he said in greeting, filling the doorway of my father's study with his magnificence. "I was angry and unprepared, which is no excuse to be hurtful and chauvinistic."

I could have taken the high ground and claimed there was nothing to forgive, but this was still a confrontation. He had hurt me. He had been chauvinistic. And he wasn't going to give me credit for Ed being the last man I'd slept with before meeting him three years later. I needed every advantage I could get.

So instead, I said, "I know." Our eyes met, and I watched as he mentally ticked one item off his to-do list. "I forgive you."

One corner of his mouth curved, but was devoid of humor.

"What would you like to know, Todd?"

"Did you fuck him?" he asked, without missing a beat.

"I didn't," I answered, and watched him suck in a breath. And I knew he had continued grilling Ed, because there was no doubt he didn't believe me. "But Anne did."

His hands balled in his pockets. When you've lived in the uniform as long as Todd and I had, you never missed this unsanctioned use of personal storage.

"I know this is all still too fresh for you to understand," I continued, "but we are not the same. "

"This isn't a card you get to pull to excuse the things you do, Amy," he retorted. His face was a blank mask, but there was an avalanche of emotion in the words. He was disappointed and ashamed of me. But even more so, he was angry that I hadn't accepted responsibility – not that he would have absolved me anyway.

"I can show you," I said, and I was at peace with the decision. Like I said, I'd had hours to prepare… to anticipate the damage this would do to us. But it wasn't as if we would have been able to move past this.

Todd was proud. He had an image to uphold. He could ride the rocket that was Richard's endorsement to the highest echelons of his career, but it would be worth shit if the men he commanded knew what being inside his wife felt like.

For that reason, I had prepared a list for him. He could decide whether he still wanted to call in favors from Richard.

But that wasn't all I'd done.

I tapped on the space bar of the computer before me, bringing the machine back to life. I unfolded out of my father's chair and crossed over to him.

"Here's a list of everyone we've slept with whom you might run into."

He didn't take the list at first, but when I pressed it into his chest he had no choice but to accept. It was a courtesy I would have liked before moving to the Dominican Republic with him. I would have hated the significance – and extent – of his list, but at least I would have been prepared.

That wasn't the end of my thoughtfulness though.

"You'll find there," I indicated the place before the computer, "the proof of our separate identities. I'll wait in my room."

Technically it was our room now. But before Todd it had been my refuge. I retreated there, not out of cowardice, but out of consideration for him. He needed privacy to examine the nuances that differentiated Anne from his wife, and the video that I had stolen from Ed's hard drive three and a half years ago was full of those.

Todd knew me. He knew I would not have been able to so thoroughly give up control. As dominant as he was, Todd had a second sense for recognizing submission. The few times we had played, he had understood that I was topping from the bottom. The control was in the hands of the one who had *allowed* the other the illusion of mastery.

What Ed had done to Anne was different. Bound, gagged and blinded, the communication had been one-way. It was an anything-goes encounter that I would never have been able to support.

I knew what it was like to be raped and nearly strangled to death. I had derived purpose from it; I had changed from the fatalistic child mourning my parents' deaths to one determined to bring their murderers to justice before I followed them. And I had wrenched the control from the hands of my rapist. We'd quietly dated until I left him for someone else.

I could never willingly submit to Ed's rape fantasies, which required complete submission akin to the powerlessness I felt that first time with Adam. Todd knew this, and so the difference between Anne and I would be apparent.

The video was almost an hour and a half long. I sat at the edge of my bed facing the hallway door the entire time. Then right on time, I heard his steps echoing on the wood from the direction of my father's office. He wanted me to know he was coming.

If I weren't so determined to get pregnant, I would have completed my preparations with a Xanax. In its absence, there was no helping the near frantic pounding of my heart.

The dichotomy of the man who had stood in the study doorway and the man before me now was stark. Either he had tried to make himself comfortable, or Todd had tried to crawl out of his skin. His uniform coat was gone; his tie askew, and shirt unbuttoned to the waist. The five-o-clock shadow seemed more like a full beard now, and the eyes that were so vibrant in their blue a couple hours ago were now nearly black and lined with concern. He wasn't standing as erect anymore. His spine was stiff, but he seemed to have folded in on himself.

He was still the most beautiful man I had ever seen, and something quailed inside me to see his vibrancy dimmed. I watched as his throat worked over the words he wanted to say.

"How could you," he said, but it came out as a gasp. He swallowed hard again. "How could you let him do that?"

"It wasn't me," I answered weakly. The whole point of showing him the video was so he would know that.

"Then let me talk to her," Todd said into the silence. "I want her to explain how she could let him do that to you."

"It wasn't me," I insisted, because at some point Todd was going to have to face that truth.

It was the straw that broke the camel's back. He lunged at me. He held me and shook me with unforgiving hands until my teeth clicked together. I knew he would leave bruises.

"It is you!" he shouted, shaking me again. "Why can't you see beyond your father's bullshit? It's always been you!"

All weekend we had flirted with this, Todd's disapproval of my father. It was a condemnation I could not allow to stand forever, so while we were clearing the air, I dealt with it. I broke his grip on me and pushed him away.

I had always demurred from using force against Todd. The one time our confrontation had become physical, I had only fought back half-heartedly. I never wanted to hurt him like that; I never wanted to challenge him like that. Perhaps he knew it too, because he seemed genuinely surprised that I'd been able to break his hold and force him back.

"Don't," I protested. It enraged him – not the fact that I would fight back, but that the defense of my father was worth the fight.

"You want to be different from her, do you?" Todd asked, cooling the blood in my veins. The change in him was too abrupt to have been anything but menacing. He was tucking away all consideration for me, his wife. "Give me Anne."

"No," I said, well aware that no good would come of that.

"Don't make me ask again."

"No."

With our eyes locked, Todd unfastened his belt. I knew he wouldn't beat me, not even with Anne in control. But my heart tripped over itself anyway. His belt was still a weapon that could be used to restrain me; incapacitate me; and if we fought and I lost, he could call Anne. I'd told him how.

I faced him. With deliberate intent, Todd removed his tie and shirt.

The last time we'd fought, I was constrained by stilettos and a narrow skirt. Not this time. I was barefoot, dressed in comfortable sweats and a tank, and my hair was pulled into a tight bun. Still, I was no match for him even if I had beaten larger, more powerful men. The things I loved about him – his intimidating size that made me feel small and feminine, and his raw masculinity – were not the things that would leave me outmatched.

Todd was the only opponent I had ever faced whom I did not *want* to beat.

"Please don't do this," I said, but came to my feet to prepare.

"Give me Anne."

I shook my head. "No."

After that, Todd didn't give me a chance to reason with him. He was beyond rational thought, because the man he was at his core – not the cultivated image of a charismatic diplomat, but the efficient killer – would not allow me to stand in his way.

His fighting style was unexpected. I was so accustomed to men relying on their strength – an asset they developed at the cost of speed – that the fluidity of Todd's movements surprised me.

I blocked the first series of grasps, pacified a little that he wasn't trying to hit, just hold. At the tail end of the second bout of blocks, his fingertips momentarily gripped the spot above my wrist. Once became twice, and then on every pass, as he tested the limits of my agility. It caused a strain on the tendons in my forearm that slowed me down.

I tried to compromise by exaggerating the weakness, only to strike harder and faster with the opposite hand. I managed to break his hold and push him back – a move that surprised him, but which I could not replicate. He was on to me and my right hand was still weak.

It was all downhill from there. Todd pressed me harder and faster, hitting me mercilessly where it would hurt most – on my painfully sensitive breasts, the weekend's bruises on my shoulder, back and arms, my abdomen. The latter I guarded at the risk to the rest of me. In a toss up between Anne and the child I hoped to carry, there was no contest.

The first sign that this would not end in a stalemate was when Todd captured and held on to my weakened right arm. He paid with a painful blow to the throat that left him gasping and doubled over. But he valiantly held on to my arm, raising it painfully behind me and above my head. The hold sent me crashing to my knees with a cry. I might have been able to twist out of the awkward position, but Todd was faster on his follow-up even as he struggled to recover from the coughing fit.

He protected his groin with a quick spin that left him standing behind my prone form. He also had his belt looped like a noose around my neck. He pulled tightly with one hand and continued to hold my arm prisoner with the other. My free hand fought to create a gap between the leather and my skin, but I was a fraction of a second too late. The belt pinched, trapped the breath in my body. I couldn't have cried out even if I wanted to.

The fight seeped out of me as Todd tightened his grip on the makeshift leash, holding it high enough to apply pressure to my carotid. The blood in my head pounded in my ears. I tried to push back the euphoria that preceded unconsciousness and ended up emptying my bladder instead. The warmth seeping down my legs mimicked the heat in my face. The darkness at the edge of my vision began closing in, and I would have ripped off my own arm to keep it at bay. Todd took the choice from me.

He released my arm, aware that with the time that had already passed, my oxygen-starved muscles were too weak to put up an effective assault. Releasing my arm was not an act of mercy either. Because even as all my fingers grasped desperately at the edges of the belt, digging into my already bruised skin, searching for the slightest gap, Todd's knee pressed into the middle of my back. His hold was unbreakable. Panic had the dark edges rushing together faster.

This is it, I thought. *He won't stop at Anne. He won't stop. Todd is killing me, and I let him. For the dream of having his child, I let him kill me.*

FIFTEEN

I didn't just lose consciousness that night; I also lost a part of Todd I would never be able to reclaim.

Up to that point, he had spared me the worst of his ruthlessness. Now there was nothing holding him back.

I was naked, cold and alone; the house void of life. It had never bothered me before: the silence. But in the morning I awoke to an emptiness that resounded heavily in my being.

I was also sore. There were the old bruises; yellow, green and brown stains shrinking in on themselves. Then there were some fresh ones; angry swaths of flaming skin almost everywhere I looked. My throat was raw on the inside and outside. My skin was broken where the buckle of Todd's belt had pinched. All the makeup at the MAC wouldn't hide that much damage. Judging by the stiffness and general discomfort on turning my head, in all likelihood I might also need a cervical collar.

Seeking medical attention was out of the question however. My eyes were bloodshot, and even a blind doctor would know I had been strangled long enough and hard enough to cause the broken capillaries in my eyes, and on my face and neck. While I could blame the cold for the hoarseness and difficulty drawing a full breath, cumulatively, my injuries painted a damning picture of abuse.

There were ligature marks on my wrists – zip ties, judging by the width; an ache in my shoulders that could only have come from being restrained in a specific stress position – arms fully extended and tied behind my back. My knees had been skinned; my ass burned, the cheeks brick red.

A domestic abuse investigation would be the least of my concerns though. The map of bruises on my thighs, the soreness between my legs, and the dried semen tracks, taken in context with all the rest, suggested a sexual assault. As much as I could argue consensual albeit rough play, the gag marks would belie that claim. With Todd's whereabouts unknown, his office would be contacted – and consequently mine.

Colonel Townsend had once told me, *"You can excuse murder, but in America, you can't get away with not paying your taxes or beating up on your girl."*

At the time, he didn't believe that my bruises were the by-products of rough sex. If I told anyone my submissive alternate identity had most likely consented to everything that had passed between herself and Todd…well, Todd wouldn't be the only one locked away. So brushing off this episode wasn't all about protecting Todd. I had to protect myself too.

At least that's what I told myself anyway.

Yes, I was disappointed, angry… hurt even, that he had obviously fucked Anne. She would have accepted him any way she could get him, because that was Anne, and she had been obsessed with him for months now. I had relied on his affection for me to keep them apart, and now that that had failed, I knew there was nothing tying him to me anymore. Todd had proved that he could – and would – fuck anyone he wanted. That was the source of the emptiness.

His absence, all day and all night Tuesday permeated the void with dread. A run to the dry cleaners in Wednesday's fresh snow had the cold seeping into my bones. Todd had collected his uniform shirts and left my heavy coat. On my return home, I discovered the bags with which he had moved in over the weekend were gone.

He'd been trying to coax me into moving into the master bedroom – my parents' bedroom. When at first I noticed his missing toiletries from my bathroom, I thought he'd simply wanted distance between us. Venturing into my parents' sanctum was hard enough; proving Todd's abandonment was worse than I could have imagined.

As devastated as I was – to the point of becoming physically ill – I refused to call him. Whoever said love had no pride didn't know what it was like to have only pride. Todd had already stripped me bare of everything else. He knew more about me than anyone else, and he had used that knowledge to deliberately wound me.

I fell back on my work. Work was safe; it filled the void and numbed the ache in the center of my body. It helped that I was good at it... so good in fact, that I turned Blitzner's reservations about detonating a car bomb in the center of Paris into a resounding 'yes'.

"Things are a little tricky right now," he had first said. "We don't want to offend the French."

My skepticism was evident in the silence flowing between us over the secure line. It asked, "When are the French ever not offended?"

"The DCRI – " (*Direction Central du Renseignement Intérieur* – the intelligence agency responsible for domestic threats) "—have been generous allies," Blitzner had persisted, but I could tell his heart wasn't really behind that protest.

"So they share what they have." I shrugged. "It doesn't change the fact that we don't have what we need yet."

I could sense his frustration from being worn down. "What if you're wrong, Amy? What if this yields nothing at all?"

"What if I'm right?" I countered.

"Start working on the specs. Let's see how we can eliminate flashover on this."

Flashover meant, if we raised the temperature under Selim high enough, the ensuing blast could pin us down too.

The specifications were simple enough; we knew Hasan al-Qasim's signature by heart. However, a few variations were required to adapt the car bomb to suit the operating environment. Paris' eighth arrondissement was as far removed from Lebanon during the 1980's as Mars was from the sun. The target was a familiar one to the civil war – a deliberate ploy that, if all went according to plan, would shake Selim's faith in the ability of the French to protect him and his family.

As much as Blitzner wanted to appear like the good guy, intent on preserving relations with our intelligence allies, I knew his act was bullshit. Anyone with a conscience would have been more concerned with the potential loss of life than having responsibility pinned on us.

Blitzner might argue the human concerns were a given, but he knew as well as I what a car bomb was like. Even with remote detonation, impact was difficult to predict.

And I was banking on impact to conceal an ulterior motive. I needed a distraction – a powerful one – to separate and extract Alexei Afanasenko from a birthday party at the Baranets' residence on January 7.

On Wednesday afternoon, I took a call from Richard. If he suspected Todd and I were having difficulties, he chose to ignore it. He would hold Todd to whatever bargain they had made, and I was expected fulfill my promises in time too.

"Have you spoken with your husband about your honeymoon?" Richard queried.

I hadn't spoken to my husband at all in over thirty-six hours, and all indications were that the break in communication would be a prolonged one. "Actually, I haven't," I admitted.

"Have you given any thought to my offer, Amy?" There was the faintest hint of disapproval, as if he suspected I hadn't. While a honeymoon was the last thing on my mind right then, Paris was high on the agenda.

"I have," I answered, forcing enthusiasm I didn't feel. My throat burned with the lie and it was a pain I welcomed. It kept my focus off phantom aches; there was no medical reason why my heart should hurt.

"Are you OK, Amy?"

I cleared my throat and ended up scraping the scab off my trachea. At least that's what it felt like. "I'm fine, Richard. Just a little sore throat." The best lies were the ones rooted in truth after all. "With the move Todd's schedule is a bit up in the air, so I haven't been able to confirm with him as yet. But I have to be in Paris right after the New Year, and I was thinking of killing two birds with one stone."

I let the silence stand, because it felt comfortable. The near absentminded manner in which I offered the information was consistent with the idea I was currently engrossed with work. I was certain Richard had a number of things vying for his attention too at the precise moment.

"You plan to work on your honeymoon, Amy?"

"Only in short bursts."

I crossed my fingers and toes, wishing on every available star that he didn't ask what I was working on. I was sure he had a general idea, since he had made the deal with Blitzner to keep me occupied and close to home.

Thankfully Richard did not press me, making it clear that my value to him was no longer career-based.

"As long as you keep in mind what's really important," Richard said.

There was no need to draw me a map of what he thought was 'really important'. He was officially on womb watch, a fact I could not protest because I had bargained my privacy in order to get Todd home.

And now I had no privacy and no Todd.

"Tell you what," Richard began, his tone suddenly conspiratorial. "I'll make sure Todd's schedule is clear for the first couple of weeks in the New Year. How does that sound?"

It sounded like Richard was in a hurry to implement his succession plans.

"Don't worry, don't worry," he hurried to stave off my anticipated protests. "I'll cover us on this, so he has no concept of our influence." Richard chuckled. He clearly had no misgivings about messing with people's lives.

Did I ever mention that we were great at our jobs because we were selfish, manipulative assholes?

"Whatever you think is best, Richard," I conceded.

"In the meantime, you may want to raise the matter with him."

"I'll do that as soon as he gets home." Whenever that was… if that day ever came. If not, I was prepared to go to Paris on my own. I'd survived this long without Todd Birch. I wouldn't curl up and die because he had left me. My father always said pain couldn't kill.

"How does January 2nd sound for departure?"

"Make that December 31." I would arrive on New Years Day. There was nothing like a fresh start for new perspective.

"Great. I have to go now, Amy." He paused for a second, either distracted by an interruption or setting out on an exploration. "Unless there's something else…"

Classic Richard.

I fell back on a tried and true tactic. Diversion. "Actually, there is. I was going to talk to Abby about getting some help for the house. It would help if you could point her towards a cleared field to move our discussions along faster."

It defied logic that we would rely on Abby to act as intermediary when Richard could just as easily send me a list of candidates with security clearance. But it not only made sense to him; it made his day. Clearly, I had found my correct place in his world. I beat back the surge of anger, because unless Todd returned, I had no intention of following through with this exercise in futility.

Richard promised to facilitate us then offered his farewells. I dove back into work, refusing to fall into despair at Todd's absence or silence.

With any luck, I had already conceived and my gamble had survived Monday night's ravages. As angry, disgusted, disappointed as he might be, Todd wouldn't jeopardize his child. That was one thing he wanted more than anything else. It was a desire he had only recognized with the news of Mona, his former fiancée's pregnancy. Her death had wiped out that dream. The pregnancy hadn't progressed far enough to be his; it was suspected to have been Colonel Townsend's in fact.

As imperfect as it would be to add a child to the morass that was our marriage, I couldn't think of a more effective or efficient way to secure Todd's loyalty and Richard's favor.

Nevermind the fact that I had to decide whether I still wanted Todd's loyalty after this.

He had proclaimed his freedom to do as he pleased, fuck whomever he wanted, come and go as he wished. I knew I couldn't live with that. I couldn't give him every bit of me knowing my portion had been shortened and was to be shared with others.

That had been my breaking point when we were living in the Dominican Republic - the realization that he had brought a woman - a prostitute no less - into our home. That I would have to share my space and my husband with her and a league of others had driven me out of our marriage. I had left him, because staying and accepting those terms would have been unbearable, even at a time when I was much less invested than presently.

The truth was a marginal improvement over my suspicions. Todd was a whore, but at least he hadn't fucked one in our home. That pleasure had gone to his friends who had arranged his surprise bachelor party. And the prostitute had become one of my best assets yet.

The second shift nanny employed at the Baranets' residence had encountered unexpected immigration problems, and was being held in detention since December 18. While her transfer from a provisional *local de retention administrative* to a longer-term *centre de retention administrative* would be complete in the next two days, the Baranets had already made in-roads in her replacement. Their preference was for native Ukrainian help, to maintain cultural homogeneity within their home. The suddenness of the nanny's departure and the difficulty identifying a suitable replacement in time for St. Nicholas Day (the day following the nanny's arrest) and days before Western Christmas, had coincided to propel Angelika's application to the top of a pool of candidates.

An urgent call was made to the owner of the Russian teashop to whom Angelika had repeatedly inquired about available positions. The owner, cognizant of the side his baguette was buttered on, had sent several employees on the lookout for the girl with the pointe shoes hanging by their laces from her bag. They were in luck, because by mid-morning she was already on her way to the teashop for a hot drink and some *pryaniki*.

"I got the job!" Angelika squealed, her excitement registering clearly over the line. "How did you know they would want me?"

How did I know their nanny would suddenly become unavailable? How did I know it would be worth her time to stop by the teashop first thing on Monday morning? How did I know she would be invited for an interview at the Baranets' mansion at the end of a private lane off rue de Liège?

How did I know, for a fresh start at a new life, she would do anything for me? How did I know that for a better price, she would turn on me?

Angelika had spent years in sexual slavery awaiting a better opportunity to fall in her lap. She would never understand that half my work entailed creating opportunities that I could exploit, while the other half was devoted to ensuring people walked through the doors I had opened for them.

Take the Baranets, for example. Alone they were of no value to me, but their son, Michel, was best friend to Alexei Afanasenko. It was virtually guaranteed that Alexei would attend Michel's birthday party, celebrated each year at the Baranets' home on January 7, because it also doubled as the Ukrainian Christmas Day.

According to the reports I had received from my contractors – mercenaries, really – tasked with watching both families, the

Afanasenkos had already purchased their gifts and the Baranets had already reserved a snowmaking machine to ensure *Ded Moroz* and *Princess Snigorichka* – Father Frost and Little Snowflake – felt right at home in their backyard.

The hardest part of my job was the capriciousness of timing. Thankfully, tradition and an insider were the great equalizers. The families would part by late afternoon, because the Baranets, who were intent on preserving their culture for their only child, would take him to the homes of other Eastern friends for caroling.

The Afanasenkos would return home. Sergei's career as an arms dealer, and general trafficker and procurer of illegal merchandise, stymied his welcome into the fine Parisian homes of fellow Eastern expats.

The small window of opportunity supported the use of a remote detonation device in Alexei's abduction.

As his father's most prized possession, Alexei was the key to breaking Sergei. It was a gamble to prescribe a higher value on the life of his cherished son than an American traitor who used to protect him over a decade ago. It was one I was willing to take, because whether or not he gave me a name, I would kill Sergei Afanasenko.

The only question was whether he would watch me kill his son.

In the meantime, I had to clean up after myself. I couldn't afford to leave any witnesses behind. I was running a skeleton crew of six men, because only critical functions were required this late in the game. The contractors who had outlived their usefulness had been permanently reassigned. With Angelika now in place, I could afford to sever ties with another.

I sent instructions to the cleaner Blerim Nesimi had sourced for me.

Even I had to admit the man was good at his job. Of the six men he had already retired, only one body had been recovered. The coroner's report blamed a hunting accident for his demise. I suspected the others had ended up on his pig farm in Bretagne, ten kilometers from the woods where that body was found.

Maybe I would keep the cleaner in a more official capacity.

As much as I would have liked to loose him on my father's former asset, Blerim Nesimi would spot him coming a mile away. After all, the man who had traded Sergei Afanasenko's secrets – that his backer promised American support to the Kosovo Liberation Army and other post-Cold war era militias for the right price – had employed the cleaner often in his current role as facilitator for the Camorra.

Todd had promised to kill Blerim Nesimi for me, but that was looking iffy now.

In exchange for his silence on my search for answers, we would try to have a child. Todd had even thrown in the hit on Nesimi for free. He had no clue how advanced my hunt for answers was, and he didn't know I'd been forcing the conception side of our deal to bind him to me. I would need Todd's unequivocal support long before he would know it. Falling in line with Richard's plans for my future also meant he would be my ally.

I'd known long before I'd married Todd that my father's killer was a senior government official – one with enough clout to sell political support for revolutionaries, secessionists and terrorist groups.

The deterioration of my marriage meant I had to rethink my strategy to silence Blerim Nesimi.

SIXTEEN

I hadn't begun to scratch the surface of the dilemma of my marriage by Friday when the question became urgent. Todd had returned.

I didn't know what to do with myself. Should I meet him downstairs? And if so, how? Should I pick up where we had left off on Monday night, resuming a combative stance I had no chance of winning? Or should I pretend he hadn't fucked me over despite the physical evidence to the contrary? Should I stand my ground but cover the worst of the damage he had wrought – a compromise that acknowledged the difficult position in which I had put him? I had no clue, so I did nothing.

It wasn't late by any standards – barely after seven – but I had worked almost non-stop for the past four days. I had showered and crawled into bed with a bowl of cereal, and was looking forward to a good night's sleep. Whatever were Todd's intentions for returning, I doubted anything I did at that point would have an impact.

After several tense minutes of waiting, pretending my stomach wasn't so badly twisted into knots that digesting a simple meal had become a painful ordeal, Todd appeared in my doorway. The low glow of my bedside lamp was good for hiding the mix of emotions conjured by the first sight of him.

Todd was beautiful, despite being so disheveled we might have bent the boundaries of time and were once again on the verge of Monday's fight. The only difference was he had exchanged his service alphas for casual attire. I couldn't tell from his dark jeans and thermal undershirt if he had been at work at any point during the past three days. His boots were wet, as were the hems of his jeans. They hinted at more exposure to the elements than would have been normal moving between shelter. Yet, the rest of him was dry – unusually so.

He was unshaved and lacked other signs of external grooming. His hair fell in thick curls around his ears and nape, too full and unrestrained for his professional position. It was an easily achievable look for Todd, requiring only a shower and a tousle of his fingers. It didn't mean he hadn't been to work though, because the shower could have come after.

What pricked my curiosity however, was the condition of his skin. His hands and face – the only parts of his body that would have been exposed to the same weather conditions that his jeans and boots had faced – were both dry and warm. No hint of pink on his nose or cheeks beneath the tan. Hands that looked perfect, as if they had been sheltered inside thick gloves.

He looked dangerous too. It was more than just the dark clothing. There was something watchful and sinister about him as he stood in the doorway, staring at me. His easy posture said he was comfortable... had been so for at least a few hours. His eyes catalogued, moving over me with an impersonal quality that was unnerving.

I set aside my dinner and sat up to face him. There was nothing outwardly threatening about him, but I sensed danger. I couldn't see the shade of his eyes, but his gaze on me felt black. He was too intense, his focus deliberately casual, as if to throw prey off the presence of a predator.

Todd had awakened in me a sensation I had never felt for him before – not when he showed me the lethal side of him as we killed and disposed of Lionel and his men in the Dominican Republic... not even a few days ago when I realized I had lost, was losing consciousness, and would be left completely at his mercy.

I was afraid of Todd.

Then he left, turning on his wet heels and disappearing as suddenly as he had appeared. I heard his quiet tread down the hall, fading as he neared the stairs, retracing the path he had made only a minute ago. I didn't doubt that he would be back though, because there was no sound where the closing of the front door should have been. He planned on returning soon, but for what I had no clue. I just knew he scared me.

I fished my Sig from under my mattress, checked the clip and chambered a round. I sat facing the door, bare feet planted firmly on the ground, waiting for whatever it was the stranger I married had in store.

This time the closing of the front door was clear. It was more ominous than reassuring. He made no attempt to conceal his advance, perhaps aware that I would be straining to decipher the other sounds behind his footsteps. Those would give away clues to his intentions, but all I could hear was the slight rustle of plastic.

I relaxed my grip on my gun, not wishing to betray any tension in my kill arm. I repositioned the pillow that obstructed sight of the weapon but not its effect. Did I want to kill Todd?

Absolutely not.

Would I, if forced?

Absolutely. I had things to live for... a promise to fulfill to the only man who could, and had, really loved me.

Would it kill me to hurt Todd like that?

Only in the figurative sense.

The choice of him or me was no choice at all. And it might very well come to that. I knew the contents of Todd's kill kit... had fetched the plastic sheeting from his car that we used to wrap the four bodies.

I was prepared, though far from ready, to face him when he once again filled my doorway with his dark presence. Did he expect me to take whatever he planned to dish out lying down?

He didn't seem surprised to find me sitting up, waiting, my kill arm tucked under a pillow while the rest of me was as taut as a bow.

He tossed a garment bag at me, which I half-caught, half swatted aside with my left hand. I was relieved to see he had one of his own, but that was no cause to relax just yet. I slowly set aside my catch, still too wary to examine its contents while this disconcerting stranger blocked my exit.

"Get dressed, Amy. We leave in thirty minutes."

Although I found his behavior and that demand troubling, my voice gave no indication of my thoughts, or the fact that I had a gun pointed at the man I loved. "Where are we going?"

"DOD holiday party," he answered simply before turning on his heel and abruptly leaving me once again.

I strained to track his progress. This time he entered the bedroom I refused to inhabit. With the door open, the sound of water running at the bathroom sink was unmistakable. I sprang to close and lock my own bedroom door with its key. Only then did I examine the bag he had tossed to me, which contained either a dress or a black burial shroud.

Close examination revealed a navy ponte evening gown, with full sleeves, a high neckline, and floor-kissing hem. Its simplicity was broken by a pattern of pearlescent beadwork, liberally hand-sewn across the front to evoke a starburst in the night sky. It was unlike anything I would have chosen for myself. It had an Old World, Hollywood-style glamor that was too classically sophisticated to suit me.

But Todd had clearly put a lot of thought into his selection. After all, he had catalogued every bruise he had made and had chosen a dress that would conceal all of them. His familiarity with women's clothing was also on display. The dress fit like a glove, down to the train that had been altered to lay just right once I stepped into four-inch heels. It even left room for a thigh holster and my Sig.

Even so, I was not prepared for a gown like this, and once I was dressed, that fact became abundantly clear. The grooming required for such an ensemble was extensive. I did the best I could with the contents of my small makeup arsenal, and home-styled hair. I pulled my hair into a basic, classic chignon – a teased-out and rolled-up ponytail, really. It left my face open to the world, including my cheeks and chin that were still marred by the toll of the fertility treatment. The worst of the discoloration was hidden beneath several layers of concealer, but texturally there wasn't much I could do. Manicures were not my thing and I had roughly butchered my nails days ago to spare my face. Tonight I would be hiding my bare hands in the folds of the gown.

By no means did I match the man who called out to me from behind my bedroom door.

He did not knock, nor did he test the closed door. Perhaps it was his way of refusing to acknowledge the shift between us. He would not ask permission for access to his wife... while the union lasted. I opened up for him, making sure he could hear the lock turning. I was still unconvinced he wouldn't hurt me, but a door wasn't going to stop him either. I chose to face him, and as should have been expected, Todd knocked the breath out of me.

He was dressed in Marine Corps evening dress blues, freshly shaved, hair slicked back, expression inscrutable. The only indication of his mood was the slapping of his white gloves against the stripes on his navy pants – either impatience at my delay or frustration at my sub-par appearance. He did not elaborate and I refused to ask anything of him.

"Lose the firearm, Amy," he said, proving again how well he knew me. There were no lines to betray the fact that I was armed. Todd looked into me eyes. "You won't need it where we're going. I can protect what's mine for one night."

But who would protect me from him? Just one look, one word, and I would fall for him all over again.

His assertion answered one question, but created more doubt. Todd would stay, but I didn't know if I wanted him to. I didn't want the Todd I would have to share with others. I didn't want him if he threatened my sense of self-preservation. And I couldn't go back and settle for less, having experienced the protection and devotion of this beautiful man.

He had protected me in every sense that mattered – beyond the standard physical security. I could keep myself safe. Todd had not only kept my secrets, like Angelika; we had forged new ones together. It was ironic that the secret I thought would have broken us – Anne – was not the game changer I had expected. But the fact I had never hidden… the sexual freedom that had brought us together in the first place… ended up being too much for him.

As strange as it might seem, I understood. My vulnerabilities sparked a protectiveness in him that was firmly rooted in the man's pride. But the moment my actions struck at that fierce pride – threatening the rapport with the men he commanded – my value had been greatly diminished in his eyes.

"Meet me downstairs," Todd threw over one shoulder. And if there was any doubt that I had been demoted from cherished wife to a subordinate, Todd had just provided the clarification. His impersonal words were the law, and his departure implied his immovable expectation: compliance.

So Todd wasn't going to kill me… not that night anyway. Todd wouldn't rely on deception to end me. The one courtesy I could expect from him was a fighting chance… and not only because he had beaten me – twice. So I unstrapped my firearm and met him unarmed.

From the entry hallway, Todd watched me descend the stairs. He was as unmoved by me as I was affected by him. My heart thumped fast and heavy in my ears as I watched him watching me with a stone mask. I had to yank the train of the dress high around my calves, and grip the banister tightly despite my sweaty palms, to avoid falling. I *felt* that I looked as though I was navigating knee-high floodwaters, making Todd wish he had someone else on his arm. Preferably a woman whose face didn't remind him of a meth-head's, and who could navigate a simple staircase with grace. But for some reason he had chosen me.

That reason became clear after we had made the thirty-minute drive to the Ritz Carlton in silence, and were greeted by the Secretary of Defense at the head of the receiving line. This wasn't the standard Pentagon holiday party. That had been held a couple days before. This was a special meet-and-greet for the who's-who of the Department of Defense forces, and Uncle Richard was their special guest.

"Good to see you again, Colonel Birch." Our host greeted Todd with a brisk handshake before turning to me. He was as much part of my family as the man who had raised me upon my father's death. "Amy, sweetheart, you're a dead ringer for Mary-Anne tonight."

Coming from the man who, every time we had met, used to remind me of how much I look like my father, I wasn't sure how to take that. Was he in on Richard's plans for me? Had they been plotting together all along? He'd been present at the family BBQ when Todd had done the right thing – asked Richard for my hand in marriage before making our engagement official. Did my marriage render me unworthy of being my father's heir? Was being the wife to a man like my father the next best thing?

Or was I over-thinking things, according significance where none belonged? Was his comment simply a reaction to witnessing my softer, more feminine side?

What was clear was Todd's motive for dragging me along. And drag he did… He was more affectionate with me during those few hours than he had been since his reemergence. One hand was firmly rooted to either my back or elbow. But the fact that that was the extent of the contact between us was a painful reminder of what we had had before. He never spoke to me; barely looked at me even.

I was oblivious to the names and faces milling around us, and that was just fine – expected perhaps – by the men in my life. They greeted each other; laughed together; made plans with each other; ate, drank and were merry together. All the while, my world was chiseled down to vacuous smiles exchanged in bathrooms over lipstick and face powder.

Even Colonel Townsend who knew me and who, in another time and place, respected my work as some of the best in the field – better even than what some of the men present could have accomplished – accepted the lines that had been drawn in the sand at the door. He had come unaccompanied and still kept his distance.

By the time Richard had left, I was ready to follow. The gathering had thinned, the bar open and dinner tables cleared. I had no doubt the quality of the evening would take a nosedive. While Todd did not disappear completely, I was left to my own devices for extended periods of time while he shared stiff drinks, raucous jokes and exaggerated laughter with old and new friends.

About an hour after I wished I had followed Richard out, Todd picked up some extra weight. As far as baggage went, she was top of the line – Hermès, compared to me, Todd's ALICE pack.   She wasn't on the original guest list although she was dressed the part; she'd come in after hours on the arm of a Navy Commander. She didn't stay there long.

I liked to think she had been professionally styled. Otherwise, life was simply unfair.

She was beautiful – at least six inches shy of my natural five-eight. Four of those feet were all legs, as displayed by the thigh-high slit on her dress; the rest was hair, sun-kissed skin, white teeth and too-blue eyes. She wasn't the airhead I wanted her to be either. According to Colonel Townsend – who finally crossed the line in the sand after twenty minutes of watching her hang off Todd – she was a journalist. She freelanced for the *Post* and the *Times*, and at least once a month her work was run by the Associated Press.

Surprise, surprise! She covered Department of Defense policy, contracts, and newsworthy personnel. And judging by the arm Todd had hooked around her waist and the ease with which she brushed the front of his evening coat, she was quite thorough at exploring her niche.

If Todd wanted to humiliate me, he failed for the simple reason that no one seemed to remember or care that his wife was present. Except

Colonel Townsend. Oddly enough, Townsend was not intent on rubbing salt into the wound Todd was inflicting. He had never failed to do so in the past, so I wondered if he had bought my bullshit about not caring where Todd kept his dick wet. Perhaps the splinters of my shattered heart weren't strewn across my face after all.

"Come on, Koehler," Colonel Townsend said with a hand on my elbow. God, I was fed up with being led around like a fucking dog on a leash! "Let me buy you a drink."

I acquiesced, because I had no phone, keys or cash with me – Todd hadn't thought to get a purse to go with the dress – and I might need a ride home, preferably sooner than later. In addition, I wasn't pregnant yet, and the fire of straight whisky down my throat might numb the ache in my chest. The first shot went down smoothly, but wasn't enough to achieve the desired effect. The second would have been fast on its heels too if Todd and his designer arm candy hadn't interrupted.

In keeping with his resolve not to speak to me, my husband faced off with his rival. "What are you doing here, Townsend?"

Colonel Townsend raised his drink in a mocking salute to Todd before clinking glasses with me. "I believe I received the same invitation as you." He signaled another round to the white-coated bartender, so I saw no reason not to bottom up.

Hermès was even prettier up close, and either she had no clue who I was to the man whose arm she was attached to, or she didn't care. Why should she when Todd did not?

"I didn't see Tammy tonight," Todd continued with an easy smile that only raised the tension in our corner of the bar. Whether consciously or not, fellow partygoers were slowly inching away. "Where's your wife?" A classic case of pot name-calling kettle, if ever there was one.

Townsend accepted the new drinks and thoughtfully placed one before me. "Didn't bring her," he confessed. "Yours is more fun. Cheers, Amy."

Todd only acknowledged the salvo because Hermès did. So our relationship was news to her.

She retreated ever so slightly from their very public PDA, but Todd tugged her back into the light. He held on to her hand, hooking their fingers together in a plea for her not to go just yet.

It was an unnecessary stab at me; I couldn't feel anything anyway. His only achievement was to increase the woman's unease.

"Hi, I'm Erika. Erika Harris," she offered weakly with a brittle smile that didn't reach her eyes, and an outstretched hand.

I raised my glass in acknowledgement and took a healthy swallow, because as awkward as this was, at least we were all being civilized. She turned to Colonel Townsend. Why she thought he might rescue this sinking ship was a mystery to me.

"How is Tammy? I'm ashamed to say it's been a while since I spoke with her or saw my nephews. We've all been so busy."

Maybe she didn't think she owed me anything. After all, I'd passed on shaking her hand. But the least she could have done was wait for me swallow.

It was unfortunate for her, because the twelve-year-old whiskey spewed from my nostrils all over her pretty dress.

SEVENTEEN

Erika Harris was Tamara Townsend's sister.

Standing before me was the woman at the source of the rancor between Colonel Townsend and Todd Birch. The former had actually loved her – a claim I believed because it had come from Todd during a confession, and because only love could have driven a man to the lengths Townsend had gone. The two men used to be friends before their rivalry got out of hand and Todd had slept with Erika. Todd claimed not to have known the extent of his friends' affections for the woman and boasted of the encounter, as was their custom. The result was a broken brotherhood that over time had disintegrated into its present state, and a rebound marriage.

I couldn't imagine the sisters being as close as Erika wanted me to believe.

Maybe there was some truth to Townsend's four-month-old claim that he and Tammy were divorcing. He made no pretense of caring for her. She could have easily made his 'plus one', but clearly he had had no interest in her tagging along. What he did care about was his career, which was cause for discretion in his extra-marital affairs.

I had only ever paid Tammy the barest attention, even when I was plotting to sleep with her husband. But on closer reflection, the sisters did look somewhat alike. Tamara Townsend was the embodiment of California health and happiness, often clad in Daisy Dukes that proved she and her sister shared their best assets. I was certain that if I scratched the surface of Erika's cosmopolitan veneer, I would find the same homegrown wholesomeness as her sister.

For all his air of don't-give-a-shit, I could tell Colonel Townsend had not put Erika behind him. For one thing, he hadn't rubbed my nose in Todd's insensitivity yet. For another, he was intent on pretending the woman wasn't standing three feet in front of him, dabbing at her dress with paper napkins Todd had helpfully supplied. All Colonel Townsend's attention was focused on making sure I was alright – offering napkins, rubbing my back, dabbing at my watering eyes. Aspirating whiskey was a painful ordeal, and I still hadn't caught my breath when Erika excused herself to find the ladies' room.

Her escort, Commander Castillo, took her place at Todd's side.

"Amy, you look tired, so I've arranged for Commander Castillo to escort you home."

If not for my name, I wouldn't have realized I was being addressed. Todd was more intent on mapping Erika's progress than looking me in the eye. Commander Castillo offered an anemic smile, catching onto the awkward vibe pretty fast.

I knew what I looked like; Todd didn't need to remind me I wasn't at my best. Unlike Erika, I had had no notice and only thirty minutes to prepare for this outing. I thought I was at least presentable considering I'd ravaged my skin while turning my body into an incubator for his child. Not to mention spending four days recovering from his assault, and missing out on precious sleep to arrange the capture of a notorious terrorist.

If he chose to dwell on the fact that I'd fucked his subordinate three and a half years before I even knew Todd Birch existed, then he was welcome to his hurt feelings. But Todd could go fuck himself if he thought I would make excuses for my appearance.

"No need. I've got Amy." Townsend counter-offered without as much as a raised eyebrow in my direction.

A 'right, Amy?' would have been appreciated, made me not feel like a chewed-up toy between two dogs. Todd didn't really want me. He had spent the past four days conveying that message, and the better part of the evening making sure everyone here knew it too.

As for Townsend, perhaps he had wanted me once. That was back in Jamaica, before Todd had emerged on the scene. I was convinced his interest in me since then was solely for Todd's benefit. More revenge for Erika. Townsend could deny it all he wanted, but if not for my relationship with his rival, he would have moved on long ago. Colonel Townsend didn't strike me as the type to waste six months chasing pussy he would never get.

Tonight though, I served another purpose in his life. It seemed misery did indeed love company.

"Stay out of this, Bob. She's my wife."

"How convenient of you to remember that now."

"It's none of your business."

"Actually, she is. Did you not see us together on Monday? What do you think that was?"

I sucked in a breath at that, and it was a good thing too, because all the air seemed to have been vacuumed from the room. The stone mask Todd wore cracked. His eyes flicked to me for the briefest second – a silent accusation of betrayal. They warned me that it would be like this every time someone connected the dots between my sexual partners and my husband.

I was less understanding than a few hours ago however. Todd had made his point tonight. While we were married in the eyes of the people who mattered, like Richard, we were also – or rather, he was – free to do as he pleased.

"Why don't I give you a few minutes?" Castillo offered, extricating himself from our minefield, while the two blue coats stared each other down.

"I don't need you to shuttle me around," I said, succeeding in breaking the standoff only because Todd directed his anger at me. And it was a good thing I'd waited for Castillo's escape too, because the fewer witnesses there were to my complete humiliation, the better for me. Todd wasn't holding back.

"You'll do as you're fucking told," he told me in no uncertain terms. I almost stepped back from the blast of heat that hit me full in the face. "That means getting your ass into the fucking car when and with whom I tell you."

He didn't touch me; he didn't have to. I was unequivocally cowed. My face flamed from the verbal slap. I was so embarrassed that even Townsend looked away to accord me some much-needed privacy.

"Castillo will come get you in a few minutes, and I expect you to leave with him then."

Todd left right after that. Erika had emerged from the general direction of the ladies' room, but she seemed hesitant about her direction. I didn't blame her for not wanting to join us. I wanted to disappear from the spot. And for that reason, I would leave the moment Castillo came to collect me.

More than a few guests were stealing glances our way, watching but pretending they were not, long after Todd had abandoned me to rescue Erika from her indecision.

Another drink materialized before me. I grasped it, because what else was I going to do? Stare empty-handed after my prick of a husband while he left the room with another woman, shaking hands and offering goodnights to the friends he passed on his way out the door?

I felt the weight of a roomful of eyes on me as the realization spread that Todd was leaving with a different woman from the one with whom he had crossed the receiving line. Castillo couldn't return fast enough for me.

"I guess he told you."

"He sure did." I gave an empty laugh to match Townsend's crooked smile, and clicked glasses with him. Because if I didn't laugh I would have cried. With nothing on the line but pride, breaking out in tears was the last thing I would ever do. The water in my eyes was only from the sting of the whiskey.

EIGHTEEN

I wasn't watching the clock or the front door. It made no difference to me whether, or what time, Todd came home. He hadn't for four days. What difference did one more make?

I was stronger than I had given myself credit for. Just a few days ago I thought I wouldn't have been able to live with the knowledge that Todd was fucking other women. It was liberating to see that I was still breathing. I still slept – and for a full four hours too!—, ate, walked, talked. And did I mention breathe? It was far from painful too... quite the opposite, in fact. There was nothing; I felt nothing. Maybe I never really loved him in the first place.

I occupied myself with work, and it was as if the void had never been there. The morning after Todd had proved our marriage was irreparably broken was Christmas Eve, but there was no time like the present to catch terrorists or arms dealers whose backers had killed my father.

Not that I was waiting for any, but word from Todd would have been useful. Richard was expecting us for Christmas dinner the following day. I figured Todd would eventually resurface, because it was Richard after all. We both knew that my husband would pretend if only for the benefit of the Director of National Intelligence.

On the other hand, I was fast running out of reasons to pretend.

Mr. Bankowski, my father's gardener called at the front door, which he never did. He had an apartment above the gardening shed on the property, from which he could oversee the landscaping. It had always been his to come and go as he pleased, and store the tools of his trade. As far as I knew he had never lived there, preferring instead to share a home with his wife and three children in Wolf Trap a few miles away. I never expected to find him on my doorstep, because after twenty years, Mr. Bankowski knew exactly what was expected of him.

Apparently, Todd's emergence on the scene had changed that.

"Good day, Ms. Koehler," he greeted me, hat twisted in his hands before him. It was snowing and I could see the steam rising off his baldpate. So I invited him into the entry hall. "I wanted to talk to Mr. Birch about the greenhouse, ma'am."

We had never had a greenhouse.

At my blank expression, Mr. Bankowski's rheumy eyes hit the floor. "Well, Mr. Birch explained that you would be taking up permanent residence again and expressed an interest in an herb garden. Congratulations on your marriage, by the way." He gave me a weak smile and took the slight incline of my head as encouragement to continue.

"Well, I explained that the best time to start with seeds would be weeks before the last spring frost." He cleared his throat and I toyed with the idea of offering him a drink, but he was old and I hoped to get to the end of the tale sooner rather than later. "For the rest – the ones that we could start from cuttings or transplants – he suggested we build a greenhouse. He never decided on the size of the greenhouse, ma'am, because he was thinking of moving some of the roses inside as well. You know, so they can bloom all year round."

He faltered at my heightened interest. He knew my father's roses were sacred and was using the pretext of the greenhouse as a way to warn me of Todd's plans. Mr. Bankowski was no fool, and his loyalty was clearly unshaken by Todd's sudden appearance.

"Why don't you come in to the kitchen, Mr. Bankowski…" He followed me to the island where I offered him a choice of a hot drink or warming spirit. It was not yet noon, but we shared a drink of scotch. I sat across from him and encouraged him to help himself to the bottle, which he did. I appreciated his honesty.

"What do you think we should do with the roses?" I asked.

"I think they've done very well all these years exactly where they are, ma'am." He said more enthusiastically as the alcohol warmed him, giving a rosy hue to his cheeks and nose.

"And the greenhouse?"

He scratched his head and rubbed his hands together as the warmth seeped into his extremities.

"Well now, there is quite a bit of land." The estate was built on just over five acres; there *was* a lot of land. "There's enough room for one, but it wouldn't make sense for just herbs. We could grow them in pots and move them in and out as the mood strikes you. But it's entirely your choice, ma'am."

Mr. Bankowski was right; it was entirely my choice. Todd had taken away my reason to pretend.

I smiled at the gardener. "I agree with you. We don't need a greenhouse."

He nodded, then leaned back in his seat and finished his drink.

"Don't worry about Mr. Birch. I'll take care of everything." And I would too. As I escorted him to the front door, Mr. Bankowski gave me a quick run-down of the rest of his plans for the estate. It was all familiar to me; there had been no changes in nearly twenty years.

"How are your wife and children?" I asked, because it would have been rude to simply push him through the door after he had declared himself an unshakeable ally. Loyalty like his deserved some reward, and most importantly, required maintenance.

"Well, the wife is retired now, ma'am." She used to be a preschool teacher. "And the children have all moved on now – married or gone into the city." As far as Mr. Bankowski was concerned, any destination that required getting on a road with more than two lanes was the city. But I appreciated his brevity.

"It must have been a quite a change for your both." I didn't know, but that sounded like the right thing to say since they had always been surrounded by people, especially children.

"It is, it is," he nodded his head, and I caught the whiff of sadness.

I blamed my next words on hormonal balance, because like I said, I'd never really been an empathetic person. "Well, I'm looking for someone to help around the house now that I've resumed residency," I said, surprising both of us. "Just basic household maintenance and maybe some meals every now and then."

I figured if I was going to have someone in my home, I might as well get a good meal out of it. I did not need Todd Birch to eat well. Of course it had to be someone I trusted and of whom I had complete control.

My father had trusted Mr. Bankowski. The gardener's apartment was his anyway and he understood how much I valued my privacy. I doubted it would make a difference whether they chose to live there or keep their home in Wolf Trap.

"Why, Miss. Koehler," he gasped, eyes wide as saucers, "I do believe Mrs. Bankowski would welcome the opportunity to keep the house in the style of your late mother," he said, which meant we understood each other. She would limit her intervention to cleaning and cooking, and of course, make herself scarce. We made arrangements for her to stop by on Monday to discuss terms.

Back in the kitchen, I slathered Nutella on toast and sat down to eat. My eyes fell on several small potted herbs hanging over the sink. The presence of the living things mocked me. Todd had left his stamp all over my body and inside my home, while he had left our marriage.

Was this my life... what I'd been built for... the reason my father had sacrificed our family just to save me? When had I become the woman who blithely accepted being underestimated, overlooked, and humiliated? Todd could bend my body, but as far as wills went, I was unbreakable.

I had run from him once before and had no desire to do so again. This was my home, paid for with all the love my mother had had in her heart and my father's blood and sweat.

I found garbage bags at the bottom of the pantry and filled them with his marks. All the herbs, some hearty and others showing the first signs of wilting because they hadn't been watered in a week; fresh produce that had begun to rot too in his absence; eggs, meat and fish that would have been forgotten if not for my purge went into the bags.

Upstairs was bare except for a few toiletries he had moved into my parents' bathroom. The bags he had brought with him a week ago but had not had the time to unpack were gone. It seemed half my work was already done.

I drove the garbage to the gates and hoisted them into the dumpster.

Next I called the security company to reset the estate codes. It wasn't an emergency, so they promised to send someone out on Monday morning. They wanted to make sure I was who I claimed to be and was not being coerced.

I went back to work, and at midnight shut down my computers and crawled into bed. I had resolved to do more of the same in the morning before leaving around 3:00 p.m. for Richard's.

It was a safe and familiar existence – filling my waking hours with Hasan al-Qasim's sons; Sergei Afanasenko and Blerim Nesimi. Living from one minute to the next meant I did not have to think about Todd. And I didn't need a strategy for dealing with Richard either. I didn't need his honeymoon or his approval. I had made my own way to Paris and it came with access to our embassy there. I was done pretending.

I had just exited my bathroom when the sound of running water alerted me to an intruder. It could have only been one of two persons. I was getting ready for dinner at Richard's, so that ruled him out. I quickly pulled on jeans and a sweater, stuffed my feet into boots and pulled my wet hair into a ponytail. The high neck and long sleeves hid the worst of my bruises. The rest could be explained away with a bout of Eskrima at the martial arts studio.

As expected, and yet completely unexpected at the same time, I watched Todd emerge from my parents' bathroom, moist and beautiful, with a towel wrapped tightly around his hips. He took a break from rubbing a towel over his head when he spotted me in the doorway. His bags were back, one of them wide open on my parents' bed as if it had vomited its contents onto the brand new sheets.

"You moved my shaving kit," he said, then sauntered over to the bed to pick through his belongings. He picked out a pair of basic white briefs and a matching undershirt.

"Get out."

He paused. "Excuse me?"

"I said get out," I said, surprised at how steady my voice sounded, because everything I hadn't felt since Friday night was building in my chest. The pressure was painful... unbelievably so. This had to be what a heart attack felt like. "Pack your shit and get the fuck out of my house."

There was no risk of me faltering. His skin was flushed from his shower, but that could not have explained all the marks on his body.

He let her put her marks on his body. Across his shoulders, visible because his naked back was turned to me, were nail tracks. Thin symmetrical streaks, four angry, red welts running in parallel lanes, stretched down into his back. Elsewhere on the canvas that used to be mine were crescent shaped wounds where she had dug in and held on.

He turned to face me, but it was too late. I had seen enough... not that he was hiding anything from me. Todd knew all about marking; he had put his brand on me enough times to know what would last. He wanted me to know. He wanted everyone to know. That was the purpose of his little production Friday night.

If he had fucked Anne as a means of breaking me into the knowledge of his sexual liberation, then he had failed miserably. The smart of his infidelity with my alter was a whisper of a caress compared to this. Perhaps he had been right about us being the same then. Compared to this, that didn't matter at all.

"I want you gone by the time I get back, but it really shouldn't take you that long. There's nothing left for you here."

I left him standing there, face blank and jaw tense. Really, what could he say? I didn't want his excuses. A denial would have been a slap in the face. And Todd never did anything without careful deliberation; an apology would have been meaningless.

I hated him. I hated him for making me feel this much, this deeply. I hated even more that the deluge of unwelcome emotion came after days of numbness. When I thought he'd broken my heart in the Dominican Republic, I hadn't cried. Now I realized I'd been more angry than hurt. Now I realized I hadn't loved him nearly enough then, but I did now. And he had broken me.

As I navigated the barren roads on Christmas Day, I blamed the poor visibility on the falling snow – penny-sized flakes interspersed with bits of ice. I couldn't see, I couldn't breathe, and I couldn't feel a thing beyond the hurt.

There was no room for pretense anymore.

NINETEEN

There was no question of my not going to Richard's. What else would I have done... supervised Todd's removal? I had already watched him walk out on me once that weekend. A repeat, regardless of the reasons this time, wouldn't have taught me anything about him or myself. Plus, I wouldn't have been able to hide the depth of my devastation from him. I couldn't even fool Richard and Abby, regardless of how hard I tried. It didn't help that I had showed up alone, face ravaged by tears that had sprung like a geyser.

Bert took one look at me through the glass and waved me through. Either the lazy son-of-a-bitch had a heart or knew I was in no mood to trade banter with him today. If only the other guests would be as considerate. The driveway was packed with matching pairs of Tahoes and an Escalade. Richard's family – Tom, his wife and two daughters; and his bachelor brothers, Andrew and David – had already arrived.

Our relationship was difficult to explain. They were all men, though still living at home part time, when I moved in at seventeen. We used to be as close as possible given the age difference – six, eight and eleven years my senior – but that was before my parents were killed. After, I was angry at the world for not coming to an end, and Richard for trying to step into shoes that would never fit. His children hated the effort he put into me, and thought I was ungrateful for blowing off the things he had not given them.

Yet Richard had harbored dreams of us being a real family in the fullest sense of the word. To his infinite frustration, his clumsy attempts at playing Cupid were met with resounding failure – and not for a lack of interest on the part of his sons.

As Richard had so eloquently put it, "Andrew is still single and Tom will divorce Michelle if I tell him to." David got a pass because as the closest to my age, he had felt the displacement from my relocation most profoundly. At least Richard had given some consideration to our happiness.

As was my custom, I walked right into the house. The smells were distinctly Christmas – just in case I'd missed the gigantic wreath and mistletoe that festooned the front door. Seasoned pine was burning in the chimney, existing in perfect balance with the other smells permeating the house: roasted meat, cinnamon, cloves, and peppermint. The low rumble of voices could be heard in the drawing room down the entry hall and to the right. The tableau reminded me of coming home for Thanksgiving a few weeks ago... only lonelier.

I had really hoped for a few moments alone, locked inside the nearest bathroom so I could run cold water over my face. Instead, Ollie, their long-time housekeeper, was waiting inside the entry hall with a glass of eggnog ready for me. She proved why she'd been with them for as long as she had however. She took one look at my face and claimed to have forgotten the nutmeg, returning to the kitchen to right the wrong.

When I emerged from the powder room, Richard was there and Abby was not. I knew I had the wizened housekeeper to thank for that.

"Where's Todd?"

"He won't be joining us."

Richard looked deeply into me for what felt like a long time. I was determined to withstand his inquiry. The charade had been for his benefit anyway. If I couldn't survive his scrutiny of our marriage, then I risked falling apart at the least convenient times. Much worse was to come in the way of questions and stares vacillating between curiosity and pity.

"Come up to my office."

His office was where Richard considered every important decision – from official DNI matters to issues that impacted the health and welfare of his children and grandchildren. Richard's office was very familiar to me. I had stood defiantly just inside the door when he had thrown condoms at me at seventeen years old and told me to be safe. Over the years, the conversations we had had here hadn't gotten any easier. And this promised to be one such discussion that would test the bounds of comfort for both of us.

We passed Abby on the way upstairs, and it seemed the gloom I'd brought had managed to permeate her chemically induced holiday cheer. At the end of one darkly spotted hand, which contrasted starkly with her wrinkle-free face, was one of her grandchildren, Savannah. I knew Michelle, Tom's wife, wasn't far away with the other child, Sarah. After one instance of Abby falling dead asleep while holding baby Sarah, Michelle had quickly learned there was more to her mother-in-law's serenity than yoga and heavily organized staff.

"Amy, dear, is everything alright?"

I offered her a smile. It wasn't all right, but it would be. Soon. I just needed to get through this minute and then the next, then the one after that.

"What happened?" Richard asked once the thick oak paneled doors were shut behind us and he had taken his place behind the massive desk that was always bare.

I sank into the stiff leather upholstered chair he indicated. It wasn't a spot for getting comfortable. It was a place to be skewered and roasted by Richard's multi-colored stare.

"I told him to get out." I shrugged, feigning a carefree spirit that had always eluded me. "He had already left anyway. I just don't want him back."

Richard sighed. "What do you mean he left?"

I swallowed deeply and took an even deeper breath, focusing on a spot over Richard's shoulder. "I mean he packed his shit, left and was fucking another woman." See? It was already getting better.

Richard leaned forward in his seat, drawing closer to me despite the massive expanse of wood lying flat between us. "Amy," he said, with a straight face to boot. "He's a man."

The rest went unspoken but audible just the same. *'What did you expect?'*

I held my breath and remained as immovable as Richard's stony stare. When it was clear I wouldn't back down, he assumed a more conciliatory tone, as if to reason with a petulant child.

"Look, Amy. I understand your disappointment," he said, which made me believe he did not in the least. "You married suddenly and maybe he hasn't adjusted to the expectation of discretion. I don't appreciate seeing you worked up like this. You're like a daughter to me."

"You're not my father!" I shouted at him, too 'worked up' to endure his condescension. "My father would never let him humiliate me like this. My father would never have chosen him over me!"

I was 'disappointed' to find myself in this position again – yelling at Richard like a recalcitrant child, while his sons shook with outrage that he allowed me to talk to him this way. It was a terrible idea to have come here.

The tears I had held off by simply focusing on moving one foot in front of the next broke through the dam walls. Richard's expectations and mine were clearly different, but he wasn't married to them. I was, and discretion was the least of what I wanted from Todd.

I moved towards the exit.

"You don't know half as much about your father as you think you do," Richard said, the first time in living memory I had ever heard him intimate a negative thought about my father.

"I know enough. I know he would have killed Todd for treating me the way he does. He wouldn't sit there and defend him. He wouldn't expect me to accept being a doormat."

"You think choosing your battles is the same as being walked over? Your mother knew the difference. Your father knew it too."

"And look where it left them." Ashes blown in the wind.

"Amy, sit down," he said, coaxing me away from the door with a conciliatory tone. "We've never really talked about your father."

He was right. How could I ignore his olive branch? I sat, but stuck to the edge of the seat, ready to fly at the least provocation.

"We're not going to do this now," he said and raised a hand to stave off my objection or flight, "because some things are sacred."

I don't want to change the opinion you have of your father, he had meant to say.

As if he could. I understood the work my father had devoted his life to. I understood my father had made choices that would have been difficult for others... people who had the luxury of a conscience... people who weren't like us.

What else could Richard say... that my father had cheated on my mother? I wouldn't believe it. We – his family, his work – were everything to him.

"And because this is about you and Todd. We need to fix this."

"It can't be fixed."

Richard sighed. "Consider what's at stake here. You're not the first woman whose husband has been indiscreet. Do you know what the difference between Diana and Hillary is? Perspective, Amy!"

The longer he droned on, the more I regretted coming. Richard was woefully out of touch.

"For pride you would jeopardize our future? You're in an enviable position, Amy. You can be the mother of our nation, part of the most powerful family in the world!"

And crazy. Richard was definitely crazy.

"The rise and fall of the elected is subject to the whim of the masses. And who do the rabble rely on? Us! They are all puppets, limited by what we tell them they should fear. The respect we command is unquestioned, because our power is earned, not granted. And so they are ruled by our policies...our ideas...our wishes.

"One day Todd will have my job. Thomas, with the right guidance, will rise to the head of the Navy. Andrew and David will back them up from the other wings. But you, Amy, will be the cornerstone of our power. Your sons will truly lead; your daughters, and the two little ones –" the man who forgot nothing made a show of struggling to recall the names of his granddaughters " –Savannah and Sarah, will be allied to leading families in Commerce and Industry. You just need perspective."

Stark, raving mad. Richard had lost his fucking mind.

There was no point arguing with a fucking lunatic, so I held my silence and nodded. He couldn't go on forever about his bullshit legacy, so I waited for him to run out of steam. Mother of our nation, my ass!

Richard had gone full-blown David-Koresh-crazy.

Had Todd bought into this plan, or was he just riding the gravy train for what he could get out of it? How could he condemn my father for what he had done to protect me, and at the same time respect this lunatic?

"Now there's something else I need to discuss with you," Richard said in his DNI voice at the end of his sermon... delusion. "Where were you between midnight Friday and oh-two-hundred Saturday?"

There were only a few reasons why anyone would ask such a question, and it was never a good thing for the person being asked. Something of value had been taken. And considering Richard was concerned by it, I knew it had to have been a life... an important one too or he wouldn't have bothered – and neither would I.

"What's happened?" I asked.

"Where were you?"

I didn't even need to think about it. "At the party until about one-thirty."

"And then?"

"I went home. Commander Castillo drove. I got in shortly after two. You can check the log at the security company." The alarm had to be set upon entry and exit.

"Todd wasn't with you?"

"No. He'd left just before one." Richard only nodded, but his eyes never wavered from mine. "He left with someone else."

"Who?"

I swallowed, but the anger was welling up from the hole in my middle. "With the woman he is fucking. A journalist."

That sparked his interest, but I didn't know why. "Are you sure?" he asked, and it was clear he wanted me to be certain.

"About what? That he was fucking someone else?"

"That he left with a journalist."

Of all the things to make Richard rub his hands together... "I haven't done a background check, but I have it on good authority. They were all over each other after you left. Everyone saw them, Richard. What fucking difference does it make that she's a journalist?"

"Because Major Edward Cummings is dead."

I didn't know what I expected, but that certainly wasn't it. The news hit me like a kick to my stomach. It knocked the breath out of me. It certainly didn't help that Richard pressed on, forcing a gasp out of me.

"His head was blown off with a Beretta."

Ed's service weapon was a Beretta M9. Had someone killed Ed with his own gun? Did Richard think Todd and I were involved?

"I remember you two had something going on a few years ago." Richard added, which raised my hackles.

"That was nearly four years ago." I hadn't killed him after he sent his muscle after me to persuade me to destroy the video I'd stolen from him. I'd decided to let bygones be bygones after he'd had Matt Boone murdered. None of which Richard knew. As far as he should have been concerned, Ed was an old ex... nothing more, Why would I have killed him?

"I understand you had a tense run-in with him last week. You, Todd, and Robert Townsend?"

The only person missing from that reunion was Don Blitzner. A 'run-in' was information; a 'tense run-in' was intelligence. It was all the proof I needed to confirm the source of that analysis.

"So you think one of us killed him?" Why else would Richard have concerned himself with Ed Cummings? It wasn't as if he would have been notified of the death under normal circumstance. I was the only link between Richard and Ed.

Richard smiled without humor. He saw my genuine emotion. There was no love lost between Ed and I, but I'd been surprised by the news. There was no motive and no opportunity.

"It looked like a suicide," he finally confessed. "He works in a high-stress area. There was no sign of a struggle. His ex-wife is skiing in Utah with the kids and a new man. Message scrawled on the wall said he was sorry. It happens. I expect it will blow over soon enough."

It was in fact common for soldiers returning from war zones to have difficulty adjusting. And Ed had been stateside for only a couple of months. Holidays were especially difficult for those without family support. Ed's wife had full custody of both his boys, and the divorce had been acrimonious... peppered with accusations of infidelity on his part. Obviously she had moved on. And Ed had been shot with his own gun. It looked like an open-and-shut case of suicide.

So why didn't I buy it?

Because it was too perfect, that's why. One or two of those factors would have been acceptable. All of them was overkill. It was as if someone had gone down the suicide checklist and selected every box.

Jesus, Ed had been murdered.

"Don't worry about this, Amy," Richard said, noticing the lack of relief on my face. "Investigators will check out all invested parties, but you don't have anything to worry about. You said Commander Castillo, right?" I nodded. Richard made a show of jotting down the name. "And the journalist?"

"Erika Harris." Her name rolled off my tongue like tar over gravel. "Colonel Townsend's sister-in-law."

Richard paused in his note-taking to look at me... really look at me. He knew about the history between those three. How could he not? For the longest time I'd been the only person who did not know. Add my relationship with Ed Cummings to the equation and what you had was a soap opera.

Richard dropped his pencil and hit me with his full attention. The blue eye shone with disapproval. "Amy, please tell me you did not have sex with Colonel Townsend."

So Todd's *indiscretion* was a source of disappointment, but the same on my part was unforgivable?

"I did not have sex with Colonel Townsend."

There was a knock at the door. Probably one of Richard's children. Abby would never have interrupted him while he was in his study.

"Keep it that way," he warned with a thick finger pointed at me. Once again I felt like the broken teenager I used to be. "Come," he called at the door.

I was right. It was one of Richard's children... one he had adopted anyway.

TWENTY

Todd stepped into the room and sucked all the heat out.

I suddenly had a sense of David's insecurities upon my insertion into their family twelve years ago. Richard actually got up to shake hands and pat him on the shoulder, as if Todd's very presence was to be celebrated.

"I wasn't expecting you," Richard said with a meaningful look in my direction.

Neither had I. The jig was up. What new game was Todd playing at?

Todd followed the direction of the older man's gaze. He lingered to the point of discomfort. I felt it on me, but I refused to meet it after the initial notice. That first look had been devastating enough.

His beauty was a powerful thing, and the knowledge that it wasn't just mine anymore was a debilitating blow. One look and I couldn't shake the vision of the two-day old beard scratching another woman's skin as he buried his face between her breasts. Those eyes, the deep pools of indigo that I had drowned in, had gazed into her and watched her come undone. His hands, his mouth, his entire fucking body had been all over her... inside her.

My time was over. I stood, ready to leave, even if it meant having to walk right by him because he stood between me and escape. With him here, my home was safe again.

"If you don't mind, I'd like a word with Amy," I heard him say.

"Of course not," Richard said at the same time I countered with: "There's no need."

Richard threw me a look that said, "Be reasonable," and left. It was naïve of me to expect any more consideration than that. But I had hoped Richard would have at least argued for some time for tempers to cool. What did he hope to achieve by throwing us together now... a peaceful Christmas dinner?

"You shouldn't drag Richard into the middle of this," Todd said, running one hand through his hair. It was not a sign of frustration, however. I'd tossed out his hair gel and his loose curls were in disarray. His calm drove the knife deeper into my heart.

"Richard has always been at the center of *this*," I reminded him, because the purpose of a post-mortem was to figure out what went wrong.

At least he paid me the courtesy of not denying it. Instead he said, "I'm not giving you up, Amy. I'm not walking away from our marriage."

"But you already have, and I'm not taking you back. I'm done, Todd."

We simply stared at each other for a long moment. I suspected he was testing the depths of my sincerity. After all, I'd claimed to have been done with him twice before – once in Jamaica, before we had even really started; and in the Dominican Republic when I'd moved out of our home following his bachelor party.

He sighed, tiredly as if I was being a chore. "We can negotiate new terms," he said, and a part of me I didn't even know was still alive withered and died in an instant. Todd had never loved me. It was all just a deal to him.

"I don't want you anymore."

"Don't be ridiculous, Amy," he said, covering the small square of rug that separated us.

I backed away, but not quickly enough. The heat of his fingers pressing into my arms burnt through the sleeves of my sweater, acid poured onto my wounds. His scent filled my nostrils –sunlight, citrus and deep blue, smells that should have been welcome at the start of winter. But it wasn't purely Todd. This scent had come from a bottle, slathered on in a shower, to cover traces of the woman who had clung to him.

"You've always wanted me. You will always want me."

He was right, but I couldn't live with this feeling. I had to give them up.

"We can stay together," he said, words and fingers insistent even as I shrank further away, threatening to break his hold on me. "We'll be together when it matters, and lead separate lives when it does not."

Of course Todd would want that. He had everything to gain from our union.

"And can I fuck whomever I want in this separate life?" I asked, and relished the fact that he pulled away, even if it was because he thought I was soiled for even saying such a thing. "All the men under your command? All your Semper Fi brothers? How about Colonel Townsend... can I fuck him too in my separate life."

"Shut up!" he snapped at me "Shut your fucking mouth."

But I had found his weakness, and I wasn't about to let it go. If he felt one-tenth of what I'd experienced this afternoon, then I would walk out the door a happy woman.

"I'll be the whore you know me to be... fuck them within an hour of meeting them." His fists balled at his sides, crushing the mask of invincibility he'd worn while he beat me into the ground all week. "But be warned, I won't be hiding. I won't put on a show like you did Friday night, but I'm not pretending either. I'll take them to *my* home, fuck them in *my* bed, if I want. And I expect you to respect our agreement, Todd, because that's what it means to live *separate lives*."

I would have continued if not for his hand pressed across my nose and mouth. I had a laundry list of things I didn't do anymore because of him. I could have gone on for days.

I didn't fight back as he pressed me back into Richard's oak paneled walls, even though pain flared up my spine from the spot where his knee had braced into me a few nights before. Todd was physically stronger than me and just as, if not better skilled, at fighting. I wouldn't win a physical confrontation – I'd learned my lesson. But the past few minutes had taught me something else. I could flay him alive with my words if I wanted to.

With my back flat against the wall, Todd leaned into me. His mouth was a hair's breath from my ear. If I looked into his eyes, I knew they would be black. His chest heaved under the strain of pulling deep gulps of air into his lungs, grazing against my peaked breasts. I felt the heat of his body as it covered mine, and it melted my core. Our bodies knew each other well, even if I was a stranger to his heart.

"Feel that, Amy," he whispered, lips brushing against the sliver of exposed skin behind my ear. The rest of me was covered up, hiding his marks. The layers of concealing clothing couldn't hide the scent of my arousal however. "Your body knows it belongs to me. You belong to me."

His hand fell away from my mouth, but pressed my shoulder harder into the wall. He pulled away, just far enough, so as he turned his face to me, our lips would meet. I turned away. His mouth had been on hers, all over her. I didn't want them anymore.

"You're wrong. Freedom turns me on... thinking of all those angry men I can fuck." The sound of his breath was brutally cut off. I felt his energy recoiling, like the air being sucked from the atmosphere before an explosion. I reached for my coup de grace. "I think I'll start with Townsend. We've already put in all that work, and we've become close over the past few months... working together."

I knew better than to touch him. Our encounter would have undoubtedly become physical, and I would have lost. But I did look into his eyes then. His lips were pressed together into an uncompromising line. No risk of contact there. His eyes were closed, but his arms blocked me into the spot, so there was no escape.

"I'll lock you away first," he said, but it was a whisper I would have missed if we hadn't been so close. "Do you hear me?" he asked. "I'll send you away before I let anyone else touch you."

I might have laughed if only our situation wasn't fucked up beyond any recovery.

"You can't, remember?" I mocked. "That doesn't gel with Richard's plans." I watched the tension in his jaw pulse. His entire body throbbed then seemed to hum.

He opened his eyes and stared right through me. And in that moment, I knew what was the last thing Ed saw.

"And you can't kill them all, either."

Todd faltered. He looked at me... directly into my eyes. From my peripheral vision, I saw his throat working, either trying to make room for the words that wouldn't come, or forcing unwanted ones away.

"You don't know what you're talking about," he said, but his voice was thick. His eyes shuttered.

"Don't I?" I followed as he slowly eased away—a threatened animal on the retreat. "I know it was you. You couldn't stand the thought of him telling anyone about us. You couldn't stand looking at him day-in, day-out. You killed a man to save your pride."

Todd snapped, like I knew he would. After a botched retreat, it was the only course left at his disposal.

"I did it for you!" he seethed, and I was back to being pressed into the wall. I was hit full force by the blast of energy that he had tried and failed to contain. It wasn't just anger there. In him I sensed feelings that were painfully familiar… the agony of something unfulfilled.

"It had nothing to do with me," I shot back at him.

"He had to pay for the things he did to you."

"And what was the reason behind your performance Friday night?" I scoffed, but the condescension may have been lost amidst the tears that surged shamefully to the surface.

Goddammit, I hated feeling!

"You had to punish me too… for something that happened before I even knew you existed? You didn't have to humiliate me, Todd. Just knowing you were with her would have been enough."

The only good thing that came out of my pitiable sobbing was the fact that it had the same effect as a physical slap on the man before me. He recoiled, stunned, and was immediately repentant for having provoked it. He reached for my hands, and I passed the next few moments slapping away his touch.

"Don't touch me."

"Listen to me."

"I don't want to hear it. Don't touch me. I am done with you."

I really wanted to be done with these tears. Talking about it was like living it all over again. Seeing her marks on his body; watching as they held hands in plain view of anyone who wished to look; the way he smiled at her, caressed her.

"Amy, listen to me," he snapped, capturing my hands, and pinning them next to my body against the wall. I reared back, trying to establish distance between us - space he was intent on eliminating - and smacked my head into the wood paneling. I wished I could have knocked myself unconscious. I didn't want him to see me like this, wracked by sobs, face ravaged by scalding streams.

"It's not what you think. I wasn't punishing you," he said, pressing his lips against my ear. "You know I would kill for you... I *have* killed for you. And I would do it again... a thousand times to protect you... to punish the people who hurt you. But I don't ever plan on living without you, so I have to be smart about it. Do you understand?"

What did I expect him to say? He valued my connections more than almost anything. When push came to shove, when I failed to fall in line with their plans for me, of course he would excuse what he had done.

On the other hand, I understood exactly what he wasn't saying. And most importantly, I believed him.

Being smart meant he needed an unimpeachable alibi, and Erika was a journalist. Should an investigation into Ed's death ensue, she *was* the news, and Todd had been with her. He had also found an alibi for me, sticking me with Commander Castillo who had lingered at the party a full forty-five minutes after Todd had left.

Did I think Todd had somehow snuck away from his love-shack, killed Ed, and returned to the arms of his alibi?

Absolutely.

All he'd had to do was render her unconscious, and for people like us, that wasn't hard at all. I had done it to FBI agent, Jessica Byles, who had been one of Todd's many conquests in the Dominican Republic. To this day she had no clue I'd dosed her.

I was fucked up enough to give Todd credit for his noble motivations. After all, I would never have to worry about Ed again... whether he decided to share my involvement with Matt Boone/Rageman 96253, or try to kill me for 'ruining his life'. But Todd had spent two days with her since Friday, and the marks on his body said they hadn't been knitting. God only knows what he'd been up to since Monday night.

"I'd do it again, Amy. I would do anything to protect you," Todd was saying. "He didn't deserve to live. And if your father were alive today, I would kill him too for what he did to you. I'll never let anyone hurt you."

"And what about you, Todd?" I asked. The incongruity of my tears was that they burned a flaming track down my cheeks and nose, but they were cold enough to freeze my lips into stiff blocks of ice. "Who will protect me from you?"

"Baby," he said, pressing his forehead against mine. His breath against my wet cheeks stung like wind chill. "I'm sorry, but I can't walk away. I love you too much."

His eyes were closed, but for the first time in weeks, it felt like he wasn't hiding his feelings from me. The pain I felt was etched right there in the lines of his face.

"I did what I had to do. I had hoped... I hope we can find our way back to each other."

I hated being weak, and so I conjured the image of what it would have been like between them. I pictured her opening her eyes, and having the magnificence of Todd's naked body chasing the confusion away. She would have felt the strain in her body... proof that he had been there. And she would have smiled at him.

"We are stronger than this, Amy. You and I can get past this. I did it for you, baby."

"I can't."

"You have to, because I'm not walking away from you. You, Amy... not Richard. This thing between us has always been stronger than him." Todd tilted my face up to his so I could see the depth of his feelings for me. "Tell me what it will take for you to get past this."

I shook my head, clearing away the daze and the stubborn, unwelcome seeds of hope. "I can't get past..."

I couldn't finish, could not put a name to my shame. Although things had already gone terrible wrong, I still deserved to keep the single shred of pride I had left.

It was in vain. Todd knew me too well... so well in fact, he didn't need me to finish the thought.

"Listen to me, Amy," Todd said, and by his urgent tone, I knew he could feel me slipping away. For good. "We've known each other for many years now. She knows who I was before I met you, and she knows I'm not that person anymore. She accused me of being in love with you. If she could tell, why can't you?"

He brushed the tip of his nose against mine a second before he drank my tears. Todd knew what he was doing, pulling my anguish into his body, draining me of any objection. I didn't dare move; I was hardly breathing. I couldn't bear to taste my tears on his lips.

"You never have to worry about her again. It's over now. I swear it."

I looked into the eyes of the man I loved. He was everything a woman would want. I knew it would never really be over... Ever.

TWENTY-ONE

Walking away was hard.

Todd Birch made it impossible.

So we struck a new bargain. I promised him one moment at a time, and he promised to spend the rest of his life making it up to me.

What did that mean?

It meant he would restore my faith in him. It meant he would prove to me everyday that he valued me more than anything Richard could do for him. And it meant I would allow him the opportunity to do so, starting right away, at Richard's Christmas dinner table.

Richard had never been more proud of me as I took my place next to my husband.

Thomas had an idea of what had passed between us. At forty years old, he was one of the youngest Navy Captains, and although he'd been absent from Friday's festivities, he seemed to have his fingers on the pulse of the service. He had heard the rumors of Todd publicly throwing me over for another woman. He might have mentioned it to his wife, Andrew and David.

We weren't the warmest family, but Todd was still a stranger in our midst. Their welcome was more strained than it had ever been before, a marked difference from our reunion over Thanksgiving a few weeks ago. The sudden chill left Abby disoriented.

I might have appreciated their show of loyalty if it didn't come at the cost of my pride. Frankly, I would have preferred their ignorance.

But they were Richard's children, and they took their cues from him. He looked on like a benevolent ruler, smiling his approbation as Todd took my hand in his and pressed kisses to the back. Order was restored in the fiefdom, the family was reassured of the strength of our union. My face burned with fresh humiliation.

They all thought me handled... that Todd, in his supreme maleness, had tamed the shrew.

I couldn't wait to leave.

Todd in his thoughtfulness, sometime between plotting and executing Ed's murder, had gone shopping for gifts. There was something for everyone, including a gift from me to him. It was an ugly Christmas sweater that he claimed to love and begged to be the start of our private holiday tradition.

Richard presented Todd with our joint gift – a honeymoon vacation package to Paris. We would arrive by private jet on New Years Day and check into Hotel George V for fourteen days.

"You said you would be able to clear your schedule," Richard qualified without even a glance in my direction. "I hope those days are convenient."

"I thought you had a special project you wanted me to work on," Todd answered, stunned and pleased at Richard's largesse. "I had no idea. It's a wonderful surprise. Thank you!" Then Todd turned to me. "Do you think you'll be able to take a couple of weeks off, Amy?"

There was some comfort in knowing I was not the only one being manipulated by Richard.

I nodded my assent, my lackluster smile matching my withdrawn mood throughout the evening. I would await a more private time to discuss my work schedule with Todd. I was not hiding my work schedule from Richard, because there was clearly a straight line of communication between him and my boss. But I wasn't volunteering any more information either.

In the past, Richard had showed only mild interest in my work, every now and then calling to congratulate me on a significant achievement – not unlike a distracted father making up for missing his kid's soccer match by buying the team ice cream.

As we said our goodbyes, Richard pulled me into a hug. Over his shoulder, I watched Michelle look away, her disappointment at being starved of such affection evident. Tom's hand fell to her shoulder, but more in comfort. He knew his father, understood Michelle's role in the building of his legacy was negligible, recognized the production of two daughters and no son was a sore disappointment. She had conveniently miscarried her third pregnancy a year ago, shortly after the ultrasound revealed it to be another girl. How inconvenient for her the doctors had performed an emergency hysterectomy to save her life.

Richard ended the embrace, but cupped my cheek and gazed into my eyes. "Perspective," he said.

I nodded, because it was expected of me. What was the point of fighting against the current? I was walking out the door with the man who had stomped all over my dignity, his hand fixed to the small of my back, his possession of me unmistakable.

Todd shook hands with the McDowell men, and next thing I knew, we were in our respective vehicles. I was glad for the space, because although my brain had come to terms with this new arrangement between Todd and I, my heart had not. It would take much more than just *perspective* to forget what he had done. Once home, I went straight to bed, shutting my bedroom door. There was no need to turn the lock; the message was indisputable.

It was a message Todd chose to ignore. The lights hadn't been off for a minute before he was there, disregarding my insistence on distance, shutting the door behind him.

"What are you doing?" I jackknifed up in bed and tucked the covers snugly around me even though I was dressed warmly in sweats and a t-shirt.

Contrary to what he might have thought were the reasons behind the uncharacteristic wardrobe choice, I wasn't trying to repel him. I simply hadn't gotten around to doing laundry yet. Anyway, his attire matched mine as if we had planned it.

As usual, Todd didn't let anything get in the way of what he wanted. And at that precise moment, he wanted in my bed. A closed door, my killjoy outfit, the fading but still present bruises and ligature marks on my body weren't going to change that.

"I need to be with you tonight, Amy," he said, crossing to the empty side of the bed.

I shook my head then remembered he couldn't see me in the dark. "That's not a good idea." Just the night before he'd been with someone else.

"I want to hold you," he said, climbing in next to me, tugging the sheets away so he could pull my body into the curve of his.

But that wasn't us. Todd and I never just held each other. If you asked me, it wasn't possible. We couldn't put our hands on each other without the insatiable need to be closer and closer still – so close in fact, it was like crawling inside the other – consumed all rational thought. For as long as we had known each other, our chemistry had bridged the chasm that our past, our selfishness, and mistrust had opened.

This time however, the cure was tainted. I couldn't look at him without seeing her. I couldn't touch him without the fear that my hands would run across her marks. I couldn't have him touch me without knowing he had done the same to her only hours ago.

"I hate that you touched her," I heard myself say, and I blamed the show of weakness on my preoccupation with escaping him.

"Listen to me, Amy," he said urgently, because he knew the hands he held were trapped for only a moment. Here I wouldn't hesitate to fight him, because the alternative – passing the night with the images of them together -- was unbearable. "What we have is unlike anything I've ever experienced. I couldn't share that with anyone else even if I tried. And I would never try."

"How could you?" It was more an accusation than an explanation of the mechanics.

"By pretending it was you. But even so I couldn't... It's not the same. She's not you."

How shallow was I that Todd's failure to conclude pleased me?

It wasn't enough though.

"Please, Amy. Let me hold you. One moment at a time, right? Give me the chance to make it up to you."

He didn't deserve to be forgiven... and I wouldn't. But sooner or later we would have to overcome the obstacles to our physical relationship. I couldn't see myself living day-in, day-out with Todd without succumbing to the demands of our bodies. And if I didn't, I knew Anne would.

I reclined next to him, but there was nothing relaxing about it. I didn't want to feel his skin on mine, didn't want his breath ruffling the hair at the back of my neck, didn't want to hear his heartbeat echoing through me. I held my body as stiff as a board, doubtful either of us would ever fall asleep.

Todd's strategy was to wear me down... watch me thaw from the outside in. And it worked to an extent. At some point during the night my body melted into his and I awoke before dawn to find myself sprawled on top of him. He was fast asleep, the depth of each of his breaths powerful enough to lift me. His breath ruffling my hair was familiar. His arms wrapped around me, one hand cupping my bottom inside my sweats, made me think I had dreamt the past week.

I arched my neck to get a better look at him. I wanted him to be different, not to be the same man I had left in the Dominican Republic. His arms tightened reflexively, preventing any adjustment. There were shadows under his eyes and a faint bruise on his cheek, partially hidden by his thickening beard. If not for my proximity I wouldn't have noticed it. It was too fresh to have been from our fight on Monday night, and it was too slight to have been caused by a man fighting for his life. In any event, Richard had said there was no evidence of a struggle.

I didn't want to think about Ed, or the two boys, Christopher and Aiden, who would never see their father alive again.

The possibility that Erika had struck Todd was as much a relief as the knowledge that he had received no satisfaction from their encounters – fleeting, and in the grand scheme of things, totally irrelevant.

Despite his sleepy protest, I extricated myself from his embrace. The fact that he slept on was proof of the type of week he had had. Todd usually stirred long enough to send me off on my run with an unnecessary 'be safe.' When I returned three hours later, wet and half-frozen, he was gone, and Mrs. Bankowski was standing on my stoop.

Introductions were completed over coffee Todd had thoughtfully made, or so I thought.

"Mr. Birch said you like your coffee strong. I hope it's to your satisfaction."

I nodded without comment and watched as she doused hers with creamer I had missed in my purge. "Why were you waiting outside?" She'd obviously been inside long enough to have a discussion with my husband, hunt for supplies, and start a grocery list, judging by the unfamiliar script pinned to the refrigerator.

"When Mr. Birch said he was leaving, I didn't feel comfortable hanging about without first meeting you."

I silently nodded again. So Mr. Bankowski had explained things to her. That was a relief. We discussed our expectations in under five minutes; the rest of the direction she would get from her husband and mine. I left her to do whatever she felt needed to be done while I showered and prepared for work.

At some point Todd had given her cash for grocery shopping, which was urgent for him because I had tossed out all his food. I assumed her husband let her in and out of the estate, because I never heard from her for the rest of the day. She was perfect.

Around noon the security company called to confirm an appointment to update the access codes. I declined and was left to work uninterrupted until late afternoon when Todd reappeared.

To break the tension, he'd brought back a moving truck and a three-man crew to shuffle his belongings into the house. His uniform said he'd been at work, but his belongings said he'd made the time to visit his storage locker. The rest, including his SUV, which was being shipped from the Dominican Republic, wouldn't arrive for several weeks.

I turned off the security monitors and shut the door to my father's study. Todd was in his prime while being social, making the movers feel like they were more long-lost friends than hired help. I was at my best locked away, plotting the detonation of a car bomb blocks away from one of Paris' major transportation hubs, the Gare St. Lazare, in order to cover up an unsanctioned abduction.

It was full dark when he came to me, and I was painfully aware of it, because I'd had nothing to eat all day but coffee from the pot on my father's sideboard and a Snickers bar from the stash in his desk. By then there were no movers and no Mrs. Bankowski to fill the silence that felt as uncomfortable as a hair jacket in the middle of summer. It had never been like this between us. I didn't know how to fix it... how to unsee the image of a couple trapped in the heights of ecstasy that was conjured by the very sight of him.

"Amy," he called, as if I hadn't noticed his advance. He'd barely knocked before he entered, and with a casual flick of his wrist, flooded the room with light. "Why are you in the dark?"

Because it felt right… like coming home. Because I didn't have the strength to get up and chase the shadows away. Because I wished I could curl up and die as long as it ended the visions of him and her.

"Come. Mrs. Bankowski made dinner." I raised a finger in acknowledgement, but made no move to follow him.

Todd wasn't fooled. He drew closer, refusing to stop until the breadth of his body was all I could see. He picked me up from my father's chair – a seat I was finding it more and more difficult to fill, and perched me like a child on the edge of the desk. He burrowed his way between my legs while I was occupied closing the lid on the computer.

"Stop this," he said, dragging my attention back to him, tilting my chin so my face was open to him.

I wanted to stop it. God, he had no idea how much I wanted to stop it all! But I couldn't look at him without feeling a sharp ache in my center. The longer I dwelled on it, the more it grew, like a flame being fed with pieces of his betrayal, shedding more and more light onto the picture of their time together.

Todd kissed me, and it was like being slapped across the face. In fact, I wished he had struck me instead. It would have given me perspective… knocked the desire right out of me. How could I still want him? How could I accept what she had left?

His kiss was hard, bordering on painful. He sucked on my bottom lip, and when I failed to open fast enough for him, Todd sank his teeth into the plumped-up flesh. He caught my cry with his tongue sweeping inside, and stoked a forgotten ache to life. Desire was like an inferno inside me, spreading with the speed and unpredictability of a wildfire. Todd was not immune to the contagion either. His hand at my hip pulled me closer to the edge as he pressed his response deep between my legs. There was no denying he wanted me.

I should have pushed him away. I shouldn't have felt the burn so deeply through layers of clothing. But the hunger could not be contained. His was too old and too deep to have been assuaged days ago, and I was weak. I was angry too and he was desperate. In the end, the swelling of emotion was too much for either of us to control alone, like using the power of the mind to bring a speeding train to a screeching halt. It didn't help that where I lacked the strength, Todd lacked the inclination.

Before I had come to grips with my personal failing, I was being lifted just high enough for him to yank my sweats down. They pooled at his feet in a lonely pile; I still hadn't gotten around to doing laundry yet, so there was no underwear. Todd greeted the unveiling like a zealot on a holy day.

He was on his knees in a second, worshipping my body. The shock of his fingers, cold against my inner thighs, had me gasping. Then they were buried deep inside me, and I was crying out for an entirely different reason. His mouth covered my throbbing flesh, his tongue lapping greedily at me, lips pulling rhythmically. I sank into the sensation, legs falling open, fingers dipping into the lush mass of curls, my body collapsing into an abyss of pure pleasure. For the first time since he had returned home there was nothing between us – no ghosts of the past, no sense of foreboding. It was shocking in its newness and purity... not a hint of the taint I dreaded.

I shook as I came, the spasms running several courses through me. I should have known better than to try to contain the euphoric rush, but I was both afraid it would break my body and terrified of it ending. I never wanted to feel anything besides this ever again. With my eyes squeezed shut and my body pulsing it was as if we existed on a different plane, one where there was nothing but us.

It seemed impossible that I was the only one so completely shaken. But how Todd could have been as affected and still found the wherewithal to function was beyond my comprehension. Before I had caught my breath, he had unbelted, unhooked, and unzipped his jeans – surprising because I felt him in me, all over, and around me, like a Hindu god with more arms than necessary. His briefs were only a flash of white before his thick, pulsing, purple arousal was at my entrance, pushing me once more back into that parallel plane. He grunted as he sank deeply into me, pressing so hard I couldn't hold back the cry ripped from my soul.

"Open your eyes," he said. "Look at me. See me, Amy. I'm yours." One arm hooked under my raised knee, he was incredibly deep. I forced the breath from my lungs to make room for him. I couldn't do as he asked; it was too full, the feeling of him inside me. I couldn't take any more. I shook my head no.

"Yes," he insisted, pressing deeper still.

"Too much," I groaned, back arched to make room.

"Not enough," he differed and pulled back minutely only to slam into me.

"God!" I cried.

"Todd," he persisted. "Say it." He reared back again, surely a threat if ever I heard one. I bit my lip, both an act of defiance and preparation, because he was a man of his word. Mostly... well, sometimes.

"Todd!" I cried as he failed to disappoint.

"Open your eyes. Give me your eyes." Todd pushed up my shirt to expose and palm my breasts.

I shook my head. Hadn't I given enough? But he was pushing and pulling now, sawing into me slowly and incredibly deeply. His movement was unbelievably smooth for someone whose flesh was as hard and rigged as his. I could feel every hill, bump and valley from root to tip as he eased into me. It was delicious torture. I could feel every inch of him rubbing across my over-sensitized flesh, but it wasn't the jar I needed to get off. It seemed to go on forever... long enough that our bodies dripped with sweat, his landing in heavy drops on my bared stomach.

All the while I kept my face averted and my eyes closed. I didn't want to see... didn't want to break the spell, even if I knew I would never come like this. I never wanted this moment to end. I never wanted to stop the sensation and start *feeling* again.

And then incredibly, I felt my body spasm. The shock of impending climax when he was *making love to my body* was a powerful thing. It defied logic and went against everything we had learned about each other... everything I knew about my body. My eyes flew open in disbelief. I had to know if this was the same man. Our eyes met. He'd been warned by the tickle that started in my core. It had never failed him yet.

"See me," he said through gritted teeth, the effort that went into breaking new ground apparent in his locked jaw and rippling body. The veins in his neck stood out thick and throbbing, the hands that held me pinned down trembling. "Only you can do this to me. This is all yours, Amy. So what's the point of fucking anyone else if I can only get this with you, huh?"

He stared into my eyes and saw deep into my soul. And in turn, he let me see into his too.

"Do you think I wanted to fuck her? Do you think I had a choice?" he drilled into me, pushing and pulling so slowly and smoothly, it was sweet torture.

"Do you know what it was like being inside her body, knowing it wasn't you? Now imagine how I felt thinking of you, wishing it was you, knowing every minute that passed took you further away from me, and not having a choice. And I don't have choice, Amy. I can't breathe when I know there's someone out there who hurt you and got away with it. It ripped my heart out to be with her, but I had to. Do you understand?"

My brain – the rational, objective part of me – understood. My body was weak and would forgive anything where Todd was concerned. But the rest of me... my heart... That was a different story. The heart never forgets and it never forgives. I was torn between loving him, needing him, and hating him for drilling that ache so deep inside me I would never reach it.

"Answer me," he demanded.

I did. I came so hard I burst into tears... or, I burst into tears as I came. I cried and cried out as my body shook from the core, convulsions wrenching me. If I thought I had felt pain upon confirmation of his betrayal, the climax was a moment of disillusionment. What I felt at the moment of awakening of my entire being – mind, body and soul – was the sweetest agony I had never thought possible. I cried as it consumed me, great, fat tears coursing down my face, streaming into my ears and hair.

"Do you think you'll ever get this with anyone else?"

I shook my head. There was no denying Todd and I were a tragedy in the making. We were bad for each other, destined to keep hurting each other until we destroyed ourselves. But I could no more stop than he. He shouldn't love me; he deserved a much simpler woman who was more understanding and supportive than me. He deserved a woman like my mother. And I didn't want to love him; it was safer not to. But God help me, I did.

"This is it for me, Amy. This is what it's like for me every time I'm with you. Do you think I can settle for less? Do you think I'll ever risk losing this again?"

I shook my head.

"Good. Because I can't. I won't."

And still the bone-melting, mind-bending, soul-cleansing pleasure persisted. I felt him thickening inside me, throbbing in rhythmic spurts. He sank deep and filled me completely, every corner of my being replete with Todd's essence … his presence.

He didn't collapse on top of me. It was as if he was determined for me to *see him*—all of him. Todd strained against the pressure in his spine, arching painfully to set his life-force free. I felt the muscles in his body trembling from head to toe, eyes losing focus, toes curled. His groan was a guttural and incoherent hum that shook his body and vibrated through me from where we were still joined. His hips rocked into me then stilled, glutes quivering, begging for relief.

At the end of it, he fell into my father's seat, knees sapped of their strength. But it wasn't enough for him to have shaken the foundation of my finite definition of my love and desire. Todd had annihilated the boundaries of my belief in the possible, but he still wouldn't let me go. He pulled me into him until I was straddling him, refusing to break the connection of our bodies.

It was a long time before our breaths eased into something that might have been mistaken for even. How could the sustenance of our body be considered steady when our world was hanging off its axis? We were rhythmic, in sync, but completely devastated.

"I'm sorry I hurt you. I wish I could have found a way around it. I'm a coward, because I don't want to live without you, and I couldn't have made him pay and get away with it without doing what I did. Do you understand?"

I nodded on a sob. My face buried in the crook of his neck. He could feel my tears as surely as I felt his essence soaking around us.

"I love you, Amy. Do you believe me?"

I nodded, but this time, my assent was slower.

I knew he loved me relatively, but how could I account for every element against which that emotion was to be qualified? Todd felt the hesitance too, because he pulled me away to stare into my eyes. His eyes were the blue I remembered... the tortured pools of indigo from the Caribbean that assured me of his love without having to say the words. I just had to accept it... believe him.

"Believe me, Amy, because it's the truth. I will kill, steal and lie for you," he said. There was no need to be self-conscious of the tears. Todd never even saw them. "Maybe I love you too much, or not enough, but I won't leave you. Call it whatever you like. Just know that I won't lie to you, and I won't live without you. So if I have to, I will die for you. Believe that."

I had never been more torn about anything in my life.

TWENTY-TWO

For someone whose sense of purpose hinged on making it to Paris, I had never really given much thought to what the city would be like. I knew it had been spared much of the devastation Berlin had witnessed at the end of World War II. I had stopped in Germany many times on my way to places like Afghanistan, Iraq, Yemen, the Emirates, Qatar, Egypt, and Somalia, but I had never been to Paris.

My father had planned for me to visit, but tragic events had derailed those plans. As an adult, I'd never had a reason to go until I'd found the end of my father's trail there. I knew he had used our embassy in the City of Lights as a sort of base while en route to other destinations. Recently I had learned he'd met many of his assets there, tended his garden in the hunt for an American traitor.

Mohammed Idalat Al-Zuwaid, MIST, from the Libyan National Army

Hosaam Tawfeek, BLUEBELL, from the Palestine Liberation Organization

Saint Michel Mabeko, HYDRANGEA, from the Zaire People's Revolutionary Party

Lucien Hakizimana, LILAC, from the Rwandan Patriotic Army

Blerim Nesimi, IRIS, from the Kosovo Liberation Army.

I had planned to work my way into our embassy there. It was a coveted and highly competitive post, and so I had tended my professional reputation diligently, and at the first opportunity, accepted Todd Birch's marriage proposal, regardless of my personal misgivings. Nothing had gone according to plan, but months later, I found myself on board a private jet, paid for by Uncle Richard, on our way to Paris Le Bourget airport to start a honeymoon.

If the charter was a reflection of Richard's commitment to our marriage, then he had outdone the bride. A business class upgrade was the high water mark of my decadence. I'd once slept eight hours straight on a C-17 aircraft, and it was one of the best sleeps I'd ever had. Granted I'd been assigned a sidewall seat – prized real estate compared to the five-a-row palletized alternative.

Although I did have an appreciation of nice things, the exaggerated opulence of the Gulfstream jet made me uncomfortable. I would have been a fool to imagine this was a gift from a loving foster father; it was a down payment.

Whatever the price to be paid, Todd seemed remarkably unconcerned – downright at home, the more I considered it.

"Is everything alright, Amy?" he asked, leaning across the narrow aisle to caress my leg.

I didn't even have the excuse of blaming the crew for my visible discomfort. The pilots were retired Air Force – I knew because they took the time to introduce themselves, instill complete confidence in their abilities, and even offered to show us around our destination city if we liked. The cabin crew was the tanned, built, ultraviolet toothed, Scandinavian variety that predictably lingered on Todd for unnecessary periods of time. I couldn't complain however, because Todd was completely devoted today, according our steward the barest attention to avoid appearing rude, even if he was clearly barking up the wrong tree... batting for the opposite team.

I couldn't hide the fact however, that even the warm embrace of the plush cream leather made me uneasy.

"Just wondering how much this cost," I answered as truthfully as possible, because there was no point pretending all was well. Todd knew me.

"Don't worry about it," Todd said, which disturbed me no end. Not only the fact that he didn't think I should trouble myself, but mostly the fact that he seemed completely unconcerned as he reclined his seat and went to sleep.

I didn't close my eyes for a minute out of the seven-hour flight. All night and well into the European morning I scanned every niche and surface as if some clue to Richard's motivations was present there in the aircraft, like a ticking bomb I had to find before it sank us. I'd felt safer on my way to Iraq in 2003.

A car service awaited us on the tarmac at Le Bourget, as if the chartered flight wasn't already too much. The Mercedes might as well have been a limousine with privacy partition raised. Our English-speaking chauffeur was efficient, non-conversational, bordering in fact on invisible, which I greatly appreciated. I was busy mentally tallying the hidden cost.

Even at the Hotel George V, Todd seemed to take everything in stride, ignorant or deliberately oblivious to the fact that Richard might have had someone killed – possibly a Saudi prince – in order to secure the Penthouse for our relatively last-minute trip. On the eighth floor, our apartment was done in shades of gold and white – a reminder that a shitload of the former was required to pay the two-week bill, and that the former would closely resemble the ghostly complexion inspired by said bill.

The grey of the early winter afternoon outside was easily dispelled by the abundance of light in the reception area. It was not unlike walking into a solarium where the best of the outdoors had been captured and brought in… a solarium with Italian marble floors that doubled as an art gallery. Designer floral arrangements, chandeliers that mimicked royal gardens of by-gone eras existed seamlessly next to priceless pieces of art, and a mix of Louis XVI and contemporary furniture.

Each room opened onto the terrace, a space lush with both green and light. It was surprisingly quiet – within walking distance of the Champs Elysée, but far enough removed to allow the ever-present sounds of crowds and traffic to die a natural death. The sights however betrayed our centrality – the Eiffel Tower, the spire of the American Cathedral, and in the distance the Montparnasse Tower visible from the south-facing exposition.

The moment we were alone, Todd took me in his arms. We were in the bedroom – a supremely restful place that was wasted on me. My heart was pounding in my chest, and from Todd's glance as he pulled me astride him onto the bed, in my throat too.

"It's a lot," he said. It was such a gross understatement I couldn't resist the opportunity for a humorless laugh. Todd nodded. He knew. "Richard thinks he failed you."

I sighed, but my body tensed as we warmed up to the subject of the price.

"It shouldn't surprise you that I confronted him about what happened with ..."

He couldn't finish, but from the way he avoided my eyes while gently massaging my back, I recognized the battle between guilt and anger. Why Todd should feel guilt at events that occurred a lifetime before he had strolled, cigar in hand, into mine still eluded me. Of course it didn't help that I'd thrown the rape at him, deliberately hurt him by drawing a parallel between the assault and his treatment of me one day.

Yes, I knew he had confronted Richard. Richard had called me almost immediately after the fact to bemoan the damage done to their relationship. All because Todd didn't agree with Richard's handling of the matter. But really, what else could have been done? Adam Rutherford III was the son of Adam Rutherford II – the then Secretary of Defense. Besides, I had intimated consent, because Adam had done me a favor really – woken me up, renewed my purpose to live.

It was irrelevant however. Adam was killed in a motor vehicle accident not long after – a combination of speed, cocaine, alcohol and I believed, Richard.

"Adam," I filled in the name of my rapist.

Our eyes met. I watched as he painfully swallowed every emotion that name conjured. "This doesn't cover it," Todd said, gesturing to the palace around us. "Doesn't come close. But he doesn't know how to say 'sorry'."

I nodded, because he was right. Richard didn't know how to apologize. He had also failed me; he should have kept his promise to find the people who had killed my parents.

"He told me your parents stayed here for their honeymoon... in this room almost thirty-three years to the day."

I didn't know that. It made me look around with new eyes, imagining them here, alive, young and happy. It didn't assuage all my reservations about the place though. My mother was a tobacco heiress, accustomed to fine things. Our house was a custom-built wedding gift from her father, who had died the year after my birth. His business interests were taken over by his partners, the compensation for which significantly augmented the trusts he had established for us. I'd rarely thought of my mother's money... had very little use for it. I required little to be comfortable.

Besides, the money couldn't buy the one thing I wanted more than my parents' life back – the life of the man who had taken theirs.

We were so different, she and I. Her influence on me was limited to some of her expressions – things like, 'God knows' that my father found amusing and which I copied just to put a smile on his face. She would have made it a point to visit the church looming outside the hotel, even if she would have to do so alone.

My father didn't believe in an all-knowing god, which was ironic because he was a strong believer in sin.

"Why does the world need people like us?" my father would ask, hundreds of times during the course of nearly a decade of training.

"Because there are sinners," was always my answer. I knew it because he had first told me so when I was six years old.

"And?"

"It's our duty to right their wrongs and punish their sins."

Here he would press his lips together. "And what are the wages of sin, darling?"

"Death, Father. The wages of sin is death."

He would nod, and I would hold my breath waiting for my reward. He kept it from me... five seconds stretching into ten... his cheek twitching the longer he tortured me. And then finally, he would smile at me, and if I had died in that moment, they would have buried me with a smile on my face.

"You are a rose," he would say, drawing me close. "My beautiful little rose."

I was his rose and my mother was an angel... so pure and good and weak. An angel of mercy, he called her.

"I know this will never be enough, but I thought it might be good for you to experience another place where they were happy. It might help you to move on... live like they would want you to... like they did."

Our eyes collided, and I knew the price of this room at least. Todd's hands on my hips were light, casual for now, but could become restraints if the need arose. Here, in this room, I wouldn't just have to face the fact of my parents' lives, but also their deaths.

"They're not coming back, Amy, and it's time for you to live."

Perhaps it was the lack of sleep, or another side effect of the hormonal imbalance brought on by the fertility treatments. My body didn't understand what it should be doing, caught in limbo between what I wanted it to do and what it had done for years. Whatever the reason, I was weepy – something I had never been before.

Todd's thumbs stroked my cheeks, wiping away the tears as they spilled over. It was a struggle that was becoming familiar, but no less difficult – holding onto those tears. I could feel my chin quivering, and I clenched my teeth to reinforce my crumbling restraint. I held my breath to prevent a sob, because then the floodgates would have crashed in.

"Shh," Todd tried to soothe me, but it only made it worse. His eyes boring into me made it damn near impossible not to melt. I was no more accustomed to the unreserved expression of his feelings for me now than when he had asked me again to marry him with an audience in tow. "It's OK."

It would never be OK, but he wouldn't understand that.

"It's not their house anymore. It's not their bedroom, and it's not your father's study. It's time to take your place," he said. "It doesn't mean you're replacing them, or that you're going to ever forget them. Knowing you, that will never happen. But you should be creating your own memories too."

He sounded so reasonable. He made it sound like such a simple thing to do. But he didn't know how full my heart was... so full that it was a struggle to find room. How could I fill it with more without first emptying it of what was there?

"We'll go slowly," he said, the tone of his hands on my hips shifting. They caressed with intimate intent where a second before they were soothing. *Here and now,* they seemed to say, which was fitting, because

Todd and I had begun in a bedroom, and all our new beginnings since took root there. It was a new year. "Promise me you'll try."

I nodded. I didn't have a choice. Our present arrangement, where Todd's belongings were installed in my parents' bedroom yet he resided in my bed with me, was unsustainable. He was living in the present with a wife trapped in the past.

"I love you," he said, before he kissed away my tears. He spent the rest of the day loving me until I believed it, giving me a reason to smile again. It was the start of the rest of our lives together, and Todd was determined to mark it with fireworks.

He did.

TWENTY-THREE

"You've been watching him for a long time," Todd said.

I was slow to admit it, not because the truth was hard to see, or out of a misplaced sense of modesty. I *had* been watching for a long time: every day, every waking hour for months now. It was what made me good at my job, and so I applied myself diligently; there was no shame in that.

I was slow to confess, because I was afraid. I was letting Todd into my secrets... giving him the chance to prove his devotion to me.

"I won't ask," he said, one hand reaching for mine. He pressed his lips to the knuckle of the finger that held his rings. His touch warmed me. I could always count on Todd Birch to heat my blood better than a propane fire and wool coat. I needed it too.

We were playing at hard-core tourists, braving the Parisian wind and the January cold to sip coffee and red wine *al fresco* at Les Deux Magots. In truth, we used the isolation of the sidewalk seats on a bitter cold day and the incessant traffic along the Boulevard St. Germain to conceal our conversation.

"I never ask," he said, his smile slipping as he resumed reading through the life and times of Blerim Nesimi. "It's enough that you want me to."

And I wanted Nesimi dead because he was a risk to me. He knew I was after Sergei Afanasenko. He had held his silence these past months, because he had nothing to lose and everything to gain from the Russian's eventual demise. His death would give Blerim Nesimi leverage. He would know I did it, and he would hold it over me until the day I died.

Better he die first.

"When do you want me to do it?" Todd asked after the waiter had topped off his glass and quickly scurried inside. I had tried the wine, but it had soured in my mouth. My glass was relatively untouched half an hour after we had taken our seats.

Everything about this conversation left me uneasy. I was taking a chance on love.

"Saturday is probably the best time."

Todd looked at me and smiled. He didn't have dimples, but if he did they would have said: 'Oh, do you? You've given a lot of thought to how I do my job, have you?'

Agreeably, Todd was the expert at executing, but I wasn't exactly a lightweight either. I'd done nothing but think about this for months now.

"Why's that?" Todd asked, and it was plain that he was humoring me. I shrugged, as if it didn't bother me that he was dismissive of my capabilities.

"For one, he visits Claudia on Saturday mornings while her father is busy opening up the café. When the father slips out at 6 a.m., you could slip in. He's an old creature of habit; he'll leave to get fresh milk first thing. Make the best of the cover of dark and the father's inattention to get inside the apartment. The target will use the tunnels running under Saint Catherine's Church to enter unseen. Put a bullet in his head while the girl is still asleep upstairs. If you can't walk out the front door, you could use the tunnels. They'll lead you to the courtyard storage shed. Dress for mass so you can leave under cover of the faithful. In and out in under an hour. Simple."

Wine glass frozen near his lips, Todd stared at me over the rim while I toyed with the handle of my coffee cup. "Not bad, Koehler," he said with a smirk.

I shrugged again. There was nothing impressive about it. It's just what we did. I planned. We killed. I was more concerned with the ease with which Todd had been using that name over the past week. After the welcome he'd planned for me upon our arrival at the hotel, I was waiting for the other shoe to drop. One of these days he would insist on my taking his name. This time it wouldn't be a simple matter of accepting his brand. For him, it was about moving on. For me, it was a question of identity.

"Besides, I have some work I need to finish this weekend." I stuck my bottom lip out in a fake pout. "I'm afraid you'd be lonely without me."

Todd nodded, already making plans for his mini-Italian vacation. Naples was a two-hour flight from Paris. I would kiss him goodbye on Friday and welcome him with back on Saturday or Sunday.

He had everything he needed to achieve a clean job – Canadian passport, Nesimi's dossier, maps and guides, site information. He had three days to arrange the delivery of a firearm to his hotel in Naples – more than enough time for a man with Todd's resources. He didn't seem overly concerned with the logistics.

"Where to now?" Todd asked, closing the lid on my MacBook Air.

We'd already covered a few of the major sights since our arrival two days ago: Eiffel Tower, Arc de Triomphe, and Sacré Coeur. We planned on spending Wednesday morning at the Louvre, and the afternoon exploring Notre Dame and the tiny winding streets of the left bank.

I needed the rest of our afternoon to get some work done.

I had a run-in to make at the Grande Mosquée de Paris and then a stop at our embassy. Blerim Nesimi wasn't my only target. I'd done as much prep work as possible last night – or rather the early morning hours – while Todd slept. Honeymoon or not, Don Blitzner still had to get his money's worth. Thankfully, our embassy resources had been put hard at work filling in the Haddad household's schedule.

"I'm not sure how long I'll be. If you prefer, you can strike out on your own while I work."

Todd pulled out his Galérie Lafayette map of the city. "Where are you going?"

I hesitated. I wasn't accustomed to this… accountability. "Why?"

"We're in a foreign country on our honeymoon and you're taking off. I understand you have to work, but it would nice to know where you'll be and when to expect you." Put like that it seemed like a reasonable question.

"Around Place Monge," I said, because as reasonable as he might be, I was too accustomed to my independence to hand it over on a silver platter. I wasn't the only one with adjustments to make.

Our eyes met and held for an extra second before Todd nodded. He returned to his map, but the crinkle in his brow said he wasn't comfortable with my evasion. "There are a couple of things I'd like see around that area anyway."

I met that remark with silence, forcing Todd to confront it after it stretched awkwardly between us. "There are the botanical gardens," he said with an easy shrug. "It might give me some ideas for our home."

"That wasn't on the itinerary."

Todd folded his map and reached across the table to grasp my hand. Even through our gloves I could feel his energy and mine joining – the physical a reliable bridge across the divide created by our wills.

"No, but the gardens at Versailles are. We can do either or both. I would like to be near you today, there's nothing more to it. So if you're going to Place Monge, I would like to visit the botanical gardens. Depending on how long you are, there's also the Natural History museum and the Roman amphitheater nearby."

I nodded, and for the time being we allowed the dust to settle around us. We walked to metro line ten, which we rode to Jussieu, and anyone who saw us would have thought we were a normal couple, in love, in the most romantic city in the world. Bundled against the cold and walking hand-in-hand with Todd, I almost felt it too. We kissed on the platform while waiting for our train, because it was acceptable, fitting, and we had company. We parted just inside the pedestrian gates to the park, kissing slowly under the watchful eyes of the stone lions.

The rest of my day was devoted to twisting another man's love for a woman into something evil, a weapon to be used against him.

I had never been there before, but the Grand Mosque struck a familiar chord that I could not attribute to the intelligence reports I had pored over for weeks. It was open and welcoming – more so than many other mosques I had visited. For one thing, I was not shrouded in yards of black cloth, as much to conform to the standards of modesty as to conceal my identity. No one was watching for me here.

Secondly, I could hardly understand the fast-flying words of the faithful. I was fluent in Farsi, conversant in Dari and Pashto, and could hold my own in the Gulf States. The dialect of the Maghreb however was as much a challenge as the French floating above my head.

Thankfully, this was one of the places I could safely play the oblivious tourist card without risk of a confrontation. Camera in hand and fee paid, I navigated the open areas of the mosque, seemingly enthralled by the Moorish architecture: the inner garden with its fountains, groomed hedgerows, sunken pools, and rows of cypress trees. There were a few other visitors, stragglers of a concluded tour, whom I used for cover as much as my rudimentary French permitted. I loitered between the rows of Corinthian columns, demonstrating marked interest in the mosaics and calligraphy with their familiar tones of brown, green, blue and white, representing the progression from earthly to holy. Todd with his red cashmere scarf would have stood out like a sore thumb – something I wanted to avoid as I scanned the faces for Selim Haddad.

A young man seated next to a wall of intricately latticed wooden doors guarded the shoes of those inside the prayer rooms, while a couple of white-robed sentries stood outside the office of the rector, keeping a casual but watchful eye on the visitors. At precisely 3:30 p.m., my target emerged from the usher's office – a Shia face among Sunnis. It was a relief knowing I wouldn't have to troll the small confines of the space two days in a row. It had been hard enough shaking loose of Todd; I knew I wouldn't be lucky enough to elude the notice of the watchmen.

I left Selim to shake hands and offer farewells, but passed close enough to match the face with the photos I had memorized. I had already identified the neighboring Muslim bookstore as the place for our meeting, offering both shelter from the January cold and privacy while I rocked Selim's world.

While he concluded the social niceties, I made my way across the street to the small park and children's playground. The shaded, enclosed green space was used as a gathering place for members of the congregation, a place where *zakat* and *sadaqah* were given. While children played ping-pong and ran up and down the slide, alms were given to the destitute, hand-outs and offers of casual employment were offered to the marginalized young men, all under the shadow of the adjacent police health services office.

A lone woman was doubled over on the pavement outside the park, forehead nearly pressed to the cold concrete. Selim had been photographed doling coins to the women who often gathered there. On such a cold day, this one seemed too desperate to pass by. I spent a few minutes pretending to read the postings on the notice board before making my way to the woman, arriving moments before Selim.

"Do you speak any English?" I asked the woman, while depositing a few euros in her donation plate.

She nodded rhythmically, nearly knocking herself out in the process, and muttered her thanks in thick Derija. She didn't understand a word I'd said. I turned to Selim as he dug inside his pockets for loose change.

"How about you?" I asked. "Can you help me, Saad?"

I had the element of surprise, and it showed on Selim's face. I would bet he hadn't been called that in twenty years. He'd been 'Selim' the moment he arrived in France; it was even the name on his asylum papers.

He unfroze slowly, counted out a couple of euros and dropped the coins in the woman's plate. She hadn't completed her thanks when the money was cleared away, disappearing into the folds of her tattered coat.

"I'm sorry. You've mistaken for someone else." Too late, he realized the English rolled off his tongue.

"My apologies," I replied with a forced smile. "I'll find someone else to save Adeline." I shrugged, pulling the strap of my purse higher on my shoulder. The casualness of the move belied the commitment to save anyone's life.

I crossed the street, deliberately making my way to the bookstore. As expected, he followed me with his eyes first. After a cautious look around to find anyone else who might be watching, his legs ate up the distance between us. As much as he might hate giving in to me – because we both knew nothing good would come of our chat – it was a risk to ignore me.

I knew who he was. I knew about his family. I had found him once and could obviously do it again. There was less harm in learning what I had to say than to live in fear for the next twenty years. That was why he had left Lebanon: he wanted to live without fear.

I was perusing a book on the major sins when he tried to corner me in the back of the store. For the son of a terrorist, Selim was peculiarly inexperienced at inciting terror. He was like a domesticated hunting bird that had forgotten how to use its talons.

"Do you know who I am? Do you know that I can have you arrested for making threats against my wife?" Trying to shriek into the wind when my hand was already wrapped around his throat. In following me, he had already revealed his weakness. He was old enough to be my father, and perhaps thought if he relied on an authoritative tone, I would quail. That conflicted with the quiet, unassuming man I knew him to be.

Brown hair, thinned out on top; kind, brown eyes made owlish by the lenses of his silver, wire-rimmed glasses; a square face framed with a greying beard; prominent laugh lines drew the picture of a man who lived free of the shadows of his past. His clothing was modest like the rest of him: black pants sticking under a black wool coat, and a wristwatch with a brown leather strap. Selim Haddad had blended seamlessly into Parisian life despite his *zebibah* – a prayer bump – and the darkened skin surrounding it. It stood out prominently in his otherwise pale face. His brother had a *zebibah* too - bumps on the forehead acquired, in their case, from prostration during prayer – a sign of piety.

Beneath the façade of the gentleman shaking his fist in outrage at me, as if to shout *'Eh, ça va pas!'* was a brilliant nuclear chemist. A man who, with the right motivation, would tell me what I needed to know to break his brother.

"Do you want to save your wife, Saad?"

"My wife is safe. What are you talking about? And stop calling me that!"

"She is for now, but she won't always be."

"Who are you?" he asked, forcing the exasperation to the forefront, trying to hide his genuine fear.

"No one important… not like the people you know."

"I don't know what you mean. Will you say what is on your mind and be done with it? I don't have time to waste."

And Selim was right. Neither of us had time to waste. Besides, I did not believe Selim would be convinced to cooperate in a day. He had no reason to believe what I would tell him. Not yet.

"I have reason to believe your family is in danger."

"You already said as much."

"Your father had a fatwa issued against you some years ago …"

Selim scoffed. I didn't blame him. It was a twenty-year-old judgment with no teeth in his civilized world.

"One of his pupils is coming for your family."

Selim watched me caress the spine of the hard cover, his eyes lingering on the title. "Why now?"

"Why not now? You are comfortable and your guards have become complacent. You have nothing of value to them anymore."

"Do you know who I am? Do you know what I do?" he asked with a bitter laugh. A more naïve woman would have missed the ring of untruth and the fact that he couldn't meet my eyes.

"I know exactly who your are. You turned your back on your family and blamed it on a woman so you could live like a prisoner in a new country. You work for your jailers, but they would never entrust you with their secrets because of your past. They guard you so you won't run to the rogues like your father did … not that you really could anyway.

"Your father is a terrorist who runs a school for terrorists. He has vowed to kill you and your wife to restore his family's honor. You're a man with a death sentence hanging over his head. That is what you are, and I am here to tell you that there is really no place safe for you, Saad."

I watched the smile fade slowly from his face. He could try to hide in plain sight for the next twenty years, but he would never truly convince himself that he was safe. It was one thing to face his own mortality, which was why he led a good, clean life according to tenets of his faith. He fasted, he made *salat* (prayed five times a day), he paid *zakat*; he didn't drink, gamble, steal or cheat. He hoped that one day, if he were killed while performing the Hajj for example, these acts would atone for his other sins. But he was not prepared to make his wife and children pay for his transgressions.

"What do you want?"

"I want to stop your father."

So soon, Selim was back to ridicule. He dragged his eyes over me like I was a broken knick-knack at the Montreuil flea market. *'You?'* his eyes seemed to ask. But he wouldn't give credence to the notion by reinforcing it with words.

I shrugged. "Your wife is going to die," I said, adjusting the strap of my bag as I pulled out a simple ballpoint pen. Inside the cover of the tome expounding the seventy great sins of Islam, I jotted ten digits, beginning with the mobile designator 06. It was a disposable number purchased for this express purpose, untraceable, and after Saturday, totally useless. "Call me when you're serious about saving her."

I held the book out for him, but he didn't take it, eyeing it with more suspicion than he had accorded me throughout our encounter. I shrugged again, pandering to his poor opinion of me. I was a kid in his eyes, one playing at grown-up games. I re-shelved the book and turned to leave.

"You can't do that," he called after me, gesturing at the defaced property. His conscience wouldn't support leaving the damaged book now, and he would consider it an act of charity to take it off the storeowner's hands... if he couldn't get me to reconsider.

For all he knew, I had just threatened his wife's life, but he thought I would lose sleep over a book that cost fifteen euros?

"You'll need it to find me," I said, backing out of the aisle. "Don't wait until it's too late."

I had arrived at the corner of rues Quatrefages and Lacépède when I heard footsteps hurrying behind me. I didn't need eyes in the back of my head to know it was Selim.

"Mademoiselle," he called, breath fogging as he panted the frigid air, touching the sleeve of his coat to his nose. "Not that I believe you," he began, which under less dire circumstances would have made me laugh. So it was a habit of his to chase down lunatics in the street to prolong their deranged tirades of self-importance?

"You've gone through a lot of trouble for a delusional kid," I said, chin jutting at the book under his arm.

"It would be a sin to cheat an honest man of his property. The owner might never be able to sell it at full price because of what you've done. And if someone did buy it without noticing the damage, they too would have been cheated."

I smiled. There really was no place for people like Selim Haddad in our world. It wasn't enough to atone for his sins; he had to save everyone he could. Maybe there was hope for his family yet – for Adeline and his children. For his brother – the Good Son – there was none.

"You never said what you want... only what you hoped for," he said. "So tell me. If I were to believe you, what would you do to save my family and what would it cost me?" He tried so hard to make it sound conversational, but there was no denying the dire undertones.

"The only thing that would save your family is the death or capture of your father."

Already he was shaking his head. "I do not know where my father is. I couldn't tell you anything about the man that I haven't already told anyone with ears."

"I know," I assured him.

"Then what do you want from me?"

"You may not know where your father is, but your brother does."

He shrugged. "What difference does that make? If you can't find my father, then you won't find my brother."

"That's where you're wrong," I told him, scanning the figures that moved along the street. "I have your brother."

He seemed confused for a moment, the grooves of his face deepening as he struggled to follow.

"Your brother is a prisoner, Saad. He's been a prisoner for several years now." Well, technically he was a detainee. He'd never been charged with a crime and likely never would.

"What?" he asked, eyes rounded in shock. "When? How?"

I shook my head. "It doesn't matter. What's important is that he knows where your father is, and I want him to tell me. You have to make him tell me."

He nodded quickly, swallowing deeply, eyes sweeping my frame with new appreciation. "Of course I will do what I can. When can I see him?"

"You can't."

"Wh... why not?" He asked, tugging the edges of his coat closer to his body. The buildings were doing a poor job of blocking the breeze, and even I longed for a brisk walk to the metro to find warmth.

"Because that's how it is. You tell me how to persuade him and if he does, I will find your father." I could tell I was losing him. He had no reason to trust me other than my willingness to walk away, which might have been a ruse as far as he was concerned. "Think of Adeline, Saad. Your wife and your children are your family now. Will you abandon them too?"

"You're crazy," he said. "I don't know you. Why should I believe anything you've said?"

I dipped into my purse again, feeling around for the pointed edge of the envelope without taking my eyes from Selim's face. It was hard to miss, a nine-by-twelve manila envelope, the biggest thing in my purse. I ignored his outstretched hand, and instead pulled out an eight-by-eleven photo. It was a headshot of Mohamed al-Mohamed... what Selim might have imagined his brother would look like twenty years after they had parted. His head was shaved and free of the takiyah, his beard shaved to the skin, his orange jumpsuit visible to the shoulders where the photo ended.

He shared many of his brother's features: a square face, coffee colored eyes, softly greying hair thinning in the middle, and zebibah – the mark of the devout. Mohamed's features were ravaged by his confinement however, appearing gaunt and nearly emaciated in the photo. What was different was their expressions. While Selim's was contorted with sadness at the moment, mourning the condition of his brother, one could clearly see in Mohamed's fierce expression – the eyes that would have killed if they could, the stubborn set of his jaw that hinted at the reasons for his deplorable state– the driving force to destroy.

"Mohamed," Selim gasped, reaching for the photo. I deliberately held it out of reach. Saad's DNA was used to identify his brother. If the French hadn't told him that his brother had been captured four years ago and was being held at Guantanamo, then I wouldn't leave behind proof that undermined their relationship.

"What have you done to him?" Selim asked with tears in his eyes for the brother who would have considered it an honor to kill him.

"Nothing he wouldn't do to you." I gave him a moment to come to terms with that truth. "They're coming for your family, Saad, and he's the only one who can stop them." I waved the photo at him again, wishing I had brought the one of his wife too. There was nothing like a visual reminder of what was at stake.

He blinked and a tear rolled down his cheek. When he tore his eyes away from the place where I tucked the photo, he raised them to mine. All the hopelessness of his position was there to see.

"You're not just any American. You are the worst of them to hold him in that place, without rights, without hope."

I offered one of the empty smiles I'd been practicing since my marriage to Todd made them necessary. "So now we both know who we are."

"I will not help you abuse him. Do you know it is a sin to spy for the enemy of the Muslims?" he asked, outrage slowly building.

It was time for me to go.

I tilted my chin towards the book he still held securely under his arm. "Then it's a good thing you make *salat*, from Friday to Friday, from Ramadan to Ramadan, making atonement for what has passed between them," I said, which might very well have been a quote from the book he hoped would buy him a place in heaven. *"As-salaam 'alaykum, Saad."*

TWENTY-FOUR

I think I understood the draw of Paris on my father. The city was alive with history, culture bursting from the seams, and on every street, corner and alley was an opportunity to learn. One could visit a hundred times each year and discover a new reason to be enthralled. It was the perfect place for people operating in the shadows but hiding in plain sight.

Take the embassy for example. The public entrance sat prominently on the Place de la Concorde, facing the Obelisk of Luxor and Hittorf's stone, cast iron and bronze fountains; with the National Assembly and Eiffel Tower in the background. The Tuileries gardens and the Orangerie – home of Monet's Water Lilies – were a stone's throw away to the west. To the east was the most famous street in the world, the Champs Elysée. At the north end of the block was the church dedicated to Mary Magdalene, just shy of the chic Place de Vendôme, surrounded by designer shops.

To the naked eye, the face of America's operations in the country was on show, surrounded by major landmarks. The façade conformed to the French sensibilities of urban planning and order, but also addressed US security concerns in the post 9/11 world.

Ensconced on a tree-lined, cobble-stoned avenue and adjacent to the large green space of the Champs Elysée gardens, the black guard rails that regulated pedestrian access along the public pavements seemed almost decorative. Iron-spined stone bollards, color-coordinated sentries that matched the gravel beds from which black-trunked trees sprang, were tightly arranged to restrict motorized access to the perimeter wall. Gendarmerie vans and mobile security posts littered the sidewalk, the men in blue a visual deterrent to loiterers but not much else. It was an arrangement that suited our purposes fine. The installation on Avenue Gabriel was only a face.

Our priority assets were much less conspicuous. Often couched in close proximity to valuable local targets, their security was less visual but more effective... hiding in plain sight. The people who worked inside them came and went, melting in the steady stream of unremarkable faces while operating in the shadows.

Lying in the shade of the French Naval Ministry, my destination on a cold Tuesday afternoon was the brain of the organism, located somewhere on Avenue St. Florentin. It figured on the evacuation plan of only a select few from Avenue Gabriel, a veritable last stand during only the direst situations. From the outside, it looked like any other building constructed in the French style: pale stone raised around a cobblestone courtyard, and French windows offering the illusion of openness.

'Nothing to see here. Nothing of interest,' it seemed to say, and yet the surrounding area was one of the few in the city totally devoid of parking spaces for anything larger than a moped. The street-facing windows were blacked out and covered with spike-tipped black spires, while the wall sconces housed more than just light fixtures.

There was nothing about our escort inside the building that announced a military occupation... at least not to the casual observer. We, the people operating the shadows, had the uncanny ability to smell our own though. Todd and I were separated, him to amuse himself with others like us on down-time, while I was led deep into the cerebral cortex, an area devoid of natural light and sound.

My contact was Sergeant Ben Shue, an engineer assigned to the construction of my car bomb. He'd spent the three years studying IEDs in Iraq, Afghanistan, and most recently Libya and Syria. I couldn't argue with his expertise, but his conscience was as constricting as a third body. We managed to agree on a VBIED (vehicle born IED) out of necessity, the need for detonation control and authenticity paramount. Every other factor was a source of contention.

For Sgt. Shue, the IED was a weapon of war – a cheap alternative to artillery. In consideration of his European hosts, he was more inclined towards a device with aural bang and little bite. For my purposes, the bomb was a tool of intimidation, which would not be achieved if the weapon were deemed to have failed. It was imperative that Selim be impressed with his father's determination to kill him.

And a nuclear chemist who had been reared at the knees of a terrorist engineer during a war that on average was marked with the deployment of twenty car bombs every month wasn't going to be fooled by a firecracker. He would be the first to recognize the work of one of his father's pupils.

Sgt. Shue also betrayed his humble beginnings with the vehicle he had selected to deliver the mechanism. The Peugeot 306 was a French staple that in his eyes was inconspicuous. Outside the Baranets' home however, it would have been an eye sore.

"What's the point of a shriveled poison apple? Nobody's going to buy that shit," I differed. "We need a Mercedes E class." I watched his eyes bug as he tried to hold in a gasp. I tapped the screen where a stolen two-year old model was pictured. "It's low riding and long enough in the back for proper concealment. Put darker tints on it and it'll fit right in."

After a minute he nodded, but with obvious difficulty. His mind wandered to all the adventures he could have in a car like that. He probably had a Mustang or a Charger back home, a car he would have bought with his sign-up bonus so he could fuck his girlfriend in the back seat.

We agreed on a location where I would pick up the car on Friday morning. The pick-up spot was a few blocks from the St. Lazare station, which was heavily monitored because of the sophisticated transportation network running through the area. It was also a high commerce district, into which the person tasked with delivering the bomb could quickly blend. I didn't want him blending too well though.

"Who will be responsible for delivery?"

"Not me," Sgt. Shue laughed.

It was a valid point. Even a good bomb was unpredictable, and knowingly getting on top of one, driving it through a city of two million people was a sobering decision. There was no question of using a proxy bomb – a third party under duress – though, because of the proximity of the security forces and the uncertainty surrounding the movement of the targets.

Not wanting to leave anything to chance, I drew up a profile for Shue: Middle Eastern male; late twenties to early thirties; low, neat beard and thick dark hair covered by a black baseball cap; dressed in high collar, black or tan leather jacket, black t-shirt and generic blue jeans. He was a comfortable anomaly – not quite marginalized youth from the suburbs; not quite Indo-Pakistani Shia on a mission – the perfect suspect.

"Do we have anyone on call that fits the bill?"

"Possibly."

"Make sure he doesn't know what he's carrying," I said, which earned me a narrow-eyed stare from Sgt. Shue. He was unnerved by how comfortable I was with these arrangements. "It's not like we're taping his hands to the wheel and chaining him to the pedals. It's a simple delivery."

"Right," he drawled, sifting through his memory, trying to understand how someone like me could be so matter-of-fact about setting off a bomb in the heart of Europe. Of course I never said that was what we were doing. But he wasn't a fool. Why else would I source from him? "Where did you say you were from again?"

I hadn't, and I doubted Blitzner had either. It was better if people like Sgt. Shue could not put both a name and a face to things like this. He'd received an order and I wasn't going to fill in any blanks for him.

"Keep your head down, Sgt. Shue." I tilted my chin to the profile sheet. "And make sure he does too. The surveillance potential is high."

I patted his arm in farewell, deliberately avoiding contact with his hands. He was an explosives expert, I couldn't be sure what residue he carried with him.

It was dark and cold as Todd and I strolled along the Champs Elysée en route to our hotel. The noise of incessant traffic and crowds of mostly tourists was a welcome distraction during the thirty-minute journey. We held each other, sharing warmth, but walked in silence.

I had more than just the weight of a ticking bomb on my mind. I knew that at that precise moment, Sergei Afanasenko was putting his son to bed, wishing him goodnight before heading out to *Lido*. The club was five minutes on foot from our hotel. As much as I would have liked to walk up to the man who had all the answers I needed and had waited a decade for, I knew I could not. It burned a hole in my chest knowing that he was so close, that he would live one more day, carefree and merry, and there was nothing I could do about it.

We had dinner at the hotel, fine cuisine that was wasted on me. My mind was five hundred meters away. After, Todd warmed me as best he could, heating my blood until my bones melted. The effects were short-lived however, and I spent a sleepless night listening to Todd's rhythmic breathing. By morning I had made myself physically ill, my stomach twisting painfully as I heaved into the toilet.

"Do you think it's something you ate last night?" Todd asked, pressing a cold towel to the back of my neck when I wished he would just go away. It would have been awkward asking him to leave however; I had burst in on him while he was shaving.

"I don't see how," I gasped during one of the breaks. "We ate off each other's plates and you seem fine."

"Well I do feel a bit nauseous."

That had more to do with watching me puke my guts out.

I shook my head. "I'm just tired. I didn't sleep well last night."

"You've been preoccupied," Todd added, pulling away a few stray wisps of my hair from my face. He thought he was being helpful, but I felt exposed.

"It's work." Not to mention he was flying to Italy tomorrow to kill Blerim Nesimi. "It'll clear up in a couple of days. I'll be fine."

It was almost prophetic. After a warm shower and some herbal tea, I felt brand new. I scarfed down a platter of pastries from Illy at Palais Royal before moving on to the Louvre. We spent hours staring at art, navigating the labyrinth of exhibitions like hundreds of other couples around us. With half the space still left unexplored, we took a taxi to St. Michel where we enjoyed a leisurely lunch in the shadow of the cathedral. It was cold enough to snow as we strolled along the boulevard St. Michel, perusing the wares on offer at the few little green kiosks that were manned.

Todd found a 1958 copy of Albert Camus' *L'Etranger*.

"You don't speak French," I remarked. In fact, to the horror and embarrassment of the hotel staff, his command of the language was even worse than mine.

"No, but I've read the English version. I don't think this will be misplaced in the library."

I looked at him. "Why?"

Todd didn't strike me as the type to keep college textbooks around. The only other books he had acquired since our marriage were clinical in nature – the DSM IV and treatment planners. Books he had acquired to bore deeper into my psyche. This latest acquisition smacked of that relentlessness too. I wasn't fooled by the pretext of fiction; Meursault and the themes he evoked were very familiar to me.

"Why not?" he countered.

I looked away, uncomfortable with his explanation. As we resumed our stroll, concealing the stiffness in my spine was the last thing on my mind.

"Amy," Todd called, pulling us to an abrupt halt. "It's a good book – one of the best pieces of French literature of the twentieth century. We're here in Paris," he said arms wide as if to encompass our surroundings. "It was there. We have a library. Why the fuck not?"

"It seems deliberate," I said.

"Well it's not." He had a knit cap pulled over his head, but seemed to forget it as he tried to run his gloved hands through his curls. "Just like we're not deliberately fighting in the middle of the street, in the goddamned cold, like those fucking lunatics over there."

He gestured to a couple several yards away who, like us, were hashing it out on the sidewalk. They seemed more dramatic however. By their dress – black on black with only the length of hair to distinguish the male from the female, as well as the faint strains of words that reached us, I judged them to be French. To top it off, the gentleman proceeded to kiss the fight out of his companion. It was such a clichéd scene that I couldn't help the smile that tickled my insides until it was finally free.

"Come on, baby. Don't let them beat us," Todd wailed plaintively before pulling me into his arms, bending me backwards over his arm, and made a production out of kissing me. His lips were cold against mine, but there was something refreshingly warm about our shared mirth.

"Have you had enough cultural emersion yet?" he asked against my lips, refusing my efforts to stand upright. "If not we can go back to the hotel and make love. But if you've had enough for one day, we can still go back to the hotel and I'll fuck you like the savages we are. What do you say, Mrs. Birch?"

I nodded. "OK."

We returned to our temporary home and did a little of both.

After a short break, Todd and I retreated to separate ends of our suite. It was a mutual, albeit unconscious decision. He had a man to kill and was chivalrous enough to exclude me from the details.

My plans, which had been set in motion months ago, were a source of near constant digestive discomfort. The incidence of queasiness increased commensurately with the approach of my deadlines.

Without informing her of my arrival in the city, I checked in with Angelika. Her position inside the Baranets household proved invaluable, because she was able to provide timeframes that I would have otherwise had to guess.

According to Angelika, she was scheduled to work the birthday party and leave by the time the family headed out at 5:30 p.m. for caroling. Self-absorbed with freedom and the potential to finally live her dream, she gave very little thought to my preoccupation with her routines.

My four remaining contractors and one unsuspecting bomb bait were scheduled to arrive on scene to decommission the Afanasenko security personnel, incapacitate Sergei, and extract Alexei and his parents. The RDV point – a pet food processing plant just outside the city in St. Denis – had been arranged by the cleaner. It was against my natural inclination to trust a man who had no qualms about committing murder-for-hire. However, it was precisely that quality that inspired my confidence in his judgment; nothing would cause this man to jeopardize his bottom line.

Sgt. Shue had come through with a courier that matched my profile, and the vehicle had been acquired and was being retrofitted to accommodate its cargo. The remote trigger would be ready for pickup first thing Friday morning. Finally, the intermediary responsible for managing Adeline Haddad reported arrangements were in place for a 4:45p.m. tour of her apartment on Rue de Liège. While the access code to building #35, had been obtained, there was in fact no newly acquired apartment in need of Mrs. Haddad's service. It was sufficient that her proximity to the blast be interpreted by her husband as a deliberate attack orchestrated by his father.

Eight hundred yards was the outdoor evacuation limit of a full-sized car bomb with an explosive capacity of one thousand pounds. Mrs. Haddad and the Parisian authorities had Sgt. Shue to thank for the fact that our IED would fall well below that capacity.

Every element was in place, and I should have been able to trust my careful planning and enjoy Todd's last hours before he left for Rome. He didn't need to be psychic to tell I was preoccupied however… so much so that I made myself sick again.

"Tell me what's the matter," Todd tried to coax. It was midnight and I was hunched over the toilet again, emptying my stomach of the cassoulet I'd had for dinner. "What's got you so worked up, Amy?"

"It's nothing," I said, but the protest sounded weak to my own ears. "Just nerves. It'll pass by the time you get back."

"What are you working on?" he asked, but it wasn't like Todd not to push.

"I can't tell you. I want to, but I can't. It's too risky."

"Do you think I would jeopardize your work, Amy?" he asked quietly after a long moment of simply sitting at the edge of the tub and staring at my back.

I turned to face him, blinking tears from my eyes. "No. I trust you not to. But don't expect me to break years of habit in a day either."

He nodded his understanding, but he didn't leave. He waited through another bout of retching.

"I hate seeing you like this," he said.

"I know you do," I replied when I could answer. "I'm sorry."

"You have nothing to be sorry about," he said, before finally leaving.

At the time, I believed him. But I soon came to realize that Todd had never been more wrong.

TWENTY-FIVE

The waiting was the worst. It made time seem at a standstill, not very different from the fine dust of snow that clogged the air like smoke and made it hard to breathe.

The stage was set, the extras standing in the wings awaiting their cues. It wasn't my first time in a directing role. I relied on my experience orchestrating for the US Army to execute a smooth run. On the face of it, it was like any other mission with Military Intelligence. At least that was what I told myself, hoping to quiet my churning stomach.

This was the most important production of my life. For one thing, the stakes were entirely personal and extremely high.

This time, I could not count on the protection of my government should the plans go awry. If caught, what I could count on was an extended stay at Fort Leavenworth. They would most likely spare me a lethal intravenous cocktail on account of my sex, but I wasn't certain that was an improvement over the alternative.

I had the area staked out hours in advance. I drank San Pelligrino and nibbled on olives and *crudité* at the corner bistro. The simple meal should not have affected me as it did, sending my stomach into convulsions, convincing me of the need for professional help. The neighborhood pharmacy was an unplanned but necessary stop.

The less people who remembered me being in the area, the better for me.

"Madam, êtes-vous enceinte?" the fifty-something pharmacist asked. I checked over my shoulder to identify the target of such an intrusive question. Except for one other patron, a male, browsing the hair restoration products, we were alone. "Madame?"

For a long minute I tried to understand what his question had to do with my request. I needed something to settle my stomach but couldn't find the Pepto Bismal. I had stress-induced indigestion; it was just nerves. I was about to set off a bomb in the middle of a residential neighborhood in the center of Paris.

What the fuck did pregnancy have to do with anything?

And then it hit me. I must have paled; I certainly felt dizzy. The pharmacist smiled at me sympathetically and led me to the homeopathic aisle. He bagged a pack of anti-nausea pills I had to stick under my tongue before discretely tilting his head in the direction of the pregnancy tests and pre-natal vitamins.

"C'est comme vous voulez," he shrugged, but stood and waited patiently for me to decide whether it was indeed possible that I was pregnant.

I had the vague sensation of nodding and watching as he made a selection for me. Just to be sure, I added two more tests of different brands, because the man seemed too eager for a positive outcome and I didn't trust the French further than I could spit. Then with a suggestion to see my doctor first thing and a cheery "Bonne chance," the man pushed me out the door.

On the short walk a few blocks away, I had the impression of knowing what a proxy bomb felt like. The paper bag in my hand might well have been a ticking explosive. I shoved it in the glove compartment of my rental car and tried as best I could to forget it. I still had a couple of hours to burn at the bistro before show time, but the last thing I wanted to know was whether I was carrying Todd's child while actively participating in the detonation of explosives. I tried to picture myself pregnant at Fort Leavenworth, but could not. In fact, I couldn't picture myself pregnant at all, regardless of how hard I had tried to achieve it. Placebo effect or not, the pills seemed to work, but just to be safe, I nibbled on pieces of baguette and swilled sparkling water.

Holding the waiter at bay with a crisp fifty-euro note and a seat at his smallest, out of the way table, I was well-placed to keep a close eye on the happenings on Rue de Liège. However, it was a struggle to keep my mind squarely focused on the organized chaos I was about to unleash. The loaded glove compartment pulled me like a knot I could not ignore.

Until Adeline Haddad walked right by me, wrapped in a tailored trench coat and cashmere scarf. If not for the click of her knee-high stilettos on the slick pavement I might have missed her. She looked like the kind of woman I wanted to be when I grew up, when all this was settled and I could try to give Todd the best of me. She looked like the kind of woman he deserved – beautiful, elegant, professional. Pure class. If she survived today, I promised myself to study her.

And then everything was moving much too fast.

Adeline's fake contact claimed to be delayed by a few minutes. The interior decorator paced the sidewalk outside #35 looking like the least likely prostitute. It was 4:55 and the snowflakes came thicker and faster, melting the moment they hit the ground.

Todd's snowflake – a name I had given Angelika on account of her pale skin, white blond hair, and blue eyes as clear as a glass of water – sent me the 'go' signal. The families were on the move.

The guests were leaving the Baranets' home in a steady stream of traffic, exiting the private road between #29 and #33 like a disorganized convoy. The last to leave would be the Afanasenkos. That wasn't a hard guess to make. For security reasons, their cars had deposited the family members and departed, idling these past five hours a block away on Rue de Moscoue. I thought that ironic considering that was the closest Sergei had come to his capital city in a decade – not that life in exile was particularly hard for him.

With Rues de Moscoue, Turin and Liège being one-way streets, there was only one way in and out, and I was strategically placed to notice the Mercedes Benz S-class vehicles – AMG for Sergei and Natalia, 600 for Alexei, both armored with run flat tires – as they passed. To avoid being sitting ducks in a traffic jam, the two drivers had to wait out the thinning of the birthday party crowd.

At precisely 5 p.m. they streaked by me, exceeding the speed limit on the narrow residential street by 10km/hour. Seventy-five seconds behind them, a blacked out, low-riding E-class crept down the street, the driver waiting for the procession and his final act to begin.

Managing the security of a family like the Afanasenkos was a delicate dance between routine and the unpredictable. Routine was required so the personnel learned their parts by heart. It seemed a contradiction that invited threats, but the balance occurred in so far as that personnel was also prepared for the unexpected.

Whenever the Afanasenkos ventured out together, Alexei's vehicle led the convoy in order to center all threats on the father, who was more likely the intended target of any comers. Equipped with one driver who, being armed also doubled as a bodyguard, it transported Sergei's most prized possession – his son – and his constant companion, a dedicated bodyguard. Sticking Alexei with the lion's share of security was also a deliberate act, motivation to squarely focus attention on the less secure father. As an added incentive, on occasions like these, the wife, Natalia and her armed shadow traveled with the son, doubling the perception of risk should one think to attack the dependents.

Following this script, the S600 had a human cargo of five – Alexei and Natalia, Alexei's driver, his and Natalia's bodyguards; while the AMG carried an armed Sergei and his driver.

My bomb bait thought his role was to create a fender-bender, but the four contractors waiting in the wings knew better. His death would commence the beginning of the end for Sergei Afanasenko, and – Don Blitzner hoped – Hasan al-Qasim.

At 5:03p.m. Adeline Haddad, daughter-in-law to al-Qasim, fished her cellphone from her designer purse. Before she could thumb a single key, the screech of tires and crunch of metal had her nearly jumping out of her skin. The cellphone slipped from her fingers as she spun in the direction of the duel between two Mercedes. She wasn't the only one curious about the crash. Within seconds, my waiter and a couple of patrons, the helpful pharmacist and a few local residents peering down from apartment windows gawked from a distance at the unfolding scene.

As one of the only persons actually on the street and in the vicinity, Adeline was strategically positioned to notice that the initial collision was harmless. As she bent to retrieve her phone, bemoaning the cracked screen, two car doors opened as drivers prepared to hurl insults at each other. A third vehicle – the one carrying Alexei and his mother – braked suddenly at the end of the street where it bisected a portion of Rue Amsterdam, prepared to render assistance if directed. One bodyguard alighted, surveilling the scene from a safe distance and recounting the events to the occupants. A fourth vehicle arrived on the scene, pulling in front of Alexei's transport in defiance of the one-way rule.

Then all at once my production unfolded with a flick of my thumb over a remote access key fob.

Before the bodyguard who was on foot could summon a protest, an explosion rocked the residential street, in what French investigators would later conclude was a botched terrorist attack and assassination attempt. Adeline Haddad, whose husband would argue she was the intended target, was knocked face first onto the ground by the shock wave, suffering a broken nose, facial lacerations and generalized bruising.

The blast had sucked the air from the immediate fifty feet before pushing it out four hundred feet with the force of a bullet from a gun. The impact shattered windows, twisted the frame on nearby vehicles, and shook the façade of the surrounding building, sending a cloud of glass, dust and metal fragments into the air where they mixed with the wet snow.

The bomb was all bang and little bite. There was very little in the way of structural damage to the neighborhood. But the E-class paid a considerable toll – a combination of both the blast and the resulting fire that consumed its interior despite having been fueled with only a few liters of gasoline.

Selim Haddad would recognize this as a slight deviation from his father's signature – so slight in fact that he would overlook it. The French authorities, unconvinced of a Middle Eastern terrorist connections, would dismiss its significance altogether, to the effect that it was accorded two sentences in the ensuing enquiry. In fact, the only mention of the fire was limited to explaining its deleterious effect on the evidence, including the destruction of the bomber's body parts and blood.

The suicide bomber was killed on impact. He was later incorrectly credited with shooting one bystander in the face seconds before detonation in a pointed statement of contempt.

In fact, that honor went to my contractor, a Senegalese by the name Youssef who arrived on the scene within seconds of the explosion.

Dressed to withstand the heat and a dearth of air, he efficiently played his part, eliminating Sergei's guard who had been injured in the blast.

The armored AMG had survived the explosion better than most other vehicles would have, but the fact that the driver's door was open at detonation caused the occupant to be severely shaken by the shock wave. A disarmed and disoriented Sergei was pulled from the back of the vehicle and dragged away from the scene before witnesses had come to terms with the unfolding scene.

The occupants of the S600 might have thought a rescue was underway, if given the chance. However, that was not to be. By the time Youssef had dragged a confused Sergei Afanasenko past them, dumping his body in the trunk of the car blocking off the end of the street then hopping into the rear passenger seat and speeding away, both bodyguards and the driver were dead.

The decommissioning of Alexei and Natalia's personnel was a team effort. My third and fourth contractors, a Portuguese and Spaniard by the names Rodelick and Manuel respectively, were an ad hoc team created by necessity of the contract. Manuel pumped two bullets into the head of the man who had exited the vehicle to render assistance if needed but had ended up knocked on his ass by the shock wave.

While confusion reigned in the immediate aftermath of the explosion, Rodelick had the driver's door open and Manuel, the front passenger's. The execution of the driver and the second bodyguard followed swiftly, with two bullets apiece. Two bodies were seamlessly stowed in the trunk of the S600 and a third in the backseat with a screaming Natalia and terrified Alexei, who watched Sergei's body being dumped in a trunk and driven from the scene. Unlike her husband, Natalia had very little to fear. Rodelick drove while Manuel kept a gun on the mother-son pair, as they eased onto rue Amsterdam twenty seconds behind Youssef and his driver.

Before the dust had settled, before Adeline Haddad could gasp a full breath into her air-staved lungs, it was over. Five men were dead, two in the middle of a Parisian residential street and three on their way to St. Denis for a meeting with my cleaner. Six months of preparation had taken only eighty seconds to unfold.

Night came early to Paris on the Orthodox Christmas day. With the distant wail of sirens playing in the background, the cries of the residents and patrons of local establishments on rue de Liege sounded even more poignant. It wasn't exactly the tinkling bells and joyous carols the Baranets had planned, but this was a day no one would soon forget.

I slipped away into the growing darkness to find my father's killer.

TWENTY-SIX

I knew what I would find in St. Denis. I had dreamt about it for weeks. Before that, I had fantasized about it for months. And even before that I had hoped for it for years.

I hadn't yet achieved what my father had expected me to do, but I was well on my way. Before the night was over, Sergei Afanasenko would pay for his sins.

Following the coordinates that had been shared with both my drivers, I arrived at the processing plant twenty minutes after the first car pulled in. The site of my interrogation was away from the face of the facility that my cleaner had arranged. Accessed by a private road – little more than a dirt track with thick woods on both sides – the gates of the facility were conveniently unmanned.

The risk of theft was low. The smell emanating from the facility was its own defense. Also, nothing short of a semi could haul away enough material for a profitable heist. It was also situated on the outskirts of a small town, the residents of which monitored the comings and goings of large vehicles. As a number of the households relied on the facility for their livelihood, it was in their best interest to note and report suspicious activity.

The passage of three passenger vehicles was below the threshold of their notice.

My final destination was the plant where the pet food was packaged. Cans of mush and sacs of meal were moved along conveyor belts, sealed and deposited into crates for inspection. Normally the place was a bevy of mechanized activity, the sounds of industrialization so heavy it drowned out the human presence.

There were four silos, one of which was used as a compost for the plant's waste. The others were used for storage of grain and other input in the production process. There was also a small water reservoir.

Far removed from human interference, even in the event of bone chilling screams, my cleaner could not have chosen a better location for what was to come. The compost could double as a dumping ground, and the equipment might prove useful in the extraction process. The surrounding woods were suitable for hiding evidence, be it vehicles or bodies. The dirt road was far removed from any public thoroughfare, and in the darkness that had fast descended with the thickening of the snowdrift, nearly impossible to find without specific intent.

At the time of my arrival, all was still. As expected, the gates to the restricted area were open. There was a box truck – a replacement for the Mercedes S600 that had been dumped near the Porte de Clignancourt with the bodies of Alexei and Natalia's guards. I parked my rental off the road, close to the tree line, and approached the vehicle with my firearm – an untraceable loaner courtesy of Blitzner.

As scripted, there was only one corpse inside the truck – that of my third contractor, Rodelick. He'd been shot in the back of the head… retired by Manuel.

There was no sound or movement outside as I made my way around to the eastern perimeter of the facility. There, in its designated spot next to the fence was the getaway car in which Sergei Afanasenko had been transported. I skirted a small puddle of blood, bits of bone and brain matter that were fast disappearing as the snow continued to fall. Soon it would all be covered up. But for now, there were the faint outline of footprints on either side of twin channels where the body had been dragged back to the passenger side of the nearby car. Two bodies were present and accounted for: the getaway driver and Youssef. This driver too had been executed in his seat by one of his passengers. And that passenger, Youssef, had been decommissioned by the last man standing, Manuel.

Satisfied with the progress of the severance package, I made my way to the packaging plant. There was a loading area with twin industrial roll up doors. They were wide enough to accommodate the forty-foot trailers into which crates of pet food were loaded for transport to wholesalers. I bypassed those, picking my way over the snow-covered concrete loading dock to the steel-reinforced pedestrian doors. The security system had been bypassed, but for all the monitoring company knew, the St. Denis facility had been closed and armed as usual at the end of the last shift at noon.

There should have been four bodies inside, but at first I only found two. For an interminable few seconds I was afraid the plan had gone incontrovertibly awry. It was a moment of self-doubt that had my blood turning to ice in my veins.

What if the blast had been too powerful for the AMG to withstand? I had left the vehicle mostly intact next to the flaming E-class, but what if the shock wave had so severely concussed the Russian that he had succumbed to his injuries? What if Youssef had further subdued him and had as a result caused his death? What if everything I had worked towards suddenly eluded me at the last minute?

There were no more leads.

Blerim Nesimi had given all he had... in every sense. The trail ended here with Sergei Afanasenko.

I turned to Manuel. "Where is he?"

"This way, señora." Manuel inclined his head in the direction of the steel staircase. The Spaniard's courtesy contrasted with the firearm he still had in hand, the eight-inch suppressor leading the way. I holstered my firearm to reassure him he had nothing to fear from me. It was a move he appreciated, acknowledging with another slight incline of his head. He did not disarm however.

I expected nothing less, but I wasn't afraid. Manuel's role wasn't over just yet. And he had not yet received payment.

"He is well?"

"Of course," Manuel responded, half-way to offense that I would question his professionalism. He would have alerted me the moment he realized the game was spoiled.

"And the woman?"

"There." He indicated a door across the open floor space, with stacks of crates and shelves full of sealed boxes standing on either side. The lights of the loading area were on, but from the room he indicated only silence and darkness emanated. "She too is well. As instructed."

There was a hiccup from the boy seated between us at the acknowledgement that his mother was alive. It was remarkable in its contrast to the silence that met news of his father's wellbeing.

"Please," I continued to address the man who stood before me, the epitome of style in a black coat, dark suit over a black open collar shirt, and black leather gloves.

His eyes were black, and judging by the dark shadow with only a smattering of silver that covered half his face, so was the hair under the black knit cap. He wasn't a naturally attractive man, but his image was a carefully crafted one that made up for his crooked nose, too full lips and beady eyes. Beneath the designer suit, he was fit, lean... and short, at barely five feet six inches and a buck fifty.

"I'll be there shortly."

He knew what came next, and like the good soldier he was, he marched up the metal staircase. The heel of his shoes clicked all the way to where Sergei was being held.

Like mine, the soles of his shoes were smooth. It made walking in snow difficult, but at least the imprint was impossible to trace. Manuel's were customized too, the added lift of the heels more than just an act of vanity; it was meant to confuse witnesses about his height, in the unlikely event there ever were any.

With Manuel out of sight, I was finally able to face the child. If I were any other woman I might have been moved by the sight of the boy before me, bound to a metal-framed chair with a hood placed over his head. He was only eight years old – a baby – and despite who his father was, an innocent one at that.

I had been afforded the opportunity to meet children – even at Alexei's age – who weren't half as innocent as him. Looking at him now, with a black hood over his head, dressed as he was in tailored dark slacks, an oxford shirt under a cashmere sweater, an authentic knotted tie, and dark wool coat, one might have mistaken him for an adult dwarf. It was indeed a departure from the three-piece suits he usually wore to school, but this was Alexei, dressed casually for a friend's birthday party.

I removed his hood. Like his parents, he was fair. His blond hair was cut somberly above his eyebrows. His blue eyes, red around the edges, took up half his face. His cheeks were uncharacteristically – for him at least – smudged, the tracks of dried tears prominent. He would have wiped them away if his hands were not bound. It was a child's face, dominated by eyes and cheeks, with a pert nose and puckered mouth rounding out the picture. But on Alexei, the corners of that mouth were permanently turned down, an occurrence for which I could not assume responsibility.

The child's sobriety hinted at his understanding of the facts that made him different from other children. Like me, Alexei had learned at an early age that he was not an average child. Unlike mine however, Alexei's father was a criminal.

I untied his gag then slid the blade of Bill, my Benchmade knife, between his wrists, severing the zip tie.

Once unbound, he did not move beyond massaging his wrists and wiping his cheeks on the sleeves of his coat. He took his time. He also did not speak.

"Alexei." He nodded. "I mean you no harm."

"You will let us go?" he asked, high-pitched voice at odds with his grown-up attire and the emotionless eyes he raised to my face.

"If I had my way. But that is a decision for your father."

"You want something from him," the boy said, devoid of even childish hope. It was as if he had known something like this might happen one day.

"Yes. If he loves you, as a father should, you have nothing to fear. You and your mother can go free."

The child looked away as the severity of the pronouncement rang through his head. After a long moment of silence, he raised his eyes to me.

"If it is money you want, I can give it to you. You don't have to do this."

I silently shook my head at him.

"What is it then?"

"Justice," I said.

The boy folded his hands in his lap and leaned into the back of his chair. "Then I fear none of us will leave this place alive," he said.

I nodded my agreement.

TWENTY-SEVEN

"My father taught me about justice."

I found a free chair matching Alexei's pushed against a wall. A few feet away were a desk, a PBX phone system, a calendar and an empty clipboard. From that post, a soon-to-be retiree tallied the crates as they were hoisted by forklifts and loaded into the containers.

"Mine too," I said and I pulled the chair close to Alexei's. The upholstery sagged as I sat. I didn't want to patronize the boy, but there was no point intimidating him either. The next few hours would go one way or the other, whether he feared me or not. Leaning forward with my elbows on my knees, we were almost the same height. "What did yours say?"

"Not say. Do. He killed Masha," Alexei said, and for the first time since his gasp at the news of his mother's survival, his emotions were plain for all to see.

I couldn't recall there being a Masha in the Afanasenko household. At first I thought she was a pet, but there were no animals in their home, because Natalia was allergic.

"She was my mother," he said, head bowed to hide his moist stare. "She was a mother to me, and he killed her. Buried her in the backyard with lime. He made me watch. That was justice for what she had done."

That would explain why there was no information on a Masha. Not only had she disappeared, all mention of her would have been forbidden among the family and staff.

"And what did she do?" I asked, not that it mattered anymore.

"She told," he confessed in a small voice. And then apparently in an act of defiance, he raised his eyes and voice to me. "She also suckled me. She would do anything for me. She loved me. Now I have only the mother who birthed me."

And birthed him Natalia had, but not much else. The people who guarded him were more family than his own mother. Now they were dead too.

"If you kill my father, you must kill me too."

I tilted my head, curious of the perspective of a jaded eight year old. "Why is that, Alexei?"

"Because if you let me go, one day I must kill you. That is justice."

I nodded and smiled, but not cruelly. "That is true."

"So you will…"

"No."

He looked at me then, looked deeply into me, trying to discern whether I was lying to him. I looked at him and saw what I might have been if my father was the monster Todd thought him to be. It was true that John Koehler was unconventional and could have been a hard man to some. But he had never been to me, which was what made the difference between myself at eight years old and Alexei.

Some lessons a parent should never teach their children. The world was a cruel enough place on its own.

"Why not?"

"Because I won't kill your father, Alexei. You will."

He didn't dismiss me as whimsical or ridiculous. In our world, patricide was well within the bounds of reality.

"And why would I do that?"

"To save the only mother you have left. And yourself." Our eyes held for a long time before he looked away. For the first time, he seemed interested in his location. He looked around the room, took in the crates and heavy machinery, noticed the high ceilings, the metal stairs leading deeper into the factory, the locked door behind which his mother was bound and gagged just like he had been.

"You would kill women and children?" he asked, proving himself to be advanced well above his years.

I nodded. "I would," I answered without hesitation, proving myself to be beyond guilt. That was for ordinary people.

"We're not like regular people," my father would say. "People like us can't follow their road, because it wasn't made for us."

But even ordinary people could surprise themselves when placed in extraordinary circumstances. And if ever there was an extraordinary circumstance, finally getting justice for my father was it.

"Would you like to see your mother before we begin?" I offered. I didn't have all night to get what I wanted from Sergei. The cleaner was coming at midnight, and Todd would be home by noon tomorrow.

"I don't need to."

"I think you should," I counseled. "It might be the last time you see her." I didn't want to scare him unnecessarily, but I wasn't going to lie to him either.

Alexei nodded and stood and I pointed him in the right direction. I followed, giving him a few feet for privacy.

Natalia's cell was little more than a closet. With a desk, two chairs and a filing cabinet stuffed inside, there was little room for much else. She was strapped to one of the chairs, her full-length blue fox coat and matching hat were draped over the desk. It wasn't the cold that had her shivering in her designer boots however.

The woman was distraught. Long after her tears should have dried up with the adrenaline surge, Natalia continued to sob wetly. At least her son understood that tears were no relief for what was to come; pity was a foreign notion in Sergei's work.

It seemed Sergei was more indulgent with his wife than his own son. Or, Alexei's understanding of the consequences of their lifestyle was superior to his mother's. Either way, one was expected to step into the patriarch's shoes, while the other's purpose was to blissfully enjoy the fruits of his crimes.

That was all about to change.

I allowed Alexei to speak with his mother in Russian. Giving them their privacy was the least I could do. Her hood remained in place however, along with her gag. In any case, he was more prepared than she to do the necessary.

Alexei was more of a threat than she would ever be.

Sergei had raised his son to be a man, long before his childhood should have ended, and now that it mattered, the boy would not disappoint.

Natalia's contribution to the exchange was to dissolve into more tears. These were different from the ones that came before however. I recognized the exact moment when it dawned on her that nothing would be the same again. Hope was like a physical presence that got up and walked out the room. Natalia's spirit was broken, her body racked by fresh despair. Her muffled wail was a funeral cry; her dejected nod permission to lower her husband's coffin into the ground.

Alexei turned to me and nodded.

With his mother plunged into darkness and shut in her cell again, I showed Alexei the way. He preceded me up the metal stairs and down the hallway Manuel had followed minutes before. A right turn; passage through a heavy steel door; down more steps, two sets this time; and finally the cold storage room came into view.

The door was flung wide open and held in place by a wall-attached anchor. Just inside the gaping doorway that was wide enough to accommodate a small forklift, strips of plastic sheeting were hung like curtains. On the other side of the curtains was Manuel, watching our approach with the same impassive expression with which he had shot the first bodyguard in the middle of a Parisian street. His firearm hung casually at his side.

I pulled up the collar of Alexei's coat before we stepped into the room. There really was no need for him to suffer – not even the cold air being pumped into the room from above. With the doors open for more than an hour now, the fans were working overtime. As intended, the whine of the motors filled the silence. It was another barrier Sergei's screams would have to overcome.

Crates were stacked twelve feet high with boxes, beginning against the walls and working their way towards the center of the room where a green forklift had been parked. The area immediately surrounding the forklift was bare, except for the plastic sheets covering the concrete floor. The nearest crates were more than ten feet away, the outward faces of which were draped in plastic.

The machinery was also covered in protective sheeting. The twin forks of the lift were raised to the very top of the mast. Perched atop those forks was Sergei Afanasenko, hands bound behind his back, a noose secured around his neck, legs spread and posture erect to maintain his footing. There wasn't much room for relaxation here.

He would have quickly realized that the steel beams that ran across the ceiling, supporting the shelves on which the crates had been stored, were capable of bearing his weight many times over. One slip of his handmade shoes and he would slowly hang. Unlike the rest of his family, Sergei was neither gagged nor blindfolded. What I needed from him required his ability to speak.

And I wanted to see terror in his eyes.

He was free to address his son in his native language while I consulted with Manuel.

"What did he offer?"

The Spaniard shrugged. "Money."

I had expected no less, which was why I had chosen Manuel as my last man standing. The price that would move Manuel would not have occurred to Sergei Afanasenko. What the assassin wanted most was not wealth, which was not to say I hadn't provided financial compensation.

It was Sergei's associates who had treated Manuel's family like livestock, to be bought and sold and shuffled across borders. It was through an affiliate network that Manuel's sister and niece had been sold in order to satisfy his brother-in-law's debt – a debt the man's life had not satisfied.

Using all the resources available to him, Manuel had tracked them as far as Ouarzazate, Morocco, six weeks ago. I had found them in the no-man's land that was the desert between Western Sahara, Mauritania and Algeria. They were netted in a raid coordinated to rescue three American aid workers before they were handed over to Al-Qaeda in the Islamic Maghreb (AQIM) approximately fourteen hours ago. The mother and daughter were currently being processed at Cap Draa. They were expected back in Europe in twenty-four hours.

While Todd was busy plotting Ed's death, I had been far from idle.

Manuel had been bought with proof of life delivered an hour before he pulled the trigger on his first victim this afternoon. The minute he fulfilled his contract, he would be allowed a telephone call to the pair, details for their reunion, and of course, his cash bonus.

"Personal effects," Manuel said, indicating where Sergei's coat, glock and the pieces of the family's cell phones had been laid out on a nearby crate. "Data," Manuel said, pulling a micro USB card from his pocket. Another piece of Sergei's life fell into my palm. This bit I slipped into my pocket.

"See to the woman." He nodded and turned to leave, barely taking note of the child standing before me.

"You said you wouldn't hurt us," Alexei shouted, his child voice almost completely swallowed by the hum of the motors. His breath gusted white before him from the cold. He blinked quickly, repeatedly, forcing back the sting of tears before they froze.

Manuel paused on his way up the stairs. He wasn't waiting for confirmation of my promise to the boy however. He was silently offering his assistance with Alexei should I need it. The man who had gone to extreme lengths to find his twelve-year-old niece probably would not relish the killing of a child. His priorities were set however; he would not hesitate to shoot the son of the man whose criminal associates were responsible for the death and disappearance of his family.

"I won't lie to you, Alexei. You will be the first to know if your mother dies."

Alexei drew his son's attention while Manuel continued on his way. I couldn't understand what they were saying, but I was not very concerned either. The entire family lived at my will. The father would never leave here alive, and there was a fifty-fifty chance the wife and son would follow.

Many times I had imagined what it would be like to stare at the man stretched up before me and know that he was about to die. Nothing I had dreamed of came close. There was no anger, no relief, no joy or sense of fulfillment. In fact there was nothing at all. I felt nothing.

I blamed it on the cold.

The heated exchange between father and son raged on. Sergei battled strained vocal chords and a thick tongue to bark at his son; while Alexei, either buoyed by the certainty of his father's demise or stepping into the shoes his father had made for him, barked right back. After a moment, the man dismissed his son.

"Zatknis'!"

Despite his best efforts, Sergei turned his eyes on me. His gaze was contemptuous – nothing I didn't expect; I was just a girl to him.

He was a little banged up. A thin streak of blood had dried in a line behind one ear, while another had been smudged at the corner of his mouth. There was a decent sized bump above his left eyebrow. His black suit was covered in dust. Judging by the vociferous argument moments ago though, he was lucid.

Good. I wanted no misunderstanding between us.

"Where is your boss?" he asked, trying to exert some control over the situation.

"There is only me."

Alexei looked between us, then settled on his father with pressed lips and a single nod. 'I told you so,' it translated.

Sergei laughed as best he could while being stretched by the neck. He did that a lot. From his photos I had counted every laugh line, memorizing the tracks a long and happy life had made. His happiness had been paid for on the sorrow of so many others. His longevity was bought with my father's life.

Sergei shifted his feet beneath him, securing his tenuous perch. He wasn't ready to die. He thought he could bargain his way out of this.

"You?" he asked, his bark one of mockery. "You bombed Paris? Killed all those people? Just to get to me?"

I let his humor die a slow and natural death. Alexei looked to me, swallowing hard, uncertain of my reaction to his father's condescension.

"Who are you?"

I shook my head. "Doesn't matter."

He considered my answer for a moment. "You're American. I haven't had much business there. What do you want?"

He still wasn't convinced I was working alone though. He didn't believe I had the power of life or death. By the twist of his mouth, I could tell he was only humoring me.

"I want a name."

"Will any name do?" he asked before I could finish. "Bitch! Whore! Cunt!" Sergei spat at me. "Will those names do? American name for American woman," he laughed.

Under the unforgiving industrial lights his tanned skin glowed purple, the white channels of his facial wrinkles standing out pale blue. His teeth were all straight, even and eerily white. All of it was as fake as his bravado. Even Alexei seemed to understand that. He began to shiver, pulling his coat tighter around him.

"You tell me a name, girl. Tell me who you're working for. I will kill him and end your obligation. I will give you money too. More money than he pays you. You need more money to take care of your bad skin and to buy nice shoes. All girls like nice shoes." He chuckled again, but the façade was losing steam the longer I remained unmoved.

"What about diamonds?" he asked. "I have never met a girl who didn't like diamonds. Tell me what you want."

"I want to know who you were working for –"

"I work for no one!" he shouted, cutting me off. "Do you even know who I am? I am Sergei Afanasenko! I work for no one!"

Alexei tried to intercede again, with an impassioned plea. "Papa!"

Again he dismissed the boy with a curt bark.

"You want a job?" Sergei asked in the wake of the sudden death of their voices. "You can come work for me. If what you claim is true – that you bombed Paris and killed my people – then I could use your talents. I have an extensive network and important connections where you would be useful."

I waited him out. Next to come would be threats.

"But you must decide now," he tried to prompt me into action while his son shook his head in disappointment.

The child was too much of a little man. It wouldn't do to underestimate him... to leave him alive. He might have certain ideas about justice for his father.

"People are looking for me. It is only a matter of time before they find you."

It was time Sergei did not have.

"This is not the most comfortable position," he said after a pause that he used to wet his throat and catch his breath. "Tell me what it is you want."

"I want to know who you were working for during the eighties and nineties," I tried again.

Sergei shifted his weight again and rolled his eyes. "Such a long time ago," he said with a long-suffering sigh. "I cannot remember what I had for breakfast yesterday much less a likely dead *associate* from twenty years ago," he mocked.

"Yesterday you had poached eggs, caviar, *bliny* and chai," I told him. Alexei shot me a startled look, eyes wide; while Sergei narrowed his gaze at me, revising his appraisal. He seemed more impressed by that bit of information than the fact that I had 'bombed Paris' just for him.

"You were a broker," I continued. "You carried his messages, received and forwarded his payments. You were his middle-man to militias." By his continued silence while I described his less-than-exalted past, I could tell he was grudgingly alert. "In exchange for his protection, you met with militia leaders. You sold them your guns, smuggled what contraband they had. But you also offered his support for their cause at a price."

Sergei tried not to give anything away, but his silence was all I needed.

After a very long time, he spoke, again with the heavy contempt. "You don't know what the fuck you're talking about, girl."

"Rwandan Patriotic Army. Libyan National Army. Palestine Liberation Organization. People's Revolutionary Party of Zaire. Kosovo Liberation Army."

He pretended not to be interested in the names, trying his best to frustrate me. How could he not understand that I had waited years, more than a decade in fact, for this? How could he imagine that I would leave empty-handed? How could he dream of walking out of here? Even Alexei knew better.

Perhaps it was time to give him the reaction he craved.

TWENTY-EIGHT

"Turn away," I told Alexei. The boy shook his head at me, silently and furiously begging me to stay with him, not to do what he feared I would do.

I crossed the few feet that separated me from Sergei Afanasenko, the plastic crinkling beneath my cheap shoes. The forks on which Sergei stood were raised well above my head. He might have tried to kick me in the face otherwise. From my position facing the sole entrance, Sergei could not see me, but the crinkling stopped just beneath his feet. Uneasy, he began shifting from one foot to the other. He was limited by the noose however, which forced him to stand tall or choke.

He wanted Alexei to be his eyes, barking more orders at the boy who responded urgently, pleading with him. Perhaps some of those pleas were meant for me, but in his excitement Alexei forgot to use English.

There wasn't much Alexei could say to change my mind however, and his pleas fell on his father's deaf ears too. I pulled Bill from my pocket, and with a flick of my thumb had the three-and-a-half inch tanto blade springing free. Before the boy could utter more than a startled cry, I slashed at Sergei's left foot, just above the back stay of his expensive shoes. Bill cut through the leg of the wool pants and silk socks, severing the Achilles tendon.

Unprepared for the blow, Sergei floundered for several long seconds before – painfully – catching himself and applying all his weight onto his functional leg. Even without the whining motors, his cry wouldn't have traveled far, choked off as it was by the noose. He gasped and groaned, straining against the rope, shivering in pain, praying for the numbing effects of the cold. Not even the near-freezing temperature could slow the flow of blood though; Sergei had been strung up in that position for over an hour, sufficient time for the blood to settle in his lower extremities.

Alexei, however, was another matter. I was unprepared for his sudden silence, but the child stood stoic and tall, as if he had assumed all the strength that had fled his father. Why didn't he look away? Was this how he had been when his father killed his nursemaid and forced him to watch? Did I want to usurp his father in the place where terror reigned in the boy's memory?

I returned to Alexei's side, and against my better judgment placed a hand on his shoulder. "Alexei, wait outside."

He didn't want to leave. He spared a glance for his father who still struggled with the pain and his precarious position. Then he looked at the knife I still held in my hand. It wasn't meant for him; I didn't need it to subdue him.

I folded the weapon and tucked it away. Sergei Afanasenko's blood would join the other stains on my life. Later I would clean the excess away, but in the grooves and private places his presence would remain.

Without another word, Alexei obeyed. Like the lost child he was, he found a place on the metal stairs we had descended minutes before. With his elbows on his knees, he gazed into the emptiness before him.

"You fucking bitch, I'm going to kill you!" Sergei half moaned, half shouted. "Alexei, come back here! You're going to let this bitch harm us?"

"You're going to die, Sergei. Your choices are whether your family joins you and how quickly the end comes."

"*You're* going to kill *me*, girl?" he scoffed. "You don't know who you're fucking with. You think you can get away with this? You don't know *what* you're toying with. You don't know what you're asking for."

"Tell me."

"You want a name? You want to know who is going to cut you up for me? *For me! Because I demand it!*" I couldn't tell which one frustrated him more: the noose for choking the anger from his words, or the noisy motors for nearly completely covering the words.

"I want to know."

"It's your own government that will come for you! Your fucking Uncle Sam!"

At this rate, his choices were dwindling down to bleeding to death or choking to death. For wasting my time Sergei would never feel a single bullet from the gun holstered at my back.

"In September 1999, someone told you about a plan to take you. I want to know who."

"I said it was your fucking government! You deaf now, bitch? You want to know my secrets but don't want to hear the truth. You want to believe that your stinking ideals aren't rotten. You're a big girl. You should know that with any good bureaucracy, the right hand doesn't know what the left is up to. And it's that left hand that's going to put a bullet in your fucking head for this!"

If only Sergei knew how right he was. Or what a big girl I was. Here I was about to kill him, and he hadn't yet realized that *I* was the left hand now.

"Who was your backer? I want the name of the man who protected you… the one who warned you of the raid in September."

"Which September?" he spat at me. "You don't know who you're fucking with. You don't know what I am to your piece of shit government. I have your fuckers on call. They tell me everything I want to know. They protect me from all the other fuckers out there who want a piece of me."

"Give me a name."

"A name, a name, a name… That's all you can say? Are you stupid, cunt?"

I was about to bleed him more. I didn't have time for this. I wanted to spare his son from hearing his father's screams again, but it seemed I had little choice.

I fished Bill from the pocket of my coat again. There was a spot of blood on my fingers, which meant there was blood inside my coat pocket. I wouldn't burn it though. I wanted to wear Sergei's blood as a reminder that I hadn't failed my father. Because before the night was over, he would tell me what I wanted to know.

I released the blade.

"Wait, wait, wait," the man gasped. I stayed, and I watched as relief coursed through his body. "Cut me down and I'll tell you what you want to know."

I didn't move, and by my unchanging expression he seemed to understand there was no hope of that.

The man laughed. It was hollow, but at the same time respectful. I wasn't going to give him false hope. He only had to reconcile himself to his death.

"Go looking, bitch! What you find is what will kill you," he said with spite, finding comfort in the belief that even after he was gone, I would pay for this. "The name you want is Big Mac, like the piece of shit food you fat fuckers like to suck down. He's going to kill you, you understand? But if you want him, I'll give him to you. Just cut me down."

The shell of Sergei's phone was twenty-four carat gold – the male counterpart to his wife's white alligator skin affair with about half a carats in diamond trim. As per my instructions, they had been pulled apart; the batteries, SIM cards, and circuit boards with their secondary GPS locators were somewhere in the middle of Paris, discarded after the data had been extracted.

It might have been a final act of desperation, or Sergei thought me inferior to his criminal genius. He had no idea I'd been tracking phones for a lifetime – well, at least his son's lifetime. I didn't need him.

I inserted the micro USB card Manuel had passed to me into the burner phone that had made communication with my contractors possible. Within seconds, I was scrolling through over six hundred contacts until I found the one I wanted.

Big Mac. The permanent dialing country code of 870 designated a satellite phone. I was even familiar with the service provider. It wasn't guaranteed that the number was current, but it provided a basis on which I could continue the hunt. There were payment accounts, call history, and of course location mapping – all tools I could use to find him.

I returned my attention to Sergei in time to witness his disappointment. He knew he had underestimated me. It was a critical failing that would deny him the time he desperately needed to save his life. While Big Mac would not swoop down and rescue him, he knew his people were out looking for him.

The abandoned vehicles were all GPS-tagged. His wife and son's cell phones were similarly tracked. Even his SIM card, once inserted into a device, emitted a signal that would have led his staff to us. And as a last recourse, the Baranets would have contacted the authorities about Afanasenko's involvement in the city bombing: Ivan Baranets was a legitimate businessman with no apparent reason to fear an official probe.

Yet I had bypassed all those pitfalls. There was nothing to tie me to the man I was about to kill. There was no time left, and there would be no rescue.

"Alexei, come," I called after the boy who was still seated in the exact position I had left him. It was as if he had been frozen to the spot.

He looked pale, and he shivered in his buttoned-up coat. But there was no fear in his eyes; there was nothing at all. He came, fists balled and rooted in his pockets. He had lost his gloves.

"Say your goodbyes to your father."

"I have," the boy answered simply. He looked up at me, waiting for my next prompt.

He was too small, too young, still innocent. I couldn't have him do it. I would rather spend the rest of my life watching him and waiting for him to come for me. I had suffered enough imagining what had happened to my father the night he was killed. For all the hate I once had in my heart for Sergei, I couldn't sentence Alexei to a worst torture than I had endured.

"Go," I told him, indicating the door that would lead him out of this dungeon, away from years of nightmares and guilt.

"No. I must do it. It ends here."

I almost let him. I understood his twisted sense of honor. He didn't want to live and possibly die like his father. He didn't want to have to come for me... to live up to his father's version of justice.

"Go, Alexei. Take your life and your mother's as payment for this debt." He seemed to think about it, looking at the plastic floor between his feet for a few seconds while in the background his father gasped and strained to save his life.

I had to act now. Sergei would lose consciousness soon. I didn't want it to be that easy for him.

Alexei raised his eyes to me again, this time looking up to me, eager for the new moral compass I extended in his direction.

"It's a generous exchange, Alexei. Two lives for one."

He seemed to consider it forever before finally nodding his agreement.

I waited for him to leave, listening as his light steps led him away, echoing off the metal stairs until they slowly faded as he passed through the steel doors and down the corridor. It was the last time he would ever see his father. It was the last time he would have to live under his tyranny.

I was free to end this chapter. And I did it smoothly. Sergei was already dead to me; I felt nothing as I watched his blood pool on the plastic sheet beneath him. His foot still bled, but the flow had slowed, the drops falling rhythmically seconds apart now instead of in a thin, steady stream. His skin was pale beneath his tan and the blue-hued lights.

"You don't have to do this," he said hoarsely as I skirted his blood and climbed into the forklift. "Let me down and it will be over. I won't look for you. Please."

There is a science behind hanging someone. With a standard drop, the victim falls between four and six feet, immediately breaking the neck. It is considered humane, because the instantaneous severing of the spinal cord causes paralysis and unconsciousness.

With the long drop, the fall is extended up to ten feet. It too results in the severing of the spinal cord, but on account of sometimes ending in decapitation, can be messy.

Twelve years was a long time for Sergei to enjoy life while only my father's memory endured. He didn't deserve to have it over quickly. He deserved to live a little in my world – the one he had created for me.

I had reserved for him death by suspension – the steady compression of the jugular and carotid, as the noose squeezes the life out of him for ten to twenty minutes.

As I turned the key in the ignition, the shudder of the machine beneath us was the only jolt he would get. Sergei slipped and tried to find his footing again. It was a futile fight, the mind's stubborn attempt to cling to life. The man began to shout, but the words were lost among the tug of the noose, the hum of the engine, and the whir of the motors that continued pumping cold air into the room. I pulled back the lever that controlled the forks. Sergei's words were immediately cut off.

Having been responsible for destroying numerous lives, Sergei should have been prepared for his own violent demise. Yet he was unwilling to go peacefully, thrashing and groaning against the pull. I switched off the ignition to better hear his struggle. From the entrance to the cold room, I watched him die. I watched as his life and waste seeped out, and his designer shoes slipped from his feet, leaving only an empty shell behind. I stood and watched until the fight no long vibrated along the line.

And still I felt nothing.

Why should I?

He had stolen my heart from me.

TWENTY-NINE

"Why did you tell me to look away?" Alexei asked.

In his hands he held his father's folded coat, scarf, and the shells of his parents' cell phones. It was little comfort. I knew this because the flag that had draped my father's casket had given me none. But it was a signal of the finality of this day. This was the only funeral Sergei would have. There would be no urn or burial ground to mark his passing; his final resting place was in the memory of his family.

"Because there are some things a child should never see."

"I am not a child," he said, reciting by rote what he had learned from his father.

"Yes, you are," I differed quietly. He didn't argue. He looked away, the only indication that there was no meeting of minds on that score. "Why didn't you look away when I told you to?"

"He wanted me to attack you… to take your gun. He didn't care that if I failed you would kill me… and mother too. He said that was what soldiers do… die for their leaders."

"You're not a soldier, Alexei," I said, finding it more difficult to harden my heart against this child as each minute went by.

Is this who Todd saw when he looked at me? How could he compare my father to someone like Sergei? Everything my father did was meant to protect me. But Afanasenko would risk his son's life, the one thing he cherished more than anything else, to save himself.

My father had given his to preserve mine.

"I know," he said. "I die for no one."

The question now was whether Alexei would live for his father, as I had done for mine.

We were interrupted by Manuel's reappearance. I judged from the amount of snow he stomped from his shoes that there was now a thick drift outside. He had been tasked with transferring Rodelick's body into the getaway car that also held the corpses of Youssef and the driver.

"Take the woman," I instructed.

He complied while Alexei stared at me with some anxiety. I waited for Natalia to be led from her cell before I addressed the boy's concern. She was still bound, her hands tied behind her back, with her hood in place. Manuel, ever the gentleman, had draped her fur coat around her shoulders. If her sobs, which had not yet abated, were a genuine sign of her grief for her late husband, then she had really loved him.

It would be several years before she could petition to have him declared legally dead, after which she would be granted access to his accounts and other holdings. That was not to say the family would starve in the interim. Sergei would have protected his assets from bureaucracies, keeping the bulk of his wealth in currency and commodities, like the diamonds he had offered me.

"You are safe, Alexei. She will be released close to home."

"And I?" he asked, dividing his attention between his mother who was being led out into the loading yard.

"I will take you. Don't be afraid; you will soon be reunited with your mother. You may tell her so."

It was an opportunity he seized with both hands. In his maternal tongue, he shouted after his mother, his tone urgent, but reassuring.

Manuel didn't wait to extend their poignant farewells; he was nearly at the end of his contract and was eager to receive his payment. In spite of his occupation, he wasn't comfortable with me. In his eyes, no woman – and especially one as young as me – should be capable of the things I had done. The fact that I was unmoved, untouched by any tender emotion, was a source of deep discomfort. The more distance he put between us, the safer he would feel... and the sooner he would be reunited with his sister and niece.

Alexei didn't want to show it, but in his frantic words I sensed his misgivings. He was afraid to trust me, but determined to allay his mother's fears. I envied him that connection. It was a purpose I had been denied with the murder of my mother. Perhaps things would have been different for me if I had had my mother to think of... if there had been a gentle hand helping to guide my path.

Not long after Manuel and Natalia had disappeared into the darkness, the sound of the box truck being started filtered faintly into the warehouse.

I turned to Alexei who continued to stare in the direction his mother had gone, as if to look away would strip her of safety. I knelt before him so we could see eye-to-eye.

"I gave you my word, Alexei. Your mother's life and yours for your father. She will be released unharmed in the Parc Monceau."

It was only a few blocks from their home in a beautiful haussmannian mansion on avenue des Ternes. Alexei I would release near the Arc de Triomphe. From there it was a straight shot via avenue Mac-Mahon to his home.

He nodded and pressed his lips together. He wouldn't believe it until he saw it. Fair enough.

"I want you to know," I continued, "that I'll understand if one day you decide you're not able to put this behind you. He was your father."

Alexei shook his head somberly. "I had no choice."

I agreed I hadn't given him much of a choice. Faced with an inevitable outcome, at least where his father was concerned, it was unthinkable for the boy not to choose life. "You did nothing wrong, Alexei. And I won't hold you to an agreement made under duress."

"You don't understand," he said. "I had no choice in my father. I had no choice in the future he planed for me. Now I can choose the man I want to be."

"And what kind of man would you like to be?"

"An honest one," he said. "A simple one."

There was no doubt that Alexei was special. During my surveillance of the family I had wondered about the somberness of the child that contrasted with the carefree existence his parents led. His eyes and aura would have been a burden to someone many times older than him. He had about him an innate innocence that was at odds with the harsh lessons he had been taught. He made me question myself in a way Todd had tried and failed.

I thought I had chosen my own paths in life, but had there really been a choice? Maybe I only walked the way my father had designed, thinking it was what I wanted. But was that desire my own or simply an expectation I had assumed? I had never given much thought to who I would be once I had avenged my father.

And in letting Alexei and his mother live, was I choosing the path my children would follow? Did I want to keep looking over my shoulder for the rest of my life, waiting for a time when this child would step into the shoes that had been made for him since birth? It would be a simple matter to lay all doubts to rest... to completely descend into the darkness.

What was another life in the grand scheme of things, even if it was a child's?

THIRTY

Paris was a city in turmoil. Everywhere the sounds of panic could be heard in the wail of sirens, the shouting in the streets mixing with the incessant blare of car horns. The constant relay of news broadcasts was unavoidable. It would have been a good time to monitor the enforcement of the tax levied against the residents with household radios and televisions.

On the walk up to Angelika's attic apartment on rue d'Assass, from behind sealed doors newscasters speculated on the circumstances surrounding an explosion near the Gare St. Lazare. There was very little information filtering out of the authorities, but eyewitness accounts confirmed several casualties.

In the midst of the turmoil I had found a semblance of calm... the peace of being neither pleased nor disappointed... emptiness, if I was being honest with myself.

Sergei Afanasenko was dead and I had taken his secrets from him. It was a simple fact, as if someone else had dealt the killing blow to a stranger who meant nothing to me.

It was so different from what I felt for Angelika.

Her entire apartment was the size of a small bedroom, but high competition for the space meant it commanded seven hundred euros per month in rent. The futon doubled as a couch during the day. The IKEA coffee table served as a multi-purpose dining area, work table, makeup counter and prep station for meals.

The aluminum sink was deep enough to hold one small pot, a dish and a wineglass; her only cupboard had the capacity for little else. She split her cooking between a hot plate and a small microwave that had been jammed directly above the sink.

A full-length mirror was hung on the door of a broom closet where she hung her clothes. Next to that was the toilet. Seated, an average sized adult could wash their hands while still doing their business. On the opposite end of the apartment was the shower, into which I could barely fit if my arms were crossed at the chest.

At 28 m², it was adequate for a woman like Angelika – a lightweight rolling stone. On her tiptoes she was about four feet eleven inches tall, and weighed ninety pounds soaking wet and wearing every item of clothing she owned. She had traveled extensively in her twenty-four years, but had nothing to show for it besides an impressive command of several languages. Everything she had, from her clothes to her toiletries, had been acquired through me.

She had left her hometown of Kovel, Ukraine, at the tender age of eighteen. She started out as a stripper when her dreams of dancing the straight and narrow were crushed. As a failed gymnast, her flexibility, agility, strength, and creativity should have served her well, but with mounting debt and no other means of making a quick buck, Angelika descended into the world of prostitution. Although permanently confined to brothels, she was a quasi-willing victim, posing as a dancer, masseuse or translator as she was shuffled due West, inching closer to her dream of America.

Our paths had crossed in the Dominican Republic, when Todd's colleagues had rented her for his bachelor party. Her gymnastics prowess on the pole made her something of a celebrity in her underworld; her pale skin, white blond hair, and eyes that were a nearly colorless blue were exotic in the Latin American country. She had already made the rounds with a number of the embassy personnel, and on that occasion was meant to be a last hurrah to single life for my husband.

I had stolen her from her traffickers, made her an offer she couldn't refuse, and made her a key element in my plan to apprehend Sergei Afanasenko.

But this was the end of the line for Angelika. After tonight, she would become a liability. She knew too much – my name, my face, my interest in the Afanasenkos. So while in pursuit of February's rent, Angelika's landlord would find her gone.

Her meager belongings were neatly stowed in the limited spaces the apartment afforded. It required little effort to find and pocket the American passport I had arranged for her in the Dominican Republic. That was one tie severed. The police would find the one issued by the Ukrainian government. It would show an assortment of visas and work permits from her days as a dancer. If they cared enough to ask the right questions, they would know she had been rescued in an anti-human trafficking dragnet barely two months ago. They would check that she had entered the European Union on an American passport that was traced back to nothing, as if it had never existed. They would assume she had been trafficked again.

Her last confirmed whereabouts would include the Baranets' home on the night of the explosion. Certain conclusions would be drawn, and her disappearance would be tied into a much wider investigation centered on the operations of the Russian mafia.

Angelika's cell phone and laptop joined the passport in my purse, soon to be disposed of. The fine spray of blood that had already dried into the unstained wood floors would only contribute to the authorities' perception that January was a bad month for Eastern Europeans in Paris, that tensions had boiled over and come to a head on rue de Liège. The Russian teashop that Ivan Baranets and Sergei Afanasenko used to frequent would fall under intense scrutiny, but in the end no bodies – besides those of Alexei and Natalia's guards on the day of the explosion – would ever be found. My cleaner had taken care of that.

Getting rid of Angelika was a simple matter of cleaning house. She had both loved and feared me in equal parts for all the things I had done for her. I took her out of sexual slavery, murdered the men who had exploited her, and gave her the life she'd dreamed of having. But Angelika was growing comfortable in that new life, and I knew she could not always be counted on to remember all the reasons why she should be afraid… and grateful.

I had found her calling card in my home, her scent on my sheets, and her hair in my sink, but the decision to kill her was all business – nothing personal.

My biggest surprise over the past few days was the decision to save Alexei. Eliminating him and his mother would have wrapped up my Paris trip in a neat bow. But I believed the child was stronger than I would ever be. He would choose his own path in life… not the one his father had meant for him, or the one his mother may, in her grief and subsequent anger, urge him to take.

Having completely eliminated all ties to Angelika and the unfortunate Eastern Europeans, I had only one task remaining.

I dialed Big Mac from Angelika's phone. It seemed like forever that I waited. For a while I was afraid the account had been closed, that months of work still lay ahead for me. I'd waited over a decade already; a few more months was miniscule in the larger picture. But I wished that for once things could be easier as I opened the apartment's only window, praying for a connection to the routing satellite.

The windowsill was littered with cigarette butts, and I imagined Angelika standing in this very spot, gazing across the rooftops, and marveling at the miracle that was her new life.

Then it rang, and I steeled myself against any reaction. I didn't want to face disappointment again. I called on the heart of the training my father had taught me to keep the blood from surging through my veins.

"Pain won't kill you," my father would say. *"Not breathing is the only way to die. Breathe, Amy, control your breathing."*

And so, through hours of training and years of conditioning, I had breathed.

And so I breathed that night, pulling slow and steady streams of tobacco-laced air into my body. And I continued to breath, feeding my body with air in spite of the voice on the other end of the line that would have choked the life from me.

"Christ, I've been calling you all afternoon! Your wife's gone bat-shit crazy. She's yelling to anyone who will listen, claiming the whole lot of you had been kidnapped and that you're dead. I was about to send someone out to find you. Where are you anyway?"

I listened and breathed. That was all I could do, and I focused on staying alive. How could he know? Unless the satellite number was a line reserved for only one contact. Unless the only incoming calls he expected were from country code 33.

I could barely keep the phone to my ear, but I resolved not to let go. Because if this was a dream, I wanted to remember everything when I woke up. But it wasn't a dream. The winter chill seeped in through the window, pinching my skin and stinging my eyes. The air was icy as I pulled it into my lungs.

"Gay?" came the voice again, uncertain in the silence. "Is that you? What number is this?"

I ended the call, because I knew I wasn't dreaming and I couldn't take anymore. My heart was broken, and I was afraid if I listened even more I would fall apart. I smashed the phone to pieces beneath my heel. I wanted it to look like my soul felt.

'Gay' and 'Big Mac' they called each other. Sergei Afanasenko and Richard McDowell.

Admiral Richard McDowell.

Uncle Richard.

It had to be a lie. Sergei had lied to me, and I had killed him before verifying his claims. That had to be it. Because the alternative was just too terrible to imagine.

Richard was like a father to me. He had held me hours after my birth. He had stood before an altar and promised to guide me in life. He had taken me into his home and raised me as one of his own. He'd been present at every graduation and most birthdays. I was the daughter he had been denied. My father was his best friend. My father trusted him with my life; he had sent me to him the night he was killed. Richard, who had been my refuge, had promised he would find those responsible.

Never in my wildest dreams did I think Richard would betray us. It was impossible to think he had killed his best friend. This was a nightmare from which I expected to awake any minute now.

I kept pulling cold air deeper into my lungs. It burned my nostrils, and went so far as to unsettle the bile in my stomach. The apartment was small. The race to the toilet was over before it had really begun. I heaved as the spasms racked my body. But I was empty. I had nothing else to give.

'Gay' and 'Big Mac' they called each other.

Sergei and Richard.

THIRTY-ONE

Sleep was a refuge I was denied. I didn't miss it much. My eyes were finally open, and if I never slept again, that was fine by me. That didn't mean I didn't deserve a few moments of peace however.

And so I immersed myself into the luxury Richard's largesse had placed at my disposal. I sipped chamomile tea while lavender bubbles and verbena salts infused my skin with their delicate fragrance. I thought of ways to kill him.

One of Todd's honeymoon acquisitions for my father's library, a French edition of the Dickens' classic, *A Tale of Two Cities*, was my companion. I relied more on my memory than my command of the language to make sense of the words swimming before my eyes. Deeper thoughts conspired against my progress beyond the first paragraph.

> *"It was the best of times, it was the worst of times, it was the age of wisdom, it was the age of foolishness, it was the epoch of belief, it was the epoch of incredulity, it was the season of Light, it was the season of Darkness, it was the spring of hope, it was the winter of despair, we had everything before us, we were all going direct to Heaven, we were all going direct the other way – in short the period was so far like the present period, that some of the noisiest authorities insisted on its being received, for good or for evil, in the superlative degree of comparison only."*

I must have read that passage a hundred times in that tub, putting the dozens of times I'd read it while on deployment to shame. I used to think it made sense of the senselessness of the wars. The first time I read the book I thought there was very little difference between the world Dickens had imagined and the one we lived in two hundred years later; it was just another instance of *'the more things change, the more they stay the same'*.

But now that my eyes were open, I knew things would never be the same.

Dawn was slow in coming. As much as I had initially thought my world had come to an end in a closet of an apartment in Paris' sixth arrondissement, I was proved wrong in only a matter of a few hours.

What else did I expect? It hadn't ended on a cool and rainy September night in 1999, when the foundation of my existence was ripped from under me. Why would it end now?

Morning came. I was still breathing. I ate, I got sick. And there was still a lot of work to be done. My cell phones chimed incessantly, which I ignored for the most part. There were too many questions waiting for me, too many people who wanted a piece of me. I had nothing to give today. I was too preoccupied with my own questions. Well, just one question.

Why?

Why had he done it?

Because there was no doubt in my mind that he had. That at least answered the longstanding mystery of how. How had an execution team invaded the home of a senior CIA official, murdered him, and dissolved into thin air, without anyone ever being held accountable?

Richard. That's how. He had ordered it, planned it, and covered it up. But why?

Knowing the reason would change nothing. My father was still dead, my mother taken with him. I was going to kill Richard. But I wanted the truth. I needed to know why. He wouldn't just volunteer that though. I needed time to think, to find a way to force him.

So far I had decided on death by a thousand cuts for Richard. I wanted to watch him bleed as I had… to suffer as I had. I wanted him to witness the end of his dreams, the destruction of his world, piece by piece. Only then would I kill him.

Until then there was only one person I wished to hear from. I had my position to preserve. I had worked too hard for many years to submit to despair now. I set out to meet Selim Haddad in the Latin Quarter.

He was understandably paranoid after the bombing. I didn't blame him; the entire city was on edge. He found in the narrow, winding, pedestrian access only streets of the left bank a sense of security. He should have known better.

More than anyone else, Saad al-Qasim should have understood that a bomb was the least practical weapon to kill a single human being. It required extensive planning and an inefficient use of resources. But Selim believed his father wanted to send him a message, and that at least was the only good reason for the use of the weapon. More than achieving death, its purpose was to demoralize the enemy.

After several hours at the hospital, Selim had put his family on lockdown. His children were pulled from school and he had taken a leave of absence from work. The windows were shuttered, their contact with the outside world reduced to a bare minimum. He had no support from his French handlers who were unconvinced of his father's involvement.

"Why now?" they asked, the same question Selim had incredulously thrown at me. Faced with the risk of losing credibility and jeopardizing his future, Selim accepted their conclusion – outwardly at least. The authorities were chasing a Russian mob lead; Adeline was unfortunately in the wrong place at the wrong time.

After securing his family inside their home, Selim's next step in making them safe again was to call me. We met at the Luxembourg Gardens. The city was on high alert, the metros and famous landmarks overrun by police and the *gendarmerie*. It was surreal knowing I was responsible for shattering the populace's fragile perception of safety.

The calm of the gardens contrasted with the buzz of the streets, but today both Selim and I were running short on time. There would be no appreciation of the scenery, no lounging on the green spaces, no marveling at the seamless union of history, dating as far back as the Medicis, and modernity. We met as casual strangers against the austere background of the black-spired fence.

From the single-lane portion of rue Auguste Comte, Selim could monitor all passersby, searching for a threat that had never really existed.

He would spend the rest of his life looking over his shoulder, questioning the safety of his family, without ever really knowing that I was the evil that stalked him.

I made him wait for twenty minutes, because with the balance of power on my side, I could.

He was disheveled. His clothing was rumpled beneath his hastily donned coat. His hands were jammed into his pockets to make up for his lack of gloves. He'd forgotten his hat and his exposed pate appeared even more vulnerable in the cold. What was left of his greying hair stood up in clumps, uncombed but for the impatient pass of his fingers. The shadows under his eyes were deep, as deep as the fear with which he looked out on the world.

He had forgotten what it was like to live like this. Lebanon was so far removed from his day-to-day, that he had put the fear out of his mind.

"It was him, wasn't it?" he greeted me, in his urgency forgetting that we had not parted as friends days ago. "The car bomb yesterday… it was my father, wasn't it?" He shook his head.

"You know as much as I," I said, shrugging non-committally. "The authorities think it may be something else."

"You know," he charged, shaking a fist at me. If I were a different woman in a less public place, I might have been intimidated. "You know damn well it was him. They almost killed my wife! You knew and you let it happen. You didn't share –"

The way he advanced on me might have looked like anger, but I could smell the fear… and yes, guilt … oozing from his pores. It wasn't in my nature however, to empathize. I pushed him back with a firm palm planted in the center of his chest. I wasn't at my best this morning. I was starving, weak from a restless night and nearly broken spirit. But I was running short on patience and wouldn't hesitate to beat the living shit out of Selim if he looked at me the wrong way.

"I shared with *you*. I told you what would happen. You chose not to believe me. If your wife was hurt then that is all on you."

It was a low blow, exploiting his guilt, but he wanted to play hardball and I was good at it.

My methods were unconventional, cruel even, but they worked. And in my line of work, results were all that mattered. Selim Haddad was living proof of that. Days ago he had thought it a sin to help me break his brother, but today he was going to turn his back on Paradise in order to save his family here on earth. Family had a way of doing that… forcing one into sacrifices that shouldn't have been made.

Or maybe he wasn't so certain of the existence of an afterlife after all.

"I've thought about what you asked me. It's all I could think about all night." He ran his hand over his balding head, the cold only adding to his frustration. Or maybe he didn't feel it at all.

Without a word we fell into step together. I was cold and he wasn't comfortable standing in one spot, an easy target for an invisible threat.

"I don't know how to help you," he finally conceded, but it was clear he had racked his brain – still was in fact.

"Tell me about your brother."

Selim sighed. It was never easy choosing between family. But it just so happened that one side of his wanted to kill the other – or so he thought. That alone should have simplified things for him.

"Mohamed was only a boy when the war began… twelve years old. There was so much he didn't understand. I don't blame him for choosing our father. Many people looked up to our father, called him a hero for destroying the people who would have slaughtered us. My brother was proud of him."

"But you weren't," I added. I wasn't looking for excuses, and I didn't have all day to starve in the cold with this man.

"At seventeen, I was already a man. I saw the innocents being killed. How did that make us better than savages?" His hands in his unbuttoned coat fisted with either cold or chilling memories. "Later I had other reasons too."

"Adeline."

Selim nodded.

"She was forbidden to me, and not just for political reasons. Before the war, interfaith marriage was not *haram*, but it wasn't a simple matter either. Either she would have had to convert or we would have gone abroad for a civil union. It certainly complicated things that my father was a bomb-maker for Hezbollah though."

Selim shrugged as if it was of little consequence now.

"But we were once civilized people. The war drove us all to madness, but there was hope that one day life would return to normal. Adeline is a reasonable woman. She has given up wine and pork – no mean feat in France."

"So what went wrong?" I asked, tiring of Selim's unwarranted preoccupation with excuses, and at the same time amused by his naïve hopefulness.

"We ran out of time," he said, but suddenly broke off at the sound of an impatient horn a few paces behind us. It was only a bus driver protesting the refusal of a banged up Citroën to allow him to merge into traffic. I marveled at Selim's degree of stress, hoping I would get what I needed before he died of a heart attack.

"My father asked me to marry a girl," he continued. "A very important girl. Or at least, her father was."

"What does this have to do with your brother?"

"By this time, the war was nearly at an end, but Mohamed was still a child in his thoughts. He idolized our father. He was also extremely jealous of our father's approval, which inspired his zealous, competitive spirit. Every thing was a challenge to him.

"He hated that father wanted this marriage for me. An alliance with Asghar El-Shafei was a great honor to our family. I didn't say yes, but I couldn't say no either. I was in love with Adeline, but to throw over the daughter of a highly respected cleric for a Christian woman was unthinkable. My father would have killed me. So I did the only thing I could."

"You ran."

"Yes. Adeline and I eloped. To protect our family's honor, my father hid the truth. He told Asghar el-Shafei that I was unworthy of the honor, and offered my brother instead. But Mohamed was only a second son. To satisfy the family, my father disowned me and my brother took the name Mohamed al-Mohamed. But knowing my brother, I can imagine it angered him to accept my cast-offs."

"Interesting story, Saad," I commiserated. "Truly," I added when his eyes flashed angrily at me. "But how does that help me stop your father from killing your family?"

Selim shook his head, still confounded that I insisted on calling him by that name. "Americans are so blind," he said, and I was forced to stifle a laugh.

"So why don't you enlighten me."

"My brother was a jealous and possessive boy. I imagine he would become a jealous and possessive man. That is all I can, in good conscience, tell you."

Lucky for me there was no need for him to say more. Living and loving a man like Todd Birch had afforded me a thorough understanding of jealousy and possession.

"Tell me about his wife," I asked.

Selim could pretend the rest was no secret, that the facts of his brother's marriage were easily traced. He could pretend to be ignorant of my actions to come. Or he could pretend that sparing his brother physical torture at the hands of his enemies was a mercy. I would leave Selim his illusions as long as he gave me what I wanted.

"Tell me what you know about her family."

And Selim, in good conscience, did.

Everything could not be so easy however. Take my call to Blitzner, for instance.

He was fit to be tied, and not because I'd been dodging his calls since the night before.

"There were casualties," he breathed into the line. For the first time since I met him three years ago, Don Blitzner didn't sound half as smug as he used to.

"It was a bomb. That was to be expected."

There was silence for a drawn-out second. It wasn't the most appropriate rejoinder for one concerned about keeping her job. But if there was one thing I had learned over the course of the past month, it was that no one – especially not Don Blitzner – was looking out for me.

In all likelihood questions were being asked at home, but Blitzner didn't have to feel any heat if he cooled his heels. There were enough players in the intelligence community alphabet soup to provide shade. And it was to our advantage that the French were pointing the finger at the Bratva.

"You OK'ed the plans; you signed the checks. And we got what we wanted."

"What we wanted," Blitzner stressed, "was Hasan al-Qasim. What we have is an international incident."

"You're wrong," I differed, proving once again just how much I thought of the *opportunity* Blitzner and Richard had conspired to place in my lap.

Richard. Just the thought of the man set a flame to my blood.

My stomach stirred again. I didn't know how much of this I could stand. I sat up in bed and pulled the sheets around my naked shoulders. Anything to keep the urge to retch down. The windows were closed and shuttered, throwing the room into darkness in the middle of the already gloomy Paris morning. I was hot and cold from minute to minute. By contrast, I was constantly hungry, because I couldn't keep anything down longer than a few minutes. The bird-sized pieces of baguette I had forced down a few minutes ago were already on their way up. Room service had brought up tea, but not even the platter of fresh *pain au chocolate* could tempt me into lifting the silver tray cover.

"How did this happen?"

"The plan was simple enough. The driver should have parked the car and walked away. Instead, he went ballistic. Crashed into a third party, got out and shot him in the face. I could have let him go on a spree, but I chose to take back control. So there were two casualties instead of half a dozen, and we still got what we wanted."

"So how come the locals are still counting bodies?"

"Not our scheme. Someone decided to ride the waves. We were not involved." Technically it wasn't a lie.

"How likely is it the Russians got wind of the plan?" At least I had gotten him to share responsibility.

"Not at all."

"So they were waiting in the wings by chance?" Blitzner sounded skeptical, and I didn't blame him. The only way to salvage was to throw in a little sacrifice.

"I believe so. I was the only one who knew the full set. The builder didn't know. The driver didn't know either, or he would have definitely stuck to the plan."

"You didn't share with anyone? Not even your husband?" It was an accusation, and not an unreasonable one either. Unless directed at someone who had cut her teeth on secrets.

"No," I answered simply and let it hang unattended, unadorned.

"So what was this in aid of? What did my check pay for?" The worst part of the call now behind us, I could focus on what I had been paid to do here, as opposed to making up excuses for my private agenda.

"His weakness is his wife, Fatima el-Shaffei." Blitzner sighed, and even without words I understood his frustration. Mohamed al-Mohamed would have had every insult thrown at him, including having his wife and daughters gang-raped. Nothing had moved him. But Blitzner's impatience was due to his lack of understanding of both Islamic law and the youth Mohamed al-Mohamed used to be.

"I'm sending new instructions for his interrogation team. You can run it by Dr. Crofter if you would like a second opinion. Frankly though, there's no harm in trying it out to see what happen."

"I didn't send you halfway across the world for trial and error," Blitzner said in a clipped tone.

"You sent me here because you knew I could get the job done. If that's no longer the case, you should say so right about now. Otherwise let me do my job."

Blitzner didn't answer for a few seconds. It was long enough to let me know he had doubts, but not long enough to damage our relationship beyond repair. He would give me a little breathing room, but he wanted more from me than a jealous man being manipulated with news of a fickle wife.

"According to his law, a woman who doesn't know whether her husband is alive or dead can divorce him with the approval of a *marji'*. The divorce is invalid however, if the man's estate continues to provide for his family, which I imagine would be the case here. It seems Hasan al-Qasim wanted the marriage for political expediency, so it's not unfathomable that he would have continued to provide for Fatima in his son's stead.

"If we lead Mohamed al-Mohamed to believe that his father acquiesced to the divorce, leaving Fatima in the lurch in order to free her from the union and secure for himself a more profitable alliance, we might be able to break him."

"We're going to need more than just say-so to move him," Blitzner added. It was perhaps the only thing I appreciated about the man: instead of harping on the negatives, he was as committed as I to finding a solution.

"His father-in-law is Asghar El-Shafei – a notable Lebanese cleric. It shouldn't be too difficult to stage him with a contender for Fatima's affections. Since both fathers have strong ties to Hezbollah, we should be able to find an ambitious buck in the party that might be familiar to our detainee."

"Hmm," was Blitzner's only reply for a long moment. It was part-skeptical and part-considering.

I allowed him the time to think it over while I slipped out of bed and made my way to the bathroom. For now, I assumed a perch on the edge of the tub, but was prepared to mute the line and heave at the drop of a hat. "What's in it for Hasan? If the son's marriage was such a hit why would he give it up now?"

"For a better one. There were four living sisters when the family skipped out of Lebanon, the youngest being just four years old. It's a double slap in the face if Mohamed thinks he's being replaced as husband and son. Put Hasan al-Qasim in the center of both decisions, and we might just be able to flip the son."

"This is all pretty archaic," Blitzner finally said. I agreed with his objection although it exposed his bias. Blitzner didn't have the appreciation I had for Islamic culture. He would never understand the interplay of marriage, chastity, legitimacy, and the rules of inheritance to the wider social contract, because our society had annihilated those ties long ago. "What's the probability that it will work?"

"There's a good chance." It wasn't exactly the reassurance Blitzner was looking for, but it would have to do for now. I had spent the hour since meeting Selim Haddad fleshing out instructions for Dr. Crofter and Mohamed al-Mohamed's interrogators. If carefully applied, and sufficiently substantiated with photographic evidence, the plan would go a long way in at least shaking Mohamed al-Mohamed's intractability. That was progress, as far as I was concerned, even if it didn't satisfy Blitzner.

"What I can guarantee however is Saad's cooperation. He thinks we're in a position to provide better protection than his current handlers. That's not a bad handle for someone like him."

Blitzner grudgingly agreed. After quickly running through our next steps, we said our goodbyes. He would keep his head down and I would complete the instructions for the handling of Mohamed al-Mohamed.

Shortly thereafter I turned my stomach and intestines inside out and shook them dry.

THIRTY-TWO

Todd had a way of making me wish for more, even in the face of staunch objection from the rational part of me.

I wasn't recovered enough to face him on equal footing when he returned mere minutes after Blitzner's call. He found me curled around the toilet, my face pressed against the cool porcelain. It was the worst position from which to gaze up at his formidableness.

Dressed as casually as he had left me, in slacks, a button-down and sweater beneath a dark wool coat, I was instantly struck by his beauty. He was fresh-shaved, hair slightly disheveled, likely from the wool cap he had recently removed. His skin glowed against the severity of his darker layers; his eyes were bright pools of indigo, but undeniably hard too.

Todd had not completely returned to me. His stance in the doorway of the bathroom and the deceptive disinterest with which he watched me betrayed the killer he had not yet buried beneath the urbane layers. I knew without asking that Blerim Nesimi was dead. I also knew there was a reason Todd gazed at me so keenly, although the casual observer would have called it dispassionately.

There was a pressing reason why a killer stood in my doorway, staring at me.

My pulse surged and my stomach ticked.

"Still ill?" he asked. It was significant that he didn't call me by name, or that his concern didn't bring him closer to my side. Where was the man who had insisted on holding back my hair days ago?

I looked away. "I'm pregnant."

It was an inelegant confession, but a lack of grace was the least of my concerns just then. Besides, there was something deadly wrong between us, and judging by the way he was looking at me, I could guess I was at the core of it.

Because nine out of ten times, I was the source of Todd's consternation.

With Todd's efficiency at the diplomatic end of a weapon, there should not have been room for last words. But what if he had? What if Blerim Nesimi had told? How long had it taken for Todd to put two and two together? How long had it been before he called Richard?

He left me, simply walked out on me, and I was too sick to feel anything but relief at the resounding slam of the front door. I must have fallen asleep on the bathroom floor, because my next memory was of warm fingers on my cheek. I was sicker than I had thought possible. I had done too much too soon to my body, and I realized as I was propped and held into a seated position, that it might very well kill me. If that wasn't ironic…

A glass of something fizzy was pressed to my lips. Even with my eyes closed, I divined tiny effervescent bubbles tickling my nose. Ginger ale.

With my head tilted back, Todd poured the beverage down my throat to his satisfaction. It burned a path around my tongue and into my stomach, but I couldn't summon the strength to protest. My insides cramped, but the shot of sugar to my blood was just what I needed to wake up.

"Open your eyes," I heard his voice.

I did, and found him too beautiful for words. He was better composed than before, but his neutral expression was far from that of the man who had kissed me goodbye.

"Can you sit up?" he asked, but by the way I swayed when he tried to release me, he learned that I could not.

Todd pulled my panties down and transferred me to the toilet with which I had had many face-to-face encounters in the past week. He held me in place with one arm while struggling with a box just out of sight.

"This is a pregnancy test," he said, in blatant disregard of the three that were propped in plain view on the vanity. "Pee on the stick, Amy."

Even my name sounded cold on his lips. I wished it didn't have to be like this. I wished Todd could trust me even a little bit. I wished I didn't have to live with the constant threat that he would kill me. I wished I didn't have to pee on a stick to bind him to me.

But I did. It was hard going; I didn't have enough fluids in me to form a thin sheen of sweat.

Todd stripped me of my underwear and transferred me to the tub. It was as good a place as any to wait out his decision. I was not unconvinced there were traces of stomach fluids in my hair; and the last moments of Todd's last fiancée's life were in a tub. Depending on the results of his test, he could wash me clean of my sins or slit my wrists, like Mona, without much of a fight.

Propped against the side of the tub, the water rising around my hips then covering my breasts was the only sign of the passage of time. I must have dozed off again, because my next conscious thought was of stillness. I awoke to an invading sensation of warmth. It surrounded me completely like thousands of comforting hands. I could feel my hair floating around me, my body buoyed by a peculiar weightlessness.

"Have you been very ill?" Todd asked. I nodded. "How long has it been like this?"

"Since you left," I managed. "Haven't eaten, and kept getting sick. Guess it caught up to me."

There might have been a sob. I wasn't sure; I had never heard Todd cry before. There were indeed hands wrapped around me, but only a pair, and they shook, wracking my body with soundless tremors. They restrained me, fighting against my start and yearning for discovery, but were far from punishing.

"Shh," he whispered against my ear.

"Todd?"

"I'm not letting go, Amy," he said, and this time the sob was undeniable.

My feet touched bottom as I straightened, my back pressing into the wall of his bare chest. Around us, the bath water sloshed lazily, but Todd's arms were firm and strong as they tightened around my body... under my arms, over my chest, caressing across my belly. His lips pressed reassuringly against my exposed throat. I shivered despite the heat rising from the bath.

"Thank you," he said. "Thank you for our baby. And I'm sorry for ever doubting you."

I didn't say anything, because I couldn't shake my first conscious thought of a few moments ago – that Todd had drowned me. I had the sneaking suspicion that if not for this child I was carrying, he would have done exactly that. But a man who wept at the news of his impending fatherhood deserved some acknowledgement. I squeezed his arm gently.

The drink he had administered had somewhat revived my flagging body, but I was still in no condition to share my strength with Todd.

After a long time, after we had settled into a silent embrace, Todd asked, "How are you feeling now?"

I could only shake my head.

"I'm sorry," Todd said, and his arms tightened around me.

"No, you're not," I replied without pause. I felt his chest shaking beneath me.

"I'm sorry you're having such a hard time. But you're right; there's nothing I want more than this baby."

I knew it, but it still stung to hear it. Regardless, it gave me the courage to broach a more sinister topic with him.

"How did it go?" I asked.

Todd's caressing fingers stilled for a brief moment. "As expected." It was all he would say about Blerim Nesimi. It was also a poor attempt at equivocation.

"Did he say anything?"

"Should he have?" Todd answered, and I was reminded not to be swept away by his tender display of moments ago.

"Yes. I imagine he would want to know why."

"What difference does it make? The end is the same."

It surprised me that Todd would be so cold. It was one thing to be detached, but it was another thing to completely bury one's humanity. I had witnessed his efficiency only once before, and even Angelika's traffickers knew why they were being slaughtered. But to strip away the meaning of the life one took was something I could never imagine. Everyone I had ever killed understood the reasons for their demise. It was not compassion that drove me, but the drive for completion.

"What happens now?" He didn't answer for a long time, so long in fact that I was afraid he was refusing point-blank to answer. "Todd."

"We move on," he said simply. I wanted to believe him. I wished it could have been that simple. I wanted to confide in him. Todd understood betrayal. If he knew what Richard had done, he would want justice for me.

The problem was, I wasn't looking for justice anymore. Justice would have meant exposure, but it just wasn't enough. I wanted vengeance. I wanted him to feel my father's breath on his back. I would strip Richard of everything he held dear, and when his time came to die, I wanted him to know what betrayal felt like. I wanted him to know it was I all along.

The peal of Todd's cellphone provided a brief reprieve from the silence that once again began to divide us. Shifting beneath me, he sifted through his belongings and resurfaced with the phone at his ear. I knew he only passed me the rest of the ginger ale to keep me occupied while he attended to the caller. In the spirit of openness, he wouldn't put distance between us too.

"I was going to call you," he said in greeting. "Something has come up."

As close as we were, our bodies fused together in the small tub, it was impossible to make out the other end of the conversation.

"Amy's not well." I pretended to be unconcerned, sipping from the plastic bottle and melting into Todd's solid frame. One arm around my waist held me close, but he was undeniably arched away under the guise of securing the phone outside the tub. "She's pregnant. We're going to have a baby."

The response on the other end was brief... too brief, as far as Todd was concerned. I felt his body tense. His sharp inhale disturbed me. I would have tilted my head towards him, but the arm that moments ago hung loosely around my middle now strategically anchored me in place at the shoulder.

"I didn't misunderstand you, but my wife needs me, and getting her medical attention is my priority. Your matter isn't time sensitive. I'm sure if you think about it, you'll understand my position."

I didn't want to fight against his hold, saw no need to add to the waves that were beating against us inside the suddenly tiny tub. But to deny my curiosity would have been unnatural. Weak as I was, pushing against Todd's restraints was more of a plea for release than the definite demand I had intended. I turned to face him, just in time to have the shutters slam before my eyes. Todd turned away, shielding them from me.

So much for wishing for more.

"You'll have to find someone else," Todd replied tersely to a stream of distant words, shortly before the call ended. He tucked his phone away, folding the edges of his annoyance in on itself until only a shadow of the emotion remained.

"What's going on?" I asked, setting the bottle aside. I repositioned myself at the other end of the tub, facing him in what might have been misinterpreted as a challenge. Todd knew better though. In my condition, it was little more than a defensive position, and a weak one at that.

"Nothing you have to worry about," he said, which was no reassurance at all.

"Who was that?"

"It doesn't matter," he said, sloshing the tepid water over his face then raking his fingers through his hair. The moisture made the strands appear thicker and blacker, not unlike the effect anger had on his gaze. A few drops hung from his lashes, which Todd quickly blinked away with the rest of his peeve.

There was something to be said for leaving well enough alone. But the soft down on my arms prickled, warning me of danger. The only thing that kept the air between us from crackling was dampness.

"Where were you last night?" Todd asked, giving up on evasion and looking at me in the way of taking stock.

"Out. Working on my case."

He nodded briefly, unconvinced.

"What have you been doing, Amy?" It wasn't my imagination that his eyes had narrowed infinitesimally.

I hesitated for a breath, because as I had told him days ago, old habits were hard to die. "Tracking a Hezbollah target."

"He's here?" His tone was neutral, but the way Todd looked at me, he might as well have voiced his skepticism.

"He's in Iran... at least, I think so. His son is here... the straight one. The other is in Guantánamo. I'm mining one to flip the other."

"Who?" he asked, and there was no doubt of his intention to verify my claims.

"Hasan al-Qasim, seventy-three year old Lebanese national. He built the bombs that blew up the Marine barracks in '83 and the embassy annex in '84. His heir is Mohamed al-Mohamed, formerly Mohamed al-Qasim, detainee 28211, forty-eight years old. The other son, Selim Haddad, formerly Saad al-Qasim, fifty-three years old is here; he's my contact."

"And how is that going?" he asked at the end of a lengthy pause.

I nodded. "He's cooperating."

Todd sank to his shoulders under the water, hooking his feet beneath my knees to pull me closer. His eyes dipped to my mouth, wondering if he could trust anything that slipped from my lips. I didn't protest, but I would have been a fool to trust his relaxed pose. This man was dangerous to me.

"You've heard about the car bomb?" he asked, eyes dancing back to mine at the last minute.

What were the chances it was only a coincidence that I was chasing a bomb-maker at precisely the same time a car bomb had exploded in the middle of the city?

"How could I not?" Silence fell again, heavier this time. I focused on my breathing, keeping it slow and steady, defying the tension that wanted to slowly creep up my spine. "What of it?"

"I don't know," he said, his hands slowly brushing over my skin to hook under my arms. He lifted me like I was a child, but there was nothing innocent about the recognition between our bodies as I unfolded over him.

In the thick of the lies, this could always be trusted. Todd's body came to life as my breasts were flattened against his chest, the nipples abraded by the smooth mat of dark hair. His legs closed around my hips, his arousal nestled against the soft flesh of my belly.

"While I was away Richard called." He didn't say anything else for a while... just breathed. I forced my body to lull to the rhythm of his heartbeat, commanded my arms to enfold him.

I cleared the thickness from my throat, and kept my eyes fixed on the dark outline of a future beard. "Was that Richard just now?"

"Yes. He wants me to look into something for him... thinks an old contact may have been targeted."

"By a bomb?"

"We don't know." My heart stuttered at news of this fresh collective. Todd's fingers inching idly up my back chilled me.

"*We*?" I ventured. "What does he want with you? Why didn't he call me?"

"It's... sensitive," Todd replied simply. "Best not to bring us in conflict with the French. And let's face it, Amy; discretion isn't exactly your forte."

"That was very diplomatic of you, Todd." And a convenient excuse for Richard's keeping me away from the search for the man for whom he had killed my father.

The corners of Todd's mouth lifted with the shadow of a smile. His fingers gathered the hair at the back of my neck and tugged insistently. His grip was uncompromising as he stared into my face. His eyes were steel, belying the humor he feigned.

"There's no need for lies between us," he said. I couldn't breathe for a full minute, as Todd stared into my soul. "Do you understand?"

I tried to nod, but only hurt myself. Todd's hold on me tightened. "Yes," I answered hoarsely after trying and failing to force my heart back into its place.

"We're a family. You and our baby are the most important people in my life. I'll protect you with all of me, but know this: there's no more hiding from me, no more lies. It ends here. What I was doing in Naples... that's the last secret. Understand?"

"Yes," I said.

"Your father is dead. He's gone, and I'm only sorry because it breaks your heart. He did terrible things to you."

This close, it was impossible to hide the hurt of those words. They were acid poured on a wound that had been recently reopened. I gritted my teeth and braced my body against the pain, but there was nothing to help the scalding stream of tears.

"I love you, Amy," Todd said, the words incongruous with the hardness he showed. "Don't make me end you."

If only he knew the end had already come. We were a tragedy and Todd was the only one who hadn't seen the end of the script.

THIRTY-THREE

Needless to say the honeymoon was over before it had really begun. Severe dehydration earned me a bed and an IV line at the American Hospital of Paris. I was out-voted four-to-one on whether I should remain overnight for observation, with Todd siding with the medical personnel. To his credit, he never left my side, more than eager to share my sentence while gazing at the first image of our child. It was due in early September, the anniversary of my parents' murders. I tried not to dwell on that bit of serendipity, but failed time and again.

It wasn't evidence of the beating of a second heart inside me that moved me to tears.

I had worked so hard at achieving this pregnancy but I found myself in the peculiar position of having to pretend to be as surprised as Todd. My initial placid acceptance of the news may have resembled shellshock, but the shelf life of stunned disbelief was extremely short. So Todd became my point of reference; I mirrored him, but even that had a limit. His enthusiasm was borne of a deep-rooted longing that I, with my emotional handicap, could not imitate.

"I thought it was going to take months," Todd confessed to the OBGYN who, for all Todd's reverence, might as well have been an angel on a divine mission.

"Then you're one of the lucky ones," was Dr. Feldman's response, beaming under the glow of Todd's high opinion of him. I wasn't convinced. He hadn't earned my respect yet; and he would have to do much better than have me pee on another stick for that. Explaining away science with a convenient diagnosis of 'luck' was strike one against him. Forcing me into an overnight stay was the second. Lucky for him his shift came to an end before he committed a third transgression.

That night, hours after he thought I had fallen asleep, I heard Todd crying from the bed he had made out of the visitors' chair. I was torn between two very distinct emotions. On the one hand, I was deeply pleased by the accuracy of my assessment of Todd. Because of this child, he would choose me. And if his refusal to accept Richard's errand, or the fact that I was still breathing, was any indication, it had already begun.

On the other hand, I hated the implication that Todd was another subject I had studied with the intent of breaking. It inspired in me what could have been described as guilt. I couldn't shake the feeling that he deserved better, someone who could love him like he deserved. Our child certainly didn't deserve having me as its mother – a woman who had conceived to score points in a deadly game of revenge.

And broken Todd certainly was... or as much as was possible for a man like him. It was evident in the wonder with which he gazed at the sepia-hued static that supposedly was our child's first live performance. It was the reverence with which he looked at me, and the awe in his fingertips as he touched me.

"Can you tell what it is?" I asked the ultrasound technician.

"It's too soon for that," Todd answered, tearing his eyes away from the screen long enough to smile down at me.

"Your best shot of finding out is around twenty weeks," the tech added. "I would say you're barely at six weeks right now. Congratulations."

I was skeptical and it showed. The woman smiled at me and launched into a well-used spiel about the difference between conception age and gestational age, and how in my case, the latter predated the former by about fourteen days.

Todd, who had been in this position once before and was better acquainted with the workings of my body than me, nodded his agreement.

"Do you want to know the sex?" he asked, while I was still adjusting to the highly invasiveness of a transvaginal probe.

"No." More than wanting the mystery to endure, I didn't want Todd sharing that bit of news with Richard. He simply nodded his agreement, satisfied that there was indeed a child – whatever the gender.

As I lay curled up on my side, listening to the strains of his quiet weeping through the still night, I wondered if he regretted killing Mona. Because after our little episode inside the tub, I knew for certain that he had in fact killed his fiancée.

Did he wonder what it might have been like to pretend he hadn't learned the child she carried wasn't his? Did he cry for the family he could have had with her – a woman, who in spite of her faults, was a thousand times more suited to be a mother than me? Did he compare our sins: Mona's infidelity against my aversion to the truth... her weakness against my selfishness?

By noon the following day, I was better hydrated, but a sleepless night had me looking as drawn as when Todd had first carried me through the hospital doors. We met with a dietician whose counsel fell like pearls into Todd's outstretched palms. Soon thereafter we were turned out with a diagnosis of hyperemesis gravidrum – severe morning sickness –, a prescription for vitamin B-6, ginger extract, outpatient IV, and rest. We were going home.

"I promise we'll come back," Todd said the following day as we settled into the cool leather seats of our chartered flight.

After leaving the hospital, it quickly became apparent that Todd had no intention of picking up our honeymoon where we had left off before the bloody weekend. The sun had made a brief appearance that morning, long enough to start melting the snow. However, by evening, the temperature had dipped again to refreeze the slush. It was a hazard from which Todd was determined to shelter me.

My attempts at seduction were also met with resounding failure. Whether due to concerns for my poor health, repulsion from the persistent bouts of nausea that sent me scurrying to the toilet, or his refusal to defile the home of his child, Todd was unmoved by my lascivious promptings. Granted, a day out of the hospital wasn't much, but Todd had never denied me before. The rejection had the effect of a slap dealt to a woman unaccustomed to violence. At first I was equal parts incredulous and hurt. And then I was angry.

"Is this how it's going to be?" I asked, and Todd, unaware of the brewing storm, laughed.

"It's eleven at night, Amy. Go to sleep."

"Fuck you!" I screamed at him, trying to find purchase amidst the mountain of down bedding to make good my escape. A firm arm around my middle had me flailing like a fish on the end of a line.

"Maybe in the morning," he answered, not even trying to hide the fact that he found me amusing. "If you're feeling better. Now stop being hormonal and go to sleep." It was a blatant attempt at humoring me, one I didn't buy at all. Still the fact that he had been glued to my side for two days offered some comfort. Granted, he wasn't fucking me, but he wasn't fucking anyone else either.

Catching that train of thought, I instantly slapped some sense into myself. Never, never, I promised myself, would I excuse Todd's indifference to me, or be grateful for his mere presence.

I turned to him with fire burning in my eyes. "Is this how it's going to be, Todd?"

He ended up going down on me, because the last thing Todd wanted was for any trace of regret to touch his precious child.

Well after midnight when we both should have been asleep, his words whispered next to my ear tickled the tiny hairs next to his lips. "Have you thought about names?"

"No," I replied frankly, too late realizing that I should have been ashamed of the enduring neutrality with which I regarded our baby.

"Don't feel badly," Todd said, correctly interpreting my mood. "It takes time to get accustomed to the idea that you've created life."

"Have you?" I asked, knowing with every fiber of my being that he had. It was better to turn the question back on him than to dwell on the fact that I'd had eight weeks more than Todd to become accustomed to the idea of our child.

"Yes, but I want you to choose the Christian names," he said, splaying his fingers over my abdomen. "On the condition that you give our baby my name and a fresh start. None of that hyphenated crap and no namesakes. I don't want your father anywhere near our children."

How could I sleep after that? With nothing to do but watch the light shift across the sky, I found very little point in sticking it out in Paris. We left the next afternoon and arrived home that same afternoon. It was quite possibly one of the longest days of my life, and I was grateful for the extra hours of daylight. As Todd slept, I ran through the plan I had been developing these past few days. This pregnancy was undoubtedly an ace up my sleeves, but I still had to be careful not to overreach in my quest to bleed Richard.

The man sleeping across the aisle from me had taught me a lot in the half year since I'd met him. The image he portrayed to the world was the opposite of the man behind the mask. It was the key to his success… leashing the soulless machine until the prey was within his sights and the inevitable outcome was death.

For all his faults, Richard wasn't a fool. If Todd knew there was more to my goings-on in Paris than I claimed, then the thought must have occurred to Richard as well. The fact that Richard was constrained in uncovering the truth by the need for secrecy in his association with Sergei Afanasenko was a boon for me. As much as the notion repulsed me, it was imperative that I erase the shadow of doubt from Richard's mind. I would have to follow the dance he'd led for over a decade now. And I didn't have much time to quell the fires that raged deep inside me.

I was working from bed late the next morning when Richard appeared in the doorway of my parents' bedroom. The transition that had begun prior to our departure for Europe was now complete. My belongings stood in the place of my mother's.

Todd didn't share my hang-ups either. He had no love for my father, and single-mindedly sought to wipe out his presence in our home. It required some adjustment on my part, but in the end, I relented, because nothing Todd replaced could have undermined my father's legacy. I was the physical embodiment of my father's work, and at the center of my being his memory endured, whether Todd wished it or not.

It was still a shock to find Richard in this holy sanctum though – a shock I was forced to bury in a shallow grave. I recalled the slow death of his man, Gay, and comforted myself with the knowledge that Richard too would soon suffer. My face split into a grin that surprised him.

"Richard!" I called to him with enough enthusiasm to fuel Todd's approval. His hand on Richard' shoulder was both a restraint and a reassurance.

"Can you come downstairs, Amy?" Todd asked, his smile conspiratorial as he squeezed Richard.

"Are you allowing me out of bed?" My stomach contents burned at the playful banter, revolting at the presence of my parents' murderer.

"If you're up to it."

"I'll manage. Let me get dressed and I'll be right down."

I waited a full minute after the door was pulled shut before I set aside the laptop and got out of bed. My knees shakily carried me to the ensuite bathroom where I struggled to turn the lock on the door on account of my damp palms and trembling fingers. My stomach ticked, but this wasn't morning sickness. All I needed was a little courage and a liberal splash of cold water on my overheated skin.

I tested my smile in the mirror until it felt real. I pulled my hair into a high ponytail, as if to prove I had nothing to hide. The sweat on my palms went into smoothing the flyaways. Then I dressed in an oversized sweater and soft jeans – the image of comfort.

Todd and Richard were seated around the kitchen table, whispering over a stew Mrs. Bankowski had made for us that morning. The quiet hum of their voices broke off at my approach, and I pretended not to notice. Todd pulled out a chair for me... the one next to his and furthest from the block of kitchen knives on the nearby counter. Even if Todd suspected what I had in mind for Richard, it was a wasted precaution. If I were to cut my way through the Judas, it would be with Bill. His blood would mix with Sergei's as I stared deeply into his eyes and watched the life ebb away.

Todd's arms across my shoulders pulled me into the protective cove of his side. "This is the strongest she's been in a week," he said.

It was a casual lie with severe consequences. To innocent ears, it was the conclusion of his explanation of the hardships of pregnancy. My appearance certainly backed up whatever assertions he had made to Richard. I was still gaunt and the glow of pregnancy might have been a myth for all the good it did me. But I understood the words for what they truly were... Todd's guarantee of my innocence, because apparently I wasn't strong enough to do whatever Richard thought I might have done.

"I'm fine," I said, but it was a deliberately weak protest.

"See if you can keep this down," he said, pushing his bowl of stew under my nose, dismissing my predictable refusal.

The last thing I wanted then was to share a meal with Richard, talk about new life and feign fresh beginnings in a house overrun by ghosts of his making. But I would need more than just courage if I were to hold Richard to his accounts. Patience and an ally wouldn't be misplaced. I wasn't going to look Todd's gift horse in the mouth either. So I picked over the chunks of meat and vegetables in thick broth with seeming reluctance, while Richard looked on with a neutral expression.

"So when is the baby due?" he finally asked.

"September," Todd answered, passing me a piece of bread.

"That's... timely," was Richard's reply. "New memories to take the place of old ones."

Our eyes met and the burn returned to the pit of my stomach. I swallowed hard repeatedly to keep the flames down and my breathing steady. I couldn't have stopped the tears if my life depended on it, and in a sense, it did. The spoon shook in my hands, and to quell the urge to pluck the chilling blue eye from his face, I relinquished my hold on the utensil. It clanged against the edge of the bowl and splashed hot broth over my hand.

Todd's arm about me squeezed me closer to him, luring me away from the brink I was edging towards.

"See what I mean?" Todd said over my head, dragging Richard's attention away from me. "She's been up and down for weeks and it never occurred to me that a baby could be the reason."

Richard had no choice but to believe him. Hadn't I stormed his study declaring the end of my marriage just a couple of weeks ago? He had witnessed firsthand the ravages of the fertility treatment on my body on our last run together. Besides, there was no denying September was significant in more ways than one. It was also when Todd and I had married.

"Why don't you go back to bed?" Todd offered kindly. "You're still not well."

It was an offer I seized with both hands, nearly tripping over my feet in my haste to leave. They were both cold-blooded killers, but undeniable gentlemen too. They both stood as I did. I would have run away without delay, but Richard at the last minute blocked my path. Instinct would have had me cringe from his touch, but that was a luxury I couldn't afford.

With one hand on my shoulder and another cupping my cheek, Richard's thumb rubbed away the last of my tears. I watched as his eyes catalogued the ravages I had endured over the past week. His eyes that used to be a source of confusion – one distinctly blue and the other brown – seemed perfectly suited now. It explained how one part of him could have committed an unforgivable act of betrayal while the other went on as if nothing had happened at all.

"Congratulations, Amy," he said. It was a tipping of his cap to me, an open-ended gesture of respect, whether for pulling the wool over Todd's eyes as we had conspired; for gracefully falling behind the line he had drawn for me in the pursuit of his legacy; or whatever schemes I had been a part to while in Paris.

In that moment I understood his game. His neutrality was a trap, because suspicion always haunts the guilty mind. He would supply all the rope I needed to hang myself.

It was the last time he would make me cry, the last time I would cede control to him, the last time I would face this man like the helpless child I used to be. I wasn't running in the rain anymore, alone and terrified of what was happening. I would become the terror that stalked him.

I smiled through moist eyes before wrapping my arms around his middle and making of his empty chest a haven. "Thank you, Richard. I'm very happy."

As I listened to his heartbeat, knowing they were counting down to the moment when I would take his life, the words resounded with truth. It would take a lot more to fool Richard, but the approval shining in Todd's eyes told me I was well on my way.

THIRTY-FOUR

February 8, 2012

"What's one more day?" I asked the woman in the mirror. It was the same question I had been asking for four weeks now, the same question I would ask tomorrow. She had good reason to think I had forgotten our purpose. I was dressed to kill, but not in the way she expected.

Ten weeks pregnant, and I had to admit that I had never looked better in my life. The terrible skin Sergei Afanasenko had thrown in my face was nothing shy of flawless now, lit from within by a golden light. In the dead of winter I was radiant. Dark-shadowed eyes twinkled from an otherwise nude made-up face. A semi-natural beauty stared back at me.

It was as much a lie as the life I was living.

I had had my hair cut in long layers like Adeline Haddad's, and lately it moved with buoyancy rarely seen outside a shampoo commercial. Tonight, it had been professionally wound in a thick braid around my head like a crown, with a few wisps carefully arranged to imitate the natural fall of healthy wind-tousled hair. It was the perfect frame for a blue, one-shouldered Grecian style gown with a gold embroidered belt.

"Holy fuck!" Todd declared from the doorway. With one hand clutched over his heart and a stricken expression, he feigned having been dealt a punishing blow. "You trying to kill me, babe?"

For his part, Todd was as devastatingly handsome, as usual, in dress blues. But that was all Todd; he didn't need nearly as much help as I did to achieve perfection. I cut my eyes at the mirror and grinned at him.

I had arrived home late from the hairstylist and had barely had fifteen minutes to slip on the dress hidden in the closet of my old bedroom.

"Says the man who almost gave me a heart attack." He was breathtakingly beautiful, but he had also developed a habit of sneaking up on me. Todd was trying to catch me in a lie, but wishing at the same time, that I would stick to the terms of our bathtub agreement. He shrugged but was unapologetic. If his distrust could deter the naturally dishonest bent of my mind… prevent a tragedy from happening, then he would forever keep me on my toes.

"Ready?"

I slipped on my mother's diamond earrings, my only adornment, and nodded.

Drawing closer in the way of an animal on the prowl, Todd curled one hand around my waist and cupped my nape with the other. "Forgetting something?" he asked, eyes narrowed and lips pressed together. It might have been a trap, but I'd been on my Ps and Qs lately.

Or as much as I could while actively plotting the death of dear Uncle Richard.

"I don't think so," I said in all honesty. Head tilted back, I met and held his gaze with nothing but openness.

Todd breathed a deep hum before lowering his mouth to mine. The man really was breathtaking in the literal sense of the word. His kiss stole the air from my lungs. My blood surged through my veins as his lips and tongue moved over mine, teasing, tasting, driving me wild. I gasped as the nerve endings fired in rapid succession down my spine like a string of dynamite.

I couldn't believe it was still like this… always like this.

Todd pulled away before I was ready to give him up. How could I ever give him up?

"Now you're ready," he said, breath gusting against our wet mouths. He knew my body better than me. He knew I was melting for him, wet and ready to blow off the evening's engagement at the least encouragement. That was the danger with Todd. He was a temptation I could not afford. We were growing comfortable with each other, and it would have been so easy to simply accept that this was my life now. And it wasn't a terrible life either. Far from it in fact.

Except I would also have to accept the injustice of my parents' murders too.

How could I move on when the one responsible for their deaths was such an integral part of my present? I had seen and heard more of him in the past few weeks than in the past year. He was everywhere, constantly looking over my shoulder, checking that I was keeping straight. He was almost as bad as Todd.

But omnipresence didn't go hand in hand with omniscience.

Todd knew tonight's plans. He was determined that I not keep anything from him again. It was his birthday after all, and I had arranged an intimate dinner with fifty close family and friends to celebrate both the anniversary of his birth and his promotion to the Deputy Directorship of Intel J2. It was a photo op Richard had endorsed, and for which he had secured the attendance of a number of Todd's colleagues at the DIA and the Joint Chiefs of Staff.

If either Todd or Richard knew the venue of tonight's celebrations was also the site of an awards dinner for D.C.'s best in the field of journalism, they never mentioned it to me. I'd been open in my preparations, had even hired a professional at Richard's behest to take care of the details. No one could rack up the planned run-in with Erika Harris to anything but chance.

I was far from looking my best the last time we had met. It was on that account that I had paid special attention to my appearance tonight. Not only was I dressed to the nines, my accessories included the man of the hour; his parents who were visiting from Florida; and the McDowells.

My motives ran deeper than simply rubbing a rival's nose in her disappointment. My intentions were to set the stage for Richard's ultimate, and fast approaching, demise.

Really, of what consequence was one more night when we had waited twelve years and the end was near?

Todd solicitously helped me down the stairs, saving me from a fall that would have belied the image of grace we were selling to his parents. Mrs. Bankowski, who had never been far from their sides for the duration of their visit, was also waiting in the entry hall.

"Isn't she beautiful?" he asked everyone and no one at the same time. Even on down-time Todd was such a bullshit merchant.

His parents were old, too old for winter, but they had insisted on making the trip. I bore their wrinkled hands on my cheeks as they welcomed the news of their first grandchild. It wasn't their fault my parents had been cheated of this moment, that they had been forced to face death together instead of a warm retirement.

Mrs. Bankowski had proved herself a very clever woman. She took the opportunity of the Birches visit to make herself indispensible to me. Through her own initiative her household duties had been expanded to include the role of hostess to Todd's parents. She attended to their every need, driving them into 'town' whenever they wished. She helped them into coats and scarves and bundled them into the back of the car. She would even turn down their beds before finally retiring for the night to the apartment she shared with her husband on the property.

Todd and his parents carried the bulk of the conversation on the forty-minute drive to the National Press Club. Perhaps he had been lulled into quiet complacency by the privacy afforded by the venue, or he had truly put other considerations behind him, and had expected me to do the same. Whatever the cause, Todd seemed genuinely unconcerned, loitering inside the lobby while I consulted with our coordinator and the event planner on a few last minute details.

Richard arrived while seating charts were being confirmed, the presentation of courses re-worked and special diets matched to guests. He played politician for Todd's parents, but I could feel his eyes on me the entire time. There was nothing to prove that I was involved in anything deeper than what it appeared… nothing as deliberate as using the pretext of rehashing details that had long been settled and for which I was not needed to await the appearance of Erika Harris. Her awards dinner was scheduled for 7p.m., and already a steady stream on invitees were making their way to their assigned room.

With about ten minutes to spare, the woman of the night arrived. With one eye on the target, I moved to greet Richard who was a beacon of respectability in his dress whites. I spared a kiss on the cheek for Aunt Abby who was as high as a weather balloon. If she had an inkling of the monster she was married to, then I could excuse her desire to spend every day of her life in a chemical-induced haze. I wouldn't excuse the fact that she had stayed married to him however, after he had killed not only his best friend, but hers too. For the moment, she was engrossed in an at-length discussion of the décor with the elder Birches.

"Admiral," I greeted Richard with a smile and kiss that came easier each time. I had had many occasions for practice lately.

"Well, look at you," he declared, holding me at arms' length so his eyes could roam to their content. "Don't you look like a real lady!" It wasn't the heights of praise, but I had to admit this look was unprecedented for me.

"I think we're ready," was Todd's response, which was a departure from the exuberance he'd demonstrated up to that point. A firm hand at the base of my spine prompted me to lead the way. The combination of his impatience and reserve was remarkable to even Richard – and a dead giveaway that the trap had been sprung.

One casual look around and our eyes met across the dark wood paneled lobby. She was still a beauty and in good standing with her stylist. The black lace cocktail dress was anything but matronly on her svelte frame. And either she'd been on assignment in the tropics or had spent the afternoon on a tanning bed. Her hair was shorter though, hanging about her shoulders in layers that would have been right at home on a Hollywood A-lister. Interesting that she had made the cut in the dead of winter.

She looked away first. Her confusion as to what was an acceptable course of action bought me the precious moments I needed. While she was looking around, wishing she was anywhere but there, I made my move. Despite Todd's hissed protest and Richard's quiet plea for an explanation, I intercepted Erika on her way to her reunion.

"Erika," I called, intent on not being ignored. As much as she would have liked to ignore me, the insistence with which I pursued her was a clear warning against it.

Regardless of the planning that had gone into this encounter, I was not unaffected facing the woman with whom my husband had been unfaithful. This may have been rehearsed, but the tension was real. She tried valiantly to put on a brave face, turning to me with a placid expression and a shaky smile. I half-expected her to ask if we had met. I didn't give her the chance.

"I know," I said indelicately, backing her securely into a corner. She refused to meet my gaze, her cheeks tinting a becoming shade of pink. I didn't look half as appealing as she did when I was on the receiving end of the public humiliation. "I know about you and Todd."

"I don't know what he might have told you.," she said lamely, hands twisting nervously around her clutch, "I want you to know there's nothing between us."

"I know," I said with conviction she could not ignore. Her eyes rose to mine and in them I found the embarrassment but also confusion. "I just wanted to be sure *you* understand that there is nothing between you and my husband."

She might have been beaten, but Erika Harris was far from broken. The spirit I had counted on reared to life, sparking a distant light in her eyes. I fanned it.

"I don't blame you for what you did," I said, belying the commiseration of my words with a stiff spine and bared claws. "I understand his appeal. And his… indiscretion, shall we say… came at a difficult time for us. But I want you to know that we've moved past that now, and I have his assurances that it will never happen again."

Her smile was a thin line completely devoid of humor. "Why you would think I care about any of this—"

"Because I forgive you," I broke in. "I wanted you to know that. I have forgiven him. And our families have forgiven him too," I added, dragging the elder Birches and the McDowell brood to her attention in one fell swoop.

She regarded me for a tense moment from beneath her brows, her incredulity plain for all to see. She was on the verge of telling me what I could do with my magnanimity when something of greater importance snagged her attention from over my shoulder. Any D.C. journalist of even mediocre worth would recognize the Director of National Intelligence, and I could tell by the way Erika readjusted the words on her lips that she had computed my reference, and my earlier proximity to Richard, and had arrived at the intended conclusion.

"Our marriage is very important to us," I added, fully aware of the overkill although it was not misplaced coming from a spurned wife hell-bent on revenge. "As is our growing family."

On the count of two, Erika's eyes widened in shock, then flickered down my frame. Without x-ray vision, there was nothing to see. But the catty smile I conjured with little effort was adequate confirmation.

The thin line of her mouth twisted derisively. "Congratulations," she said, but what she truly meant was, "Eat shit and die, bitch!"

Her gaze caught something of interest over my shoulder again, but this time held it. I had planned for Todd, was surprised he had allowed this to go on as long as it had in fact.

"I'll be sure to share my best wishes with Todd," Erika said, the blatant intimation that she intended to share much more with him explicitly designed to wipe the smugness off my face. It was a salvo that commanded more than a little of my respect.

The gauntlet had been tossed. I accepted the challenge with a quick jab.

"He doesn't want you. I believe he's already told you as much."

"Amy." Even better than Todd, it was Richard who had come to break up the catfight. It couldn't have worked out better if I had scripted his approach. The whole purpose of baiting Erika was to ensure the destruction of Richard's dreams garnered the global coverage such a colossal fall deserved.

"Uncle Richard." I turned to him with a deliberately practiced smile. He looked between us, narrowed eyes piercing the thin fog of civility.

"Admiral McDowell," Erika said in stiff greeting. He might have been the most powerful man in the world, but she was a successful journalist. She was not unaware of the power she had at her fingertips.

How naïve of her to think people like us played by the rules of the civilized. If Richard thought she was a threat, he would kill her. He'd certainly gotten away with eliminating more important people than Erika Harris would ever be. Or so he thought.

"Young lady," he returned her greeting, but it was also a dismissal. His extended arm luring me away while he turned his back on her was a brisk wind dispelling whatever uncertainty remained. It also fanned her anger at my brazen attack, and placed me and all my attachments squarely in her crosshairs.

Perfect. Mission accomplished.

Her spite was what I wanted, a tool to destroy Richard – one he would not recognize until it was too late.

"Was that really necessary?" Richard asked while ushering me away. Either Todd had filled him in, or Richard had conducted his own research in the wake of Major Edward Cummings' death.

I met his disapproving stare with a mutinous glare. "Absolutely."

He squeezed my elbow. "Don't ruin the evening for your husband," he chided. "He's worked very hard for his position. And it's his birthday, for God's sake. I thought you'd have better sense than to call attention to yourself like that. You'd better put certain things behind you if you know what's good for you. You're going to be mother. Act like it!"

I let him go on without protest. Let him think he still had influence over me. Let him think I was beaten… that he was safe. Over the hum of his words and across the lobby of this historic building, my eyes found Todd. In an attempt to forestall an even more embarrassing spectacle, someone – likely Richard – had set him to the task of inviting the last of our guests into our dining room.

As our gazes locked, I channeled the anger, hurt and humiliation he had heaped on top of me the night he had killed Ed. He'd explained away the reasons why he had broken my heart. And in moving on with our lives, I may have given him the impression that I had forgiven him. But now he knew I had not – would never – forget.

Todd looked away, a deep blush coloring his cheeks. He knew me better than anyone, and I had counted on precisely that understanding.

"Amy, I'm sorry," he began after Richard had deposited me before him. "I didn't know she was going to be here." Of course not. How could he?

"Don't," I rejected his apology. I took my place at his side and smiled my shaky support. "Let's not talk about it." He silently patted my hand where it lay on his arm. I squeezed the arm beneath the blue coat. It was a deliberate gesture, meant to reinforce my quavering voice with some of his strength. "Just promise me it's over… you won't see her again."

He stared at me in disbelief for a moment, then shook his head in a quick recovery. " Of course," he effused. "There's nothing there. I promise. I have absolutely no intention of ever… You have nothing to worry about, Amy."

I sighed with fake relief and gifted him with a broader smile. "Happy Birthday."

Todd, eager to accept my concession, bent to accept my kiss on his cheek. He couldn't hide his relief that for once, I had no intention of making it hard for him. He took it as a sign of progress, and enthusiastically moved us towards the waiting celebrations.

"Thanks, babe."

"Do I look OK?" I asked at the last minute, a self-conscious hand patting my perfect hair in place.

"You're beautiful," he said, grateful for the dodged bullet. "Absolutely perfect. I love you so much."

"I love you too," I beamed. It being true didn't mean I wasn't disgusted by the role I had to play.

Richard, the last to enter, looked on with grudging respect at my capacity for forgiveness and willingness to move on.

THIRTY-FIVE

April 16, 2012

I was twenty weeks pregnant and getting dressed for our ultrasound appointment. The simple endeavor was harder than it should have been. The pregnancy was turning out to be more of an inconvenience than I had originally thought.

In truth though, I hadn't given much thought to the process beyond actual conception. And it was becoming more and more clear each week that I was woefully unprepared.

The morning sickness had faded halfway through the first trimester, but I had been warned to ease up on my running routine. Light caution had fallen on Todd's ears like an edict. There was little choice but to compromise on a seven-mile, five-times-per-week maximum... after he had burned the right foot of all three pairs of my sneakers. The combination of a relatively sedentary lifestyle and the mountains of food that were always on hand, thanks to Mrs. Bankowski, had resulted in twelve pounds being added to my unforgiving frame.

"Is this really necessary?" I had asked the housekeeper one afternoon back in February. Why there was a full spread laid out an hour after lunch in the middle of the week was beyond me. Chips and dips, nuts and grains, fried chicken, baked goods and a cheese board, was excessive by anyone's standards.

I didn't miss that Mrs. Bankowski's eyes flickered to a spot beyond my right shoulder.

"I asked her to put together a small variety," came Todd's breezy response. We'd been fucking for the past two hours and he had showered and was readjusting the collar of his khaki shirt over the service uniform sweater. "A couple of friends may stop by."

That was another bone of silent contention between us. Todd had an endless stream of friends and acquaintances who invaded our home willy-nilly. I avoided them as much as possible, sticking to my father's study or our bedroom after the initial – and compulsory — greeting.

"A small spread?" I had quizzed, the sarcasm dripping like warm filling from the homemade blueberry turnover I had bitten into.

"Yes," he said matter-of-factly before thanking Mrs. Bankowski with a kiss on the cheek. The only thing that kept her from abandoning all dignity under the warmth of Todd's approbation was the awareness that she wasn't completely out of the woods. In all fairness, my irritation should have been totally directed at the man of the house. But what kind of bitch would I be if I let her get off scot-free?

"Aren't you going back to work?" I asked, sensing a trap somewhere in the vicinity. I watched narrow-eyed as he slowly made his way through the house, heading for the door.

"Yes, and I'll be late for a meeting if I don't head out right now. But Steve Grayson and a couple of old friends from the D.R. should be here in an hour or so. I told them it was OK to chill for a few hours until I got home." His explanation was punctuated by his pre-departure check – phone, keys, access pass, I.D., satchel, uniform coat. "You'll cover for me, won't you, babe?" He already had the front door open, letting in a particularly blustery gust of air I wasn't prepared for in my yoga pants and running bra.

"Who the fuck do you think I am?" I yelled at him. "I'm not your fucking housewife, Todd! I have shit to do today, you know... like fucking work. I don't even like your jerk-off friends!"

"Language, Amy," he chided with an unrepentant grin. "And don't get all worked up. Remember, the baby." And then he was gone, while Mrs. Bankowski busied herself covering each dish with cling wrap that was as transparent as the both of them. As if that would stop me from passing by the kitchen every few minutes on a futile quest to satisfy a phantom, but no less insatiable, hunger. None of that food was for Steve

Grayson and his bullshit entourage. It was all for me... or rather the baby, which brought me back to my present dilemma.

I had nothing to wear. I'd been working from home nearly every day, which was the reason for the sudden realization that nothing in my professional wardrobe fit. It should have been expected, but I hadn't had the occasion to dress in anything more formal than Todd's t-shirts and yoga pants lately.

I pulled a thin tank over a sports bra that was stretched to its limits. I tugged the hem down to cover the gaping zipper of a pencil skirt that was only half way fastened. An oversized sweater and three-inch heels – my most conservative shoes – completed the unfashionable ensemble.

There was no avoiding the inevitable. I had to go shopping.

I was trying not to look at myself in the mirror while running a brush through my hair when Todd's bellow echoed through the house. It was a familiar enough occurrence that led me to accurately judge the origin of the summons. The downstairs den where Todd often held court.

"Amy, get down here!" He sounded alarmed, but I hadn't been up to much lately... nothing that would concern Todd. Not yet anyway.

There was an old Arab saying – well, the first time I heard it was from an old Arab – that said a man should beat his wife daily; because even if he had no idea what she had done, she did. So I took my time, tackling the stairs barefooted.

I was counting on being able to talk myself out of whatever transgression Todd had uncovered.

The housekeeper was in the kitchen – what else was new – and I found Todd alone, in the den, which vastly improved my mood. As mad as he might be, he wouldn't want Mrs. Bankowski knowing what was beneath the surface.

I was also pleased we had no other guests. Yes, we were heading out, but that had never been a deterrent before. I had taken to locking my father's study and carting the key around with me, after coming home from a run one morning to find Ed's replacement, Captain Joey Marshall, at our kitchen table, while Todd was in the shower upstairs. Granted Mrs. Bankowski had been with him, piling a plate high with eggs and refilling his coffee despite his faint protests. But he could have incapacitated her blindfolded with one hand tied behind his back if he'd wanted. Then what would have stopped him from invading my command central?

"What is it?"

Todd had his cell phone pressed to his ear and the television remote in the other hand. He was standing behind a desk we had found for him while shopping for accents for the house.

He had moved out most of my parents' things, claiming they were dated. The truth however, was he wanted to erase my father from my existence. Todd used the space to work every now and then, but it was kept mostly bare, consistent with the public nature of the room.

He pointed at a muted program, but made no attempt to restore the audio. I glared at him with baleful eyes, but he jabbed the remote again in the direction of the screen. A CNN panel was discussing allegations of Secret Service sexual misconduct. Without audio, I wasn't sure what Todd's motives were. I could guess, but I wasn't going to make it easy for him. If he was going to accuse me of something, he would have to come right out and say it.

He had not brought up Angelika in months, had been satisfied with the presumption that she had returned to Ukraine. And as far as I knew, the current investigation being dissected by the panelists was limited to the Secret Service. No mention had been made, as yet, of the use of escort services by embassy officials in the Dominican Republic.

My former boss, O'Brien, had thrown a wrench into the extracurricular affairs of some of Todd's closest friends at Mission. Not to mention the fact that I had subtly nudged the locals into cracking down on the prostitution ring through which Angelika had been trafficked.

The anti-trafficking unit had made headlines locally; I had recruited the prostitute-come-mole to bag Sergei Afanasenko; and O'Brien had safeguarded the embassy's image. It was a win on all counts.

Unless, it had somehow come to light and was now being debated on the news, which would inevitably lead to questions about the escorts. It was in no one's best interest to have it bandied about that one of the women had departed the Dominican Republic on an American passport – that I had acquired for her. Or that she had disappeared into thin air.

I did not hold the view that confession was good for the soul, so Todd was going to have to come up with more than just a muted debate. The main points flashed across the screen as panelists gave their 'expert' opinion, but I had yet to find anything worth commenting on. I turned back to Todd with wide, innocent eyes.

He stalled me with one finger raised in silent plea for time. I stared while he confirmed details of a meeting with the person on the other end of the line. I shifted from one foot to the other in a clear display of impatience, to which Todd responded with an endearing smile. It couldn't have been all bad news for me, I surmised. I relaxed into an ever-improving mood and sat down to put my shoes on.

"There, there!" Todd snapped at me, remote jabbing at the silent screen again, urgently this time. "I'm sorry, one second," he said into the phone then held it six inches from his ear in a bid for privacy. "Check out the runner."

I did and the smile I had gifted him melted from my lips as I caught sight of the fast moving words at the bottom of the televisions screen.

Senior Hezbollah official killed in explosion on Lebanon-Syria border, the first Breaking News headline read. It was followed in rapid succession by:

Hasan al-Qasim believed responsible for 1983 and 1984 bombings of US embassy and Marine Corps HQ in Lebanon that claimed the lives of 265 US personnel.

I schooled my features into a neutral expression, burying my irritation at Don Blitzner beneath a mask of insouciance. I'd been badgering him for weeks for an update on the Mohamed al-Mohamed case. He'd invited me to Guantánamo twice, invitations that I had declined. It wasn't that I was squeamish about the treatment handed out to the detainee during his interrogation. I had provided the information that was being used to bait him psychologically while his body's physical resistance was broken. And I had no regrets about that.

Blitzner thought my refusal was the result of Todd's interference. True, Todd had become even more protective as my pregnancy advanced. But he would not have succeeded in deterring my visit to the facility if I had been intent on going. He could have called in certain favors to achieve his ends, but at the risk of an unmendable breach in our trust. So if I had wanted to oversee Mohamed al-Mohamed's interrogation, then of course, I would have.

I didn't go for the simple reason that I didn't *need* to be there. Unlike Blitzner, I took no satisfaction from watching the suffering of others... with one exception. Richard.

Todd finished up his call and turned to me with a grin. "You did that," he said, jabbing the remote at the screen again.

I scampered off the sofa as gracefully as my new gait permitted, dodging the responsibility behind Todd's praise. "Ah, no," I said, heading for the door. "I do believe that honor has gone to Israel."

Todd intercepted my hurried departure, pulling me into his arms and holding me as if to start a slow dance. I only stayed because one hand proceeded to caress my backside, while he nuzzled my neck. His kisses burned their way through my body, settling heavily in my core. I liked it.

"You were telling the truth," he whispered against my ear.

I was grateful he hadn't insisted on eye contact while resurrecting the memory of our disastrous honeymoon. There was no accounting for what he would find on my face.

The best lies were based on truth – everyone with a golden tongue knew that. If Todd wasn't so desperate to find the good in me, he would recognize that. But I didn't want to dwell on that. As things stood, he had already dampened the heat his skin on mine had caused.

"I'm proud of you," he said, spinning me around so his back was to the exit. He kicked at the double doors, pushing them together without shutting them completely. He walked me backwards to his empty desk with lascivious intent in his eyes. Before I knew it, he had tugged the sweater over my head and pulled the straps down on both the tank and the bra. "So proud of you, babe," he whispered before his mouth closed over a breast.

I gasped from the shock of my thighs hitting the wood and his mouth closing, warm, wet and exciting around me. With rhythmic pulls, he squeezed a groan from me. I closed my eyes, but arched my back to give better access, refusing to dwell on the source of his pride. It wasn't that I had had a hand in Hasan al-Qasim's death; it was the simple fact that I had told the truth – something Todd clearly thought was beyond me. What was the point of taking offense at the truth?

"These are definitely bigger," he declared a moment before switching breasts. "D's, baby," he squeezed them. "Jesus, I can't wait to watch you feed our baby." One hand fumbled with the back of my skirt, while the other raised the hem to around my hips. In spite of my senses being rocked to the beat of his mouth, I knew the moment Todd found the gaping zipper I had tried to hide. "What's with your clothes, babe?"

"Nothing fits," I said around a moan, wordless protest to his mouth having abandoned my aching breasts.

"Jesus, Amy. Why don't you go shopping?"

I halfheartedly tried to push him away. I wanted him to keep sucking on me, work his way up to fucking me, but not if he was going to find fault too. "Because I've been busy," I snapped, "tracking fucking terrorists, that's why."

Todd laughed, but pushed away my hands that were slapping at his. He tipped me backwards unceremoniously until my back was pressed flat against the desk. Urgent hands pushed up my skirt until my panties were exposed. Then he took his time gazing down at me.

"My baby," he said. He kissed my growing bump and rubbed it in with his palm. I relished looking into his eyes during these moments. The blue was bright, shining with things I never expected from him: joy, pride, love. It didn't matter that those things were directed at his child. The fact that I could look at him and see them – so different from the frustration, anger, distrust – that I was filled to the brim with a warm effervescence.

Todd didn't seem to mind that the panties were too small; the waistband bunched low on my hips to barely cover the important parts. Those he pulled down my legs while unbuckling his pants, confirming my faith in his ability to multitask.

"Look how wet you are," he groaned as I made room for him between my legs.

That too was a side effect of the pregnancy. Todd had always been able to turn me on at the drop of a hat, but the copious amounts of natural lubricant had surprised us both.

"Watch out, kid. I'm coming in," he said, pressing another kiss to my belly, and eking a giggle out of me. This lightness during sex was new. There had always been such intensity about us. It was still there, but somehow we were able to make room for more.

He pushed inside me and we both held our breaths then sighed in unison. He wasted no time setting a smooth rhythm, stroking me inside and out with remarkable skill.

"Don't cum in me," I told him. "We have the ultrasound in an hour."

"Do you think they'll mind that I dump my wad in you? How do they think we made this baby? This is their livelihood, Amy. They look at cum all day."

I laughed despite being grossed out. But Todd soon wiped the grin off my face.

"Be quiet," Todd whispered though he was shaking with laughter. "Or Mrs. Bankowski is going to come over here to see what's wrong." The television remote was across the room, dropped onto the sofa, too far away to unmute the program now.

"What's the matter? You don't mind the doctor dipping his equipment in your cum, but you don't want the housekeeper to know we fuck?"

"She's a grandmother," he explained. He had meant to say more— make sense of that madness – but I tightened my legs around his hips and pulled him deeper. The words, rational thought, and good intentions abandoned him, to be replaced by single-minded dedication to the task at hand.

One hand clamped onto my hip and another gripped my bent knee as Todd pulled me firmer, closer, higher onto him. The baby was the last thing on his mind as he pounded into me in short, sharp thrusts. The perfectly coiffed hair came undone with the man, spilling in lush curls over his brow. His nostrils flared and jaw clenched as I came, trying and failing to contain the growl that rose from the end of his spine along with the deep blush that flushed his chest and neck and face.

And I couldn't have cared less what Mrs. Bankowski thought about us.

Todd came in streaming jets all over my exposed belly. He rubbed that into my skin too. He was considerate like that... respectful of my body and mindful of the boundaries I set.

"Nobody's going to dip their equipment in my baby batter," he said.

Later, much later, while stretched out on an examination table in a dark room, Todd came face to face with that possibility.

"Do you want to know the sex?"

"No," I said firmly enough to cover Todd's silence.

"Sure?" he asked.

I nodded. "Positive."

The sonographer shrugged, but his disappointment was plain. He turned to Todd. "What about you, colonel?"

"I'll wait," Todd replied cautiously, as if there really was a choice. Specialist he might be, but the man had taken one look at the birds on Todd's epaulets and lost his damn mind.

"Do you have a preference?" he persisted. Todd broke his gaze from the screen for the first time in a minute to search me out. His eyes were still moist from hearing his baby's heartbeat over the speakers.

"Healthy," he replied. It was just the sort of bullshit he'd fed on while hiding in the State Department these past few years. "A happy, healthy baby is all I want."

"Well, let me do some checks for you, make sure everything is as it should be," the technician replied with a marked dip in his enthusiasm.

While he went through the motions of measuring the fetus and checking for developmental issues, Todd held my hand and feathered kisses over my face. "Have you thought about names?" he asked.

I nodded. "Tyler, if it's a boy." I gave him a moment to consider it, keeping one eye on Todd's biggest fan to make sure he didn't give away any clues. He was busy clicking away at the mouse, accustomed to offering brief moments of privacy at these times.

Todd nodded and smiled, brushing the hair away from my face. "I like it. Tyler Birch." He brought his face inches from mine. "Any particular reason?"

I shook my head and smiled openly at him, having nothing to hide. "I just like it. If you're not sure, we can go for something else... I like Cole and Cade too."

Todd sighed away his suspicion, satisfied there was no connection to my father. "What if it's a girl?"

I checked on the technician again. "Rose." Todd followed my gaze, but there was nothing in his comportment to indicate the sex of our baby. And it was a timely distraction to throw Todd off the scent.

"That's a beautiful name," Todd said.

"You like it?"

He nodded and pressed his lips to mine in agreement.

A few minutes later, we were left alone so I could dress. I stowed the CD of our baby's first video inside my purse, while Todd folded the edges of the printed photo so it would fit in his wallet next to the one from France.

"Hey, Todd," I said, tugging down the hem on my sweater at the same time I stepped into my shoes.

"Hmm?" He was so focused on not creasing the photo, he couldn't spare me a glimpse.

"You do know that if it's a girl, eventually someone's going to stick their equipment in your baby batter, right?"

I tried to hold in the laugh as I watched him freeze. It was obvious he hadn't thought that far ahead, hadn't considered what it would be like raising a girl. Our eyes met and I watched as the blank expression dissolved into disgust, followed swiftly by rage.

"What the fuck is wrong with you, Amy?" he shouted, unconcerned that any number of personnel or waiting patients might hear him. "Why would you say something like that?"

I lost it, collapsing on the crinkly paper shield of the examination table in a fit of raucous laughter. Todd's mood was not improved by the mirth I had found at his expense – or rather, the chastity of his maybe daughter.

"It would be poetic justice if you had all girls, though," I said while waiting for our discharge papers. It was safer to add fuel to the fire while in the presence of witnesses. "Then you'll be that dad chasing off the little dicks. You'll know exactly what to look for, because the worst of them will be just like you."

He was still seething when we parted ways in the parking lot. We'd taken separate cars, because Todd was heading directly to work while I ran a few errands.

"It better be a boy," he stormed, slamming the driver's door behind me.

I was still laughing so hard I had to rub the ache out of my abdomen while I started my car. He'd been muttering 'fucks' all the way to the parking lot, as he silently recalled his earliest encounters with girls, starting in junior high.

Todd rapped on the window, brows crashed low on his brow, eyes a deep, dark blue. I rolled the window down all the way.

"If it's a girl, she better look like me. Because if she looks anything like you…"

I sighed my pleasure at the compliment, even if he was exaggerating. I took a moment to rest my throbbing jaw. "Really? You're the most beautiful man I've ever met!" I said.

I could tell by the flush that crept up his neck that he had just about reached his limit with me. He would never put words to his wish for an ugly daughter... would never think of wishing anything but the best on his children. But the thought had some appeal to him.

I put the car in gear and backed away, waving at him. He stepped away, turning slowly towards his car as I prepared to drive by him. I braked at the last minute and stuck my head out the window with the car still in drive. Todd already had his door open.

"You think one of Townsend's boys will like her?" I asked and burned rubber making my escape. It was a terrible thing to say, but watching Todd chase after my car from the rearview mirror was the most fun I'd had in a very long time. I don't remember ever laughing until it hurt, and it was a feeling I was happy to have experienced.

It was also a refreshing distraction from the fact that I wasted no time in betraying the man to whom I had promised the truth. Not fifteen minutes later, I walked up to the urgent care counter of an out of the way medical center and asked to have the sex of my baby determined. I had no prescription for an ultrasound, but I had a CD and cash.

"Why didn't you ask to find out the sex?" The receptionist asked.

"I just changed my mind. I realize I really, really want to know," I smiled, and it was real, because I'd had lots of practice all morning.

THIRTY-SIX

I paid for my sins that night.

In between rounds of the sweetest punishment I had ever endured, Todd went to get me some water. I drank deeply while he threw his robe over the curled-foot chair he had added to the bedroom décor – apparently for that express purpose. The house no longer resembled my childhood home; this bedroom was no longer my parents' sanctuary. Surprisingly, it didn't hurt as much as I had feared. In fact, it made times like these much easier to bear, welcome even. Todd was hard again... already.

I set the empty glass aside and he curled himself around my back with deliberate intent. "Sore?" he asked, pushing the hair away from my neck so he could drag his teeth across the sensitive skin. It was barely on the other side of painful, tentatively blurring the line between want and need.

"Baby's OK? Any last requests before I fuck you senseless?" It was a checklist we had already run through twice that evening. And it was only nine o' clock.

"Let me catch my breath, baby," I gasped. He didn't miss that I chose to pass on the out he was offering.

"Fuck, no," he replied, hand brushing down my side and sneaking between my legs. "You say disturbing shit when your mouth's not full of my cock."

I tried not to laugh, but apparently had lost control over my body. The mirth was cut short by the whisper of fingers across my wet and swollen lips at the same time Todd's teeth sank deep into the skin at my throat. I spread my legs wider for him, and in answer, his thumb breached the pucker of my ass.

"Todd!" I cried. I squeezed my eyes shut so tight, my vision blurred.

"On your hands and knees," he commanded, and I would have complied immediately if I didn't have Richard to kill.

"Give me a second, " I pleaded. "I really have to make a call."

Todd's compromise was to position himself between my legs while I dialed. I had almost given up on anyone answering before Todd wedged his shoulders beneath my bent knees. In the nick of time, or at the least convenient moment, depending on how you looked at it, Navy Captain Tom McDowell picked up.

"Amy?"

"Is Michelle awake?" I would have called her directly if I'd had her number. I'd never had any use for it before; she was never really considered family... just Tom's starter wife.

Tom was momentarily stumped by the rapid succession of surprises. That I should call him was a shock in itself, but for me to ask about his wife was unheard of.

"She is. Can I help you, Amy?"

"No. Let me talk to Michelle."

Todd shook his head at my brusque tone. That was one thing pregnancy had not changed. I was the same intolerant, anti-social mess he had married. He didn't like it, but was willing to put up with it because this was family. Since I'd brought him inside our circle, Todd had learned that Richard's boys were always fighting amongst themselves in the absence of a common enemy – usually me. But we were loyal to each other, and had never failed to meet an external enemy as a united front.

It was exactly that loyalty I was counting on.

Todd dipped his head so I could get an eyeful of his firm ass, but only for a second. The lazy lapping of his tongue had my head sinking deep into the pillow. I moaned, making only a half-hearted effort to stifle the deep hum of pleasure.

"Is everything OK, Amy?" Tom ventured, playing the good husband who would stand in the path of a bullet for his wife.

"Will you put Michelle on the fucking phone?" I snapped, one hand holding Todd in place by the back of his head. I couldn't stand it if he stopped. His body jerked with the force of his laugh, the gusts of warm air from his mouth teasing my wet and pulsing flesh.

Tom sighed, but clearly preferred the route of least resistance. I heard him mumbling. "It's Amy. I don't know what she could want at this hour."

"It's nine o' clock, jerk off!" I yelled, but either he had the phone away from his ear and didn't hear, or he preferred to ignore me.

Todd squeezed my thighs and nipped at my clit with his teeth, a silent prompt to relax. Believe me, I wanted to; the sensations were building and I was ready to chase another orgasm. Unfortunately, work came first.

"Well, she wants to talk to you," Tom was saying. "Do you have any idea what this is about?"

Finally he handed the phone over to his wife who was both incredulous and tentative at once. "Hi, Amy?"

I was confounded by her whisper. The only reason Todd and I were in bed at nine was because we'd started fucking at six and had no clear plans to stop any time soon. Michelle didn't sound as if there was any action going on in their house. So they had kids. The girls had to go to sleep some time.

An impatient flick of Todd's tongue urged me to get to the point without delay. "Are you busy tomorrow?"

"Tomorrow?" she sputtered. "I-I don't know. Let me think. There's school tomorrow, then the girls have dance on Tuesdays, but that's not until late, like five. I was hoping to get my hair done in between –"

"I need clothes that fit and Aunt Abby said you were the best person to ask."

In truth, Abby had volunteered to accompany me to the mall. I'd suggested Michelle instead. She was shocked, but was quick to agree that made more sense. At the end of the brief conversation this afternoon, Abby went on her hazy way thinking it had been her idea from the start. There were no plans in place to replace Michelle just yet, so of course anything I could do to make her feel welcome was … well, welcome.

Nevermind that Tom and Michelle had been married for seven years, and had dated for two years before that.

"Me?" Michelle asked, convincing me that the longer I kept up this call the more I would have my words thrown back at me. "Well, I would be happy to share some of my maternity items, but I'm not sure about the fit, Amy."

"I don't want your old clothes, Michelle," I forced through clenched teeth. Only by the grace of Todd's wicked mouth was I able to hold back from naming her the moron she certainly was. "I meant for us to go shopping. Abby said you would be up for it. We can go tomorrow after you drop off the kids."

Right on cue, she was struck dumb. I didn't blame her. I hadn't technically asked, but my willingness to walk into a social situation with Tom's wife was unprecedented.

"What does she want?" I heard Tom ask.

"She wants us to go shopping," she gasped. "Your mother suggested it."

There was no reply before Michelle returned, so his response must have been non-verbal. "Um, OK. I guess. What time?"

"I'll be there at ten."

She thought about it for a second, then found her backbone at the last minute. "Don't you have work tomorrow?" she asked with some bite. I wasn't the only one to have thrown my career in Michelle's face. Richard may have wanted a more gender specific role for me, but he wasn't above using my achievements to reinforce his daughter-in-law's inadequacies.

"Even I deserve a break from keeping your ass safe all the time," I bit right back. Todd nipped again, making me jerk. "Tell Tom we're taking the Porsche."

"I don't think ... well, I'm not so sure—"

"If you're afraid to tell him, I will. Put me on speaker." She did, eagerly. She knew Tom's Porsche was forbidden.

He was the happy father of two girls with a hefty social calendar and daily extracurricular activities that would help to mold them into the trophy brides of Richard's dreams, but Tom's car only had one passenger seat. He had steadfastly refused to give up his Porsche, trading in every few years for a new one.

"Tom, we're taking your car tomorrow. You'll just have to drive the Escalade."

He barked a mirthless laugh. "You've gone and right lost your goddamn mind, Amy."

"Don't make me call Abby," I said on a pant. "You know she's just going to nag Richard until he gets pissed off at you."

"I don't give a flying shit," he laughed. "You're not driving my car."

"Fine. Michelle will drive." He laughed even harder, and even I had to admit that was funny.

"Michelle doesn't drive stick."

"I don't really care which one of us drives, Tom, but we are taking your car. Now we can go hard or we can go easy. Your choice."

The fact that he didn't flatly refuse right away was a sign of victory. He really was just an overgrown child if at forty years old, his parents still held that much sway over him. At seventeen Richard couldn't get me to do anything I didn't want to.

"One scratch, Amy," he said, the dire warning and seething voice wasted on one of the few people in the world Captain McDowell couldn't intimidate. "If there's one scratch on my car..."

"Yeah, yeah," I replied disinterestedly. "Ten o' clock, Michelle." I ended the call before Tom started making promises he knew he couldn't keep.

Todd pulled himself up to my level while I placed the phone on the nightstand. Slowly... much slower than I ever thought he was capable of, he entered me.

"You're a brat, you know that, right?" His deep kiss prevented me from answering. I shuddered, tasting myself on his lips. "Really, Amy, you're going to tell his mother?" he continued to tease, easing in and out in a slow and steady rhythm that had my fingers clutching at the sheets.

"Do we want to talk about Aunt Abby right now?" I asked, lifting my hips to meet his slow descent. It was too slow. Todd was going to make me lose my mind.

"No. Let's not," he whispered, and sank to the hilt. It was so filling, so thrilling, I couldn't breathe. And Todd knew it too. "Breathe, baby," he cooed.

In answer, I wrapped my legs around his hips, my inner muscles tightening around him. We gasped, then groaned, and dissolved into laughter together.

"I'm proud of you, Amy." There was that word again.

At least he recognized I had worked my way around Abby.

"You're happy?" he asked.

The laughter died, but a soft smile touched my lips. Todd traced it with his tongue, rocking his hips deeply until I gasped again and again. His tongue slipped inside, tasting the edges of my moans. Satisfied, he reared back to stare at me, mapping the lines around my eyes and mouth that didn't always come easily to me.

"I'm very happy," I said. "You make me so."

Of course, I knew it couldn't last. I was going to kill his mentor, destroy people he cared about, and betray the trust we had been building over the past few months. Todd would never forgive me... would end me, as he said, if I gave him the chance.

But what harm was there in enjoying these moments? They were so precious... so rare.

THIRTY-SEVEN

When I got to their house the following morning at precisely 9:55, Michelle was waiting on the doorstop with her best Mrs. Tom McDowell suit on. Her white linen crop pants had seams running down the middle of each leg. The navy shell with white polka dots was soft and billowy, but was weighed down by a double strand of pearls and a severe haircut. In consideration of the flighty April weather, she had a white jacket folded over her arm. Her shoes were sensible ankle boots with a kitten heel – tan, like the Coach purse slung over her shoulder. She looked like a mother, a housewife, and the most boring individual I had met all year – all of which she truly was.

And I was willingly throwing myself into her company.

A sweep of the front yard and my eyes landed on Tom's Porsche: a 911 Carrera Cabriolet. It was silver, but I called it grey to piss him off. The reason for my sacrifice.

I stepped out of my car and toed the line of civility, pasting on a brittle smile for Michelle's benefit. She didn't need to know how much I was going to hate the next couple of hours.

Perspective, I told myself. *Do what you have to do to get what you want.*

"Are you going dressed like that?" Michelle called, peering over my shoulder as if she expected a beauty squad to step out of the car too.

My running shoes crunched on the gravel of their driveway as I covered the space between us. The distance passed too soon, unconstrained as I was in yoga pants and a light sweater. It didn't offer much of an opportunity for me to think of a diplomatic response.

Besides, that was Todd's forte, and Michelle was accustomed to my lack of social grace by now.

"I was going to ask you the same thing."

She seemed taken aback, eyes widening and one hand grabbing for a pearl. "What's wrong with what I'm wearing."

I considered her for a moment. She even stood ramrod straight so I could do the honors of cataloguing every piece of her getup, all of which came with a label. I shook my head, refusing to be dragged into Michelle's superficial world, and focused instead on the silver sports car that was parked on the paved walkway.

If it didn't suit my purpose to have Tom driving the car as much as possible after I was done with it, I would have made a point of revving it through the gravel. See if I could connect the dots on the chipped paint job to autograph my name. As much as I would have loved to see the look on Tom's face when he realized I'd fucked up his ride, I had my eyes on a much bigger prize. Richard.

"Nothing," I responded absently to Michelle. "It's very 'you'. Sorry, I don't know what I was expecting. Keys?"

Her mouth puckered like she'd taken a bite out of sour fruit, but she did slap the keys into my outstretched hands. She looked like she was marching off to war as she made her way to the passenger side, but Michelle would rather gnaw off her arm than call it quits. Too much was riding on this jaunt.

She had no idea.

I played around with the navigation system in plain view, then headed north. Michelle, unfortunately had visions of our bonding over lunch and the wind whipping through our hair on the hour-long drive to Annapolis. It was unfortunate in the sense that I had a set itinerary that was limited to the Alexandria-Arlington area, and a time budget that only allowed us to eat on our feet. Michelle may have been the expert on all things maternity, but this was not a social call.

The first order of business was downloading Tom's GPS history. I pulled into one of the busiest gas stations off I-95 and had her run in for flavored water and lottery tickets.

"Birthday present," I said to explain away the scratch-off tickets. She shook her head with equal parts disgust and disbelief while clambering out of the car. She returned three minutes later before I was done stealing Tom's information.

"What do you mean that's the wrong water?" she asked from the sidewalk.

"That's flat. I distinctly said gassy." In truth I'd told her I was feeling a little gassy, but she wasn't going to debate semantics with a pregnant woman. I didn't feel the least remorse for what I was doing however. Tom was more Richard's son than her husband. It was unfortunate that she would be caught in the crossfire, but unavoidable.

With the memory card full of Tom's information safely stowed in my purse, we spent the next three hours replenishing my wardrobe. Michelle had her first drive-thru hamburger since becoming Mrs. Tom McDowell – or so she claimed – which came with a complimentary ketchup stain on her starched pants.

At the end of our day, I insisted on putting the last of our bags in the trunk. Space was tight, but half the show of rearranging purchases to make room was a distraction. While Michelle dabbed at the fading shadow of the stain on her thigh from the comfort of the passenger seat, I slipped a GPS tracking device inside the packaging for the compressor used to inflate his spare tire. A quick signal check from my cell phone, and I was almost guaranteed thirty days of real-time access to Tom's comings and goings.

"So..." Michelle led as we transferred my purchases to my car. "When can we do this again?"

I knew the hunted feeling men must face at the end of a one-night stand. Michelle stood a few feet away – not quite close enough for me to feel her breath on the back of my neck, but too close, as far as I was concerned. In her desperation she apparently forgot the litany of complaints I had faced all day, the least of which was the food. She had complained about my pace as we raced from one shop to the next, and my intractability as she urged me to try new styles; and my flat-out disdain for her mothering advice.

"I think this stuff will go a long way," I said. "Can't think of anything else I might need."

Her smile dipped and she started playing with her hair. Even with the show of youthful vulnerability, she still managed to look much older than her twenty-nine years. I slammed my trunk shut with finality and smiled as she backed away from my car. Somehow she had caught on that I would be spraying gravel on my way out. She was smarter than I gave her credit for.

However, as much as I deplored the idea of ever having to spend another minute in her company, burning the bridge was inadvisable. In the event I had to replace the tracker, or needed access to Tom's home, having a quasi relationship with Michelle was an easy 'in'.

"I could use some pointers on baby stuff, though."

Michelle didn't care that I carelessly threw the offer out. "Sure," she beamed. "Maybe we should invite Mrs. McDowell too."

It took a moment for me to understand she meant Abby. After seven years of marriage, she still called her mother-in-law 'Mrs. McDowell' even though she was also a 'Mrs. McDowell'.

"No."

She wasn't going to curry favor on my time.

"OK. Well, who's planning your shower? We should check your register to make sure we're not doubling up."

I shrugged and opened my door, not sure what that had to do with anything. "I don't know. Todd?"

Her face wrinkled with the beginnings of crow's feet. "Your husband?" she asked incredulously, giving rise to the sneaking suspicion that I didn't know what she was talking about.

"Wait... what shower?" While she had herself a good laugh at my expense, I arranged myself comfortably behind the wheel and started my car. Unlike her, I actually had places to be and things to do... like fuck over her husband... so she was welcome to keep her shower. She explained the concept between slowly fading bouts of giggles. "Like a bachelorette party, but for mothers," I surmised.

Her headshake said my analogy wasn't perfect, but would do. I wasn't sure what she thought my idea of a bachelorette party was, but the truth was I hadn't had one of those either... wouldn't know who to invite regardless. My social anxiety disorder meant I'd never been one to collect social acquaintances. That was, again, Todd's forte.

"You don't invite people," Michelle corrected me. "A close friend or family member usually coordinates the party and you just show up."

I shrugged again and adjusted my seatbelt, betraying how much I cared for her or a shower.

"Oh, I forgot," she trailed, the mirth fading from her eyes to be replaced with something darker. "You and Todd didn't have time for all the formalities."

I arched a brow at that, which sent a surge of heat straight to her face. And here I was thinking we'd managed all the necessary formalities... that Todd and I were actually man and wife in every sense that counted – the legal one. Why a month-long engagement should have detracted from our bond, I had no idea. It just meant we were goal-oriented and knew exactly what we wanted.

"I could do your shower for you. All you would have to do is send me a list of friends you would like to invite," she offered. In her haste to extricate herself from the awkward silence, she only dug herself deeper into no-man's land.

"No shower," I said, shifting the car in reverse. "I'll call you."

Michelle nodded and waved. In my last glimpse of her, she was standing on one foot, biting her lip, probably assuming I had no friends. She would have been right.

That wasn't the reason I didn't want a shower however. I simply didn't care for the open speculation of one's body that pregnant women were forced to endure. I was a naturally private ... maybe even secretive ... person.

The old woman at the supermarket check-out register who had dared to ask when the baby was due and the sex was met with a firm "Mind your own fucking business," much to Todd's embarrassment.

As I'd told him in the parking lot, "Fuck you, and fuck her too!"

Besides, Michelle was about to have her own affairs to mind.

THIRTY-EIGHT

The phone rang three hours after Todd and I had gone to bed. It was long enough for me to have fallen into a deep sleep, but thanks to my expanding girth that never lasted long. I was tired all the time. It was particularly ironic that now that I really needed a Xanax, I wouldn't have it.

I did not know when it occurred to me that this baby was mine. I had always thought of it as Todd's alone, which had nothing to do with the possibility that it might not survive Richard's death. Creating attachments was difficult enough for me, that after Todd, I didn't think I had the physical capacity to love. I didn't love the child growing inside me – at least not like I loved my husband, and certainly not like I had loved my parents, especially my father. But I felt something, and that indefinable quality prevented me from hurting it when I didn't have to.

I'd gone days without sleep before; five hours a night wouldn't kill me.

The whispering would though. It began shortly after 2:00 a.m. After a few seconds, Todd pulled on his robe and left our bedroom. A few minutes later he returned, moving stealthily in the dark as he quickly dressed. I turned in the direction of his shadow, as there was no sound by which to judge his position.

"What's going on?"

"Nothing to worry about, babe. Go back to sleep," came Todd's reply. Judging by his tone alone, I might have believed him, but this behavior was uncharacteristic. I would dare any wife to obey that command.

I hit the bedside lamp and sat up in bed. Todd had socks in hand and a suit shirt buttoned up. "Where are you going?"

He sighed and sat to put on the socks, conveniently turning his back to me. "I have to go out for a bit. It's nothing to worry about though. Go back to sleep."

"So why won't you tell me?" He didn't answer. He pulled on his pants and belt. By the time he emerged from the closet with shoes in hand, I was out of bed and looking for the fur-lined slippers he had bought me. "Why aren't you wearing your uniform?"

"This is personal, Amy. Will you get back in bed? It's two in the morning. Go back to sleep."

"What the fuck is going on, Todd?"

He sighed again and rubbed his hand over his face, both tired and frustrated, ill-equipped to deal with me and whatever emergency had him out of bed, both at this hour.

"Sit down," he said, and this time I quickly complied.

My heart was beating hard and fast in my chest. Todd could not have missed the hammering of my pulse. He sat next to me and held my hand, his thumb caressing my palm. I looked down at our joined hands, and marveled at how delicate mine looked next to his. I wasn't a small woman, and far from fragile. But when I looked into his eyes, I knew he could crush me. I was suddenly afraid.

"No, don't be afraid," Todd said. After a deep breath he pushed on. "Tom was arrested last night. There's been a misunderstanding and I'm going into DC to help clear things up."

"Arrested for what?"

"Solicitation of a prostitute. But it's a misunderstanding, and he doesn't want to alarm Michelle… or Richard."

My eyebrows must have hit my hairline. I wasn't sure what surprised me more: that Todd was selling the bullshit 'misunderstanding' line, or that he hoped to keep Tom's arrest from his father.

Tom had been trolling the corner of 12th Avenue and M Street in D.C. once per week, every week since I tagged his car three weeks ago. Three visits did not a habit make, but his GPS history proved that something was dragging Tom out of bed and to that precise location between 10:00 and 11:00 at night. It sufficed to raise my suspicions, prompting a closer look at the environs.

The historic Logan Circle neighborhood had undergone a facelift shortly after my parents were murdered. The derelict buildings were torn down and replaced with retail and entertainment spaces; the blacks moved out, and the young whites moved in. The one thing that remained constant however, was the prostitution.

After my day with Michelle, I understood Tom's yearning for something else. But never in my wildest dreams had I expected to discover that the decorated Navy Captain and highly respected father of two was paying for sex. I had recovered from the shock quickly enough to make the 911 call using a re-routed internet based line.

"This john in a Porsche is freaking me out," the anonymous caller said. "He's been following me two blocks. 12th and M. Please hurry."

Then I went to bed. It was a bit more complicated than a shot in the dark. Even an arrest for harassment would have left a paper trail that my on-call vindictive journalist could later exploit.

"The best thing you can do right now is go back to bed," Todd said, leaning over to kiss me. He rubbed my belly and tucked me in. In a few minutes he was gone.

Todd had not returned by 9:00a.m, but I resisted the urge to demand answers. In the four months since Sergei's death, I had surprised myself with my capacity for patience. For twelve years I had struggled, knowing each day that passed took my chances of finding justice for my parents farther away. Now, every hour brought me closer to Richard's end, and I relished each one, even as I tore his world apart brick by brick.

So instead of calling Todd, I made polite inquiries with the Police Service Area 307. The list of arrests made the previous night did not include Captain Thomas McDowell. So Todd was not as ineffective at fixing Tom's woes as I would have liked.

I wasn't discouraged however. In truth, I did not expect a walk in the park. I had no illusions of who my adversaries were. If it wasn't Todd, then it would have been Richard.

I got dressed and drove to work, where I pried into the law enforcement database and found Chester Williams. Chester was the sole solicitation arrest that night, coincidentally close to 12th and M Street. The twenty-four year old transgender prostitute, who also went by Chastity Williams and had one prior collar for prostitution, was arrested for offering to perform fellatio for $40. There was no record of the prospective client, but Chastity was processed and released that morning.

Ding ding ding.

I spent the rest of the day on Florida Avenue, watching Chastity's apartment building from a borrowed car. At 9:00 p.m., she emerged with two possible females, dressed for work. I trailed their twenty-year old Pontiac to a gay bar on 14th Street. An hour later, the group – short one member – raucously made the walk ten blocks back to Chastity's corner on M street. She was facing one hundred thirty-five days in jail and a $750 fine. It made sense that she would try to make back the money and live up her remaining days of freedom.

At home, Todd had waited up. The television in the den was on, but if quizzed, he wouldn't have been able to tell me what was on. He met me at the door, eyes running all over my body as I shrugged out of my trench.

"Where have you been?" he asked, hands crossed over his chest, lounging deceptively casual against the doorframe.

"Hey, babe," I greeted him, casual tone matching his façade. I kissed his cheek, which he stiffly allowed. "Were you waiting for me? You shouldn't have."

I made for the kitchen, but Todd firmly gripped my elbow. It was just shy of painful. I stared pointedly at the offending hand, before locking eyes with him.

"Where have you been?" he asked again.

"Work," I answered, with another slow and deliberate look at his fingers closed around my arm. They eased without compromising his hold.

"I've been calling you for hours." I didn't doubt it. I also knew he would have checked my office, which was why I had left both my cellphone and car there while on my surveillance mission. Returning to the office added an hour to my return home, but it also meant I wouldn't be tracked.

"I left you a note."

Todd quirked an eyebrow in a manner that silently expressed his incredulity to perfection. I brushed by him and rounded his desk in the den. It was bare, but on the floor, stuck to the rug under his desk was a strategically placed Post-It note. It read:

Working late today. On the road. Incommunicado. A.

I stuck it to his chest and made my way to the kitchen, where Mrs. Bankowski had plated dinner for me. I washed my hands and dug into the food, waiting for Todd to come to grips with my uncharacteristically thoughtful behavior. It wasn't often that I considered others' feelings while going on my way, and Todd never wanted to miss an opportunity that proved I was trying... that he was changing me.

He took the seat opposite me at the island, more contrite than angry... but still visibly upset. "I'm sorry. I didn't see your note and I was worried."

I hummed my acceptance of his apology around a mouthful of herb potatoes. "I would have called before I left, but I figured you were busy."

Todd looked away, raking fingers through his hair. He had showered. The smell of soap was faint behind his natural scent – a blend of clean blue, sunlight and tobacco. His hair was loose, sucking at his fingers as they dug furrows along his scalp. Winter, his promotion and building a life with me had taken their toll on him: upon close inspection streaks of silver could be found among the jet locks and in his weekend stubble. It made him more appealing somehow.

"What happened with Tom?" I asked, setting aside my fork to give him all my attention.

"Don't worry about it."

I sighed, and Todd met my gaze with silent challenge. "So he wasn't caught with his pants down with a hooker?"

Todd flinched. "No, he wasn't," was his firm reply.

I knew better, and I wasn't afraid of letting Todd know it too. This story struck too close to home. After all, Todd had brought a prostitute into our home back in the Dominican Republic. It would have been suspicious of me not to pick a fight over this.

"Like nothing happened with your hooker," I retorted with enough sarcasm to drown him in guilt. So what if I knew nothing had happened between them? There was always room for doubt. I got to my feet and Todd was all around me in a second, sucking the air from the room.

"You know nothing happened." I wouldn't meet his gaze, even if he cupped my face, tilting it up to his.

"I know nothing. I don't know what's between you and Tom... why he would call you and not his brothers, or his father, or any number of his friends. Why you? What do you know about him and his fucking hookers?"

I was righteously indignant. Todd demanded openness from me, but it was perfectly OK for him to keep his secrets. It was also an excellent distraction from what I had been up to all day... what I would do tomorrow.

"This isn't mine to tell. I need you to trust me." I could tell by the set of his mouth and his impenetrable expression that that was all I would get from him.

I slapped his hand away from my face and pushed him away. I succeeded because Todd was too consumed by guilt to hold me back.

"I did trust you, but you fucked that to shit," I told him on my way out of his sight. "I'll be sure to remember some secrets aren't ours to tell."

That night we slept on separate sides of the bed, with an ocean of recriminations between us. That was Todd's fault, because he refused to have me sleeping in my old room. He'd come to collect me an hour after I disappeared with my toothbrush.

"You're upset; I get it. You're entitled to that. But you don't get to keep my baby from me," he said from the doorway.

That was a battle I wasn't going to win, so I climbed out of bed and made my way back to our bedroom with Todd two steps behind. Besides kissing his baby goodnight, he didn't touch me, and I had the distinct feeling that I was cutting off my nose to spite my face.

The warmth of his body mocked me from two feet away. His scent sent a shock of electricity through my body, and even the down on my arms stood on end. I was aroused, the proof of it thick between my thighs left me awake and aware most of the night. The sounds of Todd's restless sleep said he was aware of it too. When I finally fell asleep, I dreamt of him touching me, easing the tension in my body.

I awoke to the heat of his body curled around me from behind. One busy hand was trapped beneath my body, massaging a pert and heavy breast. The other tested the slickness between my legs, feathering across my sensitive lips, tickling my clitoris.

"Open for me, babe." Todd's voice was thick and tortured next to my ear. "I need to be inside you."

I did as told, lifting one leg so he could ease into me. It was like a deluge after a drought. All resistance, all pretense was washed away with the ferocity of a mudslide. The earth moved beneath us as Todd hoisted my leg higher and pumped into me. His teeth sank into my shoulder, as he tried and failed to hold onto a guttural cry. I didn't care that I should have been angry with him. My body craved his and that was a fact I could never deny. I cried out my longing, arched my body so he could fill me with sensations I could never get enough of.

It didn't last long; it couldn't. We broke through the clouds like a shot, flying too high, too fast, too close to the sun. It seemed we were doomed from the start, but lying in his arms in the first few seconds after our fall, it felt like heaven. I fell asleep to the sound of Todd's breathing and loving words in my ear.

But in the morning we were like two strangers keenly aware of each other, but afraid to bridge the gap. And that was entirely my fault. Wordlessly, I left the house, dressed to prominently display my growing belly. The proof of a restless night was written plainly on my face – proof I deliberately left uncovered.

I went through the same motions of reporting to office as the day before, making sure Blitzner remarked my presence. There had developed an understanding between us since the breaking of Mohamed al-Mohamed. There was nothing more important to Blitzner than results. I delivered them, and he was ruthless enough not to be overly concerned by my methods. As long as the repercussions didn't come back to him. He was the perfect boss.

Shortly before 11:00 a.m., I knocked on Chastity Williams' apartment door. She lived alone. While I was counting on there being only one occupant of the third story walk up, I was prepared for more. Chastity's building sat across the street from a salon and beauty supply store with an array of synthetic hair in the window. Just down the street was a burnt out liquor store and opposite that, a strip mall with bars over all the windows and doors.

Climbing the stairs to her apartment, I stood out like an heiress in a crack den. Cracked concrete, peeling paint and broken stairs were the perfect backdrop to the distinct odor of ether and sulfur and the sound of barking dogs behind closed doors. Someone was cooking meth and drugs were being sold from more than one of the apartments. I didn't pass anyone in the stairwell, but even if I had, no one would have noticed me. Chastity's neighbors were guaranteed to see no one and hear nothing, especially not an uptown girl in Jackie-O glasses covering half her face and a wide brimmed hat and scarf that took care of the rest.

I spent a full minute knocking on Chastity's door. I was quiet enough to be overlooked by the resident who did not wish to be disturbed, but determined enough to force her to answer. She had clearly assessed me through the indispensible peephole and determined I was harmless, because the door was suddenly yanked from beneath my knuckles. She stood in the doorway, wrapped in a satiny robe that fell high on a shaved thigh, with a stocking covering her hair. Above her stubbly cheek, angry black eyes stared down at me.

"What the fuck you want?"

"Chastity?" I asked hesitantly, determined to win me points. "I'd like to speak with you for a moment, please."

"Ain't got nothing to say to no white bitch." She looked down on a nail, but made no move to shut the door in my face.

"Please," I said, removing my sunglasses and opening my trench to reveal my baby bump. "It's about my husband." Her eyes flicked over me a couple of times. Except for the bobbing of her adam's apple, she revealed nothing. "I believe you met him a couple of nights ago… in a Porsche. I'll compensate you for your time?" I dug inside of my purse and pulled out a wad of bills.

Chastity's lips twisted as she considered my condition and the folded bills for a long moment. Finally, she stepped aside and opened the door wider for me to enter. She checked the hall for witnesses before slamming the door and twisting the three deadbolts.

"I hate a cheating asshole," she said, turning to me with one outstretched hand. "But I'm in the business of not caring. See? Can't afford to."

I pressed a couple of fifties into her palm as she watched the rest of the folded bills disappear into my purse, already wondering whether to talk or muscle me out of the money. Her hundred went into the pocket of her robe.

"Are we alone?" I asked.

She brushed by me, walking deeper into the apartment. There wasn't far to go. She stopped at the opposite wall. It was a studio, but still too big to clean by the look of things. It stank, but with the general mess of the place I couldn't decipher the origin of the odor. The windows were closed, and the place sweltered with the stench and swirling dust motes. The bed was unmade, the stained sheets hanging off and joining the trail of clothes and one foot of platform thigh-high boots in the direction of the bathroom.

"Ain't nobody here but us chickens. Not that it would matter if your man was."

"What do you mean?" I asked, inching closer to the bathroom and the sole window. As far as I could see, the closet with a stand-in shower and seatless toilet was empty. From the closed window, the faint strains of traffic could be heard, but there was no one on the fire escape either.

"Means you married Houdini, cause they got me booked on turning tricks but can't find head or tail of the john they dragged in with me. Even if his car was down at the impound lot." She laughed without humor and pulled a cigarette from the pocket of her robe. "You'd think I was blowing a ghost or something," she said lighting up. "So tell me how come you're here. He confess or something? Promised it was the first and last time? You wanna hear my side?"

"No," I said, moving back towards the door. "There's been a mistake." I turned to face her, pressing, my back to the door.

"Now, now, don't be in such a hurry, honey. We just talkin'." She laughed again, but remained on her side of the narrow entryway, reassured by my rifling around in my purse.

The smile melted off her face when I came out with a nine millimeter with a suppressor already attached. I shot her in the head before she could muster a scream. Her blood, bone and brain matter painted the wall behind her in a stark spray, then patchy streak as she slid lifeless to the floor. Solely for insurance purposes, I shot her again in the heart.

I methodically checked the apartment, covering every space that could hold a body. It was empty. I spent the next few minutes lightly tossing the place, adding deliberation to the pre-existent disarray. Inside the tank of her toilet I found four dime-bags of crack and an eighth of weed wrapped up in plastic. I rubbed the bills she had stuffed into her pocket on the inside of one of the bags and crumpled them into her lifeless hands. I flushed the contents down the toilet – all except one – and scattered the empty bags around the apartment. Then I left the apartment just as unseen as I had entered. The gun and suppressor were dumped into separate points in the Potomac.

I was home, showered and fed by the time Todd arrived at 7:00p.m. As he sat down to eat, I took the seat across from him. He seemed surprised, but didn't comment, and so we sat in silence. After a long few minutes in which neither of us tried to dispel the thick tension, I reached across the gulf and plucked a spear of asparagus from his plate. He watched me feed on the vegetable inch-by-inch, reaching across to take my hand when the end disappeared between my teeth.

I didn't realize I'd been holding my breath until he sucked the juice from my fingers and I melted in a sigh. The heat of his mouth traveled down my arm, settling heavily in the pit of my stomach. My pulse throbbed as he pulled me deeper and deeper into the blue abyss of his gaze.

"How are you?" he asked, as if he couldn't see my flushed skin and quickening breath. I shrugged as if there was nothing new, and in fact there wasn't. Todd had always affected me like this. He always would, even when he chose Richard's own over me.

"I'm sorry," he said, lowering my hand to the table and twisting our fingers together. When it wasn't enough, he circled the kitchen island and lifted me into his arms.

"I know it's unfair to expect complete honesty from you at the same time I've kept this from you. But I want you to know that there's nothing here to hurt us. Tom is your family. He asked for my help, and in order for me to do that, I have to keep this secret. Even from you."

But as I looked into Todd's eyes, I knew he was lying. What he really meant was *especially from me*. He believed the less I knew the better chances I would not later use information he had given me. He wouldn't give *me* the opportunity to hurt us. In his own way, *he* was protecting us from *me*.

As he kissed me, wiping away the anger and distrust that had hung between us for the past couple of days, I was keenly aware that we were living a lie. I loved him and he loved me, but we couldn't help hurting each other. I had to find justice for my parents, and Todd would be forced to stop me.

In that seemingly small secret he chose to keep from me was the seed that would eventually destroy us.

Chester Williams' murder made the 10:00 p.m. news, but it took days before it made headlines.

THIRTY-NINE

Sometimes before a powerful earthquake, there are silent tremors deep inside a fault that do not generate seismic waves. The murder of Chester Williams was one such foreshock. The first ripple of awareness of trouble in Richard's world was an after-hours call by the indomitable Erika Harris. In a calculated blow beneath the belt, she called Todd at 10:00p.m. on a Sunday night.

We were still coming down from the high of sexual repletion when the vibration of his phone shook his nightstand. Todd innocently reached for the device, recognized the caller, and declined the request to parlay. His uneasiness was hard to miss. One second he was light and playful, and the next he was tense and evasive.

"What is it?" I asked, pulling the sheets over my cooling body.

"Nothing," he said, fluffing the pillow behind him. He pointedly ignored the renewed vibrations of the phone.

The smile slipped off my face like a piece of wood crashing from a great height. "Nothing is calling you again," I said.

His cheeks flushed at the accusation. "It's Erika," he said, looking like a kid caught with his hand in the cookie jar. "I don't know what she wants."

"Then answer," I said, sitting up in bed. "Let's find out."

Todd stared at the phone for a moment, then back at me. I didn't need to be psychic to know he was weighing his options. Unfortunately, he chose to bury his head in the sand, hoping to avoid a confrontation.

"No," he said. "She can leave a message."

"She doesn't want to leave a message. She called right back."

Todd insisted on playing ostrich. The buzzing stopped after a few more moments. His ill-fated relief died suddenly however, when she chose to call a third time.

"I get it. You want privacy," I said with deceptive neutrality, kicking off the sheets and jumping out of bed. It was getting harder to transition from horizontal to vertical, but I made it, easily shaking off Todd's half-hearted hold. "I'll leave you to her." I grabbed my robe and was out the door despite his weak protest.

After everything I'd done, I expected our staged run-in at the National Press Building wouldn't be the last I would hear from Erika Harris. In fact I was counting on it. So why did her resurgence burn a hole deep in my chest? Was it because she had chosen to call Todd instead of launching headfirst into an investigative piece on the goings-on of the McDowell's? After what Todd had put her through, why would she give him the courtesy of a heads-up? I was suddenly plagued with doubts that that night in February was the last Todd had heard from her.

I paced the floor of my childhood bedroom, anxiety building with the passing of each second. Less than a minute in and there was a cramp in my side. Why had I taken him at his word? The man lied for a living, and maybe in my preoccupation with plotting against Richard I had overlooked some things. Todd had certainly missed a few things in my case.

It felt like an hour before he came to find me. It couldn't have been that long though, because his chest was still dewy from our recent exertions. The lightness of our encounter was gone; the light in his eyes replaced by something more sinister.

"I have to go out," he said. The only reason I'd noticed the moistness slicking the mat of dark hair on his chest was because Todd's fingers drew me there. He was buttoning a shirt, preparing to leave.

I didn't answer. The ability to form words eluded me as I watched him dressing, trying to look anywhere but at me. I felt frozen to the spot, the only part of me moving was my heart, and it pumped furiously in my chest.

What was Todd willing to do to fix Tom's mess? What wouldn't he do to save Richard?

He stood in my doorway long enough for the tension to build thick and deep around us. When there was nothing else to do, he trudged through it and tried to kiss my cheek. My limbs unglued from the spot, and without my accord, my palm struck him. The slap resounded like a crack of thunder. My palm throbbed to the beat of Todd's clenching jaw. It stung so sharply, it brought tears to my eyes.

"It's not what you think, Amy," he said. But to the slap, he only nodded and rubbed it into his cheek. He knew he deserved it.

"You don't know what I'm thinking." My voice was thick with unspoken emotion.

"I do, and you're wrong." His fists balled at his sides.

His fists clenched at his side? He had cause for self-containment?

He was the one throwing a good life after a rotten family. And if our disagreement over the handling of Tom's misadventure had proved one thing, it was that Todd and I had a good thing going, as long it was only us.

"Tell me, Todd. What am I thinking?" I laughed, because being as confused as I was by the jumble of feelings, it was only natural that the least appropriate one should come out on top. At least there was no humor behind it; the tears streaming down my face belied that.

"I have to see Tom... and maybe Richard too. They may need me to handle ... Erika."

My eyebrows skyrocketed at that. "Yes, we know how good you are at that." He reached for my arm this time, holding me just above the elbow where his fingerprints could be hidden against my body.

"I told you it was over between us. Stop torturing yourself, imagining shit that isn't happening," he forced through clenched teeth, his anger strong enough for him to brave another slap.

If there was one time Todd would let me beat him, this was it. He wouldn't risk his child fighting back, or even trying to restrain me. It never occurred to me that he would simply walk away, because Todd never walked away. Except for now. I guess there was always an exception.

"So she didn't call you out of our bed in the middle of the night? Did I imagine that, Todd?" His only answer was to grind his teeth. I pulled my arm away. He didn't let go fast enough to prevent a bruise. "Go. Do what you have to do."

And the son-of-a-bitch did. He took my dare for permission.

Four hours later, my phone rang. It was Richard. It was 2:00a.m., and I hadn't had a wink of sleep since the front door slammed behind Todd. I ignored the call. Richard wasn't going to be able to talk sense into me this time. I didn't want his protestations of Todd's innocence. I'd deliberately chosen to have his child, foolishly thinking it would give me leverage... that when pitted against Richard, Todd would take my side. But twice now Todd had proved that it wasn't enough.

If Richard told Todd to fuck Erika so he could wring her neck, he would. At least if he was going to throw this marriage away he might as well enjoy himself while doing it. Why shouldn't he? He'd still get what he wanted from me – a child and Richard.

Fuck it.

The calls came steadily all morning, every twenty minutes. Still, I was determined to have my run. I needed the escape that running had always provided. I left a message for Blitzner, explaining I would be incommunicado for a couple of hours, then left the phone to charge.

I made it as far as the gates, which were blocked by a black-on-black Tahoe. David, the youngest of Richard's children, glared at me from the rolled-down window.

"Get in."

I put in my ear buds and turned in the opposite direction. It took him a minute to catch on to my plan to ignore him and his order, proving David wasn't the sharpest tool in the shed. Because really, when had I ever done as told, especially by him?

He pulled the oversized truck right into my path, almost running over my foot. He couldn't care less that he could have hurt me and the baby. Like a one-trick pony, David pursued his father's wishes with single-minded determination, regardless of the consequences. And that, I gathered, was the reason he had been sent to collect me.

He exited the vehicle and faced me with hands on his hips, as if we were caught in a western standoff. I pulled out one ear bud. "Get in the fucking car, Amy. Don't let me tell you again."

"Or what? You're up early for an ass-kicking."

It was 4:30 a.m., and by the looks of him, he'd had as much of a sleepless night as me. He was unshaved, dressed in a white undershirt and sweats. His fingers were raking through his already disheveled hair

– pulling out the short spikes actually. He kept it short, because unlike his brothers who took their brown hair from their father, David favored Abby, who was a true redhead.

"I don't know how Todd puts up with your shit everyday. Or why. Because you're definitely not worth the aggravation, Amy." I shrugged my unconcern, rounding the car to continue on my way. "Just letting you know, if I had to deal with you, I would have fucked that bitch too. Fucked her good and dirty."

It stung. It was too fresh not to. But I was above knee-jerk reactions. I wouldn't fall into the trap and throw out the fact that his brother had paid a male hooker to suck his cock. Because I shouldn't have known the specifics of the case.

Instead, I took off at a steady lope, hand under my belly to provide support until my body adjusted to the gentle jarring. It was hard to breathe with my throat clogged with unshed tears, but I pushed through it. David was on my heels, following in the car until I veered off the lonely road and into the woods. I was forced to go slower there, eyes peeled to the floor, on the lookout for rocks and roots in my path.

Todd had put me in that position, made me an easy mark for people who wanted to hurt me. I would never outlive his transgression. And while I couldn't hurt everyone who thought less of me because of Todd's actions, I could hurt David.

An hour and a half after, I returned home to find not only David, but Michelle and her two children camped out in my house. The girls were dressed in their nightgowns, the younger one still asleep while being transferred from her mother's arms to Mrs. Bankowski's. The housekeeper led the other by the hand, no doubt having colluded with Todd to abet the invasion of my home. Michelle was a wreck, eyes swollen, face splotchy, and dressed in flannel under a hastily donned trench coat. David was watching t.v. over a cup of coffee in the den, at the same time flipping through three different newspapers, no doubt looking for any story that featured Chester Williams or Tom's non-arrest for solicitation.

"Oh, my God, Amy," Michelle rushed to embrace me, fresh tears streaming down her face. I held my hands stiffly at my side, and waited three beats for her to recognize I hadn't changed my mind about physical contact with her. She pulled away and had the grace to look embarrassed. She waited for me to ask about her wellbeing, and when I stood resolutely still and silent, she finally turned the question on me. "How are you? You've been running. Should you be... with the baby and all?" She sniffed, pulling back her tears.

"What are you doing here?" I asked, as if I didn't already know. Richard had obviously decided that if Mohamed couldn't be brought to the mountain, then the mountain should come to me. Their problems, which Todd had tried to keep from me, and for which he was willing to cause irreparable damage to our marriage, was being dumped in my home.

"Well, Richard suggested that I take the children and leave for a bit while they discussed...things." She looked away, her cheeks flaming with embarrassment. "Todd said it was OK for us to come," she finished lamely, twisting her fingers around each other. She took a step back and then another, unsure what next to do, while I stared between her, David and the two bags cluttering my entryway.

"How long?" I asked, coming back to her after a while. I could hear Mrs. Bankowski in the kitchen, puttering around with the children. The younger one, four-years-old Sarah, was crying.

"I-I don't know... I'm not sure," she said, staring at me with wide eyes. "I'm waiting for Richard's instructions." That made one of us. "I don't want to impose, Amy," she said with some bite.

"OK," I said, keenly aware now of David's sudden interest in our dialogue. He'd noted the uncharacteristic steel behind her tone too. "Who should I call for you? Maybe one the friends who arranged your bachelorette party, or baby shower."

"Amy!" David called in a futile attempt to caution me. He should have known better. After all, it was he who had thrown caution to the wind and Todd's infidelity in my face. As if my husband's failings were my fault. I should have been a good, obedient wife, like Michelle, and he wouldn't have had cause to stick his dick in someone else.

I turned to him. "Get the fuck out of my house." I brushed by Michelle, who stubbornly held on to her pretenses, dissolving into soft sobs with her face hidden behind her hands. Mrs. Bankowski was working on fresh batter for pancakes for the children, who were sipping cocoa with fluffy white marshmallows floating on top.

"After breakfast they're going to visit one of their mother's friends. When you're done here, I need you to move my belongings from the master suite to my other bedroom."

"Yes, Ms. Koehler." She knew which bedroom. She also knew the rules of our house: the last command overruled the one that preceded it, with zero consequence to herself; and stay out of Todd's and my disputes.

I showered and dressed, having decided it was a good day to work from the office. On the way to my car, I discovered Michelle's family gone. But both David and eighty messages were waiting for me.

"I could swear I told you to get out."

"There's a special place in hell waiting for you," he snarled at me. "How could you turn them away? She's family, Amy. We took you in when you had no one."

"Fine. I'll leave, but I want you gone by the time I get back."

I held my breath and walked away, shutting off his angry flow of words with a slam of my car door. The only reason I'd had no one was because his father had taken away everything from me. His family had murdered mine. If there was a hell, I would gladly go. But I was going to send Richard there first.

Two hours into my research of another one of Blitzner's targets, my boss knocked on my door. I didn't have a window and the overhead lights were off. The only source of light was a desk lamp that provided a tiny circle of clarity. It was a trick I'd picked up early in my career to dissuade drop-ins; it proved especially useful now that I was working from home more days than not. Blitzner wasn't buying it today. He opened the door without an invitation.

"Your husband is on the line," he announced without preamble.

"I'll call him back soon. I'm in the middle of something here," I offered with the barest glance in his direction.

"What I meant was, why is your husband on my line?" he drawled, getting comfortable in my doorway. "I thought you didn't want me in the middle of your marriage."

He had a very good point. Once again, Todd had put me in a position that was impossible to defend. I plucked my cell phone from its drawer and dangled it before Blitzner. There were another thirty missed calls, all from Richard's minions who would rather stalk me than report their failure to their boss.

"I'm calling right now."

Todd answered on the second ring. I could tell he was in the car. Possibly on his way to or from Erika's, the angry part of my consciousness helpfully added. "Jesus Christ, Amy. Why can't you trust me?"

"I'm busy. Hold on," Blitzner hadn't left yet. "Is there something else, sir?"

"Isn't there always, my dear?" he asked with that smile again before slithering out and closing the door behind him. Personally, I hated Blitzner... didn't trust him farther than I could throw him. But who else would allow me free rein?

"What do you want, Todd?" I sighed into the line. My eyes hurt from the strain of working in dim conditions.

"Give me three days, Amy. Three days to make this right."

"There's really no hurry," I said, rubbing my eyes so hard I saw stars dancing behind the lids. "Take all the time you want."

"Goddammit, Amy!"

"I'm being fair, Todd. You've made your choice, now you have to live with it."

"I chose to help your family, Amy!"

"No, you chose Richard. You always have and you always will. And that's fine. Really, it is. Just don't expect me to be content with coming in second place."

Todd sighed, and I swear I heard him gulp. "God, Amy, you're not making this easy."

"Actually, it was a simple choice, but you made it hard. I hope you get everything you want out of it. Now, please stop calling, and tell Richard to stop too. It's not fair for you drag my boss into this. Goodbye, Todd."

He didn't agree with my dismissal, but I didn't give him a choice. At least he respected it. The calls stopped after that, and for the rest of the day, I lost myself in work.

The week that followed was filled with routines. At home, Todd accepted my move back into my bedroom. He nimbly stepped around the edges of the silence and distance between us, expecting that with time, I would bridge the gap, as had been the case that last time around.

We were like strangers who occasionally passed each other in the common spaces of our home.

I was alone for the next doctor's visit, which Todd learned after the fact. Either he had tracked me or inquired with the doctor's office, because he returned home the following day looking dazed. I was working from my father's study when he appeared in the doorway two hours before his normal hours.

"You went without me," he said in quiet accusation. His hurt was plain to see.

I didn't pretend to not know what he meant. There was only one thing that could strip Todd raw. "I didn't need you."

"You didn't need me," he repeated quietly, more mystified than angry.

"Everything is fine," I said. "The baby's fine." Then I went back to work, trying valiantly to ignore the fact that he stood there for a full five minutes, just staring at me. I could no more deny the prickling of my skin as he drew closer than I could tell my heart to stop beating.

Todd leaned across the expanse of my father's desk until our faces were inches apart. He was going to be heard, so I politely closed the lid on my laptop and gave him my attention.

"This is my baby too," he said.

I nodded. "I don't deny it. Don't worry, we'll figure something out once it's born. We have nearly four months to decide what we're going to do."

It wasn't an unreasonable offer. Todd and I were going nowhere fast. There was no denying that we couldn't continue on our present course. He had everything he'd wanted from our union. And I would have my revenge without him.

"Amy, listen to me. I love you –" I shook my head furiously and pushed my chair back. I couldn't stand to be near him when he was like this. I hated to think that I had a hand in making Todd unhappy. The fact was, I didn't make his choices for him. He could have picked me, so I refused to feel guilty for his choices. "What do you mean 'no'?" he asked, looking at me as if I'd said with absolute certainty that we were under attack from aliens.

"You don't love me enough," I said.

"Everything I've done has been for you," he said with incredulity.

I shook my head in denial again. "I don't want to fight about it, but everything you've done has been for you. Earning Richard's favor, making a name for yourself, protecting your reputation, removing my embarrassments… it's all been for you."

"That again?" he cried, frustrated, dragging his hand over his face, wishing he could wake from this nightmare. Of course he would focus on the part that spoke to Erika.

"Not *again*, Todd. *Still*. We never got past it."

He stalked around the desk, because he wasn't crowding me enough. His appeal wasn't potent enough with my father's desk between us. He had to box me into my seat. My response was predictable. We hadn't touched in a week and I was withdrawn without him. My skin prickled, my heartbeat kicked up, my core melted as his scent filled my head.

"I promised you it was over. Nothing… nothing! … could get me to stick my dick in her again. Yes, she called, but I didn't go chasing after her like you thought. I went to help *your* family, only to find out you didn't give a shit about them. But by then it was too late; I was already tied up in Tom's mistakes."

I looked away, focusing on nothing rather than the man who was pouring out his heart to me.

"Fine, don't look at me, but you're going to listen. You're going to hear me, Amy." And yet he crouched before me, twisting so his face was again in my line of sight. His eyes were hard, but bright blue, like colored glass.

"Tom got caught with his dick where it shouldn't have been. I talked the police department out of charges, making up a bullshit tale about ongoing investigations with national security implications. I did that for *you*, because Tom is like a brother to you. And I kept it from you, because it was corrupt, and I wanted to protect you in case it failed. But by then the hooker had already been sprung, and the cops were late in quashing his arrest too."

"*His* arrest?" I raised my eyebrows, but Todd didn't delay in his explanation to defend Tom. He leaned forward, bringing our lips close to each other, as if he wanted the words to pour straight from his lips into mine.

"Not two days later, the hooker is dead, executed in an apparent drug buy. But not soon enough apparently. He had confided in some friends, gabbed about the arrest and the John Doe." I wasn't surprised. Hadn't Chastity wailed in my ear too about the very same thing?

"So they're screaming into every microphone about the ghost in the Porsche. The PD gets antsy, thinking they're going to be implicated in a cover up. Plus they've got a murder to investigate, because the fake bitches won't shut the fuck up about it. Tom's arresting officer develops a case of bad conscience and starts talking to Internal Affairs, and they in turn start making calls to the Navy. With the high phone traffic, lips start getting loose and the 'national security' disclaimer hits the State Attorney's office. Only one car was impounded that night with a Navy plate, and although we took care of the records, erasing the memory of the towing crew wasn't such a simple matter. Anyway, guess how many men in the Navy drive silver Porsches?"

Todd took a break to bring his lips close to my ear. "Just one."

He pulled back to stare into my eyes. "All the while Tom and I were trying to keep Richard out of it was a waste of time. And you want to know why? Because of Erika. One whiff of the McDowell name and she's like a bloodhound. And you know why, Amy? Because of me. So she starts digging, and soon enough, she's shopping a story about a hooker killed so the son of the Director of National Intelligence can keep his job. The only reason she even called to give me a heads up was to hurt us.

"Richard squashed the story. It seems she underestimated his reach. But she did get one thing right, Amy. She knew this would shake us. So you're giving her exactly what she wants. Think about that while you're deciding what you want to do about us... when you're working so hard for us to end up just as bitter as she is."

A few months ago Todd would have played on our chemical reaction to speed up our reconciliation. This time, he left me to make my own choice, drug-free and lucid.

Erika had won, and there was nothing we could do to undo that. We were shaken. I knew without a doubt that when Richard called, Todd would always come running. And Todd, for his part, understood that I had spent so many years surviving with a broken heart that I had become accustomed to living with my heart torn from my chest. I could go on without him.

FORTY

Things were never the same after that. We tried to pretend, but both Todd and I had to face a truth that left a bitter taste in our mouths. I didn't trust him... expected the worst from him in fact, and he knew it; and Todd realized he might never be able to heal me from my past.

I was partially moved back into our bedroom, but even there it was evident our connection was broken. Sex was little more than a physical release... the filling of an insatiable appetite. We gorged ourselves on lust, but there was little love behind it. Whenever convenient, we reached for each other almost mindlessly, and Todd fucked me as if to restore my senses. It was senselessly violent at times, but always at the end, we would withdraw to our respective corners.

I had another hunger that was building too. It matched Erika's. Richard had killed her story, but not her spirit. I was far from discouraged too, because Erika had proved her willingness to play with fire. The heightened scrutiny was precisely what I wanted.

A week after Todd's confession, my birthday rolled around. I took the opportunity to appear to mend fences. While Richard's family had not quite rallied around Michelle, my abandonment during their time of crisis was poorly received. Todd had played his part in smoothing the waves, assuming full responsibility for my pique. The suggestion that he had been at Erika's beck and call was offered; my indignation was to be expected. Richard accepted his excuses, but put me on probation. I would work my way back into the fold.

The afternoon of May 26, I prepared myself for an early afternoon drinks date with Abby. Michelle had declined her mother-in-law's invitation. She was silent on the alternate plans that had her indisposed, putting to good use the get-out-of-jail-free card her husband's indiscretion had provided. For once, she had placed herself above the judgment of the McDowells. Whatever inroads she had assumed were made by our shopping expedition were washed away. I was glad for the end of that pretense at least.

Abby and I met on middle ground, in Baltimore, forty minutes from her home in Bel Air. She wasn't usually up for Mexican, which was why I chose to meet at Miguel's at Silo Point. I wanted her out of her depth. A 2:15p.m. RDV was early enough for her to make the trip alone.

She arrived on time, fifteen minutes after me and found me seated at a corner indoor table with two pitchers of margaritas. Her hesitance coming through the door was more than the unfamiliar surroundings; she was sluggish. The squinted gaze that scanned the room briefly before falling on me wasn't because she hadn't worn her glasses. Aunt Abby had driven high.

"Oh, Amy," she gushed through a shaky hug, "I'm so happy to see you. It's good of you to have invited me. Oh, dear, you ordered lemonade. How thoughtful! I am so thirsty."

"These are margaritas, Abby," I explained, rearranging my expanded girth behind the table. "Here, this one is for you. Be careful, there's tequila in it."

She proceeded to pour herself a glass while I sipped on my virgin drink. She drank deeply, stopping to refill her glass once, trying to ease the cotton-mouth from her Valium high.

"Ooh, this has a nice kick," she gasped after drawing breath, oblivious to the bitter undertones of the crushed pills mixed in.

"Slow down, Abby. You're driving home?"

She bobbed her head, eyes wide, and settled in her seat for a few seconds. She turned to me. "Happy Birthday, sweet Amy." But my birthday was the least of her concerns however. I thanked her and waited five seconds flat for the tears to follow. "Oh, Amy, something's wrong with Tom."

"Would you like something to eat, Abby?"

She shook her head, recognizing a poorly concealed evasive maneuver. Still, out of politeness she waited until I order some guacamole and shrimp corn cakes before she pressed again.

"I know you know what's going on."

"You're too suspicious, Abby," I said over the rim of my glass, which was of course a lie. Abby was oblivious on good days, uncaring at her worst.

"I know my boys, Amy," she said. From the tension around her unlined eyes, I could tell she was trying to frown. Her forehead was as smooth as glass, unnervingly so for a sixty-year-old grandmother. "I know when something is wrong. They've been around a lot lately, which is unusual outside of Sundays and the holidays. And Tom... a couple weeks ago Tom was walking around with this ... look on his face."

She drew closer and closed one manicured hand around her glass, preparing to take another deep pull and share things better left unheard.

"And I swear that Michelle has been a downright bitch, refusing to bring the girls around these past two weekends. And the thing is, Tom let her! I asked him about it... why he wasn't bringing the girls 'round, seeing as he comes over nearly every day. And you know what he said? He said 'Mamma, not now,' like I was a bother to him 'cause I want to see my grandbabies.

"Now, Tom is my first. It was just him and me for three years before Andrew came along. There's a special bond between us that you'll understand after you have your own children. That boy had never talked to me like he did the other day. So I know something's going on, my dear, and I believe it has something to do with that wife of his."

She looked at me from the corner of her eyes while taking a more dignified sip this time. I offered nothing, allowing her all the time she needed to warm up. I wondered how she would have managed to lay the blame at Michelle's feet if Tom's wife had agreed to join us today. And what would she have said about me if Michelle was sitting in my place.

It was always understood that, in her own way, Abby could be as vicious as her husband. I had always thought of her as harmless however, because her mercenary conduct was usually limited to protecting her family. I used to be mostly indifferent to her sons, which meant she was no threat to me. But lately, all that had changed. Her family was the weapon I needed to beat Richard; and I wondered if she knew more about my parents' murders than she had let on.

"Your husband has been around quite a lot too."

My stubborn silence was met with a dip of her toes in still waters. In a minute she would agitate... try to manipulate me into revealing what she wanted to know.

"I can't imagine where he finds the time with everything else that's going on." She cast a wary eye around the restaurant in a transparent attempt to appear conspiratorial.

"I think he's been running errands for Richard," she continued, cupping her hand around her mouth and whispering near my ear. "Something to do with that girl." Abby raised her eyebrows meaningfully and pressed her lips together.

"What girl?" I asked, feigning disinterest even though the words felt like wood in my mouth.

"You know the one... that reporter girl. The one he was caught with."

Consider me manipulated. She had my attention.

Either of her sons, Michelle, or even Richard could have confided in her about the source of the tension at her Christmas table. It was a confidence she wouldn't hesitate to betray in order to have her own way. Unfortunately for her, Abby hadn't fully grasped the danger of playing with matches.

"I don't mean to distress you, dear," she said, with a comforting hand covering one of mine, "but I heard Todd and Richard arguing over something to do with her. And I know it involves Tom, because they've been thick as thieves, I tell you: your husband, Tom and Richard – with Andrew and David hovering about too.

"Do you think Tom's finally going to do it... divorce Michelle, I mean? I wondered that they might be positioning the media on our side. You know, to contain the scandal..."

"I doubt it," I replied flatly, removing my hand from beneath hers.

"Well, why not?" Either she was affronted by my casual rejection of what she might have considered spot-on analysis – baseless speculation in fact – or by my refusal of her comfort.

"Tom cheated on Michelle," I blurted out just as the appetizers arrived. Abby flushed scarlet, her pale skin no match for the surge of embarrassment. She finished her drink and I helpfully refilled her glass.

"Well," she said, more reserved when she wasn't tossing about other people's faults. "These things happen, you know. You understand, don't you, Amy? I don't see what all the fuss is about." She picked at a nacho chip, nibbled around the edges then set it aside, reaching for her glass again. I let her.

"He was caught with a prostitute, Abby." Her eyes flew to mine, wide as the side plate on which she had rested her half-eaten chip. "A male prostitute."

I watched with a building sense of satisfaction as her face turned puce. "I don't believe it! Why, Amy, what a terrible, hurtful thing to say! My son... my son is not..."

I saw no reason why I should be reserved. Her age was no consideration. If she could dish it, then she could take it too. I nodded and bit into a corn cake.

"That reporter – the one Todd fucked – she found out about it." Abby flinched at *fuck*. "Todd didn't tell me what Richard wanted from him, but I imagine it was to persuade her to bury the story." I shrugged my shoulders, set aside my fork, and said matter-of-factly, "I didn't ask. You know how those things are.... Men cheat on their wives all the time."

Our eyes met, and I let her see what she wanted: an understanding between us. The men in our lives would always disappoint us, but we had to stick together.

"When did you grow up?" she asked with a watery smile. "I held you in my arms the day you were born. I can't believe it's been thirty years. And here you are, married with a baby of your own on the way. God, I hope you get a better hold of your Todd than your mama did with your daddy." She looked away and blotted at her eyes with a napkin.

I wasn't fooled in thinking her final shot was in fact a compliment. This was how Abby burnt her enemies, with quiet commiserations coated in broken glass.

"Will you excuse me for a moment, dear?" She was unsteady on her feet, but ambled to the ladies room where she would surely shed a tear or two, pop more pills, possibly call in to discretely verify my claims. She would re-emerge composed and convinced that the male prostitute was somehow Michelle's fault.

I ordered a refill on her pitcher. While the waiter went about fixing her drink, I emptied the ground-up Valium into my palm, using the low table and my wide belly for cover. Then I dumped the drugs into her pitcher and shook it vigorously.

"Dump it in," I told the waiter when he tried to replace the old pitcher with the new one. I used a knife to stir the cocktail, making sure there was a bit of Valium in every sip.

By the time Abby reemerged with a distinctly hazy expression and a firm resolve in her son's entrapment, the dishes were being cleared.

"Tell me about my mother."

She looked up from her glass, eyebrows hiked in surprise. She had already forgotten how she had left... that I hadn't simply picked this topic out of thin air.

"What's that, dear?"

"Before you left, you said my mother had a poor hold on my father," I reminded her. "What did you mean by that?" I turned to face her and waited while the reality of our confrontation pierced her euphoria.

"I didn't mean anything by it," she sputtered defensively.

I made sure she felt the heat of my gaze as she fidgeted with the cutlery, sipped from the laced drink, and avoided touching me with her tearing eyes. Finally, when she realized I refused to move on, she sought to dispense with my question as efficiently as possible.

"Your father had some unresolved issues, Amy," she ventured tentatively. "He suffered certain work stresses that I can imagine must have been difficult for Mary-Anne to deal with. Your mother was a saint though. She wouldn't hear a negative word about him. She was my best friend, but she loved your father with every fiber of her being... wouldn't think about living without him."

Abby reached for my hand and I allowed her to touch me. I desperately wanted her to continue. I wouldn't breathe, much less move a muscle, because I didn't want to distract her. She dissolved into tears, and as uncomfortable as it was to allow her the intimacy of drawing strength from my firmly clenched hand, I let her.

"When I heard what had happened, I fainted. I couldn't... My heart was broken, Amy. You have to understand. We were so close, she and I... the best of friends for twenty years. She shouldn't have been home that night. She was supposed to have taken you to New York for the weekend. She told me so. And then she was gone, and there was nothing I could do.

"Nothing, Amy," she continued, lost in her own little world and oblivious to the shift in the air between us. "Then you arrived, soaking wet and hysterical. And I knew she had sent you to me. She wanted you to come to me. That was what I could do for her."

Abby nodded her head and smiled through her tears, content with having fulfilled her purpose. The cloud of unbearable memories passed quickly for her. Not so much for me.

I remembered that day. My mother and I were almost out the door, heading to the airport when my father called. His plans had changed suddenly. He was on his way home. My mother had asked if I still wanted to go to New York, with a huge grin on her face, because she knew what my answer would be. I had wanted to camp out at the airport to wait for my father, but had to settle for pacing my room for hours. Shortly after 6:00p.m., he wrapped his arms around me and asked if I had missed him. I knew something was wrong; I could tell just by looking in his eyes. But he had dismissed my concern, told me it was just work.

Shortly after midnight, he forced me out my bedroom window, told me to run to Richard, and then turned around to face his death.

According to Abby, my father had *unresolved issues...* suffered *work stresses,* which of course excused her husband for murdering him. And my mother, her *best of friends for twenty years* was dead because *she shouldn't have been home that night.*

She told me so, Abby had said. And no doubt, she had passed that information on to Richard.

Abby had known all along that Richard was going to kill my father. She had helped him to plan it. And my mother must have known it too in her last minutes alive.

There was no doubt my father knew who and why he was killed. It was the reason he had sent me to Richard. The plan was never to kill my mother and me. But Richard had not counted on my father's revenge. My father wanted me to learn everything he hadn't had the time to teach me, and there was no better teacher left than Richard. My father never told me the truth, because he wanted me alive until I was better able to avenge him. He wanted me close to the man so that once I had learned of his betrayal, I would be close enough to strike at the heart of his killer.

"I'm sorry, dear," Abby sniffed and dabbed at her eyes and nose. "I'm ruining your birthday."

I smiled at her, a languid arching of one corner of my mouth. "Not at all, Abby."

"It's just that she was such a sweet soul… a dear angel." She sniffed again.

An angel of mercy who had been shown none.

"I know," I said and filled her glass again. "Let's have a good lunch." I raised my glass in cheers and Abby followed suit. "Here's to my mother."

"To Mary-Anne," Abby cheered and drank.

Todd was home when I walked through the door. He met me in the entryway, where the gigantic bouquet of flowers he had gotten me was on display.

"Did you have a good lunch with Abby?"

I rolled my eyes and pursed my lips. "I'm surprised she made it in one piece. And it only went downhill from there."

Todd nodded his understanding. "That bad?" That was the closest anyone had ever come to discussing Abby's addiction.

"She pressed me about Tom. She knew something was going on with all of you congregating at the house so often. She also overhead you and Richard discussing Erika." I shrugged as if to prove I was over it. "I saw no need to lie to her. And I guess with the anxiety, she fell down a bit on discretion."

I looked into his eyes and saw longing. He wanted to hold me, comfort me for, no doubt, having to face his infidelity again. Too bad I was still hardened from the lunch. Anyway, it wouldn't be the last time Todd's indiscretions would haunt me; I had better get accustomed to it.

I moved to pass him when he grasped my elbow. "We'll leave at 7?"

I nodded. Todd had made dinner plans to celebrate my birthday. It would have been the beginning of a romantic evening, which would be closed off with several rounds of torrid fucking. If he was hoping for another chance for reconciliation, it was not to be.

Three hours later, we were milling around a hospital waiting room, dressed in our evening finery. The smell of disinfectant and sanitizer choked out Todd's intoxicating scent. Seated on hard plastic chairs, I tucked my nose into his collar and breathed him in. I never rejoiced in death, not even for my enemies or those who had earned it. It was a simple fact of life.

Abby had been found that afternoon less than a mile from the restaurant. She had stopped before the train tracks by East McComas Street where she passed out behind the wheel with the car running. She was in a coma – the result of a toxic mix of alcohol and prescription medication.

She died of a cardiac arrest early the next morning. The investigation didn't last long. In her purse were prescriptions from three different physicians: one in her maiden name, one in her married name, and another in her middle name. Her medicine cabinet yielded Oxycontin, Percocet, Xanax and more Valium.

Her family was beside themselves. At last Richard had come to know the hell he had created.

"This isn't your fault, Amy," Todd whispered as I dug my nose deeper into his collar. "It was bound to happen sooner or later. It's not your fault."

"I know," I said. It was Richard's.

But as our eyes met across the waiting room, broken every now and then by the pacing bodies of his sons, I knew Richard would beg to disagree.

FORTY-ONE

Abby was buried on a beautiful spring day. The chaplain claimed it was a day of rejoicing, as heaven celebrated the coming home of one of their own. There were more eye rolls at that than at a *Real Housewives* reunion. Half the well-wishers had come to see if she looked as well preserved in death as she had been in life. Their other half had come to sign the attendance register. Some would describe Richard as composed, including the President. Others knew he was just a heartless bastard.

Security mimicked that of a presidential inauguration, and for good cause. In one fell swoop, half of Congress, the entire Executive, and most of the Armed Forces leadership could have been sent to meet Abby wherever she had gone. The press had also made a remarkable showing. Amidst the throngs, there was only one face I wanted to see. I read the tension in Todd's arm, which was permanently secured to the small of my back, and followed his furtive gaze above several rows of heads outside the cemetery, to find Erika Harris.

Two days ago she had tried to shop an exposition on sex, drugs and corruption among America's leading families. With the sudden death of the DNI's wife from a lethal prescription interaction, the editors of leading outlets had passed on account of the story being untimely and distasteful. Only her reputation held her back from turning to the gossip tabloids. Erika's presence at the graveside was a promise to bring down my family.

It was more important than ever for our family to face the world as a united front. Our performance was epic. Not only were Todd and I completely reconciled, it was as if Chastity had never happened to Tom and Michelle. As for Richard and I, only the most discerning eye would remark the thin layer of frost in our relations. Todd thought Richard held me partly responsible for not taking better care of Abby during our drinks date. Todd also thought I held Richard in contempt for his divided loyalties. He was wrong.

In as much as Abby had made her own choices, so too had Todd. I blamed my husband for his divided loyalties. I held Richard responsible for my father's murder. And Richard was suspicious of his friends' and family's demise. It was natural that he question the motivations behind the sudden avalanche of misfortune... it was inevitable that he cast a wary eye over all his enemies. And Richard knew we were enemies, even if he doubted I was aware of it.

So when David was pulled over in Arlington on the fourth of July for a broken taillight, of course Richard called Todd. It wasn't for help this time however; it was to question my husband about my whereabouts.

There was a small dent and what appeared to be blood on his bumper. David passed a field sobriety test by the skin of his teeth, but refused to take a preliminary breathalyzer, and claimed ignorance of the damage to his vehicle. Another McDowell son was carted off to jail, but this time on suspicion of driving under the influence. The evidentiary breathalyzer, administered at the police station forty minutes later, indicated a blood alcohol content of .08 – legal in Virginia. David sighed with relief at having dodged the DUI bullet.

Closer inspection of the Tahoe confirmed the presence of animal blood on the bumper – and an ounce of cocaine under the driver's seat. David was arrested for simple possession – a charge he staunchly denied.

His brother, Andrew, bailed him out while Richard worked behind the scenes. An anonymous tip led Erika Harris to the bond court where an attorney representing Lt. Colonel David McDowell entered a not guilty plea on the charge. The blood test conducted at his lawyer's insistence failed to reveal the presence of cocaine, and it was argued that any number of Fourth of July celebrants, valet attendants, or auto detailing personnel might have been responsible for the presence of the contraband. The charge was eventually dropped, but the damage was done nonetheless.

Todd hotly contested Richard's interrogation of me. "What are you suggesting? This has nothing to do with Amy."

True, David had stopped by our home earlier in the afternoon in a futile attempt to drag Todd out on a bar crawl with him. Instead, they had shared a few drinks in the den – a golden opportunity for access I had seized. The broken taillight and the blood had come later, while he was parked outside the venue he had communicated to Todd, and had only cost me $100. None of it could have been traced back to me, and Todd was furious at the allegations.

"She's like a daughter to you, for God's sake!" Todd ranted downstairs.

He had good cause to advocate my innocence. A couple of months earlier Todd had chewed David out for his humiliating remarks regarding the Erika affair. It was in my husband's best interest for a happy home however, to continue defending me against David.

Planting cocaine to jeopardize David's career and destroy the family's good name, was leagues beyond any prank I was capable of. And besides, Todd and I were celebrating the anniversary of our meeting. Not only had I not left the house all day; Todd and I were inseparable. As for what brought Erika Harris on the scene... well, it was just ludicrous that I would conspire against my own family with the woman who had had a liaison with my husband. The mention of her name alone had the effect of a deep freeze descending on our relationship that would require months of digging for Todd to escape.

With Todd's golden tongue at work, I emerged from David's arrest as a victim. It was unconscionable for Richard to suspect me... a consequence of his irrational grudge against me stemming from Abby's death.

"You may not want to face the facts," Todd continued, "but your family is far from perfect, Richard. We all turned a blind eye to Abby's habits... pretended it wasn't happening right before our eyes. Is it any wonder that David would make his way down that path too?"

Nevermind that the blood test proved him to be cocaine-free, David didn't escape the arrest unscathed. The Army fell short of sanctioning him, but his poor judgment that permitted a third party to access to his personal space was duly noted. His rise to the upper echelons of leadership was checked.

This latest development coupled with the drug related death of Abby and Tom's solicitation non-arrest – all of which were recycled, tied together with a neat bow, and were being shopped by Erika Harris – sparked budding interest from several editors. But the McDowell's were a powerful family, and with lives and careers on the line, media leaders were hesitant to incite his wrath. They declined to run her exposition, but it wasn't a flat-out refusal. They wanted more... more evidence of degeneration, more evidence of corruption in the handling of the family's personal crises, a smoking gun. Erika redoubled her efforts in the crusade.

Whether the result of his disgrace or Todd's advocacy, David's image was tarnished in his father's eyes. Richard was forced to reassess his family individually and as a unit. His legacy was in jeopardy. Not only was he grief-stricken by the untimely death of his wife of over forty years, his sons had become a source of insurmountable stress.

On July 14, 2012, Richard McDowell suffered a heart attack fifteen minutes into his morning run. He was rushed to University of Maryland Upper Chesapeake Health, which was where the family convened.

There was no pretense to my distress when Todd and I received word of Richard's hospitalization.

"It'll be OK," Todd kept repeating on the hour-and-a-half drive to the hospital. Todd wanted me calm so I wouldn't agitate his child.

I knocked away the hand that gripped mine. I didn't need his false reassurances. On good days I was revered as the sacred vessel that carried his child, but in moments of crises, he never failed to make me feel like a giant, fragile incubator. For both of us, the next seven weeks couldn't pass quickly enough.

But not if Richard died.

"You don't know that! Stop saying it's going to be OK, because you don't know." In my frustration, tears sprang to my eyes and streamed down my cheeks before I could wipe them away.

"Amy," Todd called, trying to lure me away from the edge of despair. I couldn't miss the awe in his voice at my lack of control. "Listen to me."

I turned to face him, as he divided his attention between the road and my crumbled composure. My eyes were red and swollen from the angry gush of tears, my nose flaring as I tried to take in deep calming breaths.

"Richard is strong. He will pull through."

It was a hope I was afraid to hold on to. Instead, I gripped Todd's hand and held on tight.

What were the chances that the man who had no heart would die of a heart attack?

Richard couldn't die... not if it wasn't by my hand. I cried for all the time I had wasted. I cried for my father and my mother who might at this precise moment, be cheated of the full extent of my revenge. It wasn't enough that Abby was dead. It wasn't enough that I had killed Sergei. It wasn't enough that his sons were perched on the brink of ruin. I had to kill Richard. And he had to know that it was I who had taken everything, including his life, from him.

Shock and fear united us again, but this time it was Richard at risk... the glue that held us all together. The rancor and weeks of tension died with the stroke of fate that had leveled our leader. Todd's supportive arm was seamlessly replaced by Tom's and then David's, as we embraced – all of us praying to gods in which we had no faith, for Richard's survival.

"How is he?" My quickened breath was more the result of the pressure of the baby against my diaphragm combined with the brisk walk from the parking lot rather than stress, but that didn't stop Todd from giving a silent caution to Tom, Andrew and David over my head. I watched their eyes moving above and around me as they struggled to find the right words. "Tell me the truth. Is he alive?"

"He was conscious when Bert called for help, and they said he was in and out on the way here," Tom explained slowly, squeezing my hands in reassurance.

It was 8:30 a.m. – three hours after Richard had collapsed. None of his children was shaved; they had left home before the crack of dawn and had been here for hours now. There had to be more news than that.

"Tell me," I implored, and not even David could doubt my sincerity. The fear that Richard was gone and I had missed my chance would break me. My voice cracked and the dam that held the tears at bay was breached.

"There's nothing to say, Amy," Andrew intervened. He was standing against a bare wall, his arms crossed over his chest, staring at the fluorescent light bulbs. "He's in surgery right now."

Michelle and the children arrived within minutes of us, and I had a vision of what my arrival must have been like. While Todd and the brothers quietly consulted on official business, Michelle pressed me for answers I didn't have.

Together, we presented a compelling picture of the American family to the gathering media. Like a pristine sheet billowing from a clothesline, the hounds couldn't resist pulling us down and dragging us through the mud.

With the world watching the hospital doors and the President on standby, the media was on its Ps and Qs. No one wanted to be the asshole to drag the American hero's name through the filth while he was staring death in the face. Should a recovery be announced however, then all was fair in journalism...

Then it was only a matter of time before Erika would have her moment to recount every transgression.

To preserve our dignity, the hospital made available a private waiting room where the family and Richard's security personnel gathered while awaiting news from the attending physicians. It wasn't until mid-afternoon that those elusive bastions of modern medicine finally appeared, led by a cardiologist.

The strain was evident on all our faces. Refreshments were brought up from the cafeteria, but the hours seemed to drag on indefinitely. The children were restless, protesting loudly and frequently their confinement to the small room. Though I longed to be free of the pacing, the crying, and the terrible coffee, fear kept me rooted in place. I was terrified that the moment I left, Richard would slip through my fingers.

We had the experience of Abby's hospitalization only a few months ago, to know he was still alive. Only a few minutes had passed between her death and the family being informed. Richard had been ensconced behind closed doors for ten hours.

"McDowell family?" one doctor asked, as if there were multiple families inside his hospital with armed security personnel manning the doors to private waiting rooms.

We all stood. Technically, Tom was the head of the family now, but he was too much of his father's son to take the lead. He knew Richard would have handed the reins to Todd, and so Tom stood behind my husband. I was not too caught up in my emotions to miss this.

Because if Richard survived, when I killed him, I would have to contend with Todd.

"Yes," Todd said, assuming the mantle of leadership with his usual ease and grace.

"Richard McDowell is your father?" the doctor asked, looking up from his clipboard long enough to note the difference in appearances. Richard's sons all had light brown hair and brown eyes, except David who was a ginger with green eyes.

"By marriage, yes," Todd replied so smoothly, so without hesitance, that it was as if he believed it to be so. "This is my wife, Amy." He pulled me closer to his side and I rubbed my belly in what I hoped was a convincing manner. "These are his sons, Tom, Andrew and David; Tom's wife, Michelle. And Richard's grandchildren, Savannah and Sarah."

Each adult nodded as the introductions were made, and the sons drew closer behind Todd and me. Dr. Stanton introduced himself as the cardiologist, then gestured over his shoulder to Dr. Leeson, the thoracic surgeon; and Dr. Finkleton, the neurologist.

"Richard presents a complicated diagnosis," the doctor started out after everyone was seated. "We believe he suffered an earlier episode that weakened his heart."

"Another heart attack?" Todd interrupted. He was the one to vocalize the question on everyone else's tongue. It would not be out of character for Richard to ignore the signs of a preliminary heart attack, moving on as if there was nothing out of the ordinary.

"Not exactly," Dr. Stanton replied, and with both hands appealed for patience. "Has there been any traumatic experiences recently? Any deaths in the family or incidents that would cause grief?"

"Yes," Todd answered, which had to be the greatest understatement ever. The doctor's raised eyebrows begged for clarification. "His wife passed away unexpectedly seven weeks ago and the family has had a difficult time adjusting."

How the fuck he had come up with *that* as diplomatic speech for being caught with a prostitute, arrested for cocaine possession, and dying of a drug overdose was astonishing, even to us seasoned liars. Half of us looked at Todd with awe, while the other half was too embarrassed to look anywhere but straight ahead.

"It says here he is sixty-five years old. Is Richard retired?" Dr. Stanton asked, and all eyes swiveled back to him. He seemed disconcerted by the incredulous stares.

"Richard is retired from the Navy, yes," Todd said, then added helpfully, "he is actually Admiral Richard McDowell." Dr. Stanton exchanged querying glances with his colleagues who all but shrugged their shoulders helplessly. "He is the Director of National Intelligence... appointed by the President to oversee the federal intelligence agencies."

"Well, that would do it," Dr. Stanton noted, scribbling onto his clipboard. "I apologize. We don't get out much."

"No apologies necessary," Todd assured him. "Richard is a modest man." Todd was pushing the boundaries of truth there, but we had more important topics to discuss than what Richard would have thought of a doctor who lived with his head up his ass.

"We believe Richard suffered a cardiomyopathic episode. To the untrained eye, it looks and feels like a heart attack. He might have had chest and/or arm pains, shortness of breath, and sweating. The difference is there is no clogging of the arteries. With cardiomyopathy, stress hormones like adrenaline flood to the heart, causing a shock to the muscles, which in turn jeopardizes the heart's ability to pump in a normal manner. As a result, the left ventricle of Richard's heart is misshapen. The condition is treatable with medication and the removal of external stressors. And while that alone should have been enough to bring him here, I'm afraid that's only the start of Richard's medical issues."

Dr. Stanton took a deep breath and rubbed his palm against the leg of his green scrubs. "Richard also suffered an acute cardiac infraction – an actual heart attack. The right coronary artery was blocked in two places, and the rupture of that plaque created a blood clot that blocked blood flow in the artery. Considering the extent and location of the plaque buildup as well as the damage to the tissue, we had very little choice but to clear them surgically. There are a couple other areas of concern, but we should be able to get those under control with medication. We'll keep him in the ICU for another day or so. Depending on his progress, he might be able to move into recovery by Tuesday, and home in a week to ten days. While it is important that he returns to regular activities as soon as possible, we want him to start slowly. Maybe return to work in about four to six weeks. Do you have any questions?"

We conferred among each other for a few moments, before Todd re-emerged from our impromptu huddle as the spokesman. Our level of organization was probably disconcerting to the staff, but we weren't the average military family. Everyone one of us, with the exception of Michelle and the children, were military brats who had become commissioned officers. Every one of us would stand behind our interim leader who had earned his position through merit.

"Can we see him?" Todd asked.

"He is heavily sedated now. We can accommodate you two at a time, but you won't get anything from him." Dr. Stanton's eyes flickered to the children who were hanging off their mother, and then to my belly. "I should caution that he's had a rough morning. There is a lot of equipment monitoring and helping him along. It may come as a shock to some of you."

Todd nodded, silently acknowledging the doctor's warning. But Todd wouldn't keep me away. I needed to see that he was alive.

"Will he be ... normal... when he comes around? Is there anything we need to prepare for?"

"Very good question," the doctor smiled and adjusted in his seat, as if he relished either this part of the conversation or the fact that he wasn't feeling questions from the entire field.

"Richard lost consciousness when his heart was unable to pump blood to his brain. Having CPR performed at the scene helped, so we're talking about a relatively short window of time when his brain was oxygen starved. Dr. Finkleton, our neurologist, has assessed Richard's MRI and DTI – diffusion tensor imaging – scans. What we've seen looks promising. At first, his reflexes may be slightly slower than normal, and there may be some weakness on the left side of his body, but that will go away in time. He will likely benefit from some therapy. We'll be able to provide a more precise prognosis when he wakes up. This is just so you're prepared.

"As for his home recovery, Richard will require constant care for a few weeks, especially if there is weakness in his extremities. He'll need someone to monitor his pulse, help with after-care... that sort of thing."

The doctor's eyes shifted between me – natural since I was assumed to be Richard's daughter – and Michelle, then quickly back to Todd. It was a silent question that Todd, easily picked up on.

"We would welcome your recommendations on professional at-home care."

The medical staff accepted that with ease, nodding their approval. After all, it seemed a reasonable alternative to pawning Richard off to the heavily pregnant daughter and the mother of two demanding girls. It would never have occurred to them that Richard was not as beloved as our presence suggested. He was the driving force behind Michelle's eventual replacement, and I... well, I wanted him well enough so I could kill him myself.

"Richard is a long distance runner. He frequently accompanies Amy on marathon distance runs – obviously before the advance of her condition. The question is: how could the damage have gotten so bad for someone as active as Richard?" Several heads behind Todd nodded in agreement, and Tom even squeezed his shoulder in encouragement.

Dr. Stanton scratched his head through his cap, as he puzzled over the strange dynamic. "Well, there is some research that suggests that excessive exercising may be damaging to the heart by promoting plaque build up. I would suggest that going forward, Richard limit his regimen. Of course, we'll see how well he pulls through today's surgery, and in a couple of months perform a stress test before making precise recommendations of what should be adequate for someone of his age and in his condition."

I liked the sound of 'a couple of months', but without seeing him with my own eyes, I wouldn't trust that Richard wouldn't die on me.

Handshakes were exchanged, cautious reassurances given, and a schedule for visitation established. The doctors departed, and Andrew and David were the first to see their father. Tom and Todd left us to discuss care and aftercare with the nurses and administrators down the hall. Michelle quietly waited in her corner, trying her best to keep the children quiet and occupied with coloring books and toys. And security maintained their silent watch from the doorway.

Bert had refused to leave, although his shift had ended at noon. Besides short breaks, he had not ventured far from this room, trapped on the outside by his position as an employee but riveted to the grounds by his loyalty to Richard. No doubt I would have to go through Bert too when it was time to kill Richard.

"Bert." Years of animosity would never really disappear, but at least for these few seconds, we could be united in our common fear.

"Mrs. Birch," he answered, and this time I knew it was from habit.

"I want to thank you for what you did," I told him, and the realization that, without Bert, Richard would likely have died, shook me. My voice broke and fresh tears sprang to my eyes. Normally I would have been embarrassed by my body's weakness, especially under Bert's scrutiny. "Thank you for saving him."

Bert nodded, his lips flattening as he blinked fast. "No need to thank me, Mrs. Birch. Just doing my job."

We both knew it wasn't his job that kept him here, and so it wasn't his job that had made him care for Richard, forcing his heart to beat when it couldn't do so on its own. But I didn't want to embarrass him too; I was grateful to him for giving me a second chance, and so I nodded and turned away.

"Mrs. Birch?" I wiped at my cheeks before facing him again. "He's strong. He'll make it," Bert said. I wasn't surprised that he had been listening. I was taken aback however, that he would try to comfort me.

"I hope so," I told him.

Todd was waiting for me inside, and he picked up where Bert, in his own hands-off way, had left off. In a quiet corner, he held me and tried – albeit weakly – to convince me not to see Richard. His words fell on deaf ears, but I appreciated my place in the cocoon of his arms.

Soon, Andrew and David returned, and Tom and Michelle were swept away. Eventually, the younger McDowells left and Todd took charge of the girls. I hated giving up my place for them, but it was a sentiment I was becoming familiar with hiding. I had already given up much for our own child, and watching Todd with Tom's children was like having a glimpse into the future.

Of course I was attached to the life growing inside me. I was moved when it moved. I gazed at its picture and marveled at its parts. I felt it at rest and was soothed by the calm within me. In my mind, it was trapped in a nebulous place between consciousness and existence. Like Anne, the fetus had a consciousness separate from mine. They both lived through me, breathing because I breathed; but were conscious when I was not. In its own way, the fetus had a voice. I heard it in its movements and in its silence. I felt its life like I felt Anne's.

But Todd said Anne wasn't real. And yet he loved his future child as if it were real.

"Are you sure you want to do this?" Todd asked, extending a hand to help me up from my seat.

I nodded and we made our way down the hall and into the elevator. Michelle had returned to take the children, while Tom awaited us outside Richard's door. At the end of another corridor he stood, bent by the weight of responsibility. He knew he was as much responsible for his father's condition as David and Abby.

With a hand on Tom's shoulder, Todd sought to imbue the shaken man with some of his strength, but right before my eyes, Tom broke. Tears pooled heavily in his eyes and he refused to let Todd go.

"Go in, Amy. I'll be there in a minute," he said to me. I resented the fact that Todd was his pillar of strength. Tom had two brothers and a wife to lean on. His reliance on my husband meant there was even less of him for me. And Todd knew it too. His eyes held mine and reached into the dark recesses of my mind. "One minute for you to be with Richard," he said.

I accepted his olive branch and left them. The shadow of anger was welcome for its distraction from the fear. Because inside the dark room that reeked of antiseptic, propped on a cushioned slab, was the shell of a man.

It didn't look like Richard... it didn't look like anyone. It was a body covered to the collar by a stiff sheet, arms resting lifelessly above the covers. The rise and fall of his chest was barely discernible, but the machines to which he was attached beeped with life. There were no chairs, only the wheeled bed, an IV line and the machines.

It was more than he deserved; I remembered only the stainless steel tables on which my parents' bodies were displayed.

I was terrified of touching anything... didn't want to disturb his recovery. It wouldn't be a mistake when he died, or his body's own failing. When I killed him, I wanted him to know... to feel the pain of betrayal. He would know I had ripped his legacy apart, destroyed his family, and ended his life.

For now, I needed him to live, and the man laid out before me didn't look alive.

I moved close enough that my belly touched the raised railings on his bed. They were cold, and as white as the hand lying next to them. There was blood beneath the skin, however; I felt its warmth as I held his hand. It was so different from my father's, but the memory had me doubling over with the force of my sobs.

I cried. The memory of sorrow was as strong as it had been that day at the morgue. I had insisted on going to see them against all counsel. In the end, it was Richard who had placed his hand on my shoulder, pouring his courage and strength into my body. He had watched with me as the curtain was lifted away to reveal my parents' bodies. He had held me when I asked to be with them, to touch them again... to hold my father's hand for the last time. Richard had made it possible. He had sworn to me that he would find the people who had done it.

And all along he'd been there at my side.

"Please don't die," I sobbed, as I pressed my forehead against the hand I clasped. "Please, come home," I whispered over and over, not caring that he was being bathed in my tears.

Time must have passed. I wasn't sure how much, but after a while, there were hands on me.

"He's going to be OK," Todd said.

"I need a second chance," I said to no one, as I stared down at my tears glistening against Richard's skin.

"You'll have it," Todd said, gently pulling me away. "You'll be a family again."

He didn't understand; Todd never would. He was more Richard's than mine... always would be.

I looked at the man whose hand I held. His face was grey, but it wasn't the pallor of death.

I wasn't sure if it was the sound of Todd's voice, or the warmth of my tears being massaged into his skin, but his eyes opened. It was so unexpected... caught me so off my guard... that I dropped his hand, and for a moment I feared that I had hurt him. Todd followed my gasp and the direction of my stare, and tensed, his fingers biting into my shoulders.

"Richard?" he called, leaning closer.

There was a flicker of awareness in the slightly cracked lids, but the eyes – one blue and one brown – were trained on me. I couldn't tell if he was conscious, if there was sight in his eyes, and so I shifted and watched as he followed me.

Richard was alive.

I took his hand again, and though he never so much as twitched, his eyes never left my face. There was a cooling flood of something through my body. It filled me with a heady lightness, as if I had shed a thick coat and had been given wings. He would live another day, and I would get the chance to kill him.

The tears that hadn't quite stopped blurred my vision as our eyes met. The sobs came again, shaking free the tears that hung stubbornly to the brim. But they were different – lighter, sweeter – as they met my relief.

I laughed and cried, and all the time I held Richard's hand, he held my stare. He had had a taste of death and had awakened to find it standing over him. He would never turn his back on me again.

FORTY-TWO

It came as no surprise that Richard was replaced as Director of National Intelligence.

The announcement was made two days after his discharge from hospital. However, it was not unlike Richard to have planned for all contingencies, including his sudden incapacitation. He had planted the seeds for the choice of his successor the day he took office, and had watered it throughout his tenure.

It wasn't Todd; that would have been impossible, even for Richard. But for all intents and purposes, it might as well have been. The replacement was as committed to Richard as my husband was. And so it was business as usual in the Office of the DNI – and so too the rest of our world.

Richard's recovery was slow, his body incapable of keeping pace with his will. For weeks he struggled to articulate the commands as instantaneously as they fired across his brain. His frustration was plain to see, and Todd used that to hold me at bay.

"Give him time," he would say after his nearly daily trips to Richard's. Neither he nor the man himself wanted me to witness such weakness.

But his body's breakdown was the cherry on top of a shit sundae, that Richard had no intention of indulging in for long. He made a point of getting dressed and moving about as much as possible without help. The nurses who supplemented the household on a shift basis found him a cooperative, if slightly unnerving, patient. He took his medication without prompting, let them change his bandages as needed, and submitted to their dietary recommendations with more grace than Ollie, the housekeeper/cook.

But Richard stared at them in stony silence as they worked. His eyes remained fixed to their faces even as they held their breath and checked that his flesh was mending as it should. Of course he knew their darkest secrets, and his unrelenting gaze told them so.

To compensate for Tom's fall from grace, and the tarnish of David's arrest, he directed Todd and Andrew with unparalleled vigor. In time, Andrew would step into his elder brother's shoes, buttressing Todd's eventual rise to the position of DNI. While plans to divorce Michelle were indefinitely shelved – a rift in the family would be cause for more unwanted attention – nothing precluded our patriarch from keeping a watch for other suitable wives for all his sons. It was only the order of preference that had changed, beginning with the youngest and ending with the patron of prostitutes.

As for my husband, no expense was spared in hawking his achievements... and lineage within the Defense Department. Not only did Todd come with Richard's endorsement, but my father's too. It was an indignity the ambitious Colonel bore with surprising alacrity considering his hatred for John Koehler.

According to Todd, the worst of Richard's frailties were on his left side: a sagging eye and impaired hearing. His kill arm was as strong as ever though, and he had taken to shooting to keep it that way. He spent hours at the range, drilling holes into the ghosts of his past that had finally returned to haunt him.

Richard knew someone was coming for him. There was nothing unnatural about the collapse of his world. And even if his heart attack were unplanned, the events of the past seven months would have leveled a lesser man. My proximity and our history made me the suspect of convenience, because to the observant, Richard's fall seemed to stem from the disappearance of his dear friend, Gay.

Or maybe that was simply my guilty conscience at play. After all, suspicion haunts the guilty mind. On the positive side of things, considering all I had done and all I was willing to do, it was comforting to know I still had one of those—a conscience.

It wasn't simply his physical infirmities that had provoked Richard's replacement however. Erika Harris had finally had her revenge.

The family had refused to comment on any of her allegations, deferring to the authorities in which the People held strict confidence. If David McDowell was cleared of all charges following an examination of the facts by the District Attorney, then who were we to question that decision?

Abby's death was a tragedy with which the family still struggled, and a strong case for improving oversight of medical practitioners.

As for the Chester Williams case, we were unaware of the status of an investigation; had no knowledge of any member of the family being considered a suspect; and could not comment on classified operations that may or may not have been linked to the family.

In light of the occupations of unnamed members of the family, some media blackout was accorded. So it wasn't everything Erika would have liked, but it reinforced the decision to have Richard quietly retired to avoid enhanced scrutiny of other members of the family who required the shroud of secrecy to be effective.

But Erika was greedy for my humiliation, which dulled her sense of self-preservation. The only reason she wasn't dead was the attention her sudden demise would have caused. And she either chose to ignore that fact, or was lulled into a false sense of security.

Erika should have been alarmed when I ran into her in early August. The meeting would have been innocuous on the face of it, but when a heavily pregnant woman walks into a hotel bar and seats herself at your booth as if she belongs, you take notice. When that woman is the wife of a man with whom you had an affair, and the presumed niece of a man you've spent months trying to destroy, then you stand on guard. And when that woman thanks the press liaison for the House Armed Services Committee for his time after your recently concluded, and in truth, unproductive rendezvous, you assess your proximity to the nearest exit.

Erika Harris did none of those things. Instead, she leaned back into the heavily upholstered seats with a self-satisfied smile, as if she had lured me there by sheer will.

She was still beautiful, professional and seductive all at once. Her skin glowed with good health and the kiss of sunlight under the pale lighting of the Hay-Adams, making it ideal for the trading of secrets. She was dressed in a simple shift dress that modestly hinted at the superb female form beneath. Her hair hung around her chin, swaying with each bat of her mink lashes. She wasn't tall by most accounts, but her designer heels made up for that shortcoming and then some. I had yet to catch her looking sub-par, and she seemed to relish that fact, while I struggled to find a comfortable position in the seat opposite her.

At thirty-six weeks pregnant, my greatest concern was comfort. I had given up my pencil skirts and four-inch heels long ago for elastic waistbands and slip-on sandals. And while my skin had markedly improved since our first meeting, my naturally flushed cheeks had filled out with the rest of me. Todd seemed to appreciate the rounding of my figure, lavishing an inordinate amount of attention on my breasts and rapidly expanding ass, but under Erika's smug gaze, I felt like a mound of sausage squeezed into too-tight casing.

The woman really had no sense of what was good for her.

"Mrs. Birch," she said in greeting, her glass raised to her lips in nothing short of a mocking salute. "What a surprise."

She didn't look surprised at all, but that was about to change.

"Do you want to live?" I asked point-blank and watched the smile slowly melt from her lips.

"Excuse me?" Her brow wrinkled and her eyes made a sweep, checking the edges of our surroundings for the warp that marked the edges of a parallel realm where crazy was common place.

"You've spent months digging your grave. But I don't think you realize it."

"Are you threatening me?" she asked, adeptly using incredulity to conceal her fear. She tried to make eye contact with our neighbors, but they were busy doing what the guests were known for – sharing confidences, laying the groundwork for their rise to eminence, or tearing down another's. Such heavy work was best conducted with heads bowed closely together. They didn't spare her a glance.

"You misunderstand," I said, folding my hands on top of my jutting belly. "In my family, we don't threaten, we don't give warnings. When we come for you, it won't be in the dead of night when you most expect it."

I watched as she leaned further into the back of her seat. Unlike before, this was not the settling of a champion in her victory. This was the retreat of quarry, the desire to become invisible. I watched the fear flicker across her face before she put her all into composing herself. I watched her with the impassive stare of one for whom winning has lost its luster.

Erika was slow but not completely stupid. Good. The tableau I had drawn for her at our last meeting was slowly being remade. I was not the weak and self-conscious woman she thought she had dragged into a brawl over a man. She much preferred the old image.

"If this is about Todd —"

"It's not. " I waved away the approaching waiter. He hesitated, having caught Erika's alarm. A pointed glance delivered from over my shoulder did the trick.

"What do you want?" she asked with a thick swallow.

"I want to help you," I said and watched the play of emotions across her face. Fear, disbelief, distrust only added to her appeal. She looked like a woman any red-blooded man would want to rescue. "But it depends on your answer to my question."

"What question?" she gasped.

"Do you want to live?"

She sucked in a quick breath and pressed her lips together in a thin line, trapping the air inside. She nodded, a tentative bobbing of her head that sent her hair dancing about her shoulders. She gasped as I dipped into my purse. I let her unease pass unremarked. Caution would serve her well in the coming years. It would keep her heart beating in her chest.

I pulled out an envelope and placed it on the table, sliding it halfway between us. She spared it the barest of glances, devoting most of her attention to the threat.

"Open it." She shook her head. "It's safe, I promise."

"Is that worth anything?" she asked, folding her trembling fingers into her lap beneath the table.

"My promise?" She nodded. "Usually, no." To move us along, I opened the envelope for her. Inside was a slip of paper with a hosting domain address and password. I waited for her natural curiosity to replace her fear.

"What is this?" she asked.

"Nothing for now, but in time it may save your life."

Her gaze shot back to mine even as she ran her fingers across the type-written note. "I don't understand."

"One day soon you're going to hit bedrock. It's the story behind the story you've been working on since that night in February at the National Press Building."

I waited for understanding to dawn. Her eyes darted between mine and the bit of paper as her brain worked.

"You'll have a choice to make. What you do with that story will decide whether you live or die."

Erika pulled her hand away from the paper as if it had suddenly burst into flames. "What if I don't want anything to do with this?"

"Then you've already made your choice. Like it or nor, you've already come too far to turn back now."

"I don't understand," she cried. Her wide-eyed gaze bored into me, forcing tears to pool around the rim. She blinked furiously to keep them at bay.

"You've spent months digging your grave, Erika. You declared war against an enemy you never took the time to know. To give up now is to throw yourself upon the mercy of people who have none." I tapped the scrap of paper that lay between us. "Someone will come for you if you don't meet us first. This is the only thing that can save your life, but you will have to decide how to use it."

"What do I have to do?"

"This is where the story ends," I said and pushed the paper squarely on her side of the table. "I will deliver it to you there, but I can't tell you precisely when. You'll have to check back daily, maybe even twice a day."

"You're not making sense. How will I know what to do?"

I smiled. "You're a smart woman when you're not angry. You'll figure it out."

I gathered my purse and my girth and pushed myself out of my chair. She stood too, scrambling to her feet to urgently grip my arm.

"Please, wait," she called. A pointed glance at the clammy fingers sliding down to my wrist eventually set me free. "I want you to know that I'm sorry." Our eyes met evenly as her heels and my flats brought us on an equal footing. We would never see eye-to-eye on this however. "About Todd. I'm sorry about what happened..."

I smiled without humor. "No, you're not. You're sorry it didn't work out the way you wanted."

"But I didn't plan it, I swear!" she pleaded. "I was under the impression that he was free to do as he wished. There appeared to be no affection between you. I didn't think it mattered..."

"Like it didn't matter the first time?" I asked. Erika gulped in a breath of air, taken aback that I knew their history. "You love him, and you didn't care then whom you might have hurt." I understood her perfectly because I was the same – selfish in my drive to get what I wanted.

Her lip trembled for a moment before she clamped her teeth into the plump flesh. "You mean Robert." I shrugged. "He never loved me. He wanted me for sure, but he never loved me."

I straightened the strap of my purse over my shoulder, annoyed with her self-pity. She was beautiful, but Erika was no Helen of Troy.

"Neither did Todd."

"What do you want me to say?" she asked, and this time, no amount of resolve could hold her tears at bay. It had been a trying fifteen minutes, fraught with shock and bitter memories.

"There is nothing to say. You have only to learn from past mistakes. Robert may not have loved you like you wanted him to. But there's something to be said of the fact that he waged a war for you, ruined innocent lives for you."

"My sister," she whispered.

"Among others."

"I can't go back and change things. Besides, he isn't mine to fix anymore. He stopped wanting me a long time ago."

"That's where you're wrong," I told her. I was impatient to leave now, shifting from one foot to the other. But besides the pressing urge to use the bathroom, I could hardly believe the irony of the situation. I was giving life and love advice to the woman my husband had fucked.

Her brow wrinkled in confusion again. She was going to give herself a headache overthinking everything. "Wrong about what? You do know Robert is married to my sister..."

"A man never really stops wanting a woman; he just learns to want other things more. For Robert, that was revenge. He will always be yours to fix, because you were the one to break him in the first place. No one else can undo what you did."

"Why are you doing this? Why are you helping me?"

"To achieve my own ends, of course. Now I really must go." I smiled in farewell, but there was no warmth behind it. Warmth was something Erika should never expect from me... Nor forgiveness. It was lucky for her I needed her alive. For now. "Stop digging, Erika. You've done more than enough of that already."

When I ran into Colonel Townsend a week later, it was not through my own contrivance. Blitzner insisted on holding briefings in preparation for my leave of absence. My caseload came under review, progress mapped and activities divested to other agents and agencies for the time being.

"No need to be nervous, Amy," Blitzner said on our way to the fourth floor conference room where coffee and my military liaisons awaited. Among them were Colonel Townsend and Major Edward Cummings' replacement, Capt. Joey Marshall. "Your place will be right here when you return."

The fact that Blitzner felt the need to reassure me made me suspicious. He would find a replacement as soon as the tides turned against me. Richard continued to direct play from the sidelines, but that would not last forever. His heart attack had proved what many had come to doubt – that he was mortal.

While Blitzner respected my work, there were others who were hungrier to please, who would have jumped at the offer of courtside seats at Guantánamo. And in our field, enthusiasm had its merits.

"I'm not nervous," I told my boss, stopping in the doorway while he held the door for me. "The eager will come and go – burn out like a candle lit at both ends. I'm the best at what we do, and we both know there's no risk of my growing a conscience at this stage."

"Why Amy, I think marriage has mellowed you out."

I smiled at him, sharing a genuine moment of levity with a man I still didn't trust. "Just wrap it up and keep things clean for me while I'm gone."

For the next two hours, I laid bare my portfolio and we agreed on the persons who would pick up the slack.

For months, Townsend and I had enjoyed an easy entente. There persisted some sexual banter, but I sensed his heart wasn't really behind it. No doubt he was disappointed in Todd's hold over me... suspected that I was truly in love with my husband. Why else would I have gone on a belated honeymoon and deliberately conceived Todd's child, both after his blatant indiscretion?

So while he had not completely abandoned his campaign to seduce me, Colonel Townsend had at least acknowledged that the likelihood of my succumbing to his ample charms was slim to non-existent.

In addition, it was my belief that my pregnancy struck a nerve with Colonel Townsend. I believed he cared for me in his own way. After all, he had wanted me before Todd had entered the scene. I thought perhaps my pregnancy reminded him of Mona, and I believed in the furthest recesses of his heart, Colonel Townsend regretted that his actions had led to her death.

Even so, he had a long way to go to earn his halo.

An hour into the briefing and he made a grand show of massaging my lower back. It wasn't my obvious discomfort or his experience as a father of two that spurred his chivalry. It was the simple fact that Captain Joey Marshall would report to Todd the minute he was out the door. Regardless, I went with it, because first and foremost, I craved the comfort, and secondly, Todd couldn't exactly accuse me of any impropriety with a roomful of witnesses.

At the end of our session, a gentle hand against Colonel Townsend's arm was sufficient to delay his departure. We weren't exactly alone, as there were several breakout conversations around the room and spilling into the corridor.

"A moment of your time, please, Colonel Townsend."

He turned in his seat to face me, stretching so the seam of his pants brushed my calves. Todd had made the case for pregnancy sex being the best yet. Having been there twice himself, Colonel Townsend might have shared his convictions. The light in his eyes said he didn't mind my expanded girth.

"If a moment is what you're accustomed to," he drawled smugly. "But I promise I can do better than that."

I rolled my eyes, but smiled good-naturedly at his shamelessness. "I'm sure you can, a moment is all I need... and a lot of patience for what I have to say."

He acknowledged my lighthearted acceptance of his flirtation with a lift of one corner of his mouth. But his eyes registered the sobering of my tone too. "What can I do for you, Amy?"

He leaned an arm against the conference table, drawing closer to preserve our privacy. Even without looking up, I could feel Captain Marshall's eyes on us. Not only had he been in our home, he knew our highs and lows; navigating them was a matter of professional pragmatism.

Happy Commanding Officer, happy life.

"It's about Erika Harris," I said, watching closely as the light shifted and his eyes changed from the lightest sky blue to glacial.

"What about her?" It wasn't just my imagination. The warmth was gone from his voice too, and the smile that graced his lips was brittle.

"I saw her last week." He remained unmoved, but his body grew stiffer the longer he remained still. "She's gotten herself in trouble."

He drew a shallow breath. "You mean with the McDowells?" I nodded. "Why are you telling me this, Amy? Aren't they like family to you?"

"They are." I inched closer to compensate from his slight retreat. It was such a slight withdrawal that normally it would have gone unremarked, but my body instantly missed the warmth of his proximity. "Todd is the heir apparent, and his relationship with her is DC's worst kept secret. But that won't matter to the McDowells. So when they move against her, it will be Todd who makes it happen."

Colonel Townsend looked into my eyes, and I held his stare. The silence stretched between us, and through it our concerns were shared. He didn't want to care, but he did. Whether it was solely for Erika's benefit, or because this was another opportunity to thwart Todd, was irrelevant.

All I needed was for him to care.

"You warned her." I nodded. "Why?"

"I think we've all suffered enough. It's time to end it."

"You didn't have to warn her for that. He could finish her easily enough."

"He could take her life, but that wouldn't be the end of it. You wouldn't let it."

He scoffed. "Because I'm married to her sister? I already told you that's over in fact if not deed."

I shook my head and held onto the hand he would have otherwise pulled away from the table. "Because you loved her once."

His gaze flashed back to mine, a denial hot on the tip of his tongue. I squeezed his arm and pleaded with him to hear me out.

"It's impossible to turn off something like that. If we could, we would. Even though you never told her how you felt and she doubts it to this day, you and I both know that you won't let him hurt her."

He swallowed deeply and looked away. I was enraptured by the glimpse of his soft underbelly. It infused me with warmth. In another life… one before Todd, and before I was broken… I would have liked to explore this man gazing tenderly into the past.

"She made her bed…" he finally whispered, but his resoluteness was a lie. It was all pride and no heart.

"She made a mistake. A day doesn't go by that she doesn't wish she could go back and undo it. Neither of you have moved on, and if it ends like this, you never will." His throat worked as he rolled all the excuses across his tongue. I squeezed his arm again.

"Robert."

I had never called him by his name, although there had been no obligation for me to defer to his command. It was a formality I had insisted on to maintain the distance between us. The sound was as unfamiliar to my ears as his.

"She's waiting for you."

He tried for sardonic humor again. "My wife's sister?"

"The only woman you ever loved."

"Jesus, Amy, why are you doing this? What's in it for you?" He pulled his arm away, and I let him go. It was enough that I had planted the seed.

"Justice," I said. "Righting a wrong from long ago."

We parted ways soon after. Colonel Townsend had made no promises, but he was the reliable sort who would gnaw relentlessly at the bone I had thrown his way. In the end, he would protect Erika from Todd. He didn't have the head for intrigue… only action.

He was such a simple man in fact that he naturally assumed the wrong to be righted was his star-crossed love affair with his sister-in-law.

In truth, it was the murder of my father. Because when I finally moved against Richard, Todd would have a choice to make: save me or protect his mentor. Should he choose the latter, it was a certainty that he would go for Erika.

And when he did, Colonel Townsend would be waiting.

The anticipation was more than a girl could bear. I didn't sleep for four days, which inevitably led to the wakening of dormant urges.

FORTY-THREE

Anne unfurled like a night-blooming flower under the rays of the moon, determined to live a year before wilting at dawn. The August evening was unusually warm and her preoccupations were heavy, but there was much to do and very little time in which to do it.

Todd would be home soon.

The urgency that fact instilled was diametrically opposed to Amy's cautious manipulations over the past eight months. But Amy's priorities had shifted, while Anne's had solidified.

Running her hand over her ballooned waistline, Anne marveled at the difference a child could make. The love of a mother for her child was a powerful distraction. Amy wanted to have her cake and eat it too, but Todd had precluded Anne from sharing in their bounty. Their family was an attachment she did not share. With only ghosts of the past in the place where her family had once stood, Anne knew there was no future for her.

"Not a day more," Anne promised, as she left her father's study.

The stage was set. She left the door wide open, a deliberate derogation from the routine that was sure to intrigue. Amy had given up her private place, because once Todd's eyes were opened, they could never be closed again. A locked door in the absence of the family was the extent of his accommodation, conceded solely for the purpose of preserving professional secrecy.

Her computer was primed for action, the speakers set and awaiting the actors to take the stage. In less than two hours, the final act would unfold.

Anne checked Amy's service firearm and the covert recording device. One was a precaution against Richard's security; the other would relay the live feed of Richard's Waterloo to the IP address to which her computer had been set. Anne had even helpfully scribbled Erika's email address and phone number on a nearby writing pad – stage directions for the would-be hero. It would be a test of the love Todd professed for his wife.

Whom would he save: his mentor or his wife? To whom would he run: the woman with whom Richard's secrets were being shared or the home in Bel Air?

"Not a day more," Anne whispered as she pulled up to the gates and smiled at Bert.

"Mrs. Birch. How may I help you?"

"You can open the gates."

Bert's mouth shifted into an implacable line that only a fool would mistake for a smile. "You're not on the list," he said without looking at his clipboard.

"When have I ever given a shit about your list, Bert?" No one expected his truce with Amy to last. Like combatants in an age-old conflict, the origins of which were long forgotten, they fell easily into their roles. "Call Todd. And hurry, because I need to pee."

"Your husband has already left for the evening," he replied, without moving a muscle to open the gates.

"Then call Richard."

He did, making a grand show of pointing out the obvious. "She's not on the list," he said to his boss. "Misplaced her husband again." They shared a chuckle, the guard oblivious to death creeping up behind him. "Passed hundreds of bathrooms on the way up here; must be the heated seats."

Richard was waiting, dressed in slacks and a button-down shirt just inside the front door. His casual dress shined a mocking spotlight on the formality between them. It had been a month since he had last laid eyes on the woman he claimed was like a daughter to him.

"Amy, how good it is to see you," he said slowly and without warmth. "It's been a long time." His slur was almost gone... making progress everyday.

"I'm not on the list," Anne replied, but smiled to take the sting away. She moved easily into his arms and pressed a kiss to his cheek – proof that the years under his tutelage had not been a total waste.

"Todd is not here. You've made a long trip for nothing." But what he meant was *why have you uselessly made a long trip?*

"So I've been told," she replied, casting an eye around the entry hall, a pointed admonishment of his cold reception. "It's not entirely pointless however."

"How so?" His direct stare would have been unnerving to those unaccustomed to Richard's manner of stripping away pretense.

"I wanted to see you, of course. It's been too long."

There was a lingering air of expectation, as Richard waited for the prodigal to reach across the breach. It never came. After a long time, he gestured to the entry hall's half bathroom. "Come up to my study when you're done. We'll catch up."

Anne took advantage of the small space to give Richard the time he needed to make the journey up the stairs. It suited her purposes for him to collect and arm himself. Let him think he held the control. Allow Todd the opportunity for discovery.

Anne splashed water on her face and carefully dabbed her skin dry. Her eyes were bright despite the shadows etched deeply by days of lack of rest.

"Not a day more," she said to the woman in the mirror, and watched pleased, as the fire burned brighter.

Richard was predictably seated behind his desk, his contingencies firmly in place. The indifference he exhibited was feigned. He was never nonchalant when in his place of power, cushioned leather at his back, a sea of mahogany between him and his subject, firearm within easy reach.

Anne pulled a pen and an envelope from her purse. The pen was heavier than most, endowed with recording capabilities only people like them would anticipate. The envelope was larger, meant to draw the eye away from the camera.

"What is this?" Richard asked with barely more than mild curiosity.

"My answer to a question not yet posed," Anne said, easing her considerable bulk into the hard seat facing him and drawing closer, so her props were easily within reach.

Richard laughed. "It's not like you to be so cryptic, Amy." Anne waited in silence until his false humor melted away. "Why don't you tell me why you've come? How is that for a question?"

"I want you to tell me who killed my father," Anne said.

Having held Richard's gaze without pause, the shift in him was plain to see. He grew harder, colder, and far more attentive to the woman before him. His gaze narrowed, the lift of the corners of his mouth arctic, making even the brown eye appear blue.

"Are you sure that's where you wish to begin?" he asked, tilting his head to the side. He had discerned a change – the subtle difference between the woman before him and the one he had raised. He could not tell precisely what it was, but he was intrigued.

"It's seems as good a place as any to start. After all, you did promise."

"Of course you would think so. You never developed an appreciation for nuances. It is always black or white with you."

Anne shifted into the hard-backed chair, as if it were made of the deepest plush. "Why don't you teach me, Richard? Then I'll show you what I've learned at your knee."

He broke their locked gaze, eyes flicking to the envelope that sat squarely on Anne's side. "*That* comes much later. Why don't you start from the beginning?"

The silence stretched like the intervening years since her father's murder before Richard reached into the past with a deceitful sigh. There was no resignation, no concession at all. His mental fatigue was another lie his cunning eyes betrayed.

"Just this once, I'll indulge you… before you start knocking on doors you don't want opened." Richard took a deep breath and rubbed his chest. The hole in his chest was healing, but no medical miracle would ever fix him. The man was heartless to put voice to the words that followed.

"John was my best friend – had been for more than twenty years. But he was ill, and close as we were, I didn't see it until it was too late. No one saw it."

"My father didn't die from an illness."

"No," Richard said, for a moment, his eyes softening. It wasn't in the manner of compassion however. It was meant to disarm. "But it explains why he died." Richard sighed. "In his last years, he became confused, and at the same time, intractable. He upset the balance and could not be contained."

Anne waited for him continue, but it seemed Richard was done for the moment. It wasn't enough... not by half.

"Did he upset you, Richard?" Anne prompted. "Is that why he was murdered?"

Richard stiffened, and dropped his hand from his chest. "Why would you think such a thing, Amy? Have I not been like a father to you? Have I not raised you, loved you, protected you like my own?"

He had stood side by side with the man and promised before God to raise her when her father could not. Their friendship had even extended to their wives. The best of friends... wolves in sheep's clothing.

"Yes, yes. You were best friends for over twenty years. I know."

Anne leaned forward, limited though she was by Todd's growing child. She slid the envelope across the polished wood so it was truly halfway between them. Richard regarded it for an eternity before he decided to humor her.

"There is your answer, Richard... the reason I would think such a thing."

It was light, the weight of a single sheet of paper, but it sent Richard's world careening off its axis. Whatever his suspicions may have been, he was unprepared for Anne's revelation. He spent another eternity assessing the picture printed on simple A4 paper.

"Did you do this?" he finally asked, lowering the sheet to assess his adversary in a new light. His throat bobbed, his jaw ticked, but that was the extent of his reaction.

Was this how he had received the confirmation of her father's murder? Was Sergei as much of a friend as John Koehler? If given the chance, would he comfort Alexei and promise him justice for the man pictured swinging from a gibbet?

Anne shook her head. "My question first. Did you kill John Koehler, Richard? Did you murder my father?"

Again, he refused to answer, unwilling to give voice to the glaring truth. The man was without honor... suffered not the least guilt. Richard would maintain his love of his friend of twenty years, even in the face of unimpeachable evidence. It was not entirely unexpected though. He knew nothing of love.

Richard stood, seeking a new advantage. Anne regarded him without fear, which he considered for a moment before turning away. He knew there was a reason she would unflinchingly face down death, but not knowing why was reason enough for caution.

Richard went to his safe, sifting through his most precious secrets that one day Todd would inherit. At the end of his search, he placed his own answers on top of hers and shifted the pile back into her court.

"I warned you before that you don't know your father as well as you think. You were a child when he died, and certain things were kept from you for your own protection."

Anne refused his denial, resolutely pushing responsibility back in his court. "Why don't you tell me, in your own words, Richard, why you murdered my parents."

His lips thinned at her stubbornness, his words came harsher than he intended. "Your father was going mad! He'd become insane. He was gifted with a superbly analytical mind, not unlike you. His bouts of coherence were becoming shorter every day. And when he wasn't, well... let's just say, that without warning he would become a religious nut, ranting about sin and right and wrong."

Richard quickly collected himself, breathing deeply to ease the strain on his newly mended heart. He turned his eyes from the source of his agitation – the woman who would force him into difficult recollections, rake him over the glowing coals of his own making. It irritated him to no end that she sat there serenely, as if nothing he said affected her... as if it made no difference that the man she idolized had had feet of clay.

Meanwhile Richard's heart was beating furiously behind its cage.

She would kill him if he let her.

"John was losing his mind," he said, forcing himself to calm. "He was spiraling slowly but steadily into insanity... paranoid schizophrenia, in fact."

Anne watched as the words slipped carefully... almost reluctantly... from his lips. Wouldn't Todd be vindicated? Even if it were true... even if her father was just as broken as she, he deserved help, not execution.

"He would have been quietly retired, if he didn't force our hand."

"He was hunting Sergei Afanasenko," Anne supplied helpfully.

Richard wondered that she received the news with admirable ease. He wondered that he had misjudged her maturity... that he hadn't used the truth long ago to make an unreserved ally of her.

"Yes."

"You chose to protect a Russian arms dealer from your best friend of twenty years?" she asked, her tone tinged with incredulity. "Was it truly the targeting of Afanasenko that was the straw that broke the camel's back; or was it your greed, Richard? You were selling legitimacy."

Slowly Richard's story unfolded. It was a story that required a full hour for the telling. Richard shared his folder full of secrets, outlining who, when and where he had used Afanasenko. Anne wasn't sure how many her father had caught on to... if he knew the extent of Richard's dealings with the Russian. She was only certain of the five her father had given her: Zaire and Rwanda – the two Richard counted among his successes; and his failures – Libya, the Palestinians and Kosovo.

The eighties and nineties were a difficult time, in which unparalleled challenges arose. The Government's strategy was to pre-empt the descent into total chaos by seizing the reins and directing the disorder. Those with the resources and support to rule, whose priorities matched Richard's, were assisted in their rise to power.

It was a decision John failed to stand behind because his mind was broken. He couldn't see the forest for the trees... so preoccupied was he with the question of morality. The end of the Cold War heralded an arms race in the developing world. Yes, Afanasenko fed it, but if not him then another would have. Many died as a result, but by supporting a side – a viable side – Richard had saved millions. It wasn't a perfect solution, but it wasn't a perfect world either.

"I chose to protect our country's interests against a madman who couldn't be reasoned with," Richard said, winding down. While not breathless, his justification – or the fact that he had to provide one – was wearying.

Anne smiled without emotion... unmoved. "You were selling political support to the highest bidding militias."

"We were assessing the viability of potential allies in a post-Communist world," he countered.

"You protected Afanasenko while he sold anarchy, then you cut the profits with him."

"We promoted the building of long-term political stability, economic development and trade. Afanasenko would have sold his weapons with or without us. Why not use him to make valuable contacts… to identify leaders we could train to share our values? We had nothing to lose."

Anne's lips twisted bitterly. "Nothing at all," she said. "What was one man worth?"

"Be reasonable," Richard said in quiet reprimand. "John wouldn't let it go… wouldn't go quietly."

"He was your best friend. He'd given his all to this country."

"And I made sure he got a star in the Book of Honor for it."

Anne wasn't sure what she had expected to feel, but surely not this emptiness. How could she feel nothing at all? It was strangely anti-climatic to hear the words from his lips. Perhaps Richard was right: she could only see in black and white. That would explain why knowing *why* made no difference. She had known for months now that it was Richard all along, and his reasons would not change that.

Her father was dead… had been tortured and murdered. What was the point in that? What sense was there to her mother's slaughter?

Someone had to pay.

"What now?" Richard finally asked.

It was a timely question, because judgment was at the door. He was a silent killer, but Anne didn't need sound or the furtive darting of Richard's eyes to know that Todd had finally arrived. There was a shift in the air as his presence charged the molecules that sparked to the roots of her hair. Her skin pricked with the unmistakable surge of physical awareness.

"That's for Todd to decide," she said, turning to face him. "Welcome."

The air stood still, hanging as thick as wet cement between them. It was a while before they all became unglued, waiting for Todd to make his choice.

Who would he choose? The man who could give him what he thought he always wanted, or the woman who had given him the things he had despaired of ever having?

His silence declared he had been watching, that he knew what Richard had done. On the one hand, he could condemn the betrayal.

There had to have been another way. How could he trust the man who had murdered his best friend? But on the other hand, Richard's excuses went to the heart of Todd's hatred of John. While it explained the madness that drove a father to torture his own daughter, in Todd's eyes, it would never be an adequate excuse.

Having been discovered, Todd was less keen on muffling the sound of his steps as he crossed the floor.

He was as magnificent as Anne remembered. He was still dressed in uniform, Richard's home having been his first stop after work. He had succumbed to the lure she had set in her father's study, but had wasted no time to change. His hair was as neatly arranged in its shell as when he had first left home that morning. Only the thickening of the shadow at his jaw spoke of the hours that had passed since then.

"Yes, Amy. That's a good question. What now?" he asked, taking his place at Richard's side. He was armed, the firearm hanging innocuously for now at his side. As if his wife would believe he posed no threat.

"Once again, you've made your choice," she said, alarming him with a serene smile.

"Is that what this about? A test, Amy?" There was no answer, only the placid smile. "You never really leave much of a choice."

Anne placed a hand on her belly where his child was awake, knowing he would follow the motion, as much with his eyes as his heart. "There's always a choice, Todd."

His eyes narrowed at her hand. She wore his rings, and they glinted under the light. His eyes flicked to her face where he looked deeper into the woman. After a long time, he broke the stare, eyes resting on the pen.

"Is that the camera?" Todd asked.

Anne watched as understanding dawned quickly on Richard's face. His gaze bounced between Todd, the pen and Anne. His fists clenched before he reached across the desk, prepared to smash it to pieces although it was much too late for that now.

"No point in that now, Richard. She has the whole thing wirelessly relayed. It's how I knew." Their eyes met, and Todd seemed to silently plead for the older man's indulgence. "Where's the gun?"

Richard didn't understand Todd's calm demeanor in the face of this threat... certainly didn't agree, but he trusted Todd. Why should he not?

His protégé had made his choice, and together they would resolve the problem she presented.

Anne saw no reason not to indulge him either. It wasn't exactly a secret anymore... Todd had his suspicions, and whether they were confirmed or not would make no difference to the outcome. She handed over her purse to Richard, who found her Sig, after which he tossed the purse and its inoffensive contents back at her. Anne made the catch with ease, with her left hand, not missing the instant the light shifted— hardened— in Todd's eyes.

She reclaimed her seat and faced him. "We meet again," she said.

Richard searched Todd's face for understanding, but no explanation was forthcoming. She found it intriguing that Todd refused to share this secret... Or did he not think it would alter the outcome? Was there no hope of her walking out of here alive, whether she was his wife or not?

"You know I can't let you do this," Todd said, readjusting his grip on the firearm hanging at his side. He seemed unsure however, his thumb caressing the grip of the gun nervously. Or was that reassuringly?

"I already have," Anne said. She turned to Richard.

"Don't be stupid. It's not too late to turn back."

"You'll have to kill Erika Harris. I'm sure the world will understand you had no choice. She's been knocking on Richard's door for months, exposing secrets she thought would hurt me."

Richard betrayed his shock with a hand pressed against his chest. "It was you all along?" he raged, gripping the edge of his desk as he slowly rose from his seat of power. "You set that bitch on us? You would destroy our family, Amy?"

Anne met his glare squarely, sending him spiraling into a rage by her lack of remorse. "Like you destroyed mine, Richard. You murdered my father, slaughtered my mother with the help of your wife, ripped apart the heart of me."

Richard sank into his seat as complete realization weighted him down. It was Amy all along. Everything that had led to the revolt of his heart – the threat to his sons, the death of his wife; and what came after – the end of his tenure. It seemed an eternity passed while they regarded each other, Anne baring herself, proving that his lessons in betrayal had found fertile soil in the heart of the girl he had wished was his own.

"Kill her," Richard said, the sound of his words as hollow and soulless as the man himself. The trance was broken by Todd's failure to act. "Kill her, damn it," he said, this time reinforcing his command with a balled fist slamming against the wood. Blood surged through his body, causing pain. He pressed a hand to his left arm as his face flushed.

"There has to be another way," Todd said, his eyes taking in everything he had to lose. It wasn't his wife, but it was his child... his dreams.

"There is no other way," Richard said unevenly, breathlessly, nodding when his protégé met his stare.

Anne stood. "He is right," she said. "I won't stop. I'll walk out that door and make sure Erika has everything she needs to grind his world to ashes." She turned to Richard. "I'll keep pushing until the world knows what you did. I'll never stop until I have justice for my parents... until you've answered for what you did."

"Shoot her," Richard commanded.

Still, Todd refused to move. Both Anne and Richard regarded him, waiting for his final act of obedience. When he only stood there, riveted to the spot, Anne smiled.

It seemed one of them was capable of love after all... even if that love was directed at a dream that would never be.

"Please," Todd whispered, "Anne."

He would have let her walk away. If she had looked at him one last time, she would have seen the tears pool in his eyes. But she never did, not even when she registered the unmistakable sound of the end galloping close. She was not afraid.

There was the crack of thunder and searing light, but no pain.

Anne hadn't felt a thing all day and never would again. She went home to be with her father.

EPILOGUE

There was a heaven and there was a hell. I had found them both on earth. They were the love of a man and the death of our dream. There was nothing better and nothing worse.

Trapped between life and death, I was a prisoner to the emptiness... denied the repose of my parents' welcome, and the miracle I had been too broken to cherish.

I had a fleeting sense of happiness, but it wasn't how I had imagined it would be. It was not a memory, but a vision. It was not to be found in the awareness of completion. Although I could not remember what my purpose had been, I knew it had been fulfilled. Still, on the fringes of my thoughts, a whisper of what might have been peaked at me from under the weight of regret. I struggled to seize it, but each time, grasped nothing. There was only the emptiness.

Until the day there was more.

I opened my eyes as if for the first time. Everything was strange and so thrilling... so thrilling in fact, that it exhausted me to take it in. The emptiness swallowed me again, though I was unwilling to go. I fought against it to little avail. Only bits of the world sneaked through, but they were unpredictable and punishing in their flimsiness. There was the moment I thought I could feel. It was neither pleasure nor pain, not an emotion or touch. It was too quickly swept away by the nothingness that I doubted it had ever happened. I dreamt I could hear beyond the void, but it was nothing I could remember. The barrenness endured, seemingly endlessly.

Until the day it was broken.

I knew where I was, but not how I had gotten there or why. Such sterility could only belong in a hospital. At first there was silence, as if I had left my hearing wherever I had been. It made the starkness of the room that more disturbing... as if it wasn't the surroundings that had been bleached, but my mind. I was aware of my breathing, slow and steady for a moment as I tried to understand what was happening. Then it came harder and faster as comprehension eluded me. I couldn't move, I couldn't feel, I couldn't hear a thing. It was as if my body had died, but my mind was still aware. I had the sense of being overwhelmed, the feel – but not the sound – of my breathing sawing in and out until the emptiness blanketed the edges of my vision again, and steadily crept in.

This time, I welcomed it. What was the point of being alive if I couldn't live? It was a long time before I became aware of the world beyond the void again.

I awoke to a voice... or rather, a voice woke me, luring me away from the nothingness. It was familiar, stirring a queer sensation within the depths of me. I seized the promise of feeling, holding greedily to the lure. I opened my eyes to the same disquieting view: a hospital's bleached walls, a white ceiling and door. I waited for the voice to reach me again, but there was nothing. The panic edged forward again, my silent breath gaining momentum.

And then he was there. He filled my view all of a sudden, startling blue eyes I instinctively knew. They were beacons I refused to let go, despite the flurry of movement I sensed in the periphery. I still couldn't hear, couldn't feel a thing, but just seeing him was a balm to my frantic mind.

Here was something worth staying for... someone worth living for.

We stared at each other until exhaustion pulled me down. But the wasteland was defeated. I dreamt of those eyes. From some distant part of my consciousness, a form was created – a face and then a body and a name.

Todd.

He invited in a sea of recollection, things I was sure I would forget once I opened my eyes again. I remembered sound and scent and what it meant to feel. Those I held close to me and refused to let go. So when next awareness dawned, my senses were filled to overflowing.

He was not there, but I could feel the touch of something foreign against my skin. My nostrils flared at the shadow of a powerful astringent, and at last, there was a steady beep to the pounding in my head. In the distant, there were other sounds too, the hum of people and machinery working together.

I remained awake for a long time, so long in fact that the light had shifted and the room dimmed. Eventually someone came to me. It wasn't the face I had dreamt of; it was a woman. But the fact that I could hear was in itself a relief. Her eyes ran disinterestedly over me before she turned away, only to suddenly freeze. After a moment, she returned, her eyes wide as they met mine.

"Oh my God," she said, chanting the words over and over again before she spurred into motion. She moved in an out of my line of sight, but that was fine too, because I could hear her and smell her.

And soon there were others too, a veritable throng. I took them in greedily, my eyes consuming the various colors of skin, hair and clothing. Their voices filled my head, the words lost in favor of the simple stimulation. And they all smelled differently, providing something new for me to seize upon.

It was exhausting and refreshing all at the same time.

Eventually, I was forced to focus on just one – a man with green eyes and silver hair. He smelled of coffee and hand sanitizer as he breathed on me, shining a light into my eyes. I flinched and looked away, only to return to him when he put the light away.

"Can you hear me?" he asked. I had the conscious thought of answering, but couldn't hear my own voice. I couldn't move either. It occurred to me that he might leave and take everyone with him if I didn't do something. And so I closed my eyes and opened them again, slowly so he would know that it was not my body's unconscious reaction.

"Hello," he said, his entire face creasing as he curved his mouth into a smile. "I'm Dr. Cuthbert. Do you know where you are?"

Here, I thought. My mind went back to the other place, *there*, and instantly the panic built at the prospect of returning to the emptiness.

"It's OK," he said, and I felt his skin against mine. I couldn't see where, but I instinctively knew it to be my hand. "Try to remain calm.

You've been asleep for a long time," he said. "It will take some time for things to come back to you. But I'll be here to help you along."

He was right. It did take a long time, and there was always someone with me. But never the man from my dreams. I marked the days by the shifting of the light until I lost count. Many days passed and I felt myself getting stronger. I remembered how to move, but progress was slow. While I could open my mouth to receive nourishment and manipulate my tongue to feel the different textures, speech eluded me for the longest while. By my calculation, it took days before I was able to create words from the sounds emanating from my throat.

Command of my limbs was more difficult. After a week, I had built the strength the lift my head, or move my fingers beyond a twitch. I felt the pressure of the bed and being manipulated by the staff, but it was as if the lower half of my body was still asleep.

"Don't worry about that," Dr. Cuthbert would say when I failed his tests. "There is significant muscle atrophy in the lower extremities. That's normal considering."

"Considering what?" I asked, having to concentrate to use my tongue to form the words. They sounded slurred, unlike the fast and easy gait of the people who came to me.

The doctor looked up at me for a moment before returning to a tablet. "Considering how long you've been … unwell."

I knew he wasn't going to say more. He wasn't the only one who had refused to say what was wrong with me. I tried a different track.

"There was a man here." The doctor looked at me curiously again, but said nothing. "I know him."

Days of questioning followed, and long periods of time during which they rolled me into machines that looked inside my head. I responded as best I could, but was disappointed that certain answers eluded me. I remembered my name, schools I had attended as a child, my mother's name, the country, my address, the name of the President. I remembered the names of the people who were caring for me, what I'd had for lunch that day and the one before. I remembered the man, Todd, but I couldn't say who he was to me. As the questions continued and I became more confused, frustration built, and I could feel the panic edging in. Dr. Cuthbert would end the sessions.

They were all recorded, and I began to think that was normal.

And then one day, it all changed. I awoke in the pre-dawn hours, sweat-soaked and in a panic, demanding to speak with Dr. Cuthbert. It was hours before he came, discovered me sitting up in bed, and staring at my legs.

"Good morning, Amy," he greeted me, but I sensed a reserve about him that had not been there the day before. "I hear you've been asking for me."

"What happened to my baby?" I asked, abandoning my preoccupation with my inability to move my legs. The partial paralysis was uncanny, considering my arms were now strong enough to pull my weight up in bed.

"Why don't I examine you –"

I held up a hand to ward him off. "I want to see my husband," I said. "Todd."

I guarded my memories closely after he left. After going so long without them, I would have rather died than lose them again. I remembered the highs and the lows, the ecstasy of heaven and agony of hell, and I would take the latter a thousand times over the emptiness.

I wasn't a good person; I was just me. I remembered the terrible things I had done... didn't make excuses. I simply accepted them for what they were. But the thought that I had harmed my child was something I did not believe. We had grown together. I had loved her. I had tried to save her.

I knew something had happened, but I could not remember.

My last memory before *here* and *there* was of home. I hadn't slept for days. I had kissed my husband goodbye after discussing the merits of a C-section with him. I was thirty-eight weeks pregnant and impatient to have the baby... impatient to make her safe so I could confront Richard.

I had called my obstetrician, told him about our change of heart. He was convinced it was only the physical exhaustion at play.

"Don't fucking patronize me," I had told him. "You're going to take this baby out of me before the end of the week."

He had agreed, invited us to an appointment the following day to discuss preparations. Todd had given his support.

"If you're sure," he had said, and I couldn't find a hint of disapproval coming over the line.

I'd had lunch and then lied down in the darkened room in a desperate bid to fall asleep. Then I was here, a thin line carved low on my abdomen. They had cut my child out of me. Alive or dead… I wasn't sure.

When Dr. Cuthbert returned hours later, he was not alone. But Todd wasn't with him. No introductions were made, but none was necessary. I knew the type of men that flanked the doctor. Beneath their suits were firearms, toys compared to the weapons behind their implacable gaze.

The questioning became an interrogation, as they directed the doctor down the alleyways that interested them. They asked about my parents, Richard, my Army years, Richard, the places I lived and worked, Richard, my life with Todd, Richard, the last day I could remember before arriving here. And again, Richard. Certain answers were provided – mundane details that were designed to help my memory along. I didn't need them. I remembered everything… everything except how I had ended up in the hospital.

It was the first time I was given details about my coma. I was stunned to hear that the current date was April 10, 2014. I'd been awake since March 26.

I had slept away five hundred and eighty-eight days.

I was moved into physiotherapy, but every few days more men would come – sometimes the same ones as the first interrogation, and sometimes new ones. No one would tell me what had happened to my baby, or why Todd never came to see me.

Richard was dead. No one would tell me how. My interrogators regarded my question with the same impassivity as I received their answer. It stirred nothing in me beyond quiet acceptance. My parents were never coming back. And apparently, neither was Todd.

Six weeks later, I knew no more than when I had awakened in the early in the morning, soaked in sweat and under siege from the resurgence of my past.

By then I had stopped asking for my husband. Either my baby was dead – killed as a result of the manipulations that had landed me in my present state; or Todd had taken her and finally left me for good.

I couldn't blame him if he had. It was imperative that he keep her safe. Even from me.

Especially from me.

I wanted to go home even if there was no one waiting for me there. I was disgusted with the demands placed on me, especially during physiotherapy. Dr. Cuthbert, who was a neurologist, was convinced my body was recovering from the injury caused by the gunshot wound to the back of my head, as well as the trauma associated with removing the slug. In the meantime he wanted me to focus on rebuilding muscle mass and strength so one day I could walk again.

What was the point? It was over, and I had nothing to look forward to. I had no job and no purpose. Not that it mattered anyway. The former was only a means to achieve the latter. I wouldn't miss it.

I wasn't interested in anything he had to say. The only answer I wanted from him, he was unable to give. Where was my family?

The days bled into weeks while I waited for them to conclude there was nothing more they could do for me. In the past week I had even refused to leave my room. The doctors began to toss around diagnoses of depression. I ignored them, devoting my time to eating and sleeping – as if I hadn't already slept through a year and a half.

And then one day I awoke to find him there. He was as beautiful as I remembered, his eyes the exact shade of blue from my dreams. The grooves at the corners seemed slightly deeper; the dark glint of mistrust familiar. His face was pale above the imprint of his beard even though he had recently shaved. His hair was slicked back in its customary shell. The hints of grey just above his ears were now clearly defined streaks. That was how I knew it wasn't a dream.

Even so, I was afraid to take my eyes away… terrified of returning to find him gone. I struggled into an upright position and stared.

He seemed to look his fill too. I was different from my last memory of us together. My head had been shaved for my surgery; it no longer cascaded down my lower back as in the last months of my pregnancy. I now had about nine inches of new growth, but seeing him here made me want to do special things to it. My skin wasn't at its best either, but it wasn't the worst I could remember. And I had never been thinner, but not in an attractive way. There was no helping these things now though; my body had been ravaged by the time I had slept away.

"How do you feel?" he asked, sounding formal … distant.

I nodded, because words eluded me for the moment. My eyes drank him in greedily.

He was dressed in uniform... just like the last time he had kissed me. He'd been on his way to work then. Judging by the absence of natural light, I guessed he was on his way home... wherever that was.

"Todd," I said, when at last my throat worked. "What happened?" I asked, folding my hands over my flat belly.

"You don't remember?" He arched a brow at me, but his lips were pressed together. The look in his eyes was nothing short of stony. I shook my head. "No one told you?" Again a negative response.

Todd pushed away from my bedside, releasing the rails, and took a seat in one of two standard issue guest chairs. Until then, they had only been filled by strangers.

"Richard is dead," he said with a marked absence of emotion. "I killed him."

My eyes had been busy roaming the full extent of his magnificence, until those words struck me with the force of a blow. Still, it wasn't the truth that had shocked me to the core; it was the ease with which Todd made the confession, as if the act had presented no challenge at all.

"No one told you?" he asked. I shook my head. He opened his arms as if to show them to me and shrugged. He shrugged. "He shot you. I thought he had killed you."

"He shot me?" I gasped, my hand flying to the back of my head where my scars crisscrossed like railway tracks on a map.

"Yes," Todd replied simply. "Isn't that what you wanted, Amy? For Richard to kill you so I could kill him too?"

It was the truth, but an old one. I wanted our child. I wanted her safe before I confronted Richard. In the end the choice had been taken away from me. I couldn't remember that last day... my consciousness hidden beneath another's...Anne's. But Richard hadn't just killed that part of me – I had never gone this long without being aware of her essence – he had killed our child too. And Anne had let him do it, to punish me for choosing Todd.

My heart was broken. I cried for the child I had grown to love but would never hold. I cried for the tortured soul that was the softer part of me.

"No," I sobbed, burying my face into my hands, wishing I could hide from that terrible truth forever. "I wanted her. I loved her. It wasn't supposed to be that way."

"You didn't seriously think Richard would let you walk away, did you?" Todd asked, forcing me to stare into his angry eyes.

"I would have waited. I planned to. I wanted her; you know I did. She was supposed to be safe. Please, believe me, I wanted her."

And out of all of that, Todd came away with: "You knew it was a girl?"

"I did, and I loved her. She was my gift to you, so after I was gone, you would look at her and know I loved you both. And hopefully, you would forgive me. I wouldn't have hurt her, I swear… not after I felt her moving inside me…not after knowing she was real."

I cried for hours it seemed, and Todd watched silently. Eventually, I ran dry. So we sat in silence until the darkness sucked all the light from my room. I fell asleep.

In the morning, I was conscious of a deep pain in the center of my chest. I didn't call for help. I wanted to die. I wished I had never surfaced from the emptiness. I turned away to watch the light creep through the blinds, and was surprised to find Todd sitting in the same chair.

He had left some time during the night, because he was dressed in civilian gear – jeans, loafers and a button-down shirt. He was wide-awake and staring at me, looking as if he had been doing that for hours.

"Did you ever love me, Amy?" he asked.

My answer was unreserved. "Yes."

The silence yawned for a long time before Todd broke it. "Where did we go wrong? Where did I fail you?"

Our eyes met, and I noticed that the anger was gone. In its place was the mask. "I thought you loved him more than me. Because of what he could give you."

"All I ever wanted was you, Amy."

A few minutes later, the Saturday morning rounds began. They left their trays and their pills and their encouragements. All things I didn't need. I ignored them.

Then Todd drew my tray close and stood to hold a glass of juice to my mouth. "Come, Amy. Eat something."

I looked up at him. "Why? Why do you care after what I've done?"

"Because I know it wasn't you. And because I love you, Amy. I couldn't stop loving you if I tried. And I want you to walk out of here one day soon."

My hands started to shake. "There's nothing out there for me."

Todd smiled, the slightest shift of the corners of his mouth. But there were tears in his eyes. "The people you love, and who love you, are out there. I'll be out there waiting for you to come home."

I cried, sobbing wetly while drinking the juice. He pulled his chair closer and began spooning eggs into my mouth.

"You're all I need," I told him. "Much more than I deserve."

Todd nodded. "Maybe, but I can't change how I feel... couldn't stop loving you although I've tried." he said. "And then there's Rose. She deserves a mother, Amy."

END